Titles by Jean Johnson

SHIFTING PLAINS

BEDTIME STORIES

FINDING DESTINY

The Sons of Destiny

THE SWORD

THE WOLF

THE MASTER

THE SONG

THE CAT

THE STORM

THE FLAME

THE MAGE

FINDING DESTINY

JEAN JOHNSON

BERKLEY SENSATION, NEW YORK

THE BERKLEY PUBLISHING GROUP
Published by the Penguin Group
Penguin Group (USA) Inc.
375 Hudson Street, New York, New York 10014, USA
Penguin Group (Canada), 90 Eglinton Avenue East, Suite 700, Toronto, Ontario M4P 2Y3, Canada
(a division of Pearson Penguin Canada Inc.)
Penguin Books Ltd., 80 Strand, London WC2R 0RL, England
Penguin Group Ireland, 25 St. Stephen's Green, Dublin 2, Ireland (a division of Penguin Books Ltd.)
Penguin Group (Australia), 250 Camberwell Road, Camberwell, Victoria 3124, Australia
(a division of Pearson Australia Group Pty. Ltd.)
Penguin Books India Pvt. Ltd., 11 Community Centre, Panchsheel Park, New Delhi—110 017, India
Penguin Group (NZ), 67 Apollo Drive, Rosedale, North Shore 0632, New Zealand
(a division of Pearson New Zealand Ltd.)
Penguin Books (South Africa) (Pty.) Ltd., 24 Sturdee Avenue, Rosebank, Johannesburg 2196, South Africa

Penguin Books Ltd., Registered Offices: 80 Strand, London WC2R 0RL, England

This book is an original publication of The Berkley Publishing Group.

Interior text design by Kristin del Rosario.

PRINTING HISTORY
Berkley Sensation trade paperback edition / January 2011

Library of Congress Cataloging-in-Publication Data

Johnson, Jean, 1972–
Finding destiny/Jean Johnson.—Berkley Sensation trade paperback ed.
p. cm.
ISBN 978-0-425-23862-2
I. Title.
PS3610.O355F56 2011
813'—dc22 2010040816

PRINTED IN THE UNITED STATES OF AMERICA

10 9 8 7 6 5 4 3 2 1

Praise for Jean Johnson and the Sons of Destiny

"Jean Johnson's writing is fabulously fresh, thoroughly romantic, and wildly entertaining. Terrific—fast, sexy, charming, and utterly engaging. I loved it!" —Jayne Ann Krentz, *New York Times* bestselling author

"Cursed brothers, fated mates, prophecies, yum! A fresh new voice in fantasy romance, Jean Johnson spins an intriguing tale of destiny and magic." —Robin D. Owens, RITA Award–winning author

"A must-read for those who enjoy fantasy and romance. I . . . eagerly look forward to each of the other brothers' stories. Jean Johnson can't write them fast enough for me!" —*The Best Reviews*

"[It] has everything—love, humor, danger, excitement, trickery, hope, and even sizzling hot . . . sex." —*Errant Dreams*

"Enchantments, amusement, eight hunks, and one bewitching woman make for a fun romantic fantasy . . . Humorous and magical . . . [A] delightful charmer." —*Midwest Book Review*

"A paranormal adventure series that will appeal to fantasy and historical fans, plus time-travel lovers as well. Jean Johnson has created a mystical world of lessons taught, very much like the great folktales we love to hear over and over. It's like *Alice in Wonderland* meets the *Knights of the Round Table* and you're never quite sure what's going to happen next. Delightful entertainment . . . An enchanting tale with old world charm, *The Sword* will leave you dreaming of a sexy mage for yourself." —*Romance Junkies*

continued . . .

"An intriguing new fantasy romance series . . . [A] unique combination of magic, time travel, and fantasy that will have readers looking toward the next book. Think *Seven Brides for Seven Brothers* but add one more and give them magic, with curses and fantasy thrown in for fun. Cunning . . . Creative . . . Lovers of magic and fantasy will enjoy this fun, fresh, and very romantic offering."

—*Time Travel Romance Writers*

"The writing is sharp and witty and the story is charming. [Johnson] makes everything perfectly believable. She has created an enchanting situation and characters that are irascible at times and lovable at others. Jean Johnson . . . is off to a flying start. She tells her story with a lively zest that transports a reader to the place of action. I can hardly wait for the next one. It is a must-read."

—*Romance Reviews Today*

"A fun story. I look forward to seeing how these alpha males find their soul mates in the remaining books." —*The Eternal Night*

"An intriguing world . . . An enjoyable hero . . . An enjoyable showcase for an inventive new author. Jean Johnson brings a welcome voice to the romance genre, and she's assured of a warm welcome."

—*The Romance Reader*

"An intriguing and entertaining tale of another dimension . . . It will be fun to see how the prophecy turns out for the rest of the brothers."

—*Fresh Fiction*

CONTENTS

SUNDARA

ONE

His tongue kept getting him into trouble. Eduor Aragol knew this, yet couldn't seem to stop. When his elderly owner Midalla clutched at her chest and keeled over after a dust-induced coughing fit, only to be pronounced dead mere moments later by one of the caravan guards, the last thing he should have said aloud was, "—Thank the Gods!"

But he did, and he had. The heartfelt words had left his tongue without thought, and now he was stuck with the consequences of his carelessness. Despite the dust and sand filtering into the cave, brought in by the gusts of wind toying with the torches which struggled to provide them with some light, he could see the glare aimed at him from Midalla's niece, Famiel.

"You *slime*!" the middle-aged woman snarled, her voice rising above the whistling of the sandstorm outside. Like the rest of them in the cave, she was wearing a scarf over her nose and mouth to filter out the dust of the sandstorm, but her eyes burned with her hatred.

"My aunt was too *kind* to you! She should've whipped you like your *last* owner did!"

Eduor felt his back muscles flinch in memory. He still bore some of the scars from his first half year of captivity. Midalla had bought him from a physically cruel owner simply because he had spoken in near-flawless Sundaran to a fellow merchant on her behalf, smoothing over an inadvertent, misspoken insult for her. Eduor's father had encouraged him to learn a foreign language when he was young, and this desert kingdom still traded occasionally with both Mandare and Natallia. After witnessing his fluency firsthand, the elderly merchant had bartered for him. Once she owned him, she had given him extra lessons in the language and the laws and customs of this land, instead of extra whippings.

At first, it had seemed like a slice of heaven: lessons given to a mere war-slave instead of lashings. However, there were other things she had done, things the nearly seventy-year-old woman had demanded as soon as she found out what else his tongue could do besides speak Sundaran fluently. Things which had demeaned and tormented him worse than a lashing. Nothing physically damaging, but a mental and emotional torment all the same.

Watching Midalla's niece searching brusquely around the cave until she finally found a riding quirt warned him that those days of nonphysical torment were over. He flinched again as she slashed the stiff, braided whip through the air, making it whistle almost as loud as the storm outside.

Famiel had taken advantage of him in many of the same ways her aunt had, and the thought of her whipping him on top of that other humiliation was unbearable. She was harder and more cruel than her now-deceased relative. He would not submit to her, even if it meant his death. Eduor balled up his fists, ready to fight.

"What you with that do, woman?" That came from the Arbran Knight in their midst, Sir Zeilas of some place up north. Catching Famiel by the wrist, the Knight frowned at her. He spoke Natallian poorly and with a thick northerner's accent, his words further muffled by the linen tied over his lower face, but he did manage to make himself clear. "You *not* beat anyone in presence of me!"

Glaring, Famiel yanked on her arm, but he didn't let go. She shoved her dark hair back with her free hand and glared at him. "Unhand me! You have no right to stop me. By right of inheritance, that Mandarite scum is now *mine* to do with as I please, and I *will* beat the insolence out of him. Let *go* of me!—Guards!"

The Sundarans hired by Midalla to escort their trade caravan hesitated. A couple of them reached for their weapons, but no one drew a blade. Eduor felt his fear fade, replaced by burgeoning relief. Famiel's words had triggered a memory, a precious piece of Sundaran law.

"Wrong," he stated sharply. The dust in the air tickled his throat, seeping through the scrap of linen covering his own mouth, but he struggled to suppress it. Switching briefly to Sundaran, he ordered, "Stand down, guards, or be accounted an accessory to lawbreaking."

Famiel blinked at him. "*Wrong?*" she demanded, still speaking in her native Natallian. "What do you mean, wrong? You are *mine*, boy, and I'll teach you to remember your place!"

"In Natallia, yes, you are the heir to all that your aunt owned and held, and thus in Natallia you would inherit her ownership of me . . . but we are in *Sundara*," Eduor reminded her, returning to their shared, native tongue. "And by *Sundaran* law, any slave whose owner dies of natural causes is automatically *freed*.

"I was all the way over here, by the horses and dromids. She was all the way over there, by the baggage and bales," he reminded her, gesturing at the two ends of the cavern. "I hold no magic nor machinery to affect her health even from up close, let alone from all the way over here. She died of what looks like a heart attack brought on by too much coughing from this damnable dust. Natural causes, on Sundaran soil.

"I am *free*." Eduor folded his arms across his chest. *In for a copper*, *in for a gold.* "Furthermore, I only expressed an opinion, which free men *are* entitled to do. By Sundaran law, you cannot whip me for that—oh, and here's another thing I am now *free* to say. You taste *terrible.* Like something that crawled up out of the sea and died in a sewer. Somehow, I doubt you've ever heard of soap, let alone know what it's used for. And I'd rather cut off my own tongue than touch *you* ever again. Which, thank the Gods, I won't have to do anymore."

Rage darkened the visible half of her dusty, suntanned face. Growling, Famiel jerked her wrist free of the Knight's loosened grasp but did not try to approach Eduor and strike. Instead, she pointed at the blanket-covered cave mouth with the quirt. "Get out!"

"Ah, milady . . ." one of the Sundarans interjected.

"Get out!" Famiel repeated, ignoring him. "I may not own you anymore, but I *do* own this caravan—you want to be a free man in Sundara?" she asked sarcastically, slashing her hand and its thin crop at the cavern entrance once more. "Well, *there* is your freedom! Get out into it! You are banished immediately from this caravan. *Get out.*"

"Milady . . . *all* people be welcome to shelter in sandstorm," one of the Sundaran guards apologized in broken Natallian. "Sorry, you cannot throw out him."

Eduor fancied he could hear Famiel grinding her teeth. He smirked and countered her next possible claim. "Nor can you strip the clothes from my back without being accused of theft. Plus you *have* to unlock this collar on my neck now that I am legally free . . . and you *cannot* take my water skin from me. To deny a man water in the desert is to deny him life. As I am not a criminal *on Sundaran soil*," he emphasized, since he knew she could try to dredge up his Mandarite background, "to do so would make *you* the criminal. And, just like in Natallia, they have ways of dealing with their criminals. I do not think you would care to be *my* slave, indentured to *me*. Not after the way you've treated me."

Fuming, Famiel whirled away, stalking to the far side of the cave.

She returned after a few moments with a bag and a length of cloth, and knelt over her aunt's form, no doubt to start preparing it for burial. Safe for the moment, Eduor remained in the animal half of the cave. It was closer to the entrance and thus to the dust, not to mention the dung underfoot, but nothing would compel him to get closer to the odious woman.

The Arbran Knight watched her work for a few moments, then moved across the cavern to Eduor's side. His Sundaran was far more fluent than his Natallian, and he used it to speak to Eduor under the cover of the sandstorm's noise.

"You have made yourself an enemy. Or remade one. I will warn you, I do not agree with the Mandarite philosophy toward women. You owe me for stopping her long enough for you to tell her about the local laws," Sir Zeilas reminded the younger man. "If you can feel any sense of obligation for that much, then exercise it by staying away from her and not provoking her for the rest of this storm. Save your enmity for your return to Mandare."

His words made Eduor blink, then squint as another puff of dust swirled past the blankets stretched over the posts framing the mouth of the cave. The posts had been erected by travelers long ago for just such a need. They rattled in their holes, sounding loose and empty. *Much like I feel.*

"No," he stated, his voice low but firm. "I'm not going back. I won't be a slave to anyone or anything. Not even to an idea."

The Arbran's dark brows rose, but he didn't say anything further. Giving the younger man something between a nod and a bow, he strolled away. That left Eduor alone with his thoughts.

As soon as this storm ends, I'll be out of the cave and out of the caravan. Not that I'll have much, but I'm grateful I have the clothes on my back and a water skin to drink from . . . for as long as it lasts. It was hot in the cave, hot enough to make everyone thirsty. The cistern was at the back end of the cave, behind yet another blanket drape. Beyond the grimly working Famiel and her dead aunt, and the bundles of trade goods they had brought all the way from the jungle forests of Natallia.

Lifting the water skin slung over his head and shoulder, Eduor drank from the half-full skin carefully, not wanting to waste a drop. *I'll refill it later. The same with getting my collar removed. She cannot deny me access to the water, but I don't care to get anywhere near her right now. Once the storm ends, I'll either have to leave the cave immediately and try to find my way across the desert on my own, or I could maybe leave and hang around the area, wait until she's gone, then come back and stay here until the next group of travelers comes through. I doubt I'll be able to linger. She'll probably cite that, with the storm over, I no longer have any claim to sharing it with her and her precious caravan, and won't want me lingering nearby in case I turn thief.*

Which again leaves me with nothing but the clothes on my back and all the water I can pack into this skin . . . and no food to eat. Somehow, Eduor didn't think she'd share another bite with him. *So the question is, do I stay in the hope some other group of travelers will come by soon and take pity on me? Or leave in the hope I can make it all the way back to that last village we passed and look for food and shelter and . . . well . . . work, I guess?*

After all, he realized, *if I'm to remain not only a free man but free of the insanities back home—on both sides of the war—I'll have to make some other land my home. I* do *know a bit about Sundaran customs, and I can read and write. Not every Sundaran can, I know, so hopefully there'll be some use for a scribe, or a translator, or . . . anything, really.*

The one thing my father did *get right when teaching me was his claim that a man can be anything that he sets his mind to be. And I* will *be free. Even if it means being a Sundaran. Beyond that . . . I don't know what I'll be.* He knew he wasn't in a position to be picky. A scribe usually provided his or her own pen, ink, and paper to ply the trade, but Eduor had nothing like that. *Just my body and my mind, and what I know of Sundaran life and ways.*

TWO

Of Arbran ways, Eduor knew very little. But he was learning. Rather than letting him starve as the dust storm lingered for another full day, Sir Zeilas had shared some of his own provisions with Eduor . . . after asking Famiel politely to share some of hers with him. The Knight had also insisted on escorting Eduor to the nearest village, a place which the map he carried listed as due west of their cave shelter by two days' walk, closer than the previous one they had visited by a day and a half. And his Steed, that fabled, holy Arbran horse . . . well, the Steed refused to carry Eduor, but the otherwise magnificent mottled stallion had no objections to carrying enough water to sustain the three of them for that long a distance.

Eduor's unexpected but highly welcome traveling companion finished tilting up the water skin in his hands. Leaning down in his saddle, Sir Zeilas offered the almost-empty bag to Eduor. "More water? We'll be filling it up soon, I'm sure."

Eduor eyed the village they were approaching, licked his lips, and shook his head. "We're almost there, but . . . I don't like the looks of the men milling around in front of the village gate."

Sitting up, the Arbran Knight shaded his eyes from the glare of the sun reflecting off the ground. His odd, foreign sun hat, much broader and flatter than the rain-shedding conical ones Natallians usually wore on the northern and western coasts, sheltered him only from the sun pouring down from above. It did nothing against the pale beige glare of the sunlight gleaming off the dust powdering the ground around them.

"They have weapons, I think. You have good eyesight to spot that from this far away," the Knight praised.

Eduor shook his head. His own face was wrapped in the dirty scarf that served as sand shield and head covering. It didn't do as much to shade his own eyes, but it did protect his pale skin from the worst of the glare. "I couldn't see their weapons. But I did see the *way* they were gathering. That looks like a raiding party. A loosely organized war band."

"They have spears; they could be hunters," the older man offered. Not that Sir Zeilas was that much older, but he was nearing thirty, half again as old as Eduor.

He shook his head again. Among the collected writings of Sundaran culture Midalla had insisted he read and learn, preparing him for his now-thwarted role as interpreter-slave, had been a packet of essays and observations on village life. "They'd have their desert hounds with them if they were hunting. The beasts are bred for swiftness and keen noses. Good for scenting prey, flushing it out, and chasing it toward their masters. Besides, there are too many of them. This bush desert holds some life, but not that much."

Not that there had been much bush desert for the last half hour of walking. Bushes, yes, but most of them were hardy food-bearing perennials. Date palms and acacia trees outlined patches of soil, some of which showed signs of having been plowed, others of which held just enough grass to feed small herds of animals, like the cluster of goats off to their left. And everything was still dusty from the storm that had swept through the region.

Still, it was better than the half-sand desert they had trudged through for the first day. Here, the ground was solid beneath their feet, if dusty. Most of the palms close to the village were tall enough to provide dappled, cooling shade. The presence of all these plants and the village itself suggested a good supply of water was available, enough to share with a pair of strangers. At least, Eduor hoped.

The cluster of men in front of the village gate, with their spears, swords, and leather armor, looked like they were packing their horses and dromids for a journey. Women and children hung by the village gate, their clothing much more colorful than the duller, desert-hued shades of beige and brown being worn by the dark-skinned men. Among the brocaded reds and yellows, oranges, purples, and greens, a single woman stood out for two reasons. One, she was arguing fiercely with some of the men, and two, she wore an outfit dyed in shades of blue.

Blue, Eduor knew, was reserved for the *dyara*, the water-callers, and that meant whatever she was haranguing them about, it was important business. The coastal mountains to the west were very tall and rugged. Either they diverted the winds bringing moisture from the sea, forcing them northwest into Arbra along the Bay of Winds, or they wrung most of the water out of the clouds sweeping successfully westward over the peaks. What did make it over those peaks was not enough moisture to keep this land green and growing all year long.

It was said the first gift of the Goddess Sundra to Her people was an ability to call just enough water to feed Her people. Like magic, the ability was somewhat rare, and like magic, some *dyara* were stronger than others. Unlike a mage, all a water-caller *could* do was manipulate water, summoning or banishing, boiling or freezing, shaping and purifying, but their abilities were vital for survival in this sunbaked land. Serving as priests and priestesses, as village elders—

regardless of age—the *dyara* were a part of what made life possible in the desert.

As the two foreigners drew near enough to hear, the *dyara* stamped her foot and shouted, "*Fine!* See if we starve because you will not plow your fields. See if we *die* because we are undermanned when someone else thinks to attack *us*!"

One of the men already mounted on a horse swept his arm out. "Every other tribe within five days of here is at peace with the Suds! *You* worry like an old woman, Chanson!"

The *dyara*'s eyes widened and mouth dropped open in affront. Eduor could see the curve of her white teeth in her dark face and the whites of her eyes. Both he and Sir Zeilas stopped, not wanting to come close enough to be drawn into this particular confrontation.

Recovering, she poked her finger at the mounted man. "And *you* aren't worth the effort! You are throwing away your land, Falkon!"

"I am going so I can *save* the land. They may be distant cousins, but the Aboris *are* our kin; their land is as precious as ours. I will *not* scrabble in the dirt while their food is stolen year after year and their women and children are harmed by the Rabs!"

"Then *go*," the *dyara* ordered. She pointed back to the village, but Eduor figured she actually meant eastward, beyond this little oasis. "Go fight your little battle. Prove you are a mighty warrior. But do not expect me to wait for your return!"

"Chanson—" the man on the horse argued, his tone impatient.

"*Go!*" Turning her back on the group, she strode toward the entrance. After three steps, she stopped, turned, and gave the lot a grim look. ". . . *I* will not fail in *my* duty to my people. Even if I think you are being *idiots*." Straightening her tall, slender body, she lifted her hand. "May the waters of life bless you on your journeys."

Spinning on her heel, she strode to the mud-plastered wall circling the village and stepped deliberately over its threshold. Only then did she turn and look back at the men. Finished with their packing, they gave Eduor and Sir Zeilas a wary look. The one named Falkon, who seemed to be their leader, nudged his horse toward the two foreigners. He eyed Eduor, clad in plain, dusty versions of the tunic and tights favored by Natallians, then looked longer at the armor-clad Arbran mounted on his oversized sorrel-and-cream stallion.

Falkon lifted his chin at Sir Zeilas. "What are *you* supposed to be, an Arbran Knight?"

"I *am* one." The Knight's flat tone brooked no doubt. Then again, just the fact that he rode in plate armor with no sign of sweating, and that his stallion showed no interest in the other man's mare, proved he was no ordinary man.

The villager-turned-warrior eyed them both again, then pointed his spear at the pair. "Cause no trouble while you are here, foreigners." Turning his horse around, he nudged the mare toward the others. "Come, we ride to save our kin-tribe!"

Kicking their own steeds into movement, the dozen or so riders headed out around the edge of the village wall. Most of them were younger men, though a couple were grim-looking women. *The desert kingdom breeds fierce fighters*, Eduor remembered from his lessons. *Smart ones, too. Since they know the local land, they're setting out near sunset and will be able to travel in the cooler hours of the evening, whereas we had to be able to see where we were going and trudged through the heat of the day.*

"As if I *would* cause trouble," Sir Zeilas muttered in Sundaran. "Arbora would have my Sword and my Steed if I did so without just cause. I've worked too hard to be a Knight, and a good envoy for His Majesty, to ruin it thoughtlessly.

"On the bright side," the Knight continued thoughtfully, "if their men folk *are* leaving to ride a good distance away, warfare or otherwise, they might have need for someone like you to do some of the labor around here. Other villages may not have such a need. Of course, you could travel with me all the way to Arbra, but I have a very long way to go to reach the capital and make my report to my king."

Eduor shook his head. "I don't speak Arbran, save for the few words you've taught me so far. And if their *dyara* is so worried about the fields getting plowed, then they'll have work for me. I'll stay here for now. *If* they'll have me."

Nodding, the Knight nudged his Steed toward the village gate. Eduor surreptitiously brushed at his clothes, trying to remove some of the dust clinging to them, then followed. Knowing in advance that blue was a reserved color, and that a show of prosperity would help convince these Sundarans that she was a prosperous merchant and thus worth their time, Midalla had given Eduor new, green-dyed clothes. Plainly woven linen, but still new, from the turban-cloth on his head to the cloth and leather boots laced on his feet. They just didn't look new at the moment.

At least I don't have the collar in my way, though it did take the threat of charging her with wrongful imprisonment to prod Famiel into passing one of the guards the key. She refused to unlock it herself. Bitch. Thinking about her and her aunt, and all the suffering they had inflicted on him, was not going to put him into a friendly mood, however. Mindful of first impressions, Eduor cheered himself up with thoughts of freedom. *She and her odious aunt are in my past. The future stretches bright and rife with possibilities in front of me. And, if what we heard was true, these people will be shorthanded for weeks, if not months. I can earn my keep and a few coppers beyond it, I'm sure.*

"Peace and sweet water to you, travelers. Welcome to the village of Oba's Well," the *dyara* stated, raising her hand as they reached the village gate. One of the older children dashed off, doing her silent bidding. "Or do you even speak Sundaran?"

Sir Zeilas bowed over the dappled neck of his Steed. "We speak it well enough, *dyara* Chanson. Shade and peace to you and yours. I am Sir Zeilas, Knight of Arbra. This is Sir Eduor Aragol, from Mandare."

More than just the *dyara* frowned at that, though she was the only one to fold her arms over her chest. The other villagers just stared. "A Knight of Arbra, we can trust," Chanson stated. "Your Goddess regulates your conduct. But a son of the Mandarites, and a warrior at that? We may be isolated, but even we have heard of your madness."

"Ex-Mandarite," Eduor stated firmly. "Shade and peace to you, *dyara* Chanson. I may be noble-born," he added, knowing there was no point in mentioning his recent bout of slavery, "but I have foresworn my birth land and will not go back. I am here to look for work."

"If you want to be a warrior, you should follow the others. Though I don't see a weapon on you," the *dyara* added tartly, eyeing his dusty, plain hose and knee-length tunic, with its Natallian-style slits up the sides. It was nothing like the formal layers he had once worn as a nobleman's son, but then this was a sun-drenched land, rather than the tree-shaded hills of either Mandare or Natallia.

Only the turban wrapping his head was Sundaran. The tights were a little warm, but they did protect his legs from the sun, as did the long sleeves of his tunic. The cut of the clothes worn by these Sundarans was a lot looser and shorter, with many residents boasting bared legs and arms, but then their skin was dark enough to withstand the burning touch of the sun for hours on end. He stood out somewhat in his plain green garments by their color as well as their cut, and knew these people would be judging him all the more for his foreign appearance. Still, he had to try.

"I have no weapons, because I come in peace. And I have no need for them, for I do not care to be a warrior at this point in my life," Eduor stated calmly. "If those men who have just left did so without first helping the rest of you with the planting and the plowing, then you may have need of someone to labor for you. I offer my services, if you are willing to hire me."

Her hands shifted to her hips. Before she could speak, the boy returned with a water skin, a shallow dish, and a small bowl. Eduor noticed the youth wore a blue sash around his yellow-and-green-clad waist, indicating he was a *dyara* in training. Offering her the skin, he held the glazed bowl steady while she poured water into it, invoking the ritual of welcoming.

"May the waters of life bless you and give you rest and refreshment while you abide among us in peace," Chanson stated, filling the bowl almost to the brim.

Sir Zeilas dismounted with a clank of his armor as the youth held out the bowl. Accepting it with a bow, he gave the ritual reply. "I will abide in peace as I accept your refreshment and take my rest among you."

Drinking the water in the bowl, he drained it dry. The boy took it back, letting Chanson fill it once more.

"May the waters of life bless you and give you rest and refreshment while you abide among us in *peace*," she stated, emphasizing the last word with a pointed look at Eduor.

He didn't take offense. Sundarans were known to be as heated in their opinions as the climate of their land. They were a passionate people. Not hard like the Natallians and his fellow Mandarites had become, thanks to their constant warring, but fierce and passionate all the same. "I *will* abide in peace," Eduor countered calmly, "as I accept your refreshment and take my rest among you."

The water was cool and sweet. It soothed his parched throat. Draining the bowl dry, Eduor handed it back to the youth with a bow. "Thank you."

"So. You think you can help us, and that we would want to hire you?" the *dyara* challenged Eduor, hands returning to her hips once the boy took back the water skin. He set the broad dish on the ground and filled it, giving the Steed something to drink as well, though without the formal ceremony.

"The high heat of summer is nearly over," Eduor reminded her. "If you are to have a good harvest come spring, you will need as many fields plowed and planted as you can this autumn."

"You claim to be a nobleman. Most nobles don't bother learning real trades, and they don't like grubbing in the dirt. Do you even know how to plow?" Chanson challenged him.

He figured honesty was the best policy with this woman. "Not exactly, but I can learn."

"Well, we don't have the *time* to teach you," she said. "Not with so many men gone."

"*I'll* teach him how to plow." Sir Zeilas smiled wryly as both Eduor and the villagers eyed him dubiously. "Less than a third of the Knights in Arbora's service are noble-born, and it hasn't been that many years since I was a farmer's son. Just do not expect me to hitch my Steed to a plow."

"We would not insult a foreign Goddess with such a request," the *dyara* stated formally. "We know your Steeds are not mortal beasts . . . and if you *can* teach this man to plow, you can have the use of Falkon's fields and beasts for it while he is gone. *Maybe* he will come to his senses and return before the growing seasons are done, but they should not suffer in his absence."

Her tone suggested she doubted that. Turning, Chanson gestured for both men to follow her into the walled village. The others scattered, some heading out into the fields to do whatever they could in the few hours left before the sun set, the rest returning to their homes.

Like so much else since the sandstorm, the buildings were coated in dust. But they were well made, crafted from stone and plaster. Flat roofs covered most of the workshops and homes, the granaries and the stables, while sunshade awnings made from woven palm leaves covered those rooftops, plus the occasional stretch of street and alley between each structure. Many of the low-walled courtyards sported long palm wood poles, which supported yet more tentlike weaves.

The mix of shadow and dappled sunlight allowed plenty of light for tasks while giving the locals cool shade. At least, in the places where the sandstorm hadn't torn the awnings. Some still dangled in place, tattered and letting through large patches of sunshine, while others had been taken down to be repaired. Most of those were being repaired by gray-haired elders and the children they were minding. Other residents were tending clay ovens and cook fires in the courtyards of their simple homes.

"We are a small village and do not have an inn, but you are welcome to stay in the guesthouse of the temple. *If* you can prove yourselves trustworthy and capable, I may give you permission to stay in Falkon's home. He is the last of his family in Oba's Well, since his sister married and moved to another village north of here," Chanson informed them. Her mouth twisted for a moment before she added, "No doubt he expected *me* to care for his things, as if my duties as *dyara* were light and carefree.

"You, Mandarite, will be responsible for tending his chickens and goats, plus the two donkeys and one mare Falkon has left behind. She is due to drop her foal soon. Until she does so and has recovered, you will have to get his donkeys to pull his plow. That, or pull it yourselves. You, Sir Knight, had better teach him how to care for the animals properly. Any damage to them will be taken out of his hide."

"I know how to tend animals. I can also weed and harvest. It was just the plowing part I never learned," Eduor asserted. "And my name is Eduor, not 'Mandarite.'"

"Well, you had better learn quickly, *Eduor*," she retorted. "With so many gone, we will be hard-pressed to keep everyone fed."

Eduor estimated the village held around two hundred people, with about thirty of those infants or young children and another fifty elders too gray-haired to have the strength for a full day's farming. The rest were either youths old enough for fieldwork or fully grown adults. The loss of twelve or so people didn't seem like a lot, but he knew these villagers would feel the pinch at harvesttime.

The temple lay in the center of the village. It had a small stable, empty save for the sheaves of hay in the low loft, a palm-leaf-sheltered courtyard four times as big as any of the others, and a building two stories higher than the rest. Most of the awnings drooped down from its upper edges, in fact, and the walls had been carefully painted in geometric patterns with repeating motifs of sun and water, palm trees and abstracts in bright shades of yellow, blue, green, and red. Other than that, it was built like the other buildings, with net-covered openings down low and netted windows placed up high, spaced for creating cooling drafts and enough light to see by while hopefully keeping out bugs, snakes, and other small pests.

More netting hung as curtains over the doorways, not only into the temple itself but also to the four cistern sheds in the four corners of the courtyard. The storm doors and window shutters stood open, and someone had taken the time to sweep all the dust from the flagstones lining the ground. It was just as well; splotches of water had been dripped in a series of drying lines from one of the cistern sheds toward the nearest courtyard exit, proof that more than one person had come to fetch their supper water a few moments before. With people constantly coming to the village wells for water, a dusty courtyard would have quickly turned into a muddy courtyard.

The temple building, Eduor knew from his reading, was divided into three segments. On the roof would be the rain-cistern funnels, which led down to the cisterns carved in the bedrock beneath the village. Whenever the seasonal rains came, the *dyara*'s job was to mount the stairs to the roof and use his or her powers to funnel the precious water falling directly over the village into the collection tanks. If the storm was bad, the *dyara* diverted some of that water from over the whole oasis as well, since a heavy rainstorm too early in the growing season could wash away seeds and seedlings alike.

The middle layer contained living quarters for the village priest or priestess and his or her family, and for the *dyara* and his or her immediate family, if the *dyara* wasn't the holy representative for the village. Unlike Mandarite priests, who were forbidden to marry, the *dyara* were considered prime catches as potential mates. There could be several *dyara* in a village, too, allowing it to grow larger, though small ones like this rarely had more than one or two. Whatever space wasn't needed by the priesthood and the water-callers was often given over to storage needs for the villagers, save for the occasional room kept ready for guests.

The ground floor was always the same. The court hall stood on the right, far from the cistern sheds and their moisture so as to protect the storage room holding the tax records and other rulings. If there was a problem in the village, the elders and other influential persons would gather to discuss it and pass judgments if there were any problems. The long, open-air sanctuary sat in the middle, where the reflection pool and the eternal flame awaited the light of the midday sun for holy services. To the left, between the temple sanctuary and the courtyard, sat the bathing hall.

Eduor longed for a bath. He had dust and sandy grit in places he didn't want to think about. The facilities were built along the lines of Natallian-style showers, though every temple bathing hall also had its *mikwahs*, the purification pools where the villagers would go to soak away their sins once a week after confessing their wrongdoings and receiving their penance tasks from the priests.

It's not a bad system, he acknowledged, catching a glimpse of the blue-decorated tiles through the curtained bathing hall entrance. *In such a hot, dry climate, if you want a cooling, refreshing soak, you confess your sins and promise to be a better person, cleaning yourself on the inside before you clean yourself on the outside. Of course, I know the sins the Natallians would smear on my hide, demanding that I confess and atone before I could clean up and cool off. The problem is . . . I haven't committed nearly as many of them as they wanted to think.*

He'd barely been eighteen when his father had been commissioned by King Gustavo the Third to find and claim whatever land the Earl of Aragol could find on the western side of the ocean. What little real combat he had participated in before that point had consisted of responses to minor Natallian landing parties from ships that had slipped along the coast, looking for a weakness in the Mandarite defenses.

As for enslaving women . . . well, he hadn't actually owned more than two concubines before leaving them behind on that ill-fated voyage to the west, though he had been granted the use of his father's slaves a few times. He had definitely paid for the sin of *that* with his own two years of slavery. Particularly over the last year and a half.

The memories of what he had been ordered to do left a bad taste in his mouth. Using some of the water in his skin, Eduor washed them away. *Never again. Never will I be forced to do* that *again.*

"Would you like to wash away the dirt of your travels?" Chanson asked, gesturing at the entrance to the bathing hall.

"Yes. I must see to the care of my Steed first, of course," Sir Zeilas added, gesturing at the small stable placed on the opposite side of the courtyard from the bathing hall. He glanced at Eduor, then added, "I would also like to buy a set of clothes for my companion. Something clean for him to wear while his own are washed and dried."

Chanson eyed Eduor, but more in a thoughtful way than a disdainful one. "We don't have much to spare, since this is not a wealthy village, but . . . I think someone can sell you a *thawa* and a couple cloths for your head and your loins at the very least. Both of you, if you like. That armor must be very hot."

The Arbran Knight smiled wryly. "Actually, it's enchanted for comfort in all weather, from very hot to very cold. I do get tired of wearing it, but I have my own Sundaran-style robes to wear, thank you."

"Good. As for footwear . . . our last guest left behind a pair of sandals, one with a broken lacing. A bit of rope should make them comfortable enough for now, and I think your feet will be about the right size," Chanson added, looking at Eduor. She gave him a skeptical look. "Though with such pale skin, you should probably keep even your toes out of the reach of the sun. I'll go look for those clothes."

Eduor exchanged an amused look with his fellow foreigner. Both of them had browned quite a bit on their faces and hands in the weeks it had taken them to travel this far north. Natallians and Mandarites were born with light golden-brown skin, and Arbrans weren't exactly pale, either, but neither of them were the rich dark brown of the locals. Since his mother had been half Draconan, lending him his blond hair and blue eyes, Eduor had been born a little pale for a Mandarite, but he was still capable of tanning dark enough to be taken for a Natallian laborer.

At least, on the parts he had exposed to the hot summer sun. *Of course, if she wants to see* really *pale skin . . .*

Pulling his thoughts away from that, Eduor focused on helping the Knight with his Steed. Mostly that consisted of taking the bedroll, travel pack, saddlebags, and saddle once Sir Zeilas removed them, and fetching water from the nearest cistern to the stone-carved trough. It did not consist of helping to groom and care for the huge stallion personally. An Arbran Steed permitted no other person's touch without direct orders from his Knight. Though the animal could have carried them both, Eduor hadn't asked and Sir Zeilas hadn't offered. He didn't fill the manger with hay, either, but only because Zeilas had done so while he was bringing up buckets of water from the nearest cistern.

"Thank you for the clothes," Eduor murmured as he rubbed a lightly dampened cloth along the underside of the saddle, cleaning it of the sweat and dust accumulated in the day's journey. "It seems I keep owing you more and more for your kindness and generosity."

Zeilas, now brushing the dust from his Steed's sorrel-and-cream hide, glanced over his shoulder at the younger man. "I helped you because it was the right thing to do. Whether or not you deserved it. But . . . you seem to be worthy of it."

"Worthy or not, I do owe you," Eduor pointed out. "And I'll owe you further for whatever lessons in farming you can give me."

"You can pay me back by paying close attention. I can spare only two weeks at absolute most before I must be on my way again," the Knight warned him. "My term in the court of our envoys to southern Sundara may be done, but His Majesty will undoubtedly want to reassign me elsewhere. He might even want to make me an envoy myself, now that I've had some experience under Sir Willem and Sir Helosia. Either here in Sundara or in one of the small kingdoms dredging themselves out of the shattered remains of Mekhana—I'd love to be assigned to Fortuna, but I only learned Sundaran and Mekhanan well enough to converse."

"I'll pay close attention," Eduor promised him. "If I could find paper and ink, I could even take notes."

"I'll see what our hostess can provide—here, take the saddle soap and give it a better cleaning than just a wipe down," Sir Zeilas directed him. "I can tell you've cared well for saddles before. I'll trust you to do a good job."

"I will. I used to have a fine Mandarosa gelding—that's what we call a spotted gray with dark mane and tail," Eduor explained. "The Earldom has probably reverted to the care of one of my uncles by now, since my father and older brother are long gone, and with it, my belongings. Gelding included."

"If you returned home, would you regain your family lands from your uncle?" Zeilas asked him.

"*If* I returned home and stayed there for a full year, I'd be declared the next Earl by right of succession, since my father and brother would be considered casualties of war after three years of absence. But I've had my fill of being a slave, and no more taste left for owning one, either."

"And that's why I chose to help you," Zeilas said. "I'll be leaving in two weeks, but there will be others entering your life in the future. They'll need the things you can do for them, or teach them. Help them as I am helping you, and I'll consider my own efforts repaid."

"That's a strange way to put it," Eduor murmured. "Where do *you* get the benefit, if I help someone else?"

"Life is a cycle. When the nut is planted, it grows into a tree that makes more nuts. Some of those nuts are carried far away by squirrels and birds and other things, only to drop forgotten and sprout into more trees. And some trees may fall down, rot, and provide nutrients for yet more young saplings to grow. The more nuts are spread around, the more trees grow to make yet more nuts. Trees provide shade for our comfort, nuts for our dinner, and wood for houses, hearth fires, and furniture.

"The more trees there are, the more we can enjoy the finer things in life," the Knight told him. "Similarly, the kinder I am to you, the more it encourages you to be kind to others, and the more *that* encourages them to be kind in turn to an increasing number of people. And who knows, one of these years, one of the people *you* were kind to will be able to do a kindness to me in turn. Even if it is so indirect as a hundred payments forward, well, that's still a hundred people whose lives will have been improved, making the world that much better overall."

"I think I'd want to live in a world with a hundred people happier than before," Eduor agreed, carefully applying just the right amount of cleansing oil to the leather to get the dirt off without ruining the material by making it too damp. "I'll see what I can do, here."

"At least you can fell two trees with one axe stroke. By helping others as a way to repay my own aid, it will include tending the farm of that missing warrior, Falkon, which in turn will earn you something of an income," the Knight pointed out.

"Yes, but *what* kind of an income?" Eduor returned. "Food and shelter, maybe, but since the man won't be here to barter my wages . . . I suppose I can always invoke laborer's rights, and claim a percentage of the after-tax harvest based on how much of the overall labor I put into creating it. But that presumes this Falkon will be gone for most of the planting and growing seasons."

"Ask for a silver a day *or* a percentage of the harvest value, whichever is greater when the rightful owner returns," Zeilas advised him, lifting his Steed's hooves one at a time to check their soft centers for stones or thorns. "A silver a day isn't bad for a laborer's wages, considering you don't have all of the necessary skills just yet."

"No, it's not—don't forget to scoop that into the village composting bin," Eduor added as the Steed did what horses liked to do after munching their way through a selection of grain and hay. "Sundarans don't waste a single dropping if they can help it. The soil's too poor not to fertilize it any way they can."

Zeilas chuckled. "Maybe I should make *you* do the scooping, and myself the saddle-cleaning."

"And deny you the pleasure of being the first one to bathe? This'll take me a lot longer than it'll take you to use a pitchfork and barrow," Eduor countered lightly. "I know *about* farming practices. Western Marches is one of the bigger farm holdings in Mandare, and I was trained to help govern it. I just haven't *done* certain things, like actually hitching and guiding a plow. I spent more of my time practicing to be a warrior. But I think," he said as he carefully wiped off the saddle soap with another damp cloth, "I would *rather* learn to be a farmer, now."

"Let's hope you learn quickly," Zeilas told him. "The autumn rains are due soon, and the ground needs to be broken, dampened, and planted before they begin, so the seedlings have enough time to take root—I learned that much of Sundaran-style farming in my three years here."

THREE

Chanson knew the next wave of rains were coming. She could feel it as a dampness in her bones, smell it in the air. But she couldn't stop watching the ex-Mandarite man in their midst.

Despite what she had been led to believe about his kind, he wasn't arrogant, wasn't hateful, wasn't rude or ill-mannered toward women. In fact, Eduor was remarkably polite toward everyone, men, women, and children alike. He was also rather reserved, and that aspect of his mannerisms contrasted with her boisterous fellow Sundarans about as much as his golden skin and wheat-colored hair. Well, the parts of his golden skin that weren't reddened and browned by excess exposure to the sun. She had already treated him twice with aloe salve in the two weeks since he came to Oba's Well.

He looks like he fits in, though. Foreigner though he may be, he fits in here, she acknowledged, watching him playing a guessing game with two of the children. The young boy eyed the golden-brown fists held out to him and tapped the left one. Eduor turned his hands up and displayed the pebbles on his palms, one light and one dark.

From the boy's grin, he had guessed correctly, and Eduor rewarded him by ruffling his short, nubbly twist-locks. Mixing up the two stones, the foreigner tucked his hands into the loose sleeves of his green-and-yellow *thawa*, then pulled them out as rock-clenching fists and offered them to the young girl patiently waiting her turn. She guessed the right hand and pouted when he revealed the dark pebble in that palm. The two children, cousins and just at the age where they were responsible enough for a few simple chores, followed him into the palm-shaded courtyard of Falkon's home.

Chanson, as the *dyara* who had invited them to take care of Falkon's lands, had allowed him and the Arbran to move into it after their first week here. Both men had proven careful and methodical with the house and its contents, as well as the fields and the animals given into their care. Now that the Arbran Knight had ridden away, Chanson was ostensibly keeping an eye on Eduor to make sure he remained honest and honorable, but she watched him simply because . . . well, she didn't quite know why. Other than that she wanted to watch him. Eduor fit into the village, true, but he was still exotic.

She watched him hand the boy a soft currying brush, which would be used on the filly that had been born just three days before, then hand a bucket of wheat corn to the girl, who moved over to the coop and scattered a few handfuls for the chickens to peck at. The trailing edges of the woven fronds sheltering Falkon's courtyard made it hard to see more than that, but she did glimpse enough to figure out that much of the scene.

So that's what the betting was about, to see who got the "fun" chore of grooming the new filly and who had to deal with the mindless hens. She noted what chore Eduor himself had taken with pleasure and amusement. *He's certainly taking very seriously the rules about cleaning the guano from the henhouse and taking it to the compost heaps. Who would've guessed from their reputation that a Mandarite would so happily shovel . . . aww, Goddess, the rains are starting in the distance already?*

Wrinkling her nose, she sighed and headed back to the temple. Not that she had far to walk; Falkon's compound was just two houses and courtyards away from the court hall side of the temple. Her *dyarina* came hurrying up as she reached the front entrance.

"The rains are coming, *dyara*!" Jimeyon told her, his eyes wide. "I can feel them this time, I swear it! They come from the northwest, right?"

She grinned. He reminded her of herself at that age, all excited about the tingly damp feeling in her blood and her bones. "Good! Yes, they do. Now, up to the roof. You get to try spin-trancing for the first few minutes. A little more dampness on the village ground won't hurt it and might harden the dust into dirt."

Jimeyon nodded, accepting her advice. He would be taught as she had been taught, by lessons, observations, and careful practice under the watchful eye of a trained *dyara*. The *dyarina* knew better than to practice without supervision. There were too many stories in Sundaran lore of what happened when a *dyara* turned bad, whether from evil intent, ignorance, pride, or selfishness.

The reverend *dyara* of the village joined them as they mounted the stairs. Kedle was old, her face wrinkled and her hair solid gray; she moved with the stiffness of the joints that plagued all *dyara* in their later years and rarely left the village walls. But her mind was still sharp and her smile warmer than the sun, and everyone in Oba's Well revered and loved her.

Once they were on top of the roof, all three of them could see the silvery gray streaks in the distance, drifting like slanted veils. They could even smell the cool, musty odor of the approaching rain. Chanson pointed over Jimeyon's shoulder, giving him a lesson in weather-reading. "See that? How the rain-veils drift to the east with the wind?"

He squinted, thought, and nodded. "Yes. It looks . . . it looks like it might miss some of the village lands. It's going more to the east than southeast, isn't it?"

"Yes, and it'll miss slightly more than half," *dyara* Kedle stated. "I will call half of the clouds to the south. *Your* job, Jimeyon, will be to open yourself up to the clouds and spin the water over the village into the collectors." She nodded at the sloped tubs lining the temple roof. "Make sure you do not miss."

Each of the rectangular-mouthed bins led down to one of the four cisterns carved in the bedrock beneath the village. There were drains in the roof which also led to the cistern caves, but those would pick up whatever dust had been tracked across the roof, forcing them to purify the murky turbidity such contamination would cause. These tiled collectors were carefully patched and grouted every summer to get them ready for the rains. There were other collectors somewhat like these ones out in the fields, tall inverted cones that funneled rainwater into storage caverns for later irrigation needs. Those collectors weren't kept as immaculately clean, but then the ones here in the village were for the villagers themselves.

"Chanson, you will monitor how much water falls on the fields and how much is being collected. You will siphon off whatever excess the *dyarina* cannot yet handle."

"Yes, reverend," Chanson said.

"Now, why do we only call half of the clouds?" Kedle prompted their young apprentice. "And why do we only wring out of them what they are willing to give?"

"Because the rains belong to everybody, including the other villages that would have been in their path farther along," he replied promptly.

"Good lad. I will summon the rains, now," Kedle warned them. Lifting her arms, draped in their dark blue *thawa* sleeves, she started humming to herself and began making beckoning, almost clawing gestures with her hands. The clouds started to roil.

Mindful of her duties, Chanson reached out with her own powers, extending her mind to the north. The churning of the clouds being divided were causing the droplets inside of them to grow larger and fall faster, heavier. She quickly caught the excess, cupping her hands and turning on her heel.

Like most of the younger women of the village, she was clad in a blouse and gathered skirts instead of the one-piece *thawa*. Her hem floated outward as she began her spin-trance, echoing in sky blue the way the silvery curtains of falling rain now twisted and spun. On the top of the temple and far out to the north, the two of them danced, her in her skirts and the rain in its veil. Diverting the excess into the nearest field collectors, Chanson slowed and tapered off her efforts as the clouds finished parting.

Now the rain that fell wasn't excessive, though it was enough to darken the ground visibly even at this distance. She judged it enough to water the fields and orchards without threatening anything; it was time to let nature and the careful pulling of the reverend *dyara* handle the matter. Waiting for the clouds to reach the village gave her enough time to slip between two collector bins and peer over the edge of the temple wall. From up here, she could see into Falkon's courtyard, and could tell that the chickens had been fed and the filly groomed.

The young girl now swept the courtyard stones, while the boy . . . well, Chanson couldn't see where he was, but she knew the foreigner had bartered with their mother for chores out of them in exchange for teaching them to read and write once the busy planting season was over and the more leisurely weeding season began. All of the mothers and fathers had agreed to the bargain, after the reverend *dyara* Kedle had examined his writing skills in Sundaran and pronounced them more than adequate for the task.

The elderly woman had declared her fingers too gnarled and stiff with *dyara*'s disease to teach the children, while Chanson would be busy teaching their *dyarina* how to walk through the fields and gauge the water needs of all the various plants and animals this season.

Someone needed to teach the villagers the basics, and the foreigner needed to build up a source of wealth for himself, not just tend Falkon's farm in the would-be warrior's absence.

Despite the way the clouds darkened the late afternoon light, Eduor himself was easily discernible, his loose golden curls a match for the yellow decorating his green *thawa*. He had brought the filly's dam out of the shadows of the stables and was brushing her now; the donkeys who had pulled the plow through the tough soil had already been retired for the day and were no doubt groomed, fed, and drowsing in their stalls.

Who would've thought a Mandarite nobleman could be such a conscientious farmer? He pampers even the chickens, laying straw to catch their guano and cleaning their house every few days. Despite all the things the village could have held against him, his rank, his nationality, his unfamiliarity with Sundaran ways, he was earning the respect of her people. *And he's earning my respect, too.*

Kedle cleared her throat. Pulling her attention back to the task at hand, Chanson moved away from the edge of the roof. The clouds had moved close enough that Jimeyon would need to begin shortly. That meant monitoring him and his efforts with her instinctive awareness of the water heading their way.

I think I should tell him that he's earning our respect, she decided, getting ready to coach and praise her young apprentice. *Like I do with Jimeyon, here. It won't hurt him to know we think he's doing alright, and as I was the one who first welcomed him, if a bit tartly, I should be the one to let him know he is welcome among us. Especially now that his Arbran friend is gone and he is alone. And I did treat him roughly when he first arrived.*

Yes, he needs to know we are warming up to him now.

Several weeks later, tired from channeling the latest, late autumn storm and its worrisome lightning, Chanson found herself distracted by a burst of laughter from somewhere beyond the temple walls. Leaving Jimeyon to assist *dyara* Kedle down the steps, she crossed to the edge of the roof and leaned over the waist-high parapet.

There, on the street leading into the village, walked a very muddy, very bedraggled figure. It was so muddy, Chanson had to look twice even to realize what the gender was, let alone the identity. When she did, she winced. *Poor Eduor! He has so much quiet dignity, but everyone is pointing and laughing at him now.*

The voice of one of the younger men who hadn't left with Falkon floated up to her on the wall. "*I* think he's trying to make himself look like one of us!"

Someone else called out, "Hey, Eduor—you missed a few spots!" and a third, a grandmother, lifted her hands as she cried, "—You're supposed to leave your *palms* pale, not the back of your hands, boy!" and that set the rest of them laughing even harder.

Even Chanson felt the urge to giggle. It was quickly stifled by the silent not-smile Eduor gave in reply, and the stiff way he continued up the street, limping toward the temple. Toward the bathing halls, in specific. *I think he's hurt,* she realized. *Not just by their jokes, but physically hurt, too. I should get downstairs to see if he needs tending. Not to mention find out what happened to him.*

Now that the latest storm was over, the wind was beginning to pick up; from the heat carried in the breeze, she knew it was the *meltimi*, the hot, dry wind that signaled the start of the winter season. Not that winter in Sundara was anything more than a convenience of language; it simply meant the cooler of the two local dry seasons, with spring and autumn bringing the few but necessary rains.

She was a good enough water-caller that neither she, nor her apprentice, nor the reverend *dyara* had gotten wet. The same could not be said for the land outside the village walls. With the planting season nearly over, the trio had diverted some of the water into the cisterns, but had let the rain pound the ground; the roots of their crops were firmly established, and it never hurt to let the soil soak up the last of the rains this late in the season. Early on, the rain wouldn't penetrate the too-dry soil and would only run off into the wadis of the desert, but now, the ground was quite moist.

Muddy, even. Taking herself downstairs, Chanson headed into the men's side of the bathing hall. Normally women weren't allowed in there, nor were men allowed in the women's side, but there were exceptions to the rule. Infants and toddlers were kept with whatever parent brought them to the baths, obviously, at least until they were old enough to be trusted with bathing themselves. The priesthood and the *dyara*, by the right of their calling and their training as village priests and healers, could also enter either side at need.

And I see that he needs me, Chanson thought the moment she caught sight of Eduor trying to ease his shirt over his head, his every movement slow, stiff, and accompanied by little grunts of discomfort.

The garment was a gift from one of the older women in the village, who had hired him to write a letter to one of her sons in another village. The ink and paper had come from the temple, and normally it would have been handled by the reverend *dyara*, but old Marna had taken pity on the foreigner in their midst, promising him a set of tunic and trews. Such things were easier to farm in than an ankle-length *thawa*, and less odd-looking than the fitted hose and side-slit tunic he had arrived in. Not to mention more colorful than the bland pastels favored by the forest-dwelling Natallians far to the south.

However, the red and purple fabric, re-dyed back to cheery brightness, was all but hidden under the brown mud coating nearly every inch of the garment. It clung to his skin, and whatever had caused him to roll on the ground left his body visibly wincing with each move.

"Here, let me help you," Chanson offered, hurrying forward. He grunted in surprise and twisted, peering at her through the tangled opening of the neck hole. She bit back a smile at his wary look. "I think you have injured yourself. Was it a fall in the mud? Or several, to be so thoroughly muddy, both front and back?"

"Donkeys," he grunted, struggling somewhat gingerly to pull his head free. Chanson quickly helped peel the damp, dirty cloth from his back, pulling it over his equally muddy scalp. He straightened with a rough sigh, arms still tangled in the fabric but head and torso free. "I was bringing them back in when the rains started falling heavily . . . and then lightning struck a nearby tree."

"Why didn't you bring them in when the rains began?" Chanson asked, helping to peel the sleeves down his arms as well. The state of his arms, smeared with mud despite the cloth that had supposedly protected him, made her suck in a breath. "Ouch! Where did you get all these scratches? And those bruises!"

"I was trying to churn up the soil so the rain could penetrate deeper. It's the northeast field, the one that dries up too fast because it's too hard. Obado told me about the trick, and his fields aren't much worse off than mine . . . than Falkon's," Eduor corrected himself. "But the stupid beasts bolted, and my hands tangled in the reins. I was yanked off my feet and dragged halfway across the field, this way and that, before they darted to the side and flung me straight into the bushes. The *acacia* bushes," he added wryly.

That explained the scratches, of course; acacia bushes produced acacia gum, which could be used for many things, from a kind of edible resin to a binding agent for things like ink and glue. The trees were also known for their nasty inch-long thorns, which made them great for bordering vegetable fields, since it discouraged wildlife from pushing through to get at the succulent food.

Eduor lifted one elbow enough to peer at his suntanned arm. "The bruises . . . well, they do hurt, and they'll continue to hurt, but it just looks worse since I'm so fair compared to you. The scratches sting worse, right now."

"Yes, you'll need to get them cleaned up. You were right to come here," Chanson told him. "Let me help you get the rest of your things off, then you go shower the mud away and scrub everything. I'll bring some ointments for those scratches, so they don't become infected. I think Kedle has some herbs that can be used as a poultice on the worst of those bruises."

He kept the muddied tunic close to his chest. "Uh . . ."

"Come on, everything off, Eduor. I am a healer as well as a *dyara* and priestess. Aside from your pretty hair and your pale skin, you won't have anything new for me to see," she reminded him. When he continued to hesitate, she added tartly, "Either you remove it or I'll ask some of the other men to remove it for you. Acacia scratches are nothing to trifle with, and I *will* see you cleaned and doctored."

That seemed to render him even more tense.

"You're not *afraid* of healers, are you?" she asked, puzzled by his reluctance.

He winced. "It's . . . not that. It's just . . ."

"Just, what?" Chanson asked, beyond puzzled. Hands going to her hips, uncaring that she was getting her own clothes dirty, she cocked her head. "If you don't tell me what's wrong, how can I help you?"

His blue eyes, so different from the brown she was used to seeing, remained fixed on his tunic. ". . . I don't like being ordered around by a woman."

Disgusted, she sighed heavily. *And here I thought he was telling us the truth . . .* Eduor looked up quickly, eyes wide.

"No! Not like . . . I *told* you, I don't believe in the Mandarite philosophies of male superiority anymore," he asserted, though he clutched the muddied tunic to his scratched and bruised chest a little tighter. "I just . . . I have bad memories of being ordered around by . . . women. When I was a war-slave."

That only confused her further. "Eduor, I have *seen* you being ordered around by the women of this village! Did you or did you not agree quite readily and willingly to help Mama Jakika get that old hen off her roof, the one she wanted to roast for her daughter's birthing-day feast? And didn't you agree to help Salosi carry her wet laundry to the drying lines while her husband tended to their son's scraped knees?"

"That was clothed!" he protested, clutching—no, *spreading* the tunic over his naked chest.

She still didn't get it. "I don't understand. Aren't war-slaves ordered to do all sorts of things? Manual labor and the like?"

He looked away from her. "My first . . . *owner* . . . yes. I picked fruit and harvested grain, hauled wood, and took things to market. I was worked like an ox. And I was beaten like an ox. Then I heard this woman in the marketplace trying to say something in Sundaran, only the way she said it was almost a deadly insult to the other merchant, so I stepped in and explained things, and she . . . Midalla was so impressed, once she learned how fluent I was, she bought me from my first owner. She promised me she wouldn't beat me if I served as her interpreter so that she could expand her trade relations with this kingdom. But . . . there are worse things than beatings."

Chanson hadn't thought of her life in Oba's Well as having been sheltered. Her training as *dyara*, healer, and priestess had included ways to recognize and deal with all manner of injuries, abuses, and troubles. But the things he seemed to be hinting at made her blush with discomfort.

"Did she force herself on you? Can a woman even do that to a man?" she asked.

"She denied me food if I didn't . . . please her, first. Nearly every Gods-be-damned meal." He wrinkled his muddied nose. The heat of the *meltimi* winds outside had begun to penetrate the shaded depths of the bathing hall, drying the mud and making it crumble. He brushed awkwardly at the side of his nose, spreading more of the dirt around rather than brushing it away.

Chanson shook her head. "You don't sound very enthusiastic, and if a man cannot retain enough enthusiasm, well, how could you have pleased her that way?"

"Not my . . . not *that*," he denied, shaking his head. "She said she was too old for that. Too old, *period*, if you asked me. But nobody did." A shudder rippled through him and he closed his eyes. "No, she wanted the *other* thing."

"*What* other thing?" Chanson asked. "If she didn't want you to couple with her, and didn't ask it of you, and if you wouldn't have been able to anyway out of sheer disgust . . . I'm sorry, Eduor, but I don't understand."

Opening his eyes, Eduor drew in a deep breath to brace himself, then stuck out his tongue. The tip dangled below his jaw for a moment, then he curled it up until the tip reached the *middle* of his nose. Not quite to the bridge of it, but definitely curling over the point of his nose by a thumb-width. He retracted it with a grimace as Chanson stared.

Noise from outside broke their tableau. Blinking, she cleared her throat. ". . . Well. Rest assured I won't order you to do *that* for me. Not unless *you* want it, of course."

That earned her another wide-eyed stare, but two of the village men entered the bathing hall at that moment. Grateful for the interruption, and for the sun-dark skin of her tribe that hid the flushed state of her cheeks, Chanson changed the subject back to the one at hand. Right now was *not* the time to explain—even to herself—why she had said such a thing.

"You need to finish stripping off your clothes and bathe every inch in the showers. Since you are injured, and do not intend to use the *mikwah* bath, you don't have to confess your sins first. Not that I think you have any to confess," she added, hoping he caught on to the subtle message in her words, that his suffering at the hands of his Natallian owner wasn't a sin in her eyes. "I'd also like to send Jimeyon to help you bathe. It's about time he took some of his lessons in the theory of healing injuries and started applying them in the practicality of it. I'll go fetch him, and the salve for your scratches, then see what we have on hand for making bruise poultices—oh, the donkeys, where are they?"

"They snapped the traces when the plow tangled in the acacia bushes. Last I saw them, they were browsing in the olive orchard north of the field I was in," Eduor admitted, relaxing enough to lower the wadded protection of his tunic a little. "The last time the female got loose, she came back by nightfall. I hurt too much to chase after them right away, so I figured they'd come back in by then. If not, I'd go looking in the morning."

"Falkon's donkeys are fairly good that way," one of the two men stated. He ignored Chanson's presence as he removed his rain-damp orange-and-brown *thawa*, then stripped off the matching brown loincloth underneath. "They might stay out overnight if enough rain puddled in the ditches to drink, but that's the *meltimi* wind out there."

"Everything will dry up over the next few days, and they're smart enough to know where their watering trough is—please do send *dyarina* Jimeyon in," said the other man, acknowledging Chanson with a dip of his head. "My wife insists I suffer the sin of nightly flatulence, and must therefore confess and cleanse myself before coming to bed tonight. If farting's a sin, I figure I'll get more sympathy and a lighter penance from a fellow boy than from a girl."

Caught off guard by his quip, Chanson threw back her head and laughed. Waving her hand at the men, she took herself out of the bathing hall.

FOUR

"You," Eduor said, enunciating his words carefully, "know how to hold a party."

Chanson's nut brown eyes, slightly glazed from the date wine they had been drinking, followed his every word. Chin already propped on her hand, she leaned over a little more and sighed. "Yes . . . A party."

She wasn't actually watching his lips. He was sure of it.

"A lovely party," Eduor added, flicking his tongue on each *L*.

"Lovely . . ." She sighed.

Lovely, indeed. I see my tongue is getting me into trouble again. If the wine hadn't dulled some of the pain at that thought, if her beautiful but very, very different face hadn't thwarted thoughts of anything a paler golden shade, if it hadn't been far from either wrinkled or petulant, he might have shuddered at that thought. As it was, the village vintner, or whatever it was they called the person who made the local wine, knew how to craft a very potent brew from the fruit of all those date palm trees. Eduor was drunk enough that such considerations were few and mild and faded quickly from his thoughts.

In fact, if he hadn't been so comfortably drunk, the tiny remaining sober corner of his mind knew he would never have done what he did next. Picking up his glazed cup, Eduor drank some more of the sweet-spicy wine, then licked the near edge of the rim with his tongue, catching the stray droplet that tried to slither down. Her eyes glazed over a little bit more, following the sinuous flicks of his tongue as if entranced. He wasn't even displaying half of it this time, either.

Definitely getting me into trouble, he repeated silently, finishing off the dregs in his cup. *At least it's just with words . . .*

"Doesn't it get in the way?" Chanson blurted out, chin sliding off her hand so that she could gesture vaguely with her fingers.

"Mmm?" Mouth buried behind the solid safety of ceramic, Eduor gave her a questioning look.

She glanced around quickly, making sure they were more or less alone. While there were still several other villagers about, laughing and chatting and celebrating the odd but cheerful Festival of Mid-Dry, held twice a year during the middle of what passed for winter and summer each . . . no one was within easy hearing distance. It helped that three of the original seven musicians were still playing quietly off to one side, though their music was more for listening now, and not the long, wild, exuberant dancing tunes from earlier.

Apparently believing they were almost alone enough, but not quite, she scooted around the edge of the trestle table, one of many set up in the temple courtyard. Slipping onto the chunk of palm tree trunk that served as a seat for the end of the table, she leaned over the corner separating them and whispered, "*You* know. Your tongue? I've tried, but I just can't stop thinking about it."

This close, Eduor could smell the spicy-sweet perfume she had bathed in before donning her elaborately brocaded blue *thawa* and jewel-pinned turban for the festival. This close, he could see how her own pink tongue snaked out to moisten her lips, full and soft-looking. This close, he could see she was nothing like the last two women to get this close to him . . . except that she, too, was fascinated with his tongue.

Sort of. Her next words disillusioned him as to why, thankfully.

"Doesn't it get in the way when you talk? Or when you eat, or swallow?" she asked under her breath, propping her cheek on her palm. "And what about when you kiss? You have such lovely diction, how can a tongue that big not interfere with things like eating and speaking and such?"

Ah. Lovely. Rather than thinking of me as a sexual novelty, she's thinking of me as a freak, a demonic aberration from a Netherhell. Thankfully, the date wine in his system did a good job of blunting any possible sting accompanying that thought. Eduor shrugged. "It's just . . . there. It's always been there. I'm used to it."

"Yes, but it's in *your* mouth, where you're used to it. If you put it in a woman's mouth, wouldn't it get in her way?"

"No, I'm usually careful with it. A good . . . kiss isn't about trying to shove it down someone else's throat."

Her free hand came up, the edge of her finger brushing the underside of his chin. He liked the feel of her hand, warm, dry, and slightly calloused from the occasional non-priestly bit of labor. Chanson, like all the residents of Oba's Well, was not afraid to get her hands dirty. Like that time, a couple of months ago, when she had offered to clean him up after his ignominious adventure in the mud and thornbushes.

"You don't sound happy when you say that. Haven't you had any good kisses lately?"

Eduor choked on an unhappy laugh. "As *if*. I haven't had *any* kisses, good or bad, in a couple of years. Unless you count the exceptionally wet one little Amalie planted on my cheek a few weeks ago, but then she's only three and I'm quite sure that doesn't count."

Stretching for her cup, she picked it up and drained it dry, then smiled at him. A teasing, feminine smile. Undoubtedly some of it came from the date wine, but enough of her own warmth infused it that it enthralled him. "Maybe you just need a beautiful young woman to kiss. An *adult* young woman, I mean."

It took him a few moments to register what she was saying. At least, until her next words scattered his wits.

"Do you think *I'm* pretty enough to kiss?" Chanson asked him.

Eduor shook his head, but in agreement, not denial. "Definitely. Young, and pretty, and beautiful. But a kiss . . ."

She pouted. Eduor stared, fascinated by the slight pucker of her lower lip. Normally, Chanson was brisk, efficient, and sassy. Much more lively and opinionated than any Mandarite woman dared to be, and far more warm and welcoming than any Natallian woman he'd seen. But a pouting Chanson was undeniably charming.

"It's the wine, isn't it?" She sighed, toying with her empty cup. "I'll admit it's given me the courage to speak, but it's been on my mind all the same. I like you. Now that I've gotten to know you, of course."

It was Eduor's turn to glance furtively around. No one was looking their way, tucked into the back of the courtyard as they were, by one of the cisterns not yet tapped for use. Assured they weren't drawing undue attention, he leaned close, cupped her cheek, and kissed her. Dry lips to dry lips, and no hint of his tongue, but a kiss all the same.

She was warm, she was soft, and she was feminine. She also sighed again, leaning into his kiss with an encouraging little nibble. Eduor enjoyed his first real kiss in years . . . until the ugly thought popped into his head that his last "real kiss" had been with a concubine slave. By the coldest definition, not a free, willing woman. *The wine may loosen her inhibitions, but it also loosens her good sense . . . and I like her far too much to let her regret any of this in the morning. Other than the hangover; that's unavoidable.*

Pulling back with a sigh of his own, Eduor looked down at the table. In the glow of the lights strung across the courtyard, candles sheltered from the night breezes in carefully crafted paper globes, his now deeply tanned hands didn't look that much paler than hers. Parts of him were still quite pale, particularly from waist to knees, but months of laboring in the fields as a farmer had bronzed his skin as dark as it could go. He was happy to be a farmer, too. Happy to be here in the modest little village of Oba's Well, somewhat off the main caravan routes and thus quiet and peaceful.

He didn't want to ruin the life he was building by doing or saying the wrong thing. Still, he knew he had to say something.

"I like you, Chanson. A lot. More and more as the days go by. But, more than that . . . I respect you." He glanced up at her, wanting to gauge her reaction, to see if she knew just how important those three little words were. She looked a little surprised, yes, but also touched. Something inside him relaxed. *She does understand . . .* Nodding, he shrugged. "That's why I don't think we should do this. Um, not under the influence of date wine. But later, when we're both sober . . . I'd like to try again."

The smile that blossomed on her beautiful dark face made a small corner of his mind regret the decision to wait. The rest of him felt relief, knowing that it was the right choice.

"You," Chanson murmured, lifting a finger so she could slide it down the length of his nose, "are a romantic. Aren't you?"

It wasn't a question. Blushing, Eduor ducked his head. Deciding it was best to make a tactical retreat, he carefully stood, mindful of the wine he had drunk. Then, because he couldn't resist, he swooped down and kissed her. And very briefly, very quickly, licked her lips with his tongue.

After all, he thought as he pulled back, leaving her smiling and dreamy-eyed, *if my tongue is going to get me into yet more trouble . . .*

The music stopped. Eduor became aware that all three of the musicians were staring at the two of them. Their stares and their silence were drawing more attention. *Definitely time to retreat.*

He didn't get very far. Chanson's mother, a matronly figured woman in bright brocaded green, bustled up to him, a cup of date wine cradled casually in one hand. She poked him with her other hand, alarming the young man. The older a woman got in this corner of Sundara, he had learned, the more inclined she was to speak her mind. Apparently, this particular middle-aged mother intended to speak it to him.

"You," Marison stated crisply, "are something. You are one, and a total, total one, at that!"

"Milady, I *swear* my actions were not meant to offend anyone," Eduor replied under his breath. Her confrontation was embarrassing and awkward, and drawing a lot of interest from the other adults still up this late. The last thing he wanted to do was raise his voice and let the others know what was being discussed.

"What?" She frowned at him, then sighed and shook her head. "No, no, no, boy! You are *something*. A better something than that Falkon was. Why, when he was courting my little girl, he always treated her like the girl next door! He took her for *granted*. Just look at him!" She flipped her hand expressively at nothing, both emphasizing her point and dismissing the man in question, then sipped from her cup. "Run off to fight. Silly man. The desert's a hard enough life without adding warfare to strife . . . mmm, heh, that rhymed . . .

"But as I was saying, *you* are something. You have substance!" She clapped him on the shoulder, and being a somewhat large, well-built woman, made him stagger a little. Chuckling, Marison saluted him with her cup. "Make sure *you* stick around."

Turning, she sashayed away, gathered skirts swaying with each step. A glance at the others still lingering at the celebration showed them smiling. Apparently, if Marison gave her approval, everyone else would. Eduor swayed a little from the sensation of being accepted by this community. Either that or it was the wine, but he felt good about tonight all the same.

"She's right, you know," Chanson murmured from right behind

him, so close that Eduor jumped a little. She smirked at him as he glanced over his shoulder at her. "You *are* something, and I would like you to stick around. Preferably a good, long time."

Her hand touched his back, then slid down to pat the curves of his buttocks through the brocaded purple of his festival *thawa*. It made him jump a second time, alarmed by the touch. *That* was what Midalla had done to let him know she . . . *This is* not *that dead hag of a merchant, nor her harridan niece*, Eduor reminded himself firmly. *Chanson will* not *demand I satisfy her, nor withhold everything else in my life until I comply. She is nothing like those two harpies . . . for which, I thank the Gods.*

It helped that when he looked at her, all he saw was a beautiful young woman with deep brown skin and nut brown eyes. Her twist-rolled locks had been swept up into a sort of dark cockscomb and confined in place by the length of sky blue linen wrapped around her head, nothing like the silky brown or blond tresses of a Natallian woman. When she walked, she walked with the same feminine sway to her hips that her mother used. Her ankles were bare beneath the straps of her sandals instead of covered in hose, and her arms decked with brass and silver bangles that clinked musically whenever she made some gracefully gestured point. Everything about the lovely *dyara* Chanson was different from the women haunting his past.

Tempted to follow her, Eduor reminded himself that they were both a little bit past the slightly drunk point and carefully headed for his temporary home instead. *That's another thing I have to think about. There isn't a lot of arable land around Oba's Well. If and when that Falkon fellow comes back, the land would likely revert to him.* If *he comes back before the next planting season*, Eduor remembered fuzzily. *Something about the queen a couple reigns back declaring that any landowner who abandoned his land for a full year . . . something about losing the rights to own the land, or something . . . I can't remember. It's in the village records, I'll bet.*

Of course, with my luck, the fellow will come back right at the end of the harvest and claim all my hard work for himself. Which means I'll need to either move on . . . and leave her and all these people behind . . . or find some other way of staying here.

The thought of leaving threatened to sober him. Sighing, Eduor shook his head. *No . . . I'll figure something out. I can always spend my time being a teacher and a scribe, though there isn't much calling for the latter around here. I can try claiming further soil for farming at the far edge of the village, but that would need extra irrigation support . . . or I could try my hand at Mandarite engineering.*

There has to be a better way these people can irrigate their fields than what they're doing now. They use open ditches, but it's inefficient, since it's subject to evaporation. Maybe a system of troughs, made out of wood or even pottery, graded for a gentle slope, and a holding tank with, what, a water-screw to lift water to the top, so all three dyara *don't get tired out from casting their water-magics all day?*

Heh. Maybe I should just put boards over the tops of all those ditches? That'd be the easiest solution . . . Chuckling at the somewhat silly idea, Eduor took himself off to bed.

FIVE

Caught in the middle of polishing the brazier holding the Flame of Sundra, Chanson looked up at the sound of approaching footsteps. This close to the harvest season, it was unusual for anyone to enter the temple in the morning hours. Midday, yes, as the farmers gathered in the courtyard for half an hour before their midday meal to praise Sundra and pray for the right mix of weather. They wanted clear skies for the wheat harvest, followed by gradual light rains so the various fruits would ripen and the cisterns would refill. They didn't always get it—the world was shared by many lands and many Gods with many people and many needs—but it never hurt to pray.

She did not expect to see Eduor. He looked like he was freshly scrubbed, dressed once again in his bright purple festival *thawa*, his hair freshly washed and separated into the thin braids which were the best imitation he could give of Sundaran twist-locks, given the fine, straight strands of his hair. Balancing two stacked baskets in his hands, he padded up to the end of the reflection pool, then dropped to his knees and lifted the baskets high. Offering them formally, she realized.

Quickly giving the underside of the brazier one last rub with the polishing cloth, Chanson hurried down the length of the sanctuary courtyard. "Eduor? You're bringing something to the temple?"

Lowering the baskets, he grinned at her. "I bring the first fruits for the Goddess, and the second fruits for the *dyara*."

Bemused, she took the baskets from him, allowing him to rise. He took back the top basket, accompanying her toward the brazier. She eyed him as they walked. "I thought the consensus among the farmers was that most of the wheat wouldn't be ready for harvesting for two or three more days."

"Most of it," Eduor agreed. "But some of it ripened early. It's not much, but it's all handpicked from just an hour ago. And there are some early figs, too, and some acacia gum. I also picked some of the sweet herbs for incense during the offering. *And* I confessed my sins, few as they are, to Jimeyon while he was scrubbing the tiles in the bathing hall."

She smiled. "You've really put some thought and care into honoring our Goddess, haven't you?"

He nodded and gestured at the brazier, which currently held only a small oil lamp. It was there to symbolically keep the Flame of Sundra burning while the ashes were carefully cleaned out each evening and the brass of the exterior polished each morning. "I want to make sure I do not offend your Patron. And to show that I will honor Her, so She will accept me. I like being here. Not just in Sundara, but living and working right here, in Oba's Well. I don't want to leave."

"Even when the donkeys drag you into the thorn trees?" Chanson teased lightly.

He ducked his head, but he grinned. "Even when I'm dragged into the thorn trees."

"Well, the Goddess is happy to accept such carefully selected first fruits. It's the thought and the intent that matter most, not the size of the offering," she told him. "The full fire won't be lit until just before noon, but I'll be happy to put . . . this basket? Or that one?"

"This one," Eduor said, lifting the one in his hands.

"That basket, then, on the altar platform," she agreed. "That will be the first fruits to the Goddess. This one would therefore be the second fruits for the priesthood and the *dyara*."

The tap-tap of *dyara* Kedle's cane, which she had started using in the last month, heralded the approach of the chief priestess. "That is a very small offering of first and second fruits, young man. Important, in that you brought it so soon, and I'll trust you gave as much care in selecting the first fruits as you've shown in everything else you've done so far . . . but it *is* customary to bring a larger tithe of the harvest than that."

"With respect, reverend *dyara*," Eduor said, giving her a bow, "I did not feel right about giving the full tithe. The land is not mine, and the seed was not mine, nor the bushes, nor the trees. Only the effort in growing it has been mine. The larger share of it still belongs to the absent owner, Falkon. In his name, I will bring a larger portion in a few days' time, when the full harvest begins. This is just what I felt I could bring to represent the value of my own labors."

Kedle paused, studying the young man, then smiled. "You show wisdom . . . and the mind of a law-sayer, to parse your responsibility so fine. But only by the letter of the law. If Falkon and his followers haven't returned by now, either they are dead at the hands of their enemies or they have been indentured to their captors . . . or perhaps they have taken to the warrior's life like an animal takes to an oasis. Somehow I doubt the boy will return before the end of harvest. If he does not . . . then all but *that* portion of the first fruits would be your tithe to the Goddess of Water and Flame, and what you have brought today would be his."

"With respect, reverend *dyara*," Eduor started to protest. Kedle lifted her hand, forestalling him.

"The greatest portion, young man, comes not from the seed to sow and the land to sow it in, but the *act* of sowing it. You cannot have a good hen to lay eggs if her own egg is not first carefully tended and hatched," Kedle reminded both of them. "Now, set the first fruits on the altar dais, and take the second fruits up to the kitchen," she directed them. "*Dyara* Chanson, have you finished polishing the brazier?"

"Well, no, reverend *dyara*," Chanson admitted. "I was almost finished, but I paused so that I could accept his offering."

The elderly woman chuckled. "That's not the only thing he's been offering—have you given her a kiss yet, young man?"

Eduor blushed, his cheeks darkening further under his tan. "Well, no, but . . . I thought it best to first honor the Goddess, and to not think of such things in Her temple."

"The Goddess enjoys a good romance, the same as any of us—passion has been compared more than once to a flame, after all. Sometimes it warms us and sometimes it burns us, but it is a vital part of our life. Now, I can polish the rest of the brazier, if you will deal with the baskets. The rubbing cloth is the lighter of the two loads, after all. Go on," the reverend *dyara* urged, gesturing with the tip of her cane toward the stairs to the second and higher floors. "Make sure he shows you his appreciation as he helps you with the second fruits." She smiled, wrinkling her face with definite humor. "Just don't be late for the noon prayers. Or too noisy."

Eduor flushed with embarrassment.

Blushing herself, though she knew it wouldn't be as visible on her own brown cheeks, Chanson nudged him into moving. She guided him toward the altar, letting him set the basket of first fruits on the raised stone platform, then handed him the basket of second fruits and shooed him toward the stairs.

"Go on, take it up. Please," she added as his brow creased in a faint frown. *That's right, I keep forgetting he has bad memories of being ordered around.* "Would you please carry it up to the kitchen storeroom for me, Eduor?"

The hint of a wrinkle smoothed. Nodding, he headed for the stairs. They had kissed a few times since the Festival of Mid-Dry, but nothing further, and Chanson thought she knew why. *I'll have to phrase this very carefully, then, and be mindful of his past and its memories. Because Kedle is right, our Goddess* does *enjoy a good romance.*

When he put the basket in the kitchen storeroom and carefully added the figs to the shelves and the grain to the bin, she didn't *tell* him what she wanted to do. Instead, she smiled and held out her hand. He eyed it warily, but she didn't pressure him, just left her fingers up in a silent offering. Eduor hesitated a long moment, then placed his hand in hers. Still smiling, Chanson led him out of the kitchen area and up the next flight of stairs to her own room.

But not straight to her bed. Instead, she tugged him over to the recessed window looking out across the village, and sat on one end of the cushion-strewn bench. "This is my favorite place to sit and think," she said as she looked up at him. "Would you like to sit?"

Nodding, he settled near her. Not so close that their thighs brushed, but close enough that their hands, still joined, rested comfortably between them. His blue gaze skipped around her room, first glancing toward her bed, then toward the steel mirror by her clothes cupboard, then back to the bed, before glancing at the door that led to her private refreshing room. And back to the bed again.

Chanson didn't have to guess what was going through his mind. She figured it was in a muddle. Wanting a little more privacy, she adjusted the wooden blinds on her window, pulling on the cord, which tilted them just enough to block out the view from below. "Eduor . . . I want to ask something of you."

That pulled his gaze back to her face. "What is it?"

His reply wasn't entirely defensive, but she did notice a hint of wariness in his gaze. Choosing her words carefully, she laid out her thoughts. "I would like to ask you to do something for me. I would like you to tell me what you want. From me, with me, about me . . . about *us*. Because I like you—I really like you—but I know you had some bad experiences in your past."

He didn't bother to pretend ignorance. Wrinkling his nose, Eduor rubbed at the back of his neck with his free hand. "I don't like being *told* to . . . go share a bed with someone, or the activities involved. And I no longer feel comfortable *telling* someone else to do those things, either. It doesn't feel right. I can't . . ."

Squeezing his hand, Chanson soothed him. "I know, I know . . . but, Eduor, if you don't *say* what you want, how can I know? The Gods gave us the privacy of our thoughts, but that in turn means that we must share them of our own free will. I don't want you to tell me what to do, either. At least, not in the expectation that I'd have done it regardless of my own feelings," she allowed dryly. "It might turn out to be something that I *want* to do, but I know that you don't want to order me around. Nor do I want to boss you around. For one, it's exhausting, and for another, that would be an abuse of my power as *dyara* and the next reverend priestess in training."

"Quite," he agreed. He frowned softly, thoughtfully. "You're saying I do have to *tell* you, in the sense of just saying it so that you'll know. And then . . . let you decide for yourself whether or not you'll do it?"

She smiled, relieved. "Yes, exactly. And I promise you that I will do the same. We should also remember to ask what the other person wants, and if at any time, anything makes us uncomfortable, we should feel free to say 'stop' and know the other one of us will stop, yes? So. Do we have an agreement between us?"

He considered her offer for a mere moment before nodding. "Yes. We do. So . . . I should go first, I guess. What do you want?"

Chanson grinned, happy that he had not only agreed but asked. "I want *you*. Now would be lovely, but I can also wait for later. I made sure to buy a fresh contraceptive amulet from the mage-vendor when he visited last month, same as many of the other young ladies around here, so that worry is taken care of for the next whole year. As for what I want in specific regarding you . . . well, I want to do a lot of things with you, but the first thing I would like to see, if I may, is your chest."

"My chest?" he repeated. "Just my chest, for now?"

Chanson nodded, all but holding her breath, and he gave her a half smile of his own. Freeing his fingers, he lifted both hands to the laces holding the long, overlapping folds of his *thawa* in place. The garment was a fanciful version of the kind worn out among the fields. Once unlaced, the neckline opened down to the waist where it was usually belted or sashed, though the sleeves could also be used to tie the garment around the hips. Slipping free of those sleeves, Eduor left them puddled at his hips, baring his arms as well as his upper body.

Scooting a little closer, Chanson lifted her hand, then paused. "May I touch your chest?"

"You may."

She laid her hand on his sternum and spread her fingers. The contrast in shades of brown, hers dark and rich, his warm and golden, made her smile. "Look at that," she murmured, gently sliding her palm up, then down. "You and I together are so different, and yet beautiful."

"I've usually been called handsome, not beautiful," he allowed, following her fingers with his gaze. "But usually by women who were either ordered to think that, or . . ."

"Well, I will say there are a couple of men in this village who are *slightly* better-looking," Chanson teased, grinning, "but none so exotic, and none that I want as much as you."

Eduor chuckled. "I'm not exotic. Blond, maybe, but I'm just a man."

"Nonsense. Everything about you is different. Even your chest hairs," she told him. "They're long and straight, instead of short and curly. And your eyes remind me of spring skies between the rains. You yourself are different, inside. You're educated, and you've traveled—"

"—Involuntarily," Eduor agreed wryly.

"Yes, but you've been well beyond the next village," she reminded him. "You think about things that are larger than just the little world of Oba's Well, and it's easier for you because of your travels. I like talking *with* you, not just at you. And I like looking at you . . . and thinking about you. I do that a lot, when I sit here in the mornings."

"I think about you whenever I see the color blue," Eduor said. She looked up at his face and saw his almost-shy smile. He covered her hand with his, holding it still, then glanced down at it. "I want . . ." He flushed and looked away, biting his lower lip.

Chanson waited patiently, wanting him to feel free to say whatever was on his mind. "Yes?"

"I want you to . . . touch me. All over. And . . . And give me pleasure. But only if *you* want it," he added quickly, meeting her gaze with a directness that underscored his seriousness on that point.

She grinned. "I was hoping you'd ask. Would you please stand?"

Complying, he stood and loosened the sash. Without being prompted, Eduor pulled both sash and *thawa* over his head. He dropped them on the cushion-padded bench, leaving him in the loincloth favored by Sundaran men. He had once described to her the many layers of a Mandarite nobleman's clothing. She hadn't been able to picture it very clearly even with his attempts at drawing it for her. Now, almost naked, she couldn't imagine him any other way. He stood in his skin and his sandals, facing her with the plain linen cloth wrapped around his hips and groin, and did so with a mixture of dignity and self-awareness.

His thighs fascinated her. Chanson knew he was paler than a Sundaran; one only had to look at his golden-brown face to see it. But his thighs, between hips and knees, were as pale as sand. Wanting a closer look, she slipped off the bench onto one knee. Eduor jumped back.

"What—don't *do* that!" he exclaimed, eyes wide with shock and what looked like a little fear.

Confused, Chanson blinked up at him. "Do what?"

"Don't . . ." He flushed, closed his eyes for a moment, then wrapped his arms around his chest. "Back . . . in Mandare . . . As the son of an Earl, it was customary in our household to be greeted every day by our slave-women. Greeted by them . . . They'd get on their knees, and . . ." He couldn't seem to get the words out, though he tried. "Just *don't kneel* in front of me. Please. You aren't a slave, and I don't have any right to . . ."

She still didn't get it. "Right to . . . what?"

He flushed even redder and bit out the words with a grimace. ". . . Expect you to suckle me."

Comprehension dawned, aided by the bulge now evident in his loincloth. *If he had that done to him every day, it must have trained his body to respond in expectation from the moment a woman kneels in front of him, like the way a pampered horse or donkey would learn to expect a bit of fruit before and after being harnessed to the plow. But now he doesn't want to* expect *it, in the sense of demanding it as a right. Though surely it can't be good for him to suffer without release; Sundra knows he hasn't courted any other woman since coming to the village, or I'd have heard of it by now.*

Rising to her feet, Chanson caught his hands and gently drew them out from under his elbows. She smiled at him gently, letting him know it was alright. "Then I won't kneel . . . even though I find your pale thighs rather fascinating and just wanted a closer look." She flashed him a grin and he relaxed a little. "Maybe when *I* feel like it at some point in the future . . . but since you don't want me to do it right now, I won't. So come, sit on the bench with me. Like equals. Equals sit together, yes?"

Nodding, he relaxed further and let her guide him back onto the cushions of her window seat. "Yes, equals sit together."

A thought occurred to her, and she smiled wryly. "Actually, to be equal, I'd have to take off my blouse and skirt. Shall I do that?"

From the instant interest in his exotic blue eyes, she figured she didn't really have to ask. But she waited until he gave her a quick, eager bobble of his head, then stood. It didn't take long to untie the lacings at the ruffled neckline of her blouse, but she took her time in letting that neckline droop down over her shoulders. She also watched her soon-to-be lover, enjoying the way his blue eyes roved over her skin.

She didn't let it down quite far enough to expose her breasts just yet, but instead removed the belt holding the aquamarine fabric in place, then loosened the lacings of her skirt. That, she let slide to the floor, exposing her legs down to her sandals. That also dragged his gaze down to the floor, and he took his time bringing it back up again.

From the increased shape of his loincloth, he was enjoying the view. Once his eyes returned to her face, she loosened her blouse just a little bit more and let it flutter to the floor. His gaze lingered on her breasts, long enough to make them feel tight with the longing for a more tangible caress. He lowered his focus to her hips, next.

Like his, her loincloth was crafted from plain, undyed linen, bleached only by repeated dryings in the sun. And like his, hers had the same long, ribbonlike tapes that wrapped around her hips, as well as the fall which passed from back to front, looped around the waistband, and returned to back where it was tucked into itself once more. Unlike his, which blended in with his pale thighs, hers stood out prominently against her sun-dark skin.

"I find," Eduor murmured, staring at her loins, "your own thighs fascinating. Very dark and exotic."

Pleased, Chanson stepped out of the light blue puddle of her clothes. Before he could protest, she straddled his pale thighs and settled on his knees, bringing their contrasting flesh together. His hands lifted as if to ward her off, then hovered a moment, no doubt unsure if he had the right to touch her. She could only imagine what he had gone through. Catching his fingers, she brought his palms down on the tops of her thighs.

"I *want* you to touch me," she murmured. Sliding her fingertips to his wrists, she explored up his forearms. Here, his skin wasn't as pale as his thighs, but rather tanned to a nut brown from long exposure to the sun. "And I want to touch you. What do you want, Eduor of Oba's Well?"

Knowing he wanted to fit in, she watched his eyes brighten with her intentional phrasing. "I want . . . you. I want to touch you."

She smiled. "I want you to."

His hands, resting on her thighs, moved. They slid up and down, caressing her legs, then moved to her waist. She drew in a breath of pleasure, only to squirm a moment later when his fingertips grazed her ribs a little too lightly.

Blue eyes narrowed thoughtfully. She stared back at him. He wriggled his fingers again. She squirmed a second and gave him a dirty look, but it was spoiled by her grin. He matched it with a wicked one of his own, and attacked. Within heartbeats she was squirming and laughing so hard, she could hear her voice echoing off the walls of her room, and no doubt across the roofs of the buildings beyond her open window.

Somewhere in the middle of arching her back, he swooped down and captured the tip of her left breast. Her laughter turned into a choked gasp, then a moan as he suckled and licked. Swirling and flicking his long, agile tongue, he tasted her from one breast to the other and back.

She wasn't sure which one of them moaned first, or who groaned in reply. Nor was she sure when her fingers buried themselves among the thin braids confining his soft curls, though she did note that every time she tugged gently, he suckled more strongly. Murmuring his name, she stroked and tugged in encouragement. His arms hooked around her hips and pulled her close, until her linen-wrapped groin was snuggled enticingly tight against his. Well, as tight as her restless circling and his own rocking would allow.

He mumbled something against her breasts. She managed a noise of inquiry between moaning breaths, and he dragged his lips from her flesh.

"I *need*," he panted.

"Need?" Chanson asked, attention distracted by the way he flicked his tongue in circles around her right nipple.

"Need . . . to be *inside* you," he groaned.

"Oh, *yes*," she agreed, shivering with anticipation. He hitched her closer, then stood. Clutching at his shoulders for balance, Chanson pressed a kiss to Eduor's forehead. He crossed to her bed and laid her down, then reached for the tapes on her loincloth. Pushing up on one elbow, she reached for his, smirking as they untied each other's final garment. If one didn't count their sandals.

Before she could comment on their lingering footwear, Eduor captured her mouth in a kiss. Pressing her back onto her goat-hair-stuffed mattress, he helped her lift and part her knees, making room for him. She felt his manhood bump against her groin and reached down to grasp the hot, hard shaft. He grimaced and pulled back.

"Please . . . please don't . . ."

"Don't, what?" Chanson asked, worried at this new trouble spot in their lovemaking.

"Don't *stop* me," he all but whimpered.

Suspecting what his owners had done to him, or rather, denied to him, Chanson gently stroked his warm, dry shaft as she spoke. "I'm not stopping you," she soothed him. "I'm guiding you—wait, lie on your back. *Trust* me, Eduor. I'm going to give you pleasure, because I *want* to give you pleasure."

Hesitating, he finally nodded and eased onto his back. Curling up and over his stomach, Chanson brought her lips to his shaft. He sucked in a sharp breath, then let it out in a long, heartfelt groan. Her tongue wasn't nearly as long as his, but he clearly appreciated her efforts to dampen his flesh. She in turn enjoyed both the taste of him and the close-up view of his pale golden thighs.

Once he was sufficiently wet and restless, she debated climbing on top, but decided he had conceded enough control to her. Uncurling, she lay down beside him and urged him up over her. "Make love to me, Eduor. Please."

Groaning in relief, he shifted to climb over her. She parted her knees in invitation and drew his gaze to the crux of her thighs. Seeing him hesitate, guessing at the conflicts rising within him, she caressed his jaw, returning his eyes to her face.

"Another time, and only if you want it. Right now, I want the same thing you want. I want to feel you inside me, Eduor."

He didn't even groan, just captured her mouth with his. This time, when she reached for his shaft, he didn't pull back in fear of rejection, but let her guide him home. Right after he prodded and sank about halfway in . . . the first bell for the midday harvest prayers rang.

Eduor froze and whimpered, lifting his lips a fraction from hers. As much as she wanted to curse Jimeyon for his lousy timing, Chanson knew instinctively that she didn't dare stop her lover. Not with that look of anguish in his *dyara* blue eyes. Instead of muttering imprecations, she whispered encouragements, telling him how warm he was, how strong and how wonderful he felt. Groaning, he sank deeper, accepting her words and the fingers stroking the side of his face. Accepted the pacing of those strokes as his own, until his need took over and his hips snapped to hers.

It felt good. Like his tongue, his shaft wasn't thick, but it was long, and he wielded it with skill, lifting one of her knees and hitching his own so that he rubbed against both of her pleasure points, the one inside and the one outside, with each grinding stroke. Drawing his mouth down for a kiss, she let her tongue tangle with his, enjoying her rising desire. Until he choked, stiffened, and shuddered.

Pushing in a few last times, he sagged over her, face buried in the crook of her neck. Hidden against her skin, he muttered something. Chanson couldn't quite understand. "What was that?"

". . . I'm sorry. I didn't . . . I wanted to last, but . . . I'll make it up to you," he stated and shifted his weight to one elbow, freeing his other hand.

Chanson caught it before it could brush lower than her belly. She smiled to reassure him. "Another time. We will get to do this again."

"But you didn't have fun," he pointed out, his expression sober, serious. "I don't want it to be like I'm using you. I'm not. You need—"

Shifting her other fingers to her lips, she quieted him. "Shh. Real lovemaking is neither simultaneous nor absolutely equal in every regard. After all, some women can climax six or seven times, and her poor man is often exhausted after two or three—mostly, when he's young, and less when he's older.

"What *is* equal is that both parties enjoy themselves. And I enjoyed you, just now." Chanson grinned. "It doesn't have to be a climax. In fact, I felt *very* good when you attained your pleasure. I was giving you what you needed most, and that pleased me very much." She stroked his braids back from his face. "Later, we can see how good you might feel when giving me pleasure. But *only* if you feel good about doing it."

The bell rang out again, echoing over the oasis. Eduor wrinkled his nose. "That's the second bell. The farmers will be coming in for prayers. Dammit. I don't have time to . . . to show my appreciation for your generosity."

She nodded wryly. "Yes. I need to bathe and then purify myself in the *mikwah*, dry off, and get dressed before the fourth bell rings. I'll admit it was foolish to start this so close to the midday prayers . . . but I don't regret being so wonderfully foolish."

He stared at her, visibly thinking, then kissed the tip of her nose. "Your Goddess is very generous, Chanson, in letting me be here with you. I don't want to get you in trouble with Her." Pulling free, he shifted to the side and kissed her cheek. "Go. Bathe and purify yourself. I'll sneak out of here."

Rising, Chanson lifted her brows. "*Sneak?* Goddess, no! I want you to *swagger* downstairs," she instructed, grinning wickedly. "After you get dressed, of course. I'd rather keep those sexy pale thighs all to myself, if you're willing. I like being with you, Eduor. In *all* things. I see nothing wrong with both of us proclaiming that fact to everyone else."

"Up to a point," he agreed, watching her shrug back into her clothes. "I think I'd like to keep my pale thighs reserved just for you, too. *And* my tongue. Um, you haven't told . . . ?"

"Told anyone?" she asked and shook her head. Knotting the laces on her skirt, she tightened the neckline of her blouse with two efficient tugs and a bit of tying, then crossed to the cabinet holding her blue-dyed clothes. "The length of your tongue is your own business. As is the length of your . . ."

She glanced over her shoulder at him, giving him a feminine smile. He blushed. She chuckled and grabbed one of the linen-wrapped packets of cleaned and blessed garments. Returning to the bed, she dipped and kissed his cheek, meeting him as he sat halfway up.

"I'll see you at midday prayers, Eduor. And afterward, too, I hope?" she asked.

"Yes. I'd like that," he agreed. "A lot."

Heading for the door, she paused and looked back at him. "Thank you for understanding about my duties, Eduor. I'd rather stay with you and cuddle, and other things, but . . ."

He nodded. "We can do those things afterward. Go on."

Smiling in relief, she left.

SIX

Sagging back onto her bed as the door closed, Eduor cursed himself silently. *Fool! Fool, thousand times fool . . . Idiot. Inconsiderate ass.* It was hard dredging up enough energy to castigate himself. His first chance at intercourse in years had drained his strength along with his wits. *Yes, an ass . . . as dumb as a donkey headed for the acacia bushes . . .*

After she had soothed his fear that she might stop him from enjoying intercourse with her, he had sunk into her with the intention of showing her some of the skill he had learned back in Mandare. While his older brother Kennal had treated his women as mere tools to pleasure *him*, Eduor had been fascinated by the ways he could make his own concubines react, depending on what he did to them. Giving them pleasure had been fun, even if it wasn't expected of him.

The philosophy back home was that male pleasure was paramount, the most important thing in a sexual act, and female pleasure merely an incidental adjunct. Or perhaps something to be given as a reward for good behavior. In contrast, the philosophy in Midalla's household was that her pleasure came first, her niece's second, and that her war-slave wasn't allowed to have any sexual pleasure in her presence. In the privacy of his own bed, yes, but not in her presence.

As cruel as we were to our women, that was even worse. At least, as far as I know, my father and brother didn't punish their concubines for experiencing pleasure in their presence, and I know I encouraged it myself. But I also know that there were times when I didn't bother to please my own war-slaves . . . like I didn't please Chanson, just now.

Except she seemed to understand I couldn't help it, he reminded himself, trying to soothe the guilt of that conflict. *She is just so beautiful, so different and wonderful . . . and it had been too long. Just . . . too long. I know she doesn't demand pleasure, but she* should *have it, too. Though her comment about women being able to have it five or six times to a man's twice or so, that fits with my own observations. I should . . .*

No. He arrested that line of thought. *I should* not *feel obliged to "make it up to her" for the rest of our lives together, however long that may be. Not in the sense of being* obliged *to do it.* Wanting *to do it, yes, but not obliged, like it was a chore or an expectation, a demand. That's what she means when she says "later" and what I believe she means. I believe it.*

But . . . I do *want to give her pleasure,* he acknowledged, sitting up and looping his arms around his knees. *Even if part of that wanting is guilt-prompted, I do . . . and I'm still wearing my sandals, aren't I?* A chuckle escaped him. Looking around her room, he took in the wooden furnishings, carved in the local geometric patterns, but otherwise of modest quality. *This place is so simple and plain, compared to Father's estates. But I love it here. As . . . as I love her.*

That was another piece of conditioning he would have to overcome, hearing his father's voice in his younger ears telling him that men should never love a woman, nor especially admit to loving one, because women were treacherous creatures who would use that information to weaken and ruin them.

But if there's a treacherous bone in Chanson's body, I have yet to find it, Eduor reminded himself. *Gods! These people are so straightforward. They'll play practical jokes, yes, but they're too opinionated to keep their feelings to themselves for long. And I am not my father, nor my brother, nor any sort of Mandarite at heart anymore, thank the Gods. I like these people, I especially like Chanson, I love spending time with her, and I want to spend the rest of my life here in Oba's Well. It's a good life. Hard, but I feel like I'm accomplishing something good when I work Falkon's farm.*

That was the only flaw in his life; the farm wasn't his. Not its donkeys, its mare and her foal, its chickens, its wheat fields and ground nuts and acacia trees. None of it was his. *Yet. And I can't . . . well, I* should *tell her how I feel, but I have nothing of my own to bring to her as a husband.*

. . . Alright, enough lolling in bed. Hopefully you'll get the chance to show her all the things you do *know about making sure a woman enjoys herself in bed, too, but that'll be later. Right now, you need to get yourself downstairs for the midday prayers.*

"Oh, Eduor . . . Oh . . . ohh, Eduor . . . Ohhhh, ohhhh, *yes*!" Arching her back, pressing her breasts closer to his suckling mouth, Chanson came.

Feeling her flesh, hot and slick, spasm around his first two fingers in time with her shudders, Eduor wanted nothing more than to sheathe himself inside his lover. But he had learned over the last month that it was better to let her rest for a little bit, if she was to fully enjoy intercourse. That meant gentling the pressure of his tongue and lips on her nipple, and meant sliding his hand up to her belly, letting it rest over her trembling muscles while they calmed back down. The scent of her pleasure filtered through the cool, predawn air, and the sound of her panting breaths eased into quiet breathing.

They lay side by side on Falkon's bed. At least, the frame and mattress belonged to the absent owner; Eduor had since earned his own linen sheets and the light quilt accompanying them through his work in the village, helping his neighbors on their own farms and teaching the children. That had happened before the harvest season; now it was every man and woman and even the older children striving to bring in all that they could from their own fields. Eduor would have loved to help his fellow villagers, but Falkon's farm was all he could manage during the daylight hours.

The long hours meant spending time with Chanson mostly in the late evenings, snatching as much rest as he could, and making love in the mornings. When they had woken and started, he could barely make out the shape of his hand on her stomach. Now the gray of twilight was picking up the colors of the day, and the golden brown of his fingers contrasted with the deep brown of her skin. She covered his hand with her own, pressing it to her belly for a moment, then dragged it up to her mouth and sucked on the two fingers he had used to please her.

Watching her do that, Eduor felt each suckle like a line tugging on his groin. This time, instead of wanting her lips to wrap around his manhood, he felt the urge to suckle her. Part of him still flinched a bit at the thought, but it was a smaller part than back at the start of the harvest season.

Much smaller; the beautiful woman lying next to him never demanded more than he wanted to give, and usually only just before the deepest moments of her pleasure. She gave as good as she asked, and then some. He wanted to do for her the one thing she had never asked for, though he wasn't sure if he could, given his learned aversion. Or even if she'd want him to do it.

Her hand lifted to his face, bringing with it a hint of dampness and scent from his now-clean fingers. "I love waking up with you," she murmured, giving him a warm smile. "Even if all we do is sleep, though this is very nice, too. And I love being with you. Everyone else demands so much of my time, as *dyara* and priestess, but you . . . I know you spend time with me because you want to spend time with *me*."

"I love you." The words escaped him easily, surprising him. They hadn't been on his mind, exactly, nor had he intended to say them this soon, but he didn't retract them, either. Eduor twisted his head and kissed her palm. "I'd want to spend time with you even if you milked goats all day long. And I know how precious your free time is to you, busy as you are with the needs of the village. So when you want to spend it with *me* . . ."

"I do," she agreed. Pushing up on one elbow, she kissed him. She started to curl up further, to kiss her way down his chest as usual, but Eduor didn't want that.

"Another time," he murmured, urging her back down onto the bedding. When she complied, he rose and pushed back the linen curtaining the lattice-framed window. Eastern light filtered in, promising another bright, hot day as soon as the sun rose. Returning to her, he climbed onto the bed between her calves and lowered himself to his stomach. It left his legs dangling past the bed, but it wasn't too uncomfortable. At her startled look, he managed a smile. "I *want* to do this. If I can. I just . . . need to *see* you while I . . ."

She pushed up onto her elbows, concern pinching her brow. "Eduor, you don't *have* to. Really."

"I want to," he repeated. A thought occurred to him, making him eye her warily. "Unless *you* don't want me to?"

Her concern melted away, dissolving in an almost-shy smile. "I'd like you to. But if at *any* point you feel uncomfortable, you must promise to stop. I don't want you to feel like, well, like you used to. That you *had* to do it. I'm quite happy with everything else we do."

"Thank you." Knowing she meant it, and that she wanted it, he settled himself into position. The sight of her young, firm thighs, short, nubbly curls, and dark rose flesh were all very different than before. Her scent was different, appealing to his senses because it was hers, and because he had learned to associate it with his own pleasure in the last handful of weeks, not just with hers.

Still, it took him a few moments before he extended his tongue. Just the tip of it brushed against her folds, but she jumped and quivered as if he had tickled her ribs. The sharp intake of her breath, followed by tight-muscled silence, warned him she was anticipating his reaction. Shifting just a little closer, he flicked his tongue a second time. Again, she trembled.

She also tasted good. Better than good, clean and sweet. Dipped from the source, she tasted divine. Scooting closer, Eduor pressed his mouth to her nether lips and licked, slow and deep, before settling in for some serious loving.

Chanson moaned and clutched at his hair. At her request, he had unbound his braids last night so that she could play with the long, soft curls, and now buried her fingers in the strands, holding him close. A few moments later, she gasped and jerked her fingers free. "Sorry!"

He didn't get it for a few moments. Swirling his tongue around her pleasure peak, he realized belatedly why she wasn't touching him anymore. *She must think her hands in my hair is too much of a demand—she's always careful that way.*

Loving her thoughtfulness, but not wanting to inhibit *her* reactions—his own inhibitions were more than enough—Eduor fumbled for one of her hands. It wasn't easy since he couldn't exactly see what he was doing without stopping, but he managed to catch one by the wrist and drag her fingers back to his scalp. Her happy sigh, heard between moans, heralded the return of her other hand as well.

Humming in encouragement, he returned to his task, until her moans grew embarrassingly loud, and a freshet of liquid told him she was on the verge of another crux of pleasure. Abandoning her loins made her groan in disappointment, but it didn't take much for him to crawl fully onto the bed. The hands that had tangled in his curls now clutched at his shaft, positioning him for a perfect sheathing.

This time, the slick, inner trembling of her flesh clasped more than just his fingers. This time, as he drove into her, his name echoed off the plastered walls of the little bedroom, far more than a breathy moan. This time, he knew he was able to get over his aversion to suckling her; his tongue would no longer get him into trouble with this wonderful woman.

"Ohhh . . . Chanssson!" He shuddered and buried his face in her throat, spending himself with a groan—and flinched as she tugged hard on his locks. It seemed his tongue might not get him into trouble anymore, but his hair definitely would.

"Goddess, *yes*!" she shouted, bucking and bowing her back underneath him, before slumping and panting heavily. Rearing back to ease some of the pressure, he flexed his hips a few more times, watching her enjoying herself. Her eyes, strained shut during the peak of her climax, fluttered open. She stared sightlessly at the ceiling for a while before she finally focused on him again.

Her warm smile, clearly seen in the light of dawn, made him want to melt into her and never leave.

"Thank you," she murmured, gently untangling her fingers from his locks. Stroking his hair back from his face, she gave him a somewhat lopsided version of her smile. "Sorry about pulling on your hair, there. And for screaming so loud. I think your neighbors know what we just did."

"If they haven't figured it out by now, they haven't been paying attention," he quipped, though he blushed as he said it. Then he felt his skin from forehead to chest burn as the voice of his nearest neighbor, Frandon, wafted through the open window.

"Oh, *believe* me, we know what you two have been doing. That you even have the energy for it during harvest tells me you're not working hard enough."

Grateful the windows were placed too high for anyone to look inside, Eduor eased off his lover and pulled the sheet up over her body. "I'll get the crops in."

"Yes, you will."

That wasn't Frandon's voice. That was Marison's voice. Instinct had Eduor grabbing a corner of the sheet and whipping it over his groin, even as Chanson clutched it to her breasts. They fought for a brief second, then managed to cover themselves. Not that anyone could see inside, but it was the thought of being seen that was enough to make them cover themselves.

"Mother?" Chanson asked as she gave up half of the sheet to Eduor. "Um . . . what are you doing up so early?"

"Nothing like what you're doing." The humor in the older woman's voice was evident. "But we decided we like you, young man, and we want you to stay. That means ensuring you have a place to stay, and something to do . . . aside from spending time with my baby girl."

There's the hint of matronly censure I'd have expected, Eduor thought. *But—thank Sundra—only a hint of it.* Clearing his voice, he asked, "And that means . . . ?"

"Helping you with the harvest." That was the voice of another villager, alarming Eduor and his lover.

Kedle added her voice, startling both occupants of the bedroom anew. "You'll have time for settling all of that later, children. Get up and get dressed, you two. Marison brought you breakfast, and the whole village has decided to help bring in every last fruit and grain they can from your fields. And you'll have Jimeyon to thank for it, too."

"Jimeyon?" Chanson asked, giving Eduor a blank look.

The reverend *dyara* chuckled. "He reasoned that Eduor cannot *ask* for help with the harvest and still be able to claim Falkon's lands as his own if Falkon does not show up before the last of his land is harvested . . . but there is nothing in the law against us helping without *being* asked. So, on your feet, you two. I'm not so old I don't remember what it's like to be finished doing *that*, but the rest of the village is waking up and will be here very soon. You can cuddle in the evenings after a hard day's work."

Burning with embarrassment, yet touched by their acceptance, Eduor climbed out of the bed to start dressing. He returned for a quick kiss and to hand Chanson her clothes—and to give her another kiss—but her indulgent grin let him know she wasn't upset at this unexpected end to their privacy.

"They're right," she murmured. "If you can get in all of the harvest, then that's a stronger case for you to stay and manage the land that Falkon abandoned. Not that I expect him to return today."

"I would have him return safe and whole," Eduor murmured back, knotting a fresh loincloth around his hips, "but no, not today. Even if he does, there is some land to the northwest that could have a cistern dug and some fields scratched out. Or maybe orchards planted. I'm pretty good with trees. Not that there's much room in the village for a new house, but . . ."

"But you could live with me," she agreed, rising and finding her own clothes. Loincloth in hand, she paused to look at him. "Eduor . . . where do you want to be, three years from now? What life do you want to lead?"

The question was an unexpected one, but a good one. It was also one he had an answer for. "I want a good home to live in—whether or not it's at the temple doesn't matter—a good day's work to be proud of, and most of all, to be at your side still, three years from now. If you'll have me."

Sitting down, he strapped on his sandals. Chanson bent over and looped her arms around his shoulders, bringing their faces close together. "Do you know what I want, three years from now?"

"What would you like?" he asked, meeting her dark brown gaze openly. "If I can get it for you, I will."

She grinned. "I want you. As my husband, if you would have me as your wife. And I want you to have work that you can be proud of, just as I'm proud to be one of the *dyara* for Oba's Well. I want you to have fields and trees that I can help water. And I want to know if these gorgeous gold curls of yours are inheritable . . . if you're willing to have a child or two with me."

Children. He could see them now, a blend of her features and his, laughing and playing in the temple courtyard with the other children in the village. Swallowing, he nodded. "I'd like that. A lot."

"Then let's get your harvest in, so that the lazy, absent Falkon has nothing more to claim. He certainly lost his claim to *me* the day he rode out of here. You gained it when you walked in and stayed, and proved to be a fascinating and much better man." Kissing the tip of his nose, she released him and let him continue dressing.

Which Eduor did, in a very good mood despite the lingering embarrassment from their being overheard by her own mother and a handful of others.

SEVEN

Hearing the horns of the children tending the herds at the village edge, and the cheerful pattern that warned of a friendly caravan approaching, Eduor stood and stretched. Mindful of the hot midday sun and his paler-by-comparison flesh, he hadn't loosened the neckline of his *thawa* and wrapped it kilt-like around his hips, but that meant he had to spend a few moments flapping the fabric to cool himself down.

"Hey, Substance Man! Do you think you're allowed to stop working?" Marison called out from two rows over, digging industriously at the base of the next sweetroot plant. The last of the grains and all of the fruits and greens had been harvested with the help of her and the others, yesterday. Now the remaining vegetables had to be dug out of the ground, a laborious task at best. "You're not allowed to sell more than a tenth of this to any caravan, so keep digging."

"Yes, Mother Marison," he muttered. A couple of the other men chuckled at his quip but took a few moments to stretch as well.

Someone fetched the pitcher of drinking water from the end of the row and passed it around. Eduor accepted it gratefully and drank deeply when it was his turn, then handed it to the next harvester.

Moments later a youth pelted into view, dodging the thorn-bearing limbs of the acacia trees guarding the field. His voice carried, "Falkon! Falkon's back! It's Falkon with the caravan!"

Eduor froze, mind racing, while the youth detoured to head toward the village and deliver his message there as well. *The harvest isn't fully in. He can still reclaim the land, even if I can legally claim the larger share of this year's bounty for my own . . .*

The caravan came into view, its members apparently having decided to follow the boy who had fled to warn Eduor of its approach. There weren't more than ten riders, with maybe fifteen beasts all told, the horses bearing saddles and the dromids laden with packs. At the forefront rode a vaguely familiar man in leather armor. Next to him rode a woman, also in boiled leather. Falkon lifted his hand in greeting to some of the villagers as they crossed the harvested portion of the field. Stopping a few lengths away, he leaned on the pommel of his saddle.

"So. Who's been taking care of my fields in my absence?"

"Your fields?" Marison asked before Eduor could respond. Pushing to her feet, the yellow-clad woman dusted off her knees. "*Your* fields? When you left before they were planted and returned only after the vast majority has been harvested?"

"Marison, please," Eduor murmured.

She pointed at him. "*This* man has done all the work. He plowed your fields, sowed your seeds, weeded your plants, tended your trees, helped your mare foal, fed your chickens, harnessed your donkeys, watered your fields, pruned your orchards, plucked your fruit, reaped your grain, and *dug in your dirt*."

"I don't see him digging now," Falkon pointed out. "In fact, I see a lot of the rest of you digging."

"Well, he didn't *ask* us to help him, so the effort is still all *his*."

Hands planted on her hips, she drew in her breath to say more. Eduor touched her arm.

"It's alright, Marison. Really, it is." Facing the man on horseback, Eduor lifted his chin. "Yes, I took care of everything for you. I won't deny I was hoping you wouldn't return for a few more weeks, but the land is yours, if you still want it."

"The harvest, however, is *his*," Marison interjected.

"Actually, *we* want it."

Even Falkon turned to eye the man on one of the horses behind him. "What are you talking about, Chowrick?"

The other man nudged his mare forward. He tugged down the facecloth of his turban and grinned. It wasn't a pleasant smile. "I mean, this is clearly a prosperous village. Surely they can afford to spare some of their food . . . and their other goods."

Falkon and the woman next to him both stiffened. Eduor quickly sized up the others in their caravan. Calling it a caravan was a misnomer, he realized; all of them wore wax-boiled leather, and all of it showed signs of wear and repair. *Warriors, not merchants. This is a raiding band.*

"I did not lead you here to pillage my home," Falkon growled, reaching for one of the blades slung at his waist. He turned his horse to face the other man as he did so. Eduor quickly moved out of the way of the mare's hindquarters, putting himself closer to the would-be bandit in their midst.

"You are but one man, and the only Sud in this war band. Everyone else you rode with chose to stay with their distant kin . . . or died in the fighting." Chowrick smiled his not-smile a second, equally brief time. "Do you wish to follow them?"

"I *won't* let you raid my village!" Jerking his short, curved sword free, Falkon froze as most of the others unsheathed their own blades. One of the other men and two of the women, including the one still at Falkon's side, did not draw their own weapons, but the rest did.

"You are just one man," Chowrick challenged Falkon, lifting his own blade. "What can one man do?"

Eduor jumped. Hooking one hand over Chowrick's shoulder, he grabbed at that upraised arm and used the weight and momentum of his falling body to drag the other man out of his saddle. It helped that no one had remembered how close he was to these riders, so the element of surprise was on his side as he made his unconventional attack. The mare neighed and scrambled sideways, shying away from their falling bodies. Twisting as he fell, Eduor planted a knee somewhere on the would-be bandit's stomach, hard enough that the other man *eeped* as they landed.

Scrambling to his feet, fingers still latched tightly around that sword-bearing wrist, Eduor spun. The move, ducking under his captive's arm, flipped Chowrick facedown in the rough soil of the half-harvested field. From there, it was easy enough to plant a foot on his shoulder blade and pinch the back of his hand, pressing on those dark-skinned knuckles until the sword dropped free.

". . . *That* is what 'one man' can do," Eduor stated, loudly enough for the others to hear over the downed bandit's groaning. "And I am the *least* skilled of all these farmers."

Dropping his arm, Eduor stepped back. He kicked the sword out of reach as he did so and waited for Chowrick to stand. Thankfully, no one in the field snorted with laughter at his claim. It was the truth, after all; he was the least skilled of all the *farmers* in Oba's Well. As for being a warrior, well, he was out of practice, but probably had as much training as anyone in this little war band, if not more.

A glance at the others showed them looking at each other and resheathing their swords. Some of them gave Falkon sheepish looks. Regaining his feet, Chowrick moved to pick up his sword. Eduor stepped on the blade and folded his arms across his chest. Defeated twice, the man looked at the others in his war band. They avoided his gaze.

"Go on. Take your horse and get out of here," Eduor told him.

"There's a cave with a cistern two days' walk almost due west of here. It's on the main caravan route. You can find whatever you want *elsewhere* in Sundara. I can guarantee you won't find what you're looking for here in Oba's Well. Or at least you won't like what you *will* find."

The other villagers backed him up. "Go on!" "Get out of here!" "Don't come back!" "We're even tougher and meaner than he is!" "Yeah!" "Sands take you!"

Chowrick flinched from the clod of dirt thrown his way. A glance showed no more support from his fellow warriors. Dodging Falkon and his horse, he trotted down the field after his mare, who had stopped at the edge of the trees to nip at some of the weedy grass growing there.

As he left, one of the remaining warriors shrugged and offered, "He was the war band leader. But . . . he's been defeated by a *farmer*!"

"Yes, what do we do?" one of the women asked, eyeing Eduor warily. "I don't want to follow a dirt-digger!"

"That dirt-digger . . . is my brother," Falkon stated, startling Eduor. He looked down at the ex-Mandarite and twisted his mouth in a wry smile. "What he owns, I own . . . and what I own, he owns. You'll take care of *our* farm, won't you, Brother?"

Vaguely recalling something in the inheritance laws about adopted siblings and their legal rights—and that declaring their relationship in front of so many witnesses was the biggest part of making it official—Eduor looked around at his fellow villagers and nodded. "Sure. I'll, um, keep the family farm in good condition, and make sure your room is ready for you whenever you visit, or are ready to come home. And since you're the one with the heart for fighting, you can have the war band in my place. Agreed, Brother?"

"Agreed, Brother. And we'll *pay* for our food and supplies," Falkon stated firmly. "But . . . at a discount, I trust? In the name of family?"

"Why not?" Eduor muttered wryly. "Nothing like family to rob you blind, right?"

Thankfully, both sides chuckled, warriors and villagers alike.

The woman on the horse closest to Falkon reached out and tapped his elbow. ". . . Well? Aren't you going to mention me?"

"In a moment—ah, there she is. I see Chanson coming this way." Falkon waited until the blue-clad *dyara* finished jogging up to their patch of the sweetroot field, and held up his hand. ". . . I'm sorry I left you like I did, Chanson, but I hope you've moved on. A *dyara* deserves a man who is one with the land she blesses with Sundra's waters. I am more a man of the flame, these days, and fire and water don't always mix so well."

Panting a little from her run, Chanson nodded, shook her head, then shrugged. "I'm glad you're alive, and I hope the others are, too, but . . . it's been nine months, Falkon. I've *definitely* moved on. In fact, I have a betrothed now," she added, tucking her palms on her hips in imitation of her mother. "The man who stepped up and took good care of *your* land. And if you'd only had the good sense to stay away for a few more weeks—"

"Enough!" Grinning, he held out his hand to the woman riding at his side. "Chanson, this is Berilla, a fellow warrior and a wonderful woman. She and I are betrothed . . . just as you and my new brother apparently are. What was it you said, Brother?" he asked, slanting a pointed, sly look at Eduor. "Nothing like family to rob you blind?"

Grateful his future was settled, and settled happily, Eduor blushed when the others laughed again. ". . . Something like that."

It seemed that, try as he may, his tongue was still getting him into trouble.

GUILDARA

ONE

For a land that professes its peaceful intentions so strongly via its envoys, Sir Zeilas thought, hastily sidestepping a pair of men carrying a long piece of heavily worked metal, *these Guildarans do seem to be preparing for war. I'm not sure I like this. I'm also not sure why they're showing us how these machines are built. The engineering works of old Mekhana were a deeply guarded secret for centuries. They shouldn't be exposing their knowledge like this.*

"I don't like this," Sir Catrine hissed in his ear as they paused for another pair of figures hauling a stack of gears on a rattling, wheeled table. Her whisper echoed his troubled thoughts. "Why are they still working on their infernal machines when they say they want peace?"

Zeilas didn't answer her for two reasons. One, they had to hurry to catch up with their guide, who was wearing the same ubiquitous, knitted tunic and soft-brimmed wool hat as nearly everyone else in this cavernous, barnlike building, and thus would blend into the crowd far too easily if they fell behind. Two, he didn't have an answer for her. Hopefully, they would *get* answers out of their hosts.

It was strange that they should be led here first, though. The handful of other knights who would serve as messengers and advisors had been allowed to head straight for the suite of rooms given to them for ambassadorial quarters, but the leader of this former patch of Mekhana had insisted on talking to the chief Arbran envoy and the chief Knight-mage accompanying him. So here they were in the "motorbarn" or whatever the man guiding them had called it, surrounded by the same machines that had once been used to try to conquer Arbra.

Light poured down from the windows high overhead, strange smells oozed from the various liquids and greases in evidence, and crackling fires in pierced barrels did their meager best to warm the oversized building. There was too much space and too much metal to warm the air efficiently, though.

Their guide from the palace didn't lead them toward the largest and most imposing of the machines. Not toward the giant metal man with its giant metal mallet suitable for smashing through ranks and walls and anything else in its way, nor toward the strange round platform high up on six imposing legs, and not toward the tube things which Zeilas had never seen in action, but which reportedly could fire an explosive spell-like object hundreds of yards to devastating effect, if whatever it targeted wasn't thoroughly protected by spells.

Instead, the man led them toward several ranks of horselike things. Vaguely horselike. They looked like jointed statues of horses, with the shanks of each horse supported by a spoked wheel between their paired hooves. Handles poked out from their mane-draped necks, seams and hinges pierced their painted flanks, and the curve of their painted spines were interrupted by leather padding shaped something like a saddle, though this saddle seemed to be part and parcel of the thing, with no girth-strap in evidence. Nor were these horses very tall, more like ponies in height.

Their guide stopped in front of a partially disassembled horse thing, where two grease-smeared, wool-clad figures were poking their heads and hands into the metallic innards of the flank-bared beast, and loudly cleared his throat. "*Ahem.* Consul-in-Chief, I present Sir Zeilas, Knight and chief envoy from Arbra, and Sir Catrine, Knight-mage and sub-envoy. Envoys, I present Marta Grenspun, Consul-in-Chief of Guildara, and Gabria Springreaver, sub-Consul of the . . . Mage's Guild."

Zeilas wondered over the man's palpable hesitation in saying the word *mage* but he didn't have time to ask. The figure in the black wool tunic pulled back from the horse thing and squinted up at them, then extended a dirty, greasy hand. She—he realized suddenly that almost half the leather-and-wool-clad figures in the room were actually females—didn't get up off the ground, just held up her hand for clasping, one side of her mouth curled up in a wry-looking smile.

"Welcome to Guildara, Sir Knights," the woman stated. "I'm Marta, this is Gabria."

The other woman, clad in knit gray wool, lifted a hand long enough to flutter it approximately in their direction, but didn't look up from whatever she was doing. The one named Marta, Zeilas realized belatedly, *was* wearing a golden circlet, but it was thin, not very ostentatious in size, and half hidden between the floppy crown and soft brim of the felted cap she wore. He did recognize the motifs which the new kingdom had chosen to represent themselves by, though: the hammer, scythe, and paintbrush forming the spokes of a gear-toothed wheel. Only in this case, the top edge of the circlet had gear teeth as well as around the medallion fixed to the front.

Out of the corner of his eye, he could see Sir Catrine frowning slightly. For himself, Zeilas guessed this informality was a test, as was the oily state of her fingers. Clasping it without hesitation, he shook hands with her as if they were merchants conducting business, then tilted her fingers and bowed more formally over her knuckles. "A pleasure, Milady Chief. I'm Zeilas, and this is Catrine. Will there be a more formal reception where we can meet the various, ah . . . Guild-heads of your government? The Consuls?"

"Yes, there will be one. It's scheduled for tomorrow, so that you have time to relax and prepare. In the meantime . . . Gabria?" Marta asked, turning back to her companion.

"Sir Catrine, come here please." Scooting over, the sub-Consul made room for the lady Knight on the leather hide spread on the ground. She even patted the leather when the other woman hesitated.

Catrine quirked her brow at Zeilas, clearly taken aback. He gave her a silent, pointed look. Sighing, she moved over to that side of the machine-horse.

"We're having a problem integrating shielding spells into the engine matrix," the woman Gabria stated, pointing at something inside the metallic beast's abdomen. "The fuel which powers the mechanism is flammable, and if anything penetrates the housing . . . well, *boom*! Which is deadly for the riders. We'd rather not lose lives. But the new shielding runes themselves create heat, particularly when stressed. The number of explosions has been cut down, but they're still a serious problem. Chilling spells run the risk of locking up the mechanisms, because we can't localize them small enough with what we currently know. The priests torched their spellbooks when the Convocation disbanded everything, and the guild doesn't have a dozen years to experiment under controlled conditions with new combinations of runes, metals, and enchantments."

Catrine didn't crouch and look at the part in question. Instead, she stared at the Consul-in-Chief and her fellow envoy. "I'm . . . not comfortable giving advice on how to shield a *machine* against magics. These are war machines."

Pushing to her feet, the Consul-in-Chief pulled an oil-smeared rag out of the sleeve of her tunic and scrubbed her hands. "We're not interested in war, Sir Knight. Guildara wants peace. It's even in our kingdom's charter, ratified by the people and blessed by our Goddess—who Manifested last year, and whose Name has been placed on the list for the next Convocation. We *will* seek peace and knowledge, trade and prosperity.

"Unfortunately, our land, and with it our charter, only covers our own claimed territory. Anything north of the Endevi Ridge is still filled with chaos, warlords, and would-be conquerors," Marta told them. "Including a particularly annoying fellow by the name of Durn the Dreaded. He's proclaimed himself 'Leader of the Free North' and is trying to build enough of a following for his own Patron Deity. Even more unfortunately, he's built up the concept of a Patron God who thrives on war and conquest. *Our* Patron Goddess embodies the ideals of knowledge and prosperity. So he thinks we'll be an easy target, as soon as his armies grow big enough. Which, by our calculations, will be this next summer, possibly even this coming spring."

"Durn has the *exact* same technology we do," Gabria added, tilting her wool-capped head back so that she could squint up at Sir Catrine. "The same war machines culled from all the various Precinct motorbarns scattered throughout old Mekhana. Even the same percentage of freed . . . victims of the False God, some of which have joined his side. The only advantages we have are that Guildara was formed out of the guilds and guard precincts in the heart of the engineering district so we have the knowledge and tools to create better machines, that neither side has access anymore to the few but horrible spells the False priesthood used to wield, and that we managed to pull ourselves together fast enough to become a kingdom and thus gain stable, *educated* allies."

"We specified we wanted a Knight-mage as one of your ambassadorial staff for two reasons," Marta stated, facing Zeilas. "One, even the lies of the False God couldn't hide the fact that Arbran Knights are honorable men and women. Two, your Knights and Knight-mages have successfully repelled invasions by the False God's forces for centuries. What you know how to defeat and destroy, you *should* be able to figure out how to strengthen and defend." She flicked her gaze to Sir Catrine's face. "The Endevi Ridge is the northern border of this valley. We're half a day's march from that ridgeline, and a week's march from Durn the Dreaded's chief stronghold at most. Less, if the weather is good."

"And before you ask, *no*, we will *not* march north and reduce it to ashes," Gabria asserted. "Tempting though the idea is from a defensive standpoint, it's against our charter. No conquering anyone, no starting a war, and no using force to convince anyone to join us."

"If they want to *join* us of their own free will, they can. We have two villages north of the ridge who are negotiating with us for protection from the warlord harassing them. But we will *not* conquer anyone," the Consul-in-Chief stated flatly.

Off in the distance, someone dropped a chunk of metal which clanged, loud and sharp, on the flagstones lining the huge, drafty building. A handful of workers catcalled the fumble-fingered accident, but most of the rest attended to their own business. Marta Grenspun held the other woman's gaze, unmoved by the commotion.

"Now, you *have* the knowledge of spellcrafting which my people lack, Sir Catrine. It is up to your conscience whether or not you will stand idly by and allow your *allies* to die because you refused to teach us the knowledge we need to protect ourselves. We're willing to let you have a glimpse at our engineering abilities," she added, spreading her still-somewhat-stained hands to indicate the cold, cavernous building around them, with its strange metal machines lit by the clerestory windows high overhead. "Secrets which no outsider has ever been allowed to see before now, and secrets which we're well aware you could use against us. What are *you* willing to share, to give this alliance a chance?"

Catrine looked like she wanted to argue the point. There were too many centuries of spilled blood between Arbra and Mekhana . . . but Mekhana was no more. Having more experience at diplomacy, Zeilas could see just how much this odd Guildara version of a queen wanted to put the old enmities aside. Nobody would expose their secrets so thoroughly to foreigners, if they weren't very much interested in cooperation.

Switching from Mekhanan to Arbran, Zeilas addressed his fellow Knight. "In the interest of fairness, I should point out that we *can* walk away right now, and do so with at least some minor information about their mechanical secrets, without exposing any of our own. But to *be* fair, I will also point out that His Majesty wishes us to secure *peace* between our two lands. These people are willing to pay for that peace by exposing a potential vulnerability. If they wanted war, they wouldn't expose themselves. Certainly not without prompting or promises secured in advance, none of which they have."

"But, to shield their machines, *protecting* them against our most effective spells?" Sir Catrine protested. "Wouldn't that tempt them into using the new protections in an invasion *against* us? I don't know if I can risk that!"

From the way the Consul-in-Chief's mouth quirked up at one corner, Zeilas guessed she could understand at least part of their words. Given how open she was being about letting the two Knights see their mechanical secrets—even if he and Catrine couldn't understand most of what they saw in this oversized barn, lacking any knowledge of engineering—he didn't bother to disguise his reply, though he did keep it in Arbran.

"Diplomacy involves things like keeping an open mind toward offers and counteroffers, gauging the sincerity in offers of cooperation, an ability to weigh benefits and disadvantages, and being willing to compromise and meet the other side up to halfway. King Tethek made me the lead envoy because I have experience in these matters," he told her.

The Consul-in-Chief started cleaning more of the grease from her fingers, using a clean scrap of the rag she had pulled from her sleeve, but he could tell she was listening. So was Catrine. Sort of.

"*Fine*. What do you, in your *vast* experience, say about giving them the very means to shield their evil machines against our spells?" Catrine asked, hands shifting to her hips.

"I say, first of all, their machines are not evil. They are simply tools, just like our swords and our lances. It is the *people* who wield them that determine whether they are used for good or for evil." Zeilas could see that same half smile lurking on Marta's face, but the other woman, Gabria, watched them with the sort of blank fascination of someone understanding nothing more than vocal tones and body language. "Second, even I, a non-mage, know that for every defensive spell invented, a counterspell *will* be developed sooner or later.

"Third, we *will* extend a reasonable amount of trust, and we *will* be honorable in acknowledging these *Guildarans*' efforts to offer their half of a diplomatic compromise. We learn about their machines, and they learn about our magics—you will notice that *they* offered first, with a show of trust on their part. The diplomatic thing to do is acknowledge that show of trust, and respond with some of our own. You reward good behavior with *more* good behavior, after all," he reminded her. "Particularly when it's finally being displayed."

Out of the corner of his eye, he saw the other side of Marta's mouth twitch briefly upward. Facing the Consul-in-Chief, he switched back to Mekhanan. Or more properly, Guildaran, now that they were a new kingdom.

"Forgive us, Milady Chief," he apologized, giving her a short bow. "Sir Catrine's reluctance is typical of too many years of antagonism between your predecessor kingdom and our homeland. But King Tethek made his wishes clear. We are here to seek out and establish peaceful relations with Guildara. That you are willing to risk the secrets of your kingdom's defenses shows more than mere words how much your side is interested in establishing those peaceful relations with Arbra. We, in turn, shall do our best to meet and match your sincerity.

"Sir Catrine, please assist the, ah . . . sub-Consul, is it?" he asked, not entirely sure of her title. He knew a Consul was the head of a guild, but the rank and meaning of a sub-Consul eluded him.

"Sub-Consul Gabria of the . . . Mage's Guild," the woman still kneeling on the ground confirmed, again with that same hesitation their long-departed escort had used. "Advisory staff to the Consul-in-Chief."

"Not to mention, my good friend," Marta added, both sides of her mouth curving up in a warm smile.

Zeilas blinked, surprised at how feminine the full-mouth smile made the Consul-in-Chief look, feminine and pretty. Her face was rather square compared to Arbran features, with plain, gray blue eyes and wisps of ash brown hair showing beneath the edge of her soft-felted cap. The knitted bulk of her tunic hid most of her figure, which she carried in a straight-backed, no-nonsense stance when facing off against Sir Catrine. But that smile made her beautiful.

It returned to its previous halfway state when she looked back at him. Tearing his gaze away from her, Zeilas gave Catrine a firm look. "Assist and instruct sub-Consul Gabria, Sir Catrine—in the interest of earning enough trust on both sides hopefully to build a solid foundation for peace."

She rolled her eyes, but the Knight-mage started to lower herself to the leather mat on which the woman Gabria knelt. Zeilas switched back to Arbran, this time couching his words somewhat for subtlety.

"And do make sure to treat this machine as if *you* were going to be its very next operator. It will only do what we create and enspell it to do. It is not evil, in and of itself," he reminded her. "Evil only exists when someone acts in an evil manner."

The dark look she shot his way let him know his message had

struck home. *Good. Now she'll think twice about sabotaging the machine or offering poor spell choices that could cause harm to its operators.*

"Sir Zeilas, while your fellow envoy cooperates with my advisor," Marta offered in Guildaran, "would you like a tour of the Palace Precinct's motorbarn? It may be the first time an Arbran has had the chance to view an intact war engine from up close with no fear for their personal safety. Hopefully, it won't be the last time."

He gave her a half bow. "I am honored by your offer and would be delighted to be given a tour."

TWO

"This way, then." Gesturing at the other machine-horses, she walked beside him, pacing down the row. "These are what we call motorhorses. They can run on smooth, level roads as fast as a cantering horse, but without needing to slow down and rest every so often, as a flesh-and-blood horse needs.

"Nor do they need to graze, though they do 'eat' a special liquid every hundred miles—the distance a man can walk in three days. It's refined from common grains and grasses, empowering their movement, though it isn't magic. We understand you occasionally use magic on your own carriages and wagons in Arbra to move goods and people from place to place, yes?"

"Yes. Horseless wagons with special locomotion spells. They're expensive, but reliable when needed, such as when going up hills with heavy loads," he admitted. "Horses are cheaper, particularly in the flatter sections of Arbra, but in the northern mountains, the miners and loggers prefer to use enspelled carts despite the cost. I understand these were used as a sort of counterpoint to our Knights on the battlefield, back in the Mekhanan days."

"More for scouting than for jousting, but yes, they could be used for that. They do require both hands on the controlling rods, though, so we tend to team up in pairs for motorhorse battle. These are our small mobile *cannons*, and beyond them are the large siege cannons," she added, nodding at the next group of machines they approached, the ones with the long tubes on wheels. "They're used for firing explosive *charges*, sort of like exploding magical Artifacts. We'd rather not use them for two reasons. One, some of the minerals used to make the explosives are culled from farmlands, and Guildara is more mountainous than the northern lands, so our agricultural resources are geared far more toward feeding ourselves than in procuring the components we need."

"And the other reason?" Zeilas asked.

Her gaze, fastened on the tube things, looked haunted for a moment. "They gouge holes in the land. Ruin crops, divot meadows . . . destroy lives. We have stationary cannons at all the Precinct forts, of course, for defensive purposes, but we'd rather not see them on the move, trampling the land. These will be retrofitted for permanent posts of their own. Once they've been repaired, of course. The others that used to fill that back bay, there, were sent out before the start of winter to the two villages who wanted asylum from Warlord Durn. They've had their wheels removed and their axles filled with molten lead, so they cannot be easily returned to mobility, nor turned back against us."

"A sensible precaution," Zeilas murmured. Among the cannons, which were being repaired, over half of the men and women working on them slanted him wary looks as he passed. Deciding bluntness was the best tactic, he added, "Forgive me if I'm mistaken, but somehow I don't think everyone in Guildara is happy to see an Arbran wandering around inside this place."

"So long as you behave yourself, they'll behave themselves. At least, in my presence," she allowed. "I'm riding a tide of popularity based on a strong platform of favorable reforms, and the blessing of our Goddess Manifesting during the election process."

"Yes, the election process. You have an . . . unusual method of selecting your kings and queens," he observed under his breath. "No offense is meant, but it is unusual."

"We'd never have gotten everyone behind a single candidate for leadership, otherwise. Guildara survived the chaos of having Mekhana crumble and dissolve because the guilds have a very strong presence here in the southern mountains. Not even the priesthood could penetrate the full depths of our secrets—that's how people like Gabria survived," Marta revealed. "We figured out how to hide them and their abilities. But as I was saying, the guilds would never have agreed to a single representative, unless the Gods Themselves decreed it. Which, when I pointed *that* out, made undeniable sense to everyone.

"So we agreed each guild would put forth a candidate, who would then petition our chosen Goddess, and let Guildra decide who is the most fit to lead us. And, to make things fair, the petitions would happen once every five years, the same as the term of service for each guildmaster," Marta told him. "It was just building further on a system that was already there, and thus everyone could grasp how it would all work. Bad leaders could be ousted at the end of their term, and good leaders could be retained."

"So your guild put you forward as a candidate, and Guildra selected you?" Zeilas surmised.

The corner of her mouth quirked up. "Hardly. I was just the idiot child who figured out *how* we should pick our leader, rather than waste years bickering uselessly from inter-guild politics. I ended up being the event organizer for the great Convocation of Leadership, to prevent *that* from being turned into another round of endless committee meetings."

"Sir Orana pointed out during the Knights' Convocation just a month ago that most kingdoms cannot be successfully run by a committee," Zeilas admitted. "She said the only land she knew of that *could* be run by a committee was both isolated and well protected against invasion, which gave *them* the leisure to argue matters to death. Most other lands don't have the luxury of time for endless debate."

"Sounds like she was secretly listening in on our inter-guild meetings—I met her once," Marta added, lifting her hand and examining the pad of her thumb. She tilted it toward Zeilas. "I even signed her petition book with my own blood. Most guilds, we circulated our own books, once our ancestors realized she truly meant to help us. We saved them up for when she'd sneak back in for another visit. It was ten or so years ago that she last came through Durasburg, where I grew up, but I signed it. When she left, I didn't hold any hope that we'd see the False God removed from power in my lifetime . . . but we did. She's one Arbran Knight *everyone* in Guildara will trust, for that reason alone. People like Sir Catrine . . . well, there's reason for caution and wariness on both sides."

"She's new to politics. After hearing Envoy Jellis explain why your people wanted instruction in spellcrafting, King Tethek sent her straight from one of our top Mage Academies. She *is* good at explaining the basics. She's just . . . not trained as an envoy," Zeilas hedged. "Every Knight undergoes *some* instruction in things like negotiation and foreign etiquette, but not everyone has an aptitude for diplomacy."

"No, they don't," Marta agreed. Since they had reached the next set of machines, the platforms balanced on tall, jointed pillars, she gestured at them. "These are the hexaleg troop transports. I understand 'hex' means something different in Arbran, something to do with magic, but in Guildaran, it's just an old word for 'six.' Being machines, they weren't built with spellcasting abilities, obviously. Six legs give them a great deal of stability over a variety of terrain, much more than four. They only have trouble going over swampy or muddy ground, or loose gravel and sand."

"I wouldn't mind seeing them in action one day—in a peaceful demonstration, of course," Zeilas demurred. For a moment, both sides of her mouth quirked up, then settled back into that one-sided smile. "Anyway, you were telling me how you were chosen to lead?"

"Yes, well, as I said, I ended up organizing the whole thing. I wasn't even paying any attention when She Manifested—instead, I was busy encouraging everyone else present to focus on the thought of Guildra, and on the qualities She should consider when selecting our best leader." Marta shrugged, flicking a hand expressively. "All the candidates were up at the front of the amphitheater, with the expectation She'd Manifest there, select one of them to be the leader, and that would be that. The various guilds would grumble but deal with it, and we'd happily become a kingdom.

"I was on the upper tiers, encouraging people to concentrate. The next thing I knew, someone tapped me on the shoulder, I turned around, and there She was. She looked at me, said, 'If you can put *this* into motion, and make *them* all agree, you can pull this nation together, and make it strong. Now go do it,' and then She vanished." Marta shrugged, spreading her mostly clean hands. "If Her reasons hadn't been heard by everyone else, if I hadn't had the crown Manifest on my head the moment She spoke, there might have been trouble. But there it was. Everyone had agreed to the system, they didn't disagree at Her choice, and so here I am. Consul-in-Chief."

"Were you a member of a guild before all of this began?" Zeilas asked, remembering how she hadn't actually answered that question.

"I started out in the Clockworks Guild, but then was requested to work for one of our guard captains. He needed someone good at organizing things in Precinct Logistics . . . which I'll admit gives me an advantage of understanding how to protect Guildara, as well as provision her." She eyed him and quirked the opposite side of her mouth in a half smile more wry than amused. "Which means yes, I was in the Mekhanan military. But not as a soldier. Women weren't allowed to fight, though we did fill many of the support roles. Particularly if we presented ourselves as gender neutral as possible and deferred to men whenever a priest was around.

"The False God's patriarchal egotism took a bad beating from your female Knights over the last two hundred years. Once we were free, the women voted to fight to retain that freedom, right alongside our men. And while we now have mandatory Precinct service for everyone, it's limited to a set number of days per year, and no one *has* to be a Guardsman for the rest of his or her life. And no more whippings or hangings if you desert.

"Nowadays, most of our fines and punishments are money driven. If you can't pay it, or your family or your guild, you labor for the kingdom for a set period of time," Marta told him, sweeping her hand out expressively as she talked. "Right now, it's all indoor work, mostly refurbishing the old, defaced temples into new ones for Guildra, or crafting public artworks and facilities, or working in the hospices to care for the old and the injured. When the weather clears up, it'll be road-building and major construction work . . . including the wings of the palace. We just have the main section up, what we could get done in a year. Your quarters are small compared to what we have planned for next year, but as comfortable as we could make them."

"I look forward to seeing them. What are these things for?" Zeilas asked her as they reached the towering iron giant and his equally huge mallet. Behind him in a wing of the motorbarn, the Knight could see smaller versions. Each was still four or five times the size of a flesh-and-blood man, but all were crafted from painted metal. And each one was in some stage of construction, or perhaps reconstruction was a better term for it.

"Constructive retrofitting," was her succinct, if mysterious reply. At a glance from him, Marta elaborated. "We're removing the personnel cannons and replacing them with construction tools. The cannons can be reinstalled in case of war, but we'd rather turn our motorguards into constructor suits. Diggers and pushers, sawers and drillers, everything from mining to lumber work, ditch-digging to frame-lifting. Particularly construction work. One of these larger motormen can lift several tons of stone or steel on its own, and even the little ones can lift half a ton without straining any gears.

"There are tenement buildings in Heiastowne, the city just beyond the palace grounds, which are literally in danger of falling down, they're that badly in need of repair. If it didn't glorify the False God, it wasn't considered important. Half of all Guildarans live in what other lands would call hovels and slums. We're changing all of that," she murmured, the near side of her mouth quirking up with a hint of pride. "The fuel is expensive to process, but it frees up so many people to work on other projects, it's really made a huge difference in how fast and how far we've come."

Someone yelled and another chunk of metal dropped with a startling clang, making both of them jump. It had fallen nearby, reminding Zeilas they were indeed in a construction zone. Leading the way across the broad floor, away from further dangers, Marta brought him back to the ranks of motorhorses. Sir Catrine was busy sketching something on one of her miniaturized slateboards, with Gabria nodding and taking notes of her own in a blank-paged book. Both women looked up at their approach.

"So . . . What's the prognosis on my motorhorse?" Marta asked.

"We should have it warded and ready for testing by morning," Gabria stated, lifting the book in her hands. "Catrine's already given me a dozen ideas on how to fix the problem of shielding the fuel barrel without running into problems from impact-induced overheating."

"Good. Thank you, Sir Knight," Marta added, nodding at the woman on the ground. "I'll leave you in Gabria's hands then, and escort Sir Zeilas back to the palace. If you don't mind us leaving, that is?" she asked Zeilas.

"Catrine?" he asked.

She glanced down at her slate, then over at the sub-Consul for the Mage's Guild. "Milady Gabria learns quickly, and has some good ideas . . . but all the mages in Guildara lack certain basic instruction. We could easily be here most of the day, discussing pure theory."

"Try to save the pure theory for a classroom," Marta directed both of them. "Get the fuel shielded, produce results that can be demonstrated to Gabria's fellow guildmates, and earn *their* cooperation. The sooner, the better. We know our people are undertrained, but they've had too many years of mistrusting outsiders. The sooner you can show that *you're* earnest about helping them, the sooner they'll open up and accept that help." She paused, then switched to Arbran. Accented and not exactly grammatically correct, but Arbran all the same. "There be a number of our fellows who doubt *your* sincere self toward peace, all you Arbrans. Sharing your magical secrets to us is proof *you* will help. Such things build trust. Trust builds peace. Not to abuse it is very good, yes?"

". . . Understood," Catrine murmured. In Mekhanan. Her accent and grammar were much better. "I'll see what I can do to help, as you suggest. And I'll test one of these . . . machine-horses personally. Provided my Steed doesn't object, of course."

"He shouldn't. These aren't even real horses," Zeilas pointed out. "Just don't overwork yourselves trying to get things right."

"I'll have her back in time for supper," Gabria promised.

Nodding, Marta gestured for Zeilas to join her in working their way back out of the cavernous, somewhat crowded building. "What was that about her 'Steed' objecting?"

"Some Steeds get offended at the thought of their Knights riding any mount other than themselves," Zeilas explained. When the far corner of her mouth quirked up in a bemused look, he knew he had lost her. "Our mounts are Goddess-blessed stallions. They are immortal, never born and never aging; they simply appear from the nearest forest when a Squire successfully summons one. You don't know anything about how Knights are chosen, do you?"

"Nothing, beyond that your Goddess has a hand in it," she confessed, shrugging. "Everything we'd heard from the False priesthood involved demonic sacrifices of blood magic and pacts with the Netherhells. Naturally, most of us refused to believe them, since the False God kept claiming to be good, yet clearly was one of *them*. I am curious, though. How does someone end up as a Knight of Arbra? Are you just declared one, or . . . ?"

"It's a lengthy process. Boys—and now girls, thanks to Sir Orana's efforts at getting young women recognized for sponsorship a couple of centuries back—are tested and selected for that sponsorship, either by their family, their village, a noble household, or a local Knight. They go to an Academy for training above and beyond the usual reading and writing and figuring most children struggle to learn before heading off to follow some family trade. After six or so years," Zeilas added, shifting to the side when he did, so that a pair of women could trundle a wheeled cart loaded with tools past the two of them, "those that wish to become more than a soldier or a bureaucrat can petition the Tree of Swords at the High Temple near High Hold, the capital of Arbra."

"Does your Goddess Manifest in person?" she asked.

"Only rarely. If Arbora judges them worthy, She drops a sword at their feet. If not, they can join the government, or go back home and put their training to some good use. If they do receive a holy sword, then they go on to a Squire's Academy for an additional year or two of training—more if they're also a mage, though there are separate Mage Academies for training boys and girls who just want to be mages. But it's in the Squire's Academy that the chosen learn the additional skills of a Knight. After the first three months, the Squire sends out a special summons, and their Steed will appear.

"Even if we have no tangible magic and cannot do so much as light a candle, all Knights are granted just enough power by Arbora to summon our Steeds, and to command horses during times of great need," he told her. "Others, like Sir Catrine, spend most of their time training in the ways of both Knighthood and magecraft . . . and as a consequence, don't gain a lot of experience in other, more worldly subjects," he finished wryly as they emerged from the motorbarn.

The air was bright with early winter sunlight, and crisp with the cold air of the mountainous landscape cupping the broad valley around them. It was a far cry from the shimmering hot shores of Sundara far to the south. There hadn't been any snow on the journey here, just bitter cold and the occasional chilly rain, but he'd been warned that snow could and would fall in the coldest depths of winter.

Instead of golden sands and frond-topped palms, he was surrounded by dark evergreens and stone walls. Some of those walls belonged to the palace compound, situated on a slightly higher rise to the west, and some to the Palace Precinct fortress, where the motorbarn was housed. Those walls were necessary, with the northern border being so close, but it made him wonder about the location of their capital.

"Milady Chief . . ."

"Marta, please. We're not being formal at the moment," she demurred.

"Marta," he allowed. "Why this valley? Why a spot next to Heiastowne? You said it yourself, this valley is awfully close to the northern border."

"Several reasons. It's a rich town with several strong guilds. There are good quarries and mineral lodes nearby, plus coal mines and forests for lumber, which have made Heiastowne the center for stonecrafts, forgeworks, refineries, and other construction materials." She gestured at the broad compound around them. Some of its features were little more than stakes and ropes outlining future buildings and paths between them. Others were actual buildings, either completed, or in the process of being completed. "The original fortress belonged to a priest-lord. We razed the main buildings and used the rubble as part of the outer defensive walls, and built up the palace on newly blessed foundations.

"The promontory on which this palace compound was built is readily defensible, with a natural artesian spring for water, large plots of farmland for pastures and fields, a good sighting distance to detect approaching armies, and plenty of stone for the defensive walls. Heiastowne has similar defensive features, though instead of a spring, the wells pump up water from the underground river which feeds the spring. It's also located on what passes for a reasonable trade road.

"We don't have actual roads connecting us to Sundara, Arbra, Aurul and the like, since your ancestors wisely dug them up and made them impassable for anything more than the smallest of caravans." The near side of her mouth curved up, sharing her wry sense of humor about her country's checkered past. "At least, not without cooperation on both sides."

"Maybe that will change," Zeilas offered. "Peace offers far more opportunities for prosperity than war."

Marta nodded. "We're hoping to put our knowledge of road-building to good use in reestablishing the old trade routes. Once we do, Heiastowne will become a major trade center, since it's just about equidistant from our stable neighbors to the east, south, and west. As for the north . . . we're hoping everyone north of us will see how stable and prosperous we are, stop fighting each other, and ask politely to join. As two of the villages to the north have already done." She wrinkled her nose. "I suspect it will take successfully dealing with this Warlord Durn to show the rest of the northlands that we *can* fight, and hopefully fight well, but aren't interested in conquering anyone. *That* will gain us enthusiastic new citizens, and that's far better for the kingdom in the long run than gaining a bunch of frightened, cowed subjects."

"A wise viewpoint, and a well-considered one. I'll admit your roads are more level and better drained than ours, with far fewer ruts, too," Zeilas said. "Our journey east was quite smooth, once we crossed the border and reached the first real road. I found them all the more impressive because you haven't hired mages to make the work easier. At least, not in the past."

She wrinkled her nose. "We're still trying to get comfortable *ad-*

mitting we have mages among us. I've worked hard on it—I have to be comfortable, to set a good example as Consul-in-Chief—but even I sometimes feel like some zealous False priest is going to overhear me say the *M* word."

That particular phrase had a different meaning in Arbra. Without stopping to think about it, Zeilas quipped, "What, marriage?"

She stumbled to a halt, giving him a surprised look—then threw her head back, laughing long and heartily.

The world dropped away from him. Zeilas blinked at her, equally surprised. She was *gorgeous* when she laughed, beaming with mirth, eyes crinkling at the corners, teeth gleaming in the midafternoon light. There was a sense of *rightness* about her when she laughed, as if this was what she was meant to do. He knew even as he thought it that it was just a flight of fancy, but the feeling wouldn't go away.

It drew the attention of his Steed, Fireleaf. Smart as a child, though not quite that articulate, the blessed horse nosed his way into Zeilas' thoughts. *Something good?*

Steeds were immortal avatars of Arbora. To have one read his Knight's thoughts was no more disturbing than to have the Goddess read those thoughts. Less invasive, really, if more inquisitive. Zeilas thought back, *Something good, yes. Something . . . right.*

The last time he had felt anything this right simply from looking at it was when he had successfully summoned his Steed, and had seen Fireleaf trotting out of the royal woods beyond the fields ringing the Squire's Academy. Then, the dappled sorrel-and-cream stallion had been a gift from Arbora. Now . . . it was simply a chance meeting. Perhaps deliberately arranged by Fate, the Threefold God, or perhaps just pure luck. Or perhaps as a potential repayment for all the kindnesses he had done to others in his life.

Fireleaf nosed at his mental impression of the Consul-in-Chief, then snorted. *Lead mare. Good female. Strong, will bear fine foals.*

His mouth twitched with mirth. *Trust it to you to put it* that *way.*

Mare in season?

Not yet . . . but hopefully soon. He wouldn't have put it that way himself, but Zeilas did know he needed to capitalize on his luck, predestined or otherwise. As her mirth died down, she leveled her head and eyed him, grinning. That grin faltered as he just stared at her, until it wound up higher on one side of her mouth than on the other, dissolving into her usual wry smile.

". . . What?"

"You're exceptionally beautiful when you laugh," Zeilas told her. She blinked at the compliment, but he didn't retract it. Honesty prompted him to add a little bit more. "I shall endeavor to make you laugh more often."

"Well . . . I suppose as a diplomat you'd want me to be in a good mood whenever I—" she started to say.

Zeilas cut her off by lifting his finger to her lips. He shook his head, speaking softly. "What we do as the representatives of our governments is separate. *This* is personal, just between you and me. And, just between you and me, I think you are magnificent when you laugh." Removing his finger from her soft lips, he gave her a lopsided smile of his own. "Unfortunately, we both know that you and I must attend more to our duties than to our personal needs each day . . . though those needs do still exist . . . and they *do* deserve to be recognized. From time to time."

She stared at him, blinked, and blushed. Looking away for a moment, she shrugged slightly. "I'm not used to . . . being treated as a woman." She looked directly at him again, adding, "And not being threatened by it. Many of us women, who had the brains the Gods gave us and the wit to recognize it . . . we turned ourselves into sexless workers, to avoid the attentions of the False priesthood. Not all of them, but some, yes. Some preyed on women as well as on . . ."

". . . Marriage?" Zeilas offered when she hesitated over the *M* word. Marta burst out laughing again. As she wound down into chuckles, rubbing at the corner of her eyes with a finger, he grinned. "I'm glad to see our cultural differences are so amusing. I'll have to find other ways to make you laugh, too."

"You do that," she murmured, giving him a smile somewhere between half and whole. Glancing around at the half-grassy, half-paved courtyard, she shrugged and gestured at the palace in the distance. "We should head to your quarters, and maybe take a brief tour of the palace on the way.

"Tomorrow will be the grand reception," she reminded him. Then shrugged. "Not that we have any other ambassadors; we're still waiting to receive one from the Aurulan government, since they've claimed it isn't 'the right moment' to send one. Frankly, they make me nervous with how devoted to their Patron God they are . . . but they're not warlike, at least. The Sundarans can be warlike, but they refuse to send anyone to us until spring, citing that the cold, harsh winters found in our hills and mountains would be less distressing if their envoy crossed them instead in warmer months. So your Arbran promptness is appreciated by my people."

"Your Guildaran peacefulness is appreciated by mine," Zeilas reminded her, following her as she started for the palace gate.

THREE

". . . So when he mounted onto the saddle, for one split second he was on my Steed's back, and then Fireleaf sidestepped right out of the saddle, bit, and bridle," Zeilas told her, gesturing with his hands. "For one more brief moment, Captain Geldas just *hung* there in midair, clinging to the reins and the empty saddle—and then whump! The expression on his face was priceless as he fell, and I'll tell you, he made a very satisfying thump when he hit the ground!"

Marta laughed. She covered her mouth, since she had been caught chewing some of the food he had cooked, Arbran style, and brought to this "indoor picnic" idea of his, since the weather was too stormy and sleeting outside the palace to go anywhere. But she chuckled, swallowed, and cleared her throat. "I'm amazed your Steed didn't trample him."

"I asked him not to. We were visiting that town, looking for trade materials, and it wouldn't do to injure anything more than his dignity, and a bit of his backside . . . and he bruised his ankle, too. But I *did* warn him my Steed wouldn't tolerate anyone but me riding him," Zeilas added. "He just insisted he was a born horseman and could ride anything."

"And your Steed just . . . sidestepped the saddle and the bridle, girth strap, bit, and all?" she asked.

"He's an avatar of Arbora, and thus not entirely a creature of flesh and blood, though he can fake it well enough to fool most people. Or more like Her servant, rather. I'd be nervous, riding around on an actual piece of my Goddess," he admitted, sipping some of the wine she had brought to this odd, fireside midday meal. "Not that I'm afraid of Her, so much as I'm afraid I'd do something stupid in Her presence and offend Her. The rules governing a Knight's behavior are pretty strict as it is."

"A good distinction to make." His words did make her wonder. "About those rules . . . what do they say about you insisting on a private picnic with a head of state?"

"Neither of us are married, neither of us are being forced to attend this picnic, and everything we do here is entirely consensual," Zeilas stated, pouring more wine into both of their glasses. Not that they'd had much. He emptied the last drops of the bottle into his goblet, then set it back in the basket in which he'd brought the roasted duck, cheese-stuffed pastries, and vegetables. "My honor and my duty demand that I treat you, the Consul-in-Chief, with respect. My honor demands that I treat you, the woman, with respect as well. My duty says I must take no action that would jeopardize peaceful relations between Arbra and Guildara.

"Since my intentions are respectful toward Marta the woman as well as Marta the Consul-in-Chief, there is no conflict of interest. Provided you know that I court your attention for *your* sake, and not for sweetening your opinion of Arbrans in general." Lifting his glass, he saluted her with it.

"You don't want me to think sweetly of all Arbrans based on my interactions with you?" Marta dared to tease dryly, lifting her own blown-glass goblet.

"You've already met and conquered Sir Catrine's reluctance to deal with former Mekhanans. You know how the average Arbran will react, and what it will take on both sides to overcome those old fears," Zeilas pointed out. "Anything I do on a personal level can't change that, and won't change that, other than what I can do to encourage Arbrans like her to get past their old fears. All I can hope for is that you'll think sweetly of me, the man, in personal, private meetings like this."

"I do," she acknowledged. He smiled. Then he shifted, but not toward her. Not toward anything like a kiss, which given their conversation, she half expected.

Instead, she watched him select another log from the bin beside the hearth and tuck it into the flames providing a toasty level of heat. The parlor, one of several designed into the main wing, was meant for receiving visitors, with its inlaid wooden walls and floors, its fine-carved furniture. Not for impromptu picnics on quilts spread in front of the main fireplace. But the setting wasn't absurd. Somehow, he made it . . . romantic. Particularly when he had complimented the woodwork with high praise, comparing it to the wood-anointed chapels and cathedrals dedicated to his people's Goddess of Forests, and then looked at her with a gleam in his brown eyes that said he thought *she* was just as beautiful.

Yet, when he settled back onto the quilt next to her, he didn't kiss her. Marta had courted a time or two before, though she hadn't cared to give up her independence, since under the False God's rule that had meant giving up her work in favor of raising good little children like a good little wife should. Now that they had a freed kingdom with good attitudes about all their citizens, she was ready to court anyone she pleased, in any manner she pleased. Except a foreign ambassador wasn't necessarily the smartest choice.

But he's right. So long as we do know our duty is separate from our de-

sire . . . "You're quite right. About my own intentions," she said as the new log snapped and hissed, catching fire. "My duty and my honor say I shouldn't do anything to cause misunderstandings or troubles between our nations. My duty would have me separate what I do as the Consul-in-Chief from what I want to do as a woman. And my intent is to be respectful of you and toward you. Both toward you as Envoy Zeilas, Knight of Arbra . . . and you as Zeilas, the man. Which leaves us with a single question."

"And that question is . . . ?" he prompted, his warm brown eyes studying her, clad in her usual black knit tunic and leather trews. Sexless worker clothes, suitable for commanding respect from her fellow citizens . . . but the gleam in his eyes told her he saw her feminine side all the same.

Lit more by the fire than by the gray gloom of the storm beyond the windows to either side of the hearth, she thought he was quite possibly one of the most handsome men she had ever seen. Not for the shape of his face, or the muscles under his velvet and linen garments, but simply because he was him. Zeilas. Charming, funny, honorable, and neither intimidated by her status as Consul-in-Chief nor as inclined to treat her as sexlessly as a fellow Guildaran because of it.

Gathering her courage, since it required a different sort of bravery than the kind required to rule a nation, Marta looked him in the eye and asked, "Would it be disrespectful to share a kiss?"

Zeilas smiled. "Oh, I think I could still respect you afterward."

Pleased, Marta leaned onto her left hand, swaying closer to him. To her relief and delight, he leaned closer on his right palm. Their heads tipped, their lips met, and it was warm, soft, and sweet. Respectful. He brushed her mouth with his once, twice . . . on the third time, the tip of his tongue flicked against her lips unexpectedly, tickling her. She pulled back, stifling her giggle into a snicker.

He still smiled, not in the least offended by her brief, startled retreat. Pleased, Marta leaned in a second time, this time for a lick of her own. Once, twice . . . their mouths parted and met in open tasting, and there was no point in counting past the third time. He pulled back after a moment, just long enough to move the goblet and crumb-dusted plate between them out of the way, then shifted closer for more. More kissing, more touching as his hand lifted to cup her jaw, more tasting of her lips, more of everything.

Somehow, she ended up on her back, her coronet of braids adding their cushioning effects to the quilt protecting them from the polished wooden floor. His elbows braced some of his weight off of her, but the warmth of his body cradling hers felt even better than the fire in the hearth. Arms wrapped around his shoulders, Marta tangled her fingers in his shoulder-length brown hair. It was longer than a typical Guildaran male's and felt clean and soft. The velvet of his doublet disconcerted her fingertips, half expecting the knitted wool of a Guildaran man, but she liked the feel of it. The priests of the False God had flaunted their wealth by wearing velvets and silks in face of the average citizen's relative poverty, making it hard even now for any of her people to care openly for such things, but she could admire it secretly.

She wasn't going to reject *him*, though. Not when he tasted of apple-stuffed pastry and wine, when he smelled of musk and wood smoke, not when he felt warm and wonderful. Unfortunately, a knock at the parlor door startled both of them. Breaking off their kiss, he gave her a rueful look as he sat up. Hastily levering herself upright as well, Marta found her voice.

"Come in!"

Gabria entered, a familiar man at her side. It was Stevan, one of the palace talker box operators. "I apologize for the intrusion, Milady Chief," Gabria stated, "but we've received a rather . . . odd . . . talker relay from the eastern border."

"From Aurul?" Marta asked, her disappointment at having their kisses interrupted vanishing under the interest sparked by those words. Or rather, not vanishing so much as subsiding, since she was still keenly aware of the Knight seated beside her on the quilt. "Are they finally talking to us, then?"

"Aye, milady," Stevan confirmed. He lifted the paper tablet in his hands and read the message he had brought. "To the Consul-in-Chief. 'Finally granted audience with Seer King Devin. He said, quote, Tell your queen what she does is right and just. Seek it further from the west if you wish peace for longer than a day. If you wish the same from the east, send your friend, the girl in gray. From the south, the solution is a solution, otherwise you waste your breath. From the north, the only solution is the resolution brought by a firmly faced death. End quote, and no I do not know what he means, milady.' Signed by Envoy Pells Chartman, sent from the Guildaran border post nearest the City of Searching, Aurul, and relayed fifteen times from the border, checked and double-checked each step of the way."

The talker boxes, she knew, didn't project their sendings more than the distance a person could comfortably ride in half a day. They could also be interrupted by bad weather or heavy spellcasting. As a result, their operators tended to send back any and all messages for confirmation. The process was a little cumbersome, but much, much faster than even a scout on a motorhorse could ride. That redundancy meant the message was as accurate as its sender could make it, and she knew Pells Chartman to be quite levelheaded and reliable.

"That's a very odd message," she murmured, pushing to her feet. Dusting off her tunic, she eyed Stevan again. "Recite for me King Devin's words again, please?"

"'Tell your queen that what she does is right and just,'" Stevan repeated, checking his notes. "'Seek it further from the west if you wish peace for longer than a day. If you wish the same from the east, send your friend, the girl in gray. From the south, the solution is a solution, otherwise you waste your breath. From the north, the solution is the resolution brought by a firmly faced death.'"

Marta looked at Gabria. As usual, the other woman was clad in silvery gray wool, spun by her western-dwelling, sheep-raising kin.

"Well, *one* part is easy to decipher, even if I dislike the thought of doing without your company. That is, assuming you're willing to head to Aurul, Gabria, and be our next envoy there?"

"I'm not trained for it. I'm not even trained fully as a . . . mage . . . but if it'll secure peace on the eastern border, I'll go," Gabria said, lifting her chin a little. She lowered it after a moment, an uncertain look in her green eyes. "Except, I don't speak Aurulan, and the message doesn't say how much of a delay we can risk before I have to go."

"You have a point. We'll find someone to give you some rudimentary lessons at the very least. Stevan, send back this message to Envoy Pells Chartman," Marta instructed the talker box engineer.

Tearing off the top page, he handed it to her. Stevan then fished a charcoal pencil from the pouch at his waist and poised it over the tablet.

She nodded and began, speaking slowly enough that he could scribe each word. "To Envoy Pells. Please inform His Majesty with due courtesy that we shall send the 'girl in gray' as soon as the spring thaws have made it safe enough for her to cross the eastern mountains. We wish her to arrive alive and unharmed in the Seer King's court so that she may enact a peaceful treaty between our lands. In the meantime, and as ever, we wish His Majesty good health and a long reign. Send a reply if any, and continue to act as our envoy until instructed otherwise. Marta Grenspun, Consul-in-Chief."

When he finished, Stevan read back her words to her to confirm them, then nodded crisply. "Right. I'll get this sent out immediately. Milady Chief, sub-Consul . . . Sir Knight."

His tone wasn't rude, so much as speculative, Marta judged. Particularly since he eyed the way Zeilas was still seated on the quilt spread over the floor, and the remains of their makeshift picnic. With a brief, wordless lift of his brows, the talker box operator spun on his heel and strode out of the room.

He wasn't the only one to eye Sir Zeilas with bemusement. Gabria studied him and his position, too, before shaking her head slightly, visibly dismissing her curiosity. "Right. We still have three more Seer King verses to make sense of. I'd leave the two of you to do whatever you were doing, but . . ."

"But this is important. Not that what we were doing wasn't important in its own way, either," Marta added quickly, glancing down at her picnic partner.

The Knight pushed to his feet, dusting off his blue velvet clothes. "Nothing wrong in what we were doing. It's just that the needs of your kingdom come first. I understand completely."

The words *nothing wrong* and *just* stuck in her brain. Marta wanted to chase them down, but Gabria had moved closer, attempting to peer at the tablet page in her hand. Tilting it, she displayed it toward her friend. "What I do is right and just, apparently, which is all to the good. I'm *trying* to do what is right and just. That's what being Consul-in-Chief is all about. But this second sentence puzzles me—the start of it, I mean. 'Seek it further from the west,' that part. What is 'it' and how does it relate to what I'm doing, versus what I seek from our allies?

"Sir Zeilas, do you have any idea what this means?" she asked, turning to him. "Perhaps 'further' means I should offer more treaties?"

He rubbed his chin, which from its smoothness she suspected he had shaved just before their picnic lunch, then shrugged. "I haven't much experience in dealing with prophecies, to be honest, but . . . It seems to me they come in two types. Either they unfold their meaning when the events predicted happen, *or* they have meaning which pertains to the moment they are revealed to their intended target. This doesn't seem to have any sort of specific date or goal in mind—not an actual month or day like, oh, Fevra 7th or Mars 14th. Prophecies are never that specific. But they do refer to an event, when they *do* refer to one. This one is more like a set of instructions. 'Follow this, and such and such will happen.'"

"So, you think it has more meaning for the context of the moment in which it was heard?" Marta asked.

"Well, it did specify the 'girl in gray' who is your friend," Gabria pointed out. "I'm not your only friend, and I'm not the only person wearing gray clothes in the palace compound. But I was the first person Stevan saw as he came out of the talker room, I am your friend, and I did know where to find you, the intended recipient of the message."

"Exactly. So, what we were doing was . . . *right* and *just*?" Marta looked up at the Arbran Knight, confused.

Zeilas smiled. Smirked, rather. "What we were doing certainly seemed right, though I don't know how 'just' it was." Catching a curious look from Gabria, he shook his head. "Just getting-to-know-you things, that's all. Respectfully."

His gaze slipped back to her mouth. For a moment, Marta could once again feel the touch of his lips against hers. Clearing her throat, she focused on the paper in her hands. "Well, maybe it means respect and a cultural or social exchange of some sort. Which would make sense, if I would 'seek it further than a day' since with understanding often comes acceptance, or at least greater tolerance." She eyed the next verse. "Which means you'll be in charge of some sort of cultural exchange once you get to Aurul, Gabria."

"I look forward to it," the other woman quipped wryly. "Seers are strange enough, I don't see why someone as socially awkward as me should be entrusted with this task."

"You don't seem the least bit shy to me, milady," Zeilas offered politely.

Gabria wrinkled her nose. "Not shy, awkward. I *am* a . . . you know."

"Ah, yes. Married," he quipped.

Marta snorted. She quickly covered her nose and mouth to muffle her giggles, which were worsened by her friend's confused look. Waiving it off, she mustered some composure and muttered, "It's a private joke . . . Well. We'll load you with ideas for cultural exchanges, as well as lessons in Aurulan, so at least the Aurulans can understand you if you ask for the nearest refreshing room or what time supper will be served. As for the south . . . the solution is the solution?"

"It might be something you already know they need," Zeilas said, rubbing his chin again.

"Considering they've waited almost a full year after our Patron Deity Manifested to agree to sending us an envoy . . . which they haven't yet *sent*," Marta returned, "we don't know much of what they *need*. In fact, the only thing I know most Sundarans 'need' is water, and they get it for free from the River Ev . . . oh. Right. The River Evada." Lifting a hand to the bridge of her nose, Marta rubbed at the headache threatening to form. "Right. The tailings and runoffs from the south valley mines. Well. I *have* been after the Mining Guild to clean up after themselves."

"If the miners want peace with Sundara, like the rest of us, cleaning up the mining pollution in the river water *would* go a long way toward sweetening their feelings about us," Gabria agreed.

"I'd have to agree," Zeilas chimed in. "In my time down in southern Sundara, I did notice the locals were rather keen on pure water. The cleaner, the better. They use it ritually to purify themselves, confessing their sins and cleansing their souls even as they scrub their skin. It may not have come up yet because they may not have noticed, or they may simply be waiting for their envoy to bring it up once the preliminary stuff is out of the way . . . but they will notice. Anything you do preemptively to make the river water better will also be noticed, and appreciated."

"I'm not too up-to-date on my alchemical knowledge, but I do know they use certain extracts in the refining process for certain rare ores," Marta muttered. "Some are acidic, some are alkaline, and many require one or the other opposing kind to neutralize their effects. That could be the 'solution' the Seer King had in mind for us. I'll pressure the Mining Guild to cooperate with the Alchemy Guild on figuring out how to clean up the river."

"That leaves just one verse left. Two guesses as to what it means, and the first one's already been used up," Gabria quipped.

Marta wrinkled her nose. "The north, and Warlord Durn the Dreaded. Well, even an idiot child could tell we'd have to fight him at some point. If 'a firmly faced death' means facing him in battle, then we'll face him. But not without provocation. We're creators now, not aggressors."

"Sir Catrine has promised to show the Mage's Guild several varieties of long-distance scrying spells," Gabria said. "Combine that with some extra scout patrols from the border precincts, and we should have plenty of advanced warning on when Durn starts massing his troops this coming spring."

Marta started to comment, then caught herself. She gave her friend a lopsided smile. "I was about to ask you to contact them, and see if the Mage's Guild can offer some enchanting assistance as well, since a lot of our magical style was sublimated into alchemy over the years. But you'll have to select a replacement from among your fellow sub-Consuls before you leave. Now is as good a time as any to go pick one out, so they'll have time to learn and train."

Gabria returned the half smile, making it look more rueful than wry. "You're right. I'd better get started on that. I'll see you later. Sir Zeilas . . ."

"Sub-Consul," Zeilas returned, giving her a polite bow. She turned and left the parlor, closing the door in her wake.

"We don't have much time," Marta murmured. Turning to face him, she found her next set of words cut off by the way he wrapped his arms around her body and caught her mouth in a soft, succulent kiss. He didn't kiss her for long, and when he pulled back, it was with a slight smile.

"Sorry, but I figured we didn't have much time left in our scheduled picnic. You were saying?"

"I was about to say, if this prophecy relates to our *current* circumstances . . . then more of 'it' for her would be more of *this*," she pointed out, slipping her arms around his ribs. Then she sighed and scrunched her nose in a grimace, though she didn't let go of him. "From a political standpoint, it makes no sense. *This* isn't politically wise."

"Agreed. If we court openly, they could question our judgment. If we court secretly and we're discovered, they'll question our motives for every decision made," Zeilas agreed. "Besides, the prophecy implies that whatever we do here, the 'girl in gray' shall have something similar happen to her. That in turn would imply that she's being called to Aurul to court or be courted. People don't actually conduct politics that way. Not in this day and age, at any rate."

Standing in the circle of their interlaced arms, Marta gave in to impulse. She leaned into him, resting her cheek on his shoulder, and sighed. "I may have to go back to being Consul-in-Chief in a moment, but I'm not going to regret this moment. I'm a leader and a woman, and I'm very glad you're enjoying the company of the woman."

"It'd be easier if you weren't a leader," he agreed, dusting the top of her braid-wrapped head with a kiss. Squeezing briefly, he released her and stepped back. "But you are, and I still respect you, as both a woman and a ruler. If nothing else, you *are* an elected ruler. I need only wait patiently for your term to be up."

"Except I might get reelected," she pointed out, chuckling. Mock-posing thoughtfully, finger on cheek, she added, "*Unless* I deliberately befouled my reputation with, say, flirting openly with an honored envoy . . . oh, but to truly foul it up, you'd have to be offended, wouldn't you?"

He lifted her hands in his, bowing over them with a warm smile. "That, I think, would be very difficult for you to do."

His words warmed her from the inside out. She *liked* feeling feminine around him, for he was not only sincere, he didn't diminish her in any way. "Then to a Netherhell with what anyone thinks. What we would do is not *wrong*. Not if we mind the difference between our positions and our persons.

"You and I shall continue to get to know each other, and perhaps even to court one another," she allowed, reasoning it out loud. "We shall do so discretely in the sense of separating it from our occupational concerns, and discreetly in the sense of not being overly blatant or disrespectful about it . . . but we will still court. When we can schedule the time for it, since I do have to leave in a few moments to meet with the Consul of the Accountant's Guild. Is this course of action agreeable with you?"

Pressing a kiss to the backs of her knuckles, he murmured, "Eminently."

FOUR

The flurry of knocks on the door of the Arbran ambassadorial suite startled the three Arbrans mid-meal. Sir Collum, junior-most of those present at breakfast, got up and hurried to answer the impatient thumping. No sooner had the messenger-Knight opened the door, however, than he stumbled back, giving ground before the furious, flushed appearance of the Consul-in-Chief.

Waving a sheet of tablet paper, she stalked into their parlor without waiting for permission and shook the scrap in Zeilas' face as he hastily rose to greet her. "Your king is *impossible*! Or at least, he's *demanding* the impossible! Do you know what he's expecting us to do?"

Wiping the crumbs of his breakfast from his mouth, Zeilas swallowed not only his food but the urge to tell her she looked absolutely beautiful in her gown. The outer garment was black, like all of her clothes, and knitted from finespun wool in a complex, almost delicate pattern. A silvery gray linen undergown could be seen peeking through beneath the holes knitted into the pattern, the first sign of nonblack in any of her apparel so far. Instead, mindful that his duty came first, he asked, "Actually, no, I don't, but if you'll explain, I'd be happy to listen."

She flapped the tablet sheet in front of him again. He belatedly recognized it as the same size used by their "talker box operators" like that fellow Stevan. The talker boxes, he had learned, were a clever, complex, nonmagical solution to the scrying mirrors used for long-distance communications by most other countries. They were particularly useful for nonsensitive or time-sensitive communications; for those missives requiring discretion but which weren't time sensitive, delivering the messages personally were what his fellow Knights like Sir Collum did best.

"Your king," Marta growled, "expects us to pay for *everything*! Regarding the road-building projects," she clarified as he gave her a blank look. "I *told* you, we don't have a lot of arable land to spare—and frankly, we'll need every hand we *do* have to bring in the harvests this next year, because we're having to push for bigger farms and fields, and yes, that means taking laborers from other guilds and cross-training them in the agricultural ones. If I have to take those men and women *out* of the fields to build roads connecting us with Arbra, then how the hell am I going to *feed* them?"

Plucking the tablet sheet from her grasp, Zeilas read over the message, relayed by mirror and talker box all the way from High Hold. "His Majesty is refusing to *pay* you in coin for the roads. I don't think it is unreasonable for him to ask *your* people to build those roads. First of all, it reassures him, if the roads are first built from the Guildaran side, that you have no fear of us invading *you*, because you're making it easier for us to do so, if that were our intent. Which it isn't.

"Second . . . even our own road-builders would have to admit that *your* roads are far better constructed than ours. It only makes sense to have the best builders do the job, so that they'll last a good long time," he added. "Third, we've already agreed that trade in food items can begin immediately. You can buy whatever you need."

"With what money? Our entire economy has been self-sufficient, until now. Poor, but self-sufficient," Marta argued. "If we send you our coinage for your food—an enduring commodity for a consumable one—that means we're weakening *our* economy. We don't have *that* much in the way of gold and silver in our mines. Most of what we have is tin, copper, and iron. If your king wants *us* to build those roads—and thank you for the compliment; yes, we do build very good roads—then *he* will have to feed us for them! *And* house us. And clothe us, besides!"

"Oh, now that's asking too much," Zeilas protested. Mindful of Sir Collum and Sir Eada, who hadn't finished their breakfasts, he gestured at the table. "Would you care to sit and join us, Milady Chief? We have some fruit and some pastries left, and half a sausage."

"I've broken my fast, thank you, though some fruit juice would be nice," Marta replied, settling into the chair he quickly held out for her. "I apologize for the intrusion, but this is a ridiculously expensive request. Peace and trade both require cooperation, and if he will not compromise at least somewhat favorably for us, then we will have no incentive to comply. Thank you," she added as Sir Eada poured and passed to her a fresh goblet of apple juice.

"Forgive me my ignorance," Sir Collum offered somewhat hesitantly, "but surely this could have waited for later?"

"Yes, and no," Marta explained to the younger Knight. "Technically it could, but now that winter is on its way out, my schedule is filling up rapidly with all that we have to do once the weather improves. Sir Catrine—by the way, where is she?"

"She broke her fast early and went out to exercise her Steed, along with the others," Zeilas explained.

Marta nodded. "Right. Yes, you've certainly given our motorhorse corps some fits of envy with your horsemanship skills. For all they're nearly inexhaustible, our motorhorses are still merely machines, and must be constantly guided . . . As I was saying, Sir Catrine has been teaching our mages how to read and predict the weather. They and she both predict that the weather will start improving this next week.

"*That* means, if we're to get a head start on breaking ground for the roads, we need to clear up the details of who will be responsible for what as soon as the conditions are perfect for digging, grading, and laying new roadbeds. It will *also* be good weather for planting, soon," she finished pointedly.

"Sir Eada, would you fetch the border map?" Zeilas asked. The lady Knight nodded and rose to fetch it from the scroll rack in the room serving as their office. Once she came back with it, he unrolled it and spread it out on the table, using some of the emptied plates to hold down the corners. "If you're concerned about the food to feed all the road workers, then how about we concentrate on *one* new road . . . um . . . this one, between the Arbran town of Brightglade and the Guildaran one of . . . Poverstowne? It's a short enough distance, you can do some preliminary clearing of the trees and such, lay down a rough track, and then maybe Arbra can ship in cartloads of grain and vegetables to feed your workers while you turn the rough track into a decent road?"

"Not Poverstowne," she corrected, shaking her head. "Too many hills and trees on its west side—it's near where Gabria grew up, and she's described the terrain a time or two. It may seem a short distance, but it's actually not very good. Between these two towns up here in the north might be better. The distance is longer by several miles, but the terrain is flatter, and there isn't as much forest to clear-cut. I *do* know something of how you Arbrans revere your trees, and I wouldn't ask you to let us chop down too many of them."

"Your care for our values is appreciated," he allowed. Eyeing the map, Zeilas tapped the river valley at the southern edge. "What about the River Evada? It does turn more toward Sundara down here than toward Arbra, but you could cut a road up over this line of hills . . . ?"

He leaned closer as he outlined his idea . . . and became aware of his knee, which now brushed against her thigh. There hadn't been too many opportunities to sneak a discreet kiss or three in the intervening weeks, but there had been a few. Now, though it wasn't exactly an intimate touch, he was aware of just how feminine she looked, clad in the first dress he had seen on her. A dress which, for all it flared out over her legs in a swirl of knitted wool and linen, clung to her figure from the waist up.

The sight of her breasts from this close, which looked to be the perfect handful in size, made him flush and fix his gaze firmly on the map. He didn't remove his knee from its proximity to her leg, though. His flush deepened when he felt her leg shift, nudging her foot against his in a subtle, under-the-table caress.

"That line of hills . . . at that point . . . are actually a line of cliffs and steep escarpments," Marta said. She took a sip of juice, her boot, calf, and fabric-draped thigh brushing against his own. "There *is* a viable method of trading goods, without needing any new roads. It would require taking the caravans down this road from Arbra into Sundara, then porting them up the river on barges from this Sundaran town here . . . but we still don't have a Sundaran ambassador on hand to negotiate with and clear things up with their border guards, allowing the food to get through."

"Plus, it would add months to the journey." It wasn't easy to focus on their negotiations, but he did, tapping the northern route. "If this one has the fewest terrain obstacles, perhaps if we sent a few preliminary shipments of foodstuff via pack animals? Sending spare grains, dried fruits, and root vegetables that way might not bring you a lot, but it should supplement your workers' diets enough to get that preliminary track laid through the no-man's-land of the border. You'd be on your own for meats, since those don't transport quite as well on pack animals. Most of it tends to be salted and stored in barrels, which are better suited for cart-based travel. And carts require roads, preferably good ones."

"We have plenty of meat, if you like lamb and mutton," she said. "Though if you'd care to ship us dried fish, that'd be lovely. Dried fruit, dried fish, grains, and so forth. We'd be willing to accept food as payment for our road-building services, in lieu of coin. But it would also help if you arranged for shelter, too."

"You're not asking for much," Zeilas muttered wryly. He tucked his left hand into his lap, then shifted it over a few inches, until it brushed her thigh. Her breath caught slightly and she blinked twice, but otherwise didn't react. Unless he counted the way her calf slid against his in a caress. He returned it, though he shook his head. "His Majesty won't go for that. *Unless* it's confined strictly to his side of the border. I think if you word it as such, and point out that the buildings could then be turned into barracks for road patrols—"

"—I'd *rather* word it as future inns for traders," she countered firmly. "I suppose we could do the same on our side, as our part of the bargain. But if you want us to build those roads, you have to offer a suitable incentive for building them. Feeding and housing our workers would be a very good start. If a cheap one."

"A cheap one?" Sir Eada interjected.

Marta gave her a half-sided smile. "We build *very* good roads."

Given she had seen those roads for herself, the lady Knight couldn't dispute that fact. Instead, she rose to fetch paper and pen. With her taking notes, and Zeilas writing the final draft, the four of them crafted a reasonable counterproposal for Marta to take to her fellow Consuls. If they concurred, it could be sent back again via talker box and mirror scryings to the capital of Arbra.

Soon enough, the young Sir Collum was sent off to the talker engineers with a neatly penned sheet detailing the counteroffer. Standing, Sir Zeilas escorted the Consul-in-Chief back to the door. There, he lifted her fingers to his lips for a kiss, and a subtle caress of his thumb. "May all our morning encounters end so pleasantly, milady . . . and may they one day begin even more so."

Blue eyes gleaming with mirth—she knew what he was implying, thankfully—Marta dipped her head politely. "May every morning begin with a pleasant interaction and a cooperative proposal, Sir Knight."

She left in a swirl of black knit and gray linen, looking lovely and graceful as well as her usual competent self. Sighing, Zeilas shut the door and returned to the cold remains of his breakfast. No sooner had he seated himself than Sir Eada spoke.

"So," she asked without preamble, "when are you going to bed her?"

His fork clattered back onto his plate. Had it made it all the way to his mouth with the slices of fruit speared on its tines, he might have choked. As it was, Zeilas coughed and cleared his throat. "I beg your pardon?"

Eada, only a handful of years older than Collum and a bit younger than Zeilas, lifted her brows. "You feign ignorance, after the two of you canoodled your ankles together under the table all that time?" She smirked when he blushed. "I noticed it when I went to fetch paper. Not that we haven't noticed all the *other* courtly things you've been doing around her."

"Well, I won't deny it," Zeilas stated, composing himself. "But neither have I *bedded* her."

Eada sobered, fixing him with a slightly worried look in her hazel gaze. "Is it really wise to court the queen of this land? When you're an envoy?"

"I've wondered that myself." He sighed. "But we both know our duty comes first. And she may not *stay* queen. Or rather, Consul-in-Chief. In a few years, they'll hold another Manifestation-borne election, their Goddess will choose someone, and it just might be someone else."

Eada snorted, refilling her glass with the dregs of the apple juice. "Unlikely. She's highly competent, and her people both like and heed her. You don't switch horses midstream, if the horse is wading through just fine."

"True." That did worry him. "The more I get to know her—

Marta, the woman—the more I like her. And yet the more I admire her as I learn about the Consul-in-Chief, too. And I know I can't *bed* her," he added, emphasizing the slightly crass term. "She deserves far more respect than that. I am what I am, the chief envoy from Arbra, and she is what she is, ruler of Guildara." Sighing, he stabbed at the fruit slices again. "Nothing will happen between us, beyond a little calf 'canoodling' as you put it."

"Technically I said ankles, but yes," she agreed. "You are a Knight of Arbra. Your honor is strong. A little curved, mayhap," Eada teased, pausing to drain her cup, "but not bent or broken."

Zeilas didn't bother to say *yet*. He knew his duty and would not let things go that far. Not without approval from his own government. The only problem was how to broach the subject without looking as if he *had* bent his honor. That part would be tricky.

FIVE

The clang-clang-clang of nearby bells, beaten fast and furious, startled Zeilas out of a sound sleep. It also startled his Steed. Fireleaf reached out to him even as he fought to make sense of the noise.

What that? What that?

I don't know, he sent back, blinking and scrubbing at his eyes. He heard Sir Collum swearing, a crumpling sound, and a moment later the embers in the fireplace flared up, igniting the scrap paper the younger man had tossed onto the fire for illumination. At least, it was supposed to be scrap paper, from the bin set in their bedchamber for such things. The other two male Knights sharing this room grunted and sat up, squinting through the gloom as the bell or gong or whatever kept banging for a few moments more.

It fell silent just as he drew in a breath to speak. Caught off guard by the silence, he listened—then winced as the clang-clang-clang-clang started up again.

"What in the name of rotten trees is *that* for?" one of the others snapped.

"Hell if I know," Collum muttered, feeding more paper and bits of kindling onto the fire.

Shoving out of bed, Zeilas flung open his trunk and started pulling on his clothes. Nothing fancy, just shirt and trousers, socks and boots. He was still stamping into the lattermost when the bell stopped banging again, only to be replaced by voices shouting in the distance. Tugging one last time, he crossed to the window, unlatched it, and poked his head out, ignoring the near-freezing night air and the protests of his roommates.

Somewhere nearby, several people were yelling something. Yelling and pounding, like they were banging on doors. Noise from nearby had him hastily closing the window. The voice was muffled by distance and a few stout walls, but the words were somewhat clear.

"*Palace Precinct, arm and stand ready! This is not a drill, I repeat, this is not a drill! Precinct captains, report to the War Room! Sergeants, report to the motorbarn! Palace Precinct, arm and stand ready! This is not a drill!*"

Someone banged on what sounded like *their* door. First one out of the bedroom, Zeilas hurried down the short hall to the front parlor. Sir Catrine had beaten him to it. She was still clad in her nightclothes, loose shirt and worn trews, but a ball of flame burned over her uplifted hand, illuminating the room, the door, and the person on the other side when she flung open the panel.

The man flinched back from the sight of her hovering fire, then recovered his composure. "Begging pardon, but Heiastowne's about to be attacked. Or maybe the palace; we don't know, yet. Precinct Command says the Knight-envoy and Knight-mage need to report to the War Room immediately. 'Scuse me—I have to wake the rest."

Without waiting for questions, the man spun on his heel and strode quickly down the lantern-lit hall, banging on the walls with the edges of his fists as he went, weaving back and forth.

"*Palace Precinct, arm and stand ready!*" he shouted as he left. "*Pre-*

cinct captains, report to the War Room! Sergeants, report to the motorbarn! This is not a drill!"

Sir Catrine shut the door with a wince, for the middle-aged man had more than enough lung power for his task. She grimaced. "I don't like the sound of this."

"You heard the man, get ready. I'll go on ahead—the War Room is in the Precinct annex, ground floor. If the valley's under attack, we need to know if they'll want us to fight," Zeilas said. Catching sight of her roommate, he nodded at Eada. "You're the Knight with the most combat experience, so I'd like you with me, too. The rest of you," he added, turning to face the others who had come out of their rooms, ". . . get yourselves and your Steeds ready for battle, just in case."

They nodded and scattered. Since he was mostly dressed, if not warmly, Zeilas grabbed his riding coat from the row of pegs by the front door of the suite. It had been made from felted wool in the local style, commissioned after having seen Marta, Gabria, and others riding around on their motorhorses. While it didn't cover him from shoulders to ankles, just from shoulders to thighs, it did keep him warm as he headed down the cold halls.

The Precinct annex had technically been built first. Or rather, remodeled, since it was part of the original castle built on the rise which the locals had turned into the palace compound. Now it was reached via a stout-walled corridor that dipped underground. Joining the half dozen or more bodies headed that way, he managed to spot Marta simply from the glint of gold circling her felted black cap. She was huddling in one of her thickest-knit tunics, smothering a yawn and eyeing the map on the central table in the hall as the man known as Precinct General Stalos thumped it with his fingers.

Edging up next to her, Zeilas managed to catch her eye. And that of the Precinct General. The other man spoke first, giving him a brisk nod, but forestalling any questions.

"Sir Knight. If you'll wait a few moments while everyone gathers, we'll get the briefing done all at once." The gray-haired warrior returned his attention to the map, continuing whatever it was he had been saying. "If they do go for the palace, if we can delay two hours, we can still bring in the South Fluttersfield Precinct, but if we delay three, that might give the West Freshford Precinct time to sweep up in a pincer on the northwest flank. It all depends on whether or not they've spotted us spotting them, and if they'll want to pause their troops to refuel and refresh."

A talker box operator hurried into the room, calling for the general's attention. He elbowed his way to the edge of the table and displayed his tablet, murmuring in the older man's ear. Hands in his pockets to keep them warm, Zeilas strained to hear what was being discussed but couldn't make out any words. Too many people were murmuring and whispering around him, trying to make sense of their abrupt awakening and summoning.

Someone touched Zeilas on the shoulder. A glance back showed it was Sir Catrine, with Sir Eada at her back. Both women looked hastily dressed—Eada was still lacing the cuffs of her sleeves, in fact—and a little flushed from having raced to dress and get here, but they were more or less ready to hear what was going on. If they wanted to be ready for combat, it would take each of them several minutes to don their armor, but it looked like they might have that much time.

"Alright, listen up!" Stalos called out, silencing the speculative murmurs in the room. The air was cold and slightly smoky from the braziers hastily lit in the corners of the room. A couple of people coughed, but otherwise gave him the silence to speak. "This is the situation. Three of our border scouts due north of Heiastowne failed to report in on time. Only one of the four scouts sent by the Pliny Pass Precinct managed a partial report before her talker box failed. This was a quarter hour ago. Pliny Pass relayed the report to me, and I have called for a general mobilization from all precincts within four hours of Heiastowne. This is *not* a drill.

"Warlord Durn has crossed the border and is invading Guildara with a very large force. Scout Theress estimated that there were at least ten precincts' worth of engines mobilized and headed our way, possibly twelve. Her communication cut out before she could estimate more closely. We lost communication with her for at least ten minutes, until she managed to get outside what appears to be a magical anti-communications field cast by whatever sources Durn is fielding." Lifting the sheet most recently torn from the talker box operator's tablet, Stalos continued. "The latest report—again, only from one scout—is that there is somewhere between ten and twelve precincts' worth of troops and engines, including motorhorse ranks, hexaleg transports, at least four giant-class motormen, *and* mobile cannonry.

"We can only assume, coming from the farmlands to the north as they do, that they have more munitions than we have," the Precinct General reported grimly. He glanced over at Zeilas and the two lady Knights behind him, and switched to a grin. "On the plus side, while we don't know the full capabilities of Durn's mages, we have mages trained in Arbran magics, and we should therefore be able to neutralize the impact of those cannons and the giant-class motormen. We also have the familiarity of the terrain and the defensive construction of both Heiastowne and the palace."

"What of the missing scouts?" someone called out from off to the right.

Stalos lost his brief show of good humor. "We have to assume they've been captured or killed, and if captured, they're being tortured for information. We know this Durn the Dreaded doesn't balk at using such tactics."

"He is *nothing* more than a Godless priest!"

Those strong-voiced words came from Marta, startling Zeilas. The Knight hadn't known she could speak so loudly or so vehemently. Firmly, yes. Sternly, perhaps. But not with a tone that could cut through steel. She didn't stop there, either.

"We all know what tactics *they* used to get their way." Lifting her arm into the air, she jutted out her thumb sideways. "And by the pricking of my thumb, I say, no more torture!"

Arms shot into the air around the Knights, thumbs thrust out sideways. "*No more!*"

"No more conquest!" she shouted.

"*No more!*" the men and women in the room shouted back.

"No more death!"

"*No more!*"

Lowering their arms, everyone except the startled Arbrans faced their Precinct General in grim, determined silence. He faced Zeilas, dipping his grizzled head in acknowledgment of the younger man's attention. "Sir Knights . . . this isn't your fight. But your presence here means your lives are equally in danger, for I doubt this warlord will stop to ask for nationalities before he attacks. You also have an undeniable level of experience in thwarting Mekhanan-style war engines . . . plus an enviable level of magical skill. Any advice you can bring to this moment, please feel free to give."

"I haven't had long, but I've trained a number of your mages in several defensive magics meant to counter and disarm or dismantle your machines," Sir Catrine stated, raising her voice so she could be heard. "They know enough to be effective. I also trust you Guildarans when you say you want peace. I have no reason to expect similar sentiments from this Durn fellow. I would offer my services as a combat-trained Knight-mage against these invaders."

She's come a long way from shuddering at the thought of sharing any Arbran secrets with these people, Zeilas thought, proud.

"Is that offer acceptable to your government, Sir Zeilas?" Marta asked him. While it was clear the Precinct General was in charge of the kingdom's defenses, she was still the head of their government, and that was a government-sensitive question.

"We are Knights," he replied succinctly. "We may be mages and diplomats, teachers and couriers, but we are trained for war. Arbra has signed its initial treaties of peace with your nation. While the treaties involving mutual assistance are still some ways off in the timeline of our negotiations . . . it is understood that offering our assistance in this instance—where you are not the aggressors—is politically astute . . . and morally just. As chief envoy for the Arbran delegation, I approve of our participation.

"As for any suggestions toward your battle plans . . . I defer to Sir Eada as our most experienced military advisor. She has engaged in defensive combat against the forces of old Mekhana, the bandits of Sundara, and spent time instructing the arts of tactics and strategy to our people." Shifting a little to the side, he let Eada step up next to him. The movement shifted him up against Marta's side.

Her fingers found his, a little cold to the touch but comforting nonetheless. Zeilas twined them with hers and tucked their joined hands into the still-warm depths of the pocket on that side of his felted riding coat. Together, they listened as possibilities were outlined and plotted, pushing around tiny carved and painted counters on the map to represent different configurations of troops.

Sir Eada finally straightened and shook her head. ". . . It's a hard case to judge. They have three times as many troops, possibly four, as you can field. They don't know the terrain, and if you can get them into the right spot between Heiastowne and the palace, you can bombard them with your own cannons from both sides . . . but that puts your own troops at risk. They have to be whittled down and led to the right spot before a rapid, strategic retreat of all our forces can commence so that they *can* be bombarded in a cross fire situation.

"The biggest factors are those giant motormen, their mobile cannonry, and whatever forces they have riding those motorhorses—the hexaleg engines are easily dealt with," she dismissed. "Even if their limbs are shielded against direct attack, there are things our side can do to the ground on which they step to bring them tumbling down. One mage, mounted behind a motorhorse engineer, can take all of those out with the right spells. In fact, they could take out most of the giant motormen, too.

"If it were up to me, I'd take out the cannons or immobilize them as fast as possible, while luring the motormen and the hexalegs *to* the bombardment zone, and save dealing with the troops they carry for last. It's keeping those motorhorses from pulling fast-and-loose skirmishing, disrupting our own formations, that worries me the most. Your side doesn't have very many by comparison, and it'd be very hard to corral them in one place. In fact, they're more likely to overwhelm us."

Her words gave Zeilas an idea. "Milady Consul, how many horses would you say are within, oh, half an hour's ride of Heiastowne and the palace?"

She looked up at him with one of her bemused half smiles and guessed. "A good . . . two or three hundred?"

Sir Catrine's eyes widened. "Of course, the Stampede spell! They may be machines, but they still have to move more or less like a real horse. All we need are a score of horses apiece to anchor the magics, multiply that by the Stampede spell to two hundred or more, and then we just charge in and force them to go with the flow, wherever *we* want them to go. Brilliant! The hexalegs, giant motormen, and cannons won't be forced to go where we want them to by this method, but the motorhorse cavalry will have no choice, unless they want to risk being knocked down and trampled to death. General Stalos, if we can get their forces within a mile or so of each of the three possible battle sites, *where* do you want the enemy's motorhorses to end up?"

"Ah . . . here, and here, if they only get as far as Heiastowne," he quickly asserted, touching the map. "And anywhere along here, obviously, for the bombardment zone . . . and here and here for the palace—by preference, any place that allows us to channel them between the town and the palace compound."

"We'll do our best," Zeilas promised.

Someone pushed up to the edge of the table on Marta's other side. The ash blond woman was a disheveled-looking Gabria, her hair not even contained under a cap, let alone wrapped up in a coronet of braids. Her eyes looked a little bleary, and she still had a reddish crease along one cheek from her pillow, though it looked like it was fading. "The guild has managed to break through their anti-scrying wards, General," she reported. "They have roughly six thousand troops, dispersed among four giant motormen, two hundred megamen, ten mobile megacannons, twenty-eight chariot cannons, twelve hexalegs with munitions turrets, about five hundred chariot turrets, and almost a thousand motorhorses—practically every single motorhorse from here to the River Castar, I'd guess.

"Most of the large machinery and all of the cannonry has had some magical wardings integrated into them, but they looked a bit crude compared to what we can now do," she added, glancing at Sir Catrine. "Defensively, I think they'll be vulnerable. I don't know what they'll bring to bear offensively, though."

"Thank you, sub-Consul," Stalos praised. "You know these wardings. Do you think you can penetrate them, yourself?"

She nodded briskly. "I scryed them in tandem with Allee; two of us had more luck penetrating their cloaking wards. It'll be tricky for some, but I'm pretty sure I can remove or at least weaken most of them. They only seemed to have three types of protection spells."

"Good. Milady Chief, I believe you're her mount engineer, correct?" Stalos asked.

Marta nodded. "I'll get her there, wherever they are."

Zeilas gave her a sharp, disconcerted look, but Stalos had moved on, outlining their best battle plan. He squeezed her fingers, making her glance up from the map. Catching sight of his concern, she gave him a half smile and leaned in close, whispering into his ear.

"Don't worry," she murmured. "Sir Catrine augmented my motorhorse with the toughest defensive wards she knew, once she realized it was *my* horse. Gabria has since added a few of her own. We could probably survive a direct blow from a megaman or a midsized munition. We've also trained together for something like this . . . and I *need* to lead by example." Lifting her right thumb, the one that had been pricked to sign her name in blood against the depredations of their former False God, she smiled. "No more thinking we're helpless. No more. Not when we can *all* do something about it."

She squeezed his fingers in reassurance, though his anxiety didn't exactly ease. After nearly four months in Guildara, Zeilas knew better than to ask her to stay back and stay safe. She *did* lead by example, getting her hands dirty, working hard, and being fearless in the face of difficulty. That willingness to be at the forefront made him fear for her safety.

It was, he realized, the same reason why he loved her.

And that's *going to complicate matters*, he acknowledged with a silent groan. *I love her, and I want to keep her safe, but I don't want to stifle who she is . . . and I have no right to demand that she, the leader of her people, not lead them anywhere.*

Herd mare makes good mate, Fireleaf interjected. *Strong mare, good herd, good foals.* The stallion could follow his Knight's thoughts whenever he wished, but rarely did so. Unless he thought—in his Steedish way—that the topic was important enough to comment upon, the judging criteria for which rarely matched the ones Zeilas would have used.

Yes, he acknowledged, sending the thought back to his Goddess-wrought mount. *A herd mare does make a good mate. I'm just not sure how I can keep my job if we do.*

SIX

"Why isn't it going down?" Gabria yelled in Marta's ear. Marta stomped on the galloper pedal and leaned left, then right, dodging the huge mechanical arm swiping at them with a rush of displaced air. It smacked into several of the horses galloping around them, but luckily only the illusionary ones—they went flying, but landed on their hooves with thuds and kept cantering.

"I don't know!" Marta shouted back. They were close to the bombardment zone, so awfully close, and yet so far from turning this nightmarish chaos into a victory. Durn's forces kept skirmishing just a quarter mile short of *both* sets of cannons, just beyond the range of the walled city as well as the palace compound. The other three giant-class motormen had crashed with devastating impact early in the dawn confrontation, squashing ranks of motorhorse operators. Mostly their own ranks, luckily.

She dodged a clump of sorrel mares, then leaned harder to the right, darting between them and the next cluster. That put them out in the open, just ahead of a swinging foot which clanged as it thumped into several horses and caused one of them to whinny sharply in pain. As soon as the cluster of victims landed, nineteen of the massive herd winked out, vanishing with the death of their anchor point. Marta winced.

"Damn, we lost another—*fence*!"

Her sharp scream jolted her partner into action. Flinging out her hand, Gabria shouted a word, creating a glittering ramp almost under the nose of their mechanical mount. They thumped into the meadow grass on the far side, thighs clinging and teeth gritting against the impact. Behind them, some of the horses swerved their way, either clattering up the ramp or leaping the stone fence.

The *thoom-thoom-thoom* of the giant motorman swerved, too, heading her way when she dared to glance back. As she did so, she saw munitions exploding around its head and shoulders, concussing it with what should have been enough force and timing between steps to have knocked it off balance, like its three companions had been knocked. It staggered a little but didn't falter as it gave chase.

She also thought she saw a flash of light like a curving shield, protecting the metal skull encasing its operator. "Adaptive magics!" Marta swore, bearing around to the right again. "They're crafting new magics to adapt!"

"That was the one we hit last!" Gabria agreed, hugging her close as she went into her turn. "The others didn't have time to react before they fell and were mine-bombed, but this one might have a spellcrafter on board! I have an idea! Get around behind it, right behind its heels, and stay back there!"

"Easier said than done!" the Consul-in-Chief snapped, dodging back to the fence line as a host of enemy motorsteeds headed their way. Enemies, for they weren't clad in the black-and-gray of her own side. Runes inlaid along the neck of her own mechanical Steed glowed, making the air shimmer and warp as the foremost rank of Durn's brown-clad followers fired their hand-cannons from their second-place seats on the motorhorses bearing their way. Sir Catrine's carefully crafted magics deflected the force of *most* of the lead pellets, but some of them smacked into their leather coats, and one tore a gash on her cheek.

Flinching, Marta ramped up over the stone hedge wall on another of Gabria's ramps. A whole mob of horses swung around, following the two women as they dodged and drove in a big circle, trying to get behind the motorman kicking and swiping its way through their forces.

"*Duck!*" Gabria screamed. Marta tipped their mount almost all the way over, sliding it across the dew-damp grass. A low-flying munition case whistled past. Righting the engine, she stomped on the galloper, taking off in a spray of turf clods even as the case struck into the heart of the enemy motorsteeds pursuing them. The metal runes glowed a second time, protecting them from the backlash of the explosions—multiple, for the munitions charge set off the fuel stomachs in each of its metal victims—though not from the sight of torn, bleeding, smoldering, *human* limbs mixed in with the chunks of metal and leather raining down around them.

The carnage did give them the opening they needed, for the motorman diverted to go after one of the few mobile Guildaran cannonry that had made it out to this war field. The herd of solid but still mostly illusionary horses swerved to follow the two women on the mechanical horse. Reaching around Marta, forcing her to lean forward a little, Gabria opened up the talker box panel, churned the crank, grabbed the talker horn, and pulled it back to her ear. That forced Marta even lower, for the cord connecting horn to talker wasn't all that long.

"Relay to the cannons on the . . . northwest flank!" she shouted into the device while Marta swayed their engine back and forth behind the massive legs of the motorman, bouncing them up and down across the ruts and gouges left by its equally massive feet. "All concussive fire to the giant's head in one minute—That's right, all concussive fire in one shot to the giant's head. *Only* the northwest cannonry!"

She fumbled the horn back into place, but couldn't get the hatch closed again as they bumped through a deeper rut, only to have to dodge around piles of broken machines and bloodied men on the other side. Marta swerved to join the stream of illusionary horses on her right; that gave her enough time to shove the cord back into its compartment, resecure the horn, and slap the hatch shut. Shoving on the stopper pedals, she scrunched backward into her friend as the front wheel skidded and the back wheel lifted up off the ground a few inches, then slammed her foot back onto the galloper, narrowly avoiding an armor-clad rider on a sorrel-and-cream real horse, one whose withers stood a full arm's length taller than their own mount.

Darting away from Sir Zeilas—though it warmed her fast-beating heart to know he was still alive—Marta swerved to avoid another swiping blow from the motorman's arm, and daringly dodged between its feet before swerving to the left to avoid horses from their side and machines from the enemy. Gabria squeezed Marta's waist on her right side, signaling which way to go.

"Get behind it now, right past its feet! We have twenty seconds—ramp! *Cushoga!*" This time, Gabria cast her ramp-building spell over a fallen chunk of hexaleg limb. As soon as they slammed down on the far side, Marta swerved them to the right. That brought them racing past the motorman's heels. Gabria flung out her arm, her skills crude but her magic potent. "*Aputoma! Aputoma!*"

The soles of the giant, Marta realized upon a quick backward glance, now glowed an odd shade of yellowish green.

Gabria thumped her on the shoulder. "Back again! Go back! Now, now, now!"

Skidding them into a turn required a complex touch of the stopper, galloper, and steering posts. It also kicked up clods in the face of the swerving, returning herd. Once again, Sir Zeilas was using his mob of illusion-expanded horses to give them cover, though the two women were at the head of the pack this time, not buried in its midst.

Just as they came within stomping range of the metal giant, the northwest cannons opened fire in a single, near-simultaneous boom that rattled the air. Gabria screamed something, flinging out both arms to their left at the motorman's feet. Mindful of their terrain, Marta still looked back, wanting to see what her friend had done. High up in the air, the head jolted from the smoky, fiery impact of all those munitions . . . and at the base of those massive heels, Gabria's spell impacted with a blast of purple white light. The new spell-shield sheltered it from damage, but that wasn't what her friend meant for it to do.

Instead, the chartreuse glow on the soles of the giant's feet flared—and both shot up and out from under it, as surely and swiftly as if they had been heavily greased. Marta looked ahead and quickly slowed their mount, swerving to avoid the downed hexaleg transport they had ramped over moments ago. Several of the horses from the herd caught up with them, parting on either side to go around the hexaleg remnants. At the same moment, two other things happened. The giant-class motorman slammed into the ground, shaking them, forcing her to stop and steady the two-man engine for balance . . . and the majority of the horses flanking them abruptly vanished.

No . . . Oh, Gods . . . no! The whistle of incoming munitions warned her. Hitting the galloper, she tore forward, joined by the now neighing and whinnying, frightened remnants of Zeilas' stampede-enspelled herd. They scattered, scampering off in whatever direction looked safest to their now unguided equine minds.

Part of Marta grieved. The rest of her ignored the tears stinging her eyes, seeking instead to get as far away as possible from the magnetic mine-bombs being lobbed at the downed motorman. They clanged into its painted metal body, clamping onto its hide. Somewhere back there, if the operator crew were conscious after such a hard, concussive fall, they would be scrambling to get free of the machine and its impending blast zone. Most likely, they wouldn't make it. Not when enough bombs were being lobbed its way by the two remaining hexaleg transports, heavily mage-shielded, on Guildara's side of the battle.

The horses . . . Sir Catrine swore the horses wouldn't vanish . . . unless something happened to the Knight controlling their illusions! Zeilas! Damn *you, Durn, you bastard!* Skidding to a stop by a pile of twisted metal, Marta grabbed and yanked out a chunk of pipe, what looked like a piece of iron hydraulics tubing from one of the limbs of the fallen hexaleg platform.

She shoved the length of metal back at Gabria with a terse command. "*Sharpen* it!" As soon as the other woman had it in her grip, Marta sent their ride roaring forward again. "Get ready to cast a really *big* ramp!"

It didn't take long for Gabria to realize what she meant to do. "You can't attack Durn!" she shouted. "That's the most heavily shielded platform he has left!"

"No more!" Marta growled, glaring at the trashed fields and meadows and pastures, once green with early spring grass and now charred and fouled with mangled machines and murdered men. Off to her left were the bulk of the remaining forces, swirling and smoking, banging and bellowing in the chaos of combat. Off to the right, yet more fields damaged by the enemy's munitions, with Heiastowne in the distance. "By the pricking of my thumb, *no* . . . what in the *Netherhells*?"

She slowed the motorhorse, startled by the sight of horses leaping down out of the air. Leaping in twos and threes out of thin air, no less. Out of at least ten *patches* of thin air, forming a shallow curve as long as a giant motorman would have been, felled end to end. The foremost of these cantered forward by a dozen yards, left hands raised and voices chanting, making the air glow in a wall in front of them.

"Mirror-Gates," Gabria stated, awe coloring her voice. "They're invading us with *mirror-Gates*! They're . . . wait, those aren't Durn's colors! Everyone in Durn's forces is wearing brown! Those are . . ."

"Those are the livery colors of the *Aurulans*!" Marta finished, equally astonished. Before she could voice the question of why they were even here, if it was an invasion or what, several riders carrying long poles leaped through the mirror-Gate portals. As soon as they gained level ground, they lifted the poles and tugged on ribbons, releasing the banners wrapped around the wooden shafts. What little Marta knew of mirror-Gates suggested that brushing up against the edges of the gate ran the risk of breaking the transportive link between its originating mirror and the location it was focused upon, so the ribbon-wrapped banners made sense.

What didn't make sense were the banners themselves. On the left was a purple background sporting the Eye of Ruul mounted within a golden crown, symbol of the Aurulan kingdom. On the right side, the black length of cloth bore the bright yellow gear wheel of Guildara.

The mage-warriors at the forefront advanced, pushing their shield-wall past Marta and Gabria. A final man, clad in purple, gilt-edged armor, leaped through the centermost ripple responsible for this unanticipated army, and then no more appeared. He was more than enough, though. It only took him a moment, despite the distractions of the ongoing chaos and confusion behind them, to focus on the two women. Trotting his horse up to the two of them, he bowed over the animal's armor-draped neck.

"Your Highness." Pulling a ribbon-wrapped scroll from beneath the baldric strap of his sheathed sword, he nudged his Steed closer and held it out. "It was foretold that I would meet Marta Grenspun, Consul-in-Chief and ruler of Guildara, right here and now. Is this correct?"

"Ah . . . that would be me," she offered, stunned further by his accuracy. Too much had happened, between the horrors of battle, the loss of her Knight, and now this Manifestation. Marta struggled to regain her wits. "You are . . . ?"

"Mage-Captain Ellett of the Royal Guard. I bring you a signed peace treaty straight from His Majesty's hands, countersigned by the Prime Minister, and sealed by the Will of Ruul. Contingent, of course . . ." He had to pause as something exploded and fell in a noisy mess of shredded metal off in the distance, then continued as soon as he could be heard. ". . . That we are permitted to escort Gabria Springreaver to His Majesty at the end of this matter."

"Ah . . . of course. We would have sent her earlier, but the passes . . . and the battle . . ." Giving up trying to explain—wincing as something else exploded noisily, though the purple-clad mages seemed to be sheltering them from any possible shrapnel—Marta quickly accepted the scroll. "You'll have to forgive me, but we're a *little* busy at the moment."

"Yes, we know. With your permission, Consul-in-Chief, now that we are bound as allies, I would be honored to direct my troops in mopping up these insurgents," the Mage-Captain stated. "As you have reassured us many times in the last year, there should only be peace within these lands, and it would be our pleasure to teach them to properly behave."

She eyed the thirty or so mounted men and women, their painted armor inlaid with gilded runes similar to the ones protecting her motorhorse, and nodded quickly. "By all means! Let there be peace!"

His smile visible through the grille of his helm, Ellett flicked up his hand. A sizzling line of light shot up, much like a festival-rocket, and exploded in bright purple sparks. All but a dozen of the mage-warriors surged forward, leaving the rest to cluster defensively around their captain and the two Guildaran women. They looked somewhat like Sir Catrine did, chanting spells and flinging them as they entered the fray, glowing with powers and mowing down the warlord's troops with each fierce attack, save that they mostly used magic instead of the weapons slung at their backs, and that no riderless horses, illusionary or otherwise, accompanied each warrior.

Absently, Marta shut off the engine of her motorhorse, conserving its fuel. She was sick of fighting, and neither she nor Gabria were the level of warriors and mages that these people were.

". . . Your Highness, are you injured?" the Mage-Captain asked solicitously, diverting her attention.

Marta was fairly sure she had told her envoy, Pells, to tell them that her correct mode of address was Milady Chief, not Highness, but she didn't quibble over protocol. The Aurulans were here to save her people, outnumbered by Durn's forces, and she'd accept anything they called her, unless they called for her surrender. His inquiry did make her aware of her aches and pains, now that she wasn't trying madly to steer a safe course through the destruction ruing the outer reaches of the Heiastowne Precinct fields.

"Um . . . just some cuts and bruises. The worst one is on my cheek. Minor things, really. Gabria?" Marta asked, glancing back at her friend.

"A bruised ankle, a hoarse throat, and a couple scratches of my own from shrapnel and pellets, but I'm fine—save your healing spells for those out there who'll need them far more than we will," Gabria added, lifting her chin at the mess the warlord had wrought.

That reminded Marta of all the other casualties out there. The men and women groaning and bleeding from their injuries, the lives lost to munitions and machinery . . . and the charred, exploded lump that had been the last giant-class motorman. Now that she wasn't focused on her own survival, the tears came back, wavering her view of the battlefield.

This was why she didn't like nor want war. Zeilas was only the most personal loss she knew of, so far. Undoubtedly there were plenty of others whose names and faces she knew, and far too many she didn't.

The battle didn't end instantly. It did end, though, particularly once Durn's hexaleg transport, with its banner of a round, bronze munition on a white background, was immobilized by crackling violet-hued lightning. That banner burst into flame as the transport stumbled, faltered, and sagged to the ground, its limbs folding up awkwardly.

A swirling herd of horses cantered their way. They slowed and milled a short distance away as Sir Catrine, clad in the surcoat of Arbra with its brown-and-green tree on a white background, emerged from the mass of enchanted equines. She pushed up the visor of her helm, eyed the Mage-Captain warily, then nodded briefly to Marta. "Milady Chief, the battle is won. Thanks to these . . . Aurulans, yes?"

"Mage-Captain Ellett of the Royal Guard of Aurul, sent here to protect Her Highness and lend aid to our western neighbors on this day," the armored man explained. "You are a Knight of Arbra?"

"Sir Catrine, Knight-Mage. Milady Chief, where is Sir Zeilas?" Catrine asked Marta. "He set himself to provide cover for the two of you."

She had to close her eyes against a fresh sting of tears. Tugging off a riding glove, she scrubbed them from her face, then pointed at the fourth fallen metal man. "He was behind us when we toppled that last giant-class, and . . . was caught under it."

The other woman twisted in the saddle to look that way, her Steed pivoting with her. "Was he with his Steed when it fell? Was Fireleaf with him?"

"Yes, but . . ."

"Then there's a chance he's still alive. Gabria, I'll need your help; it's too big for one mage to lift," Sir Catrine ordered.

"We will go with you and provide help, as well as an escort," Ellett offered unsolicited.

I am not *going to look for the made-by stamp on a gift toolbox*, Marta warned herself, twisting the ignition crank on her motorhorse's neck. *I am* not *going to ask why they acknowledge us* now, *after over a year's wait for more than merely acknowledging our existence. Never mind giving us this much help so freely! I am just going to nod and say thank you, and leave it at that.*

Some of her own people rolled up on rumbling motorhorses. A few were missing their combat teammates, others were injured. All of them bore a mixture of emotions on their battle-grimed faces, somewhere between grimness over the gore and hope for all of the help. A look she suspected was echoed in her own eyes. The dozen riders with the Mage-Captain made room for them, along with Sir Catrine once she had dismissed the spells linking the illusionary horses from the real ones, and dismissed the real ones to trot obediently toward either Heiastowne or the palace, to await collection and tending by their rightful owners.

Many of whom had gone on to ride into battle on machine-made beasts, and some of whom wouldn't return.

By the time they reached the towering chunks of brass and steel, pipes and gears that had been the last of the giant-class motormen, most of the fighting seemed to have stopped. More than that, a knot of purple-clad riders cantered up, two of the mages holding a bound and gagged, brown-clad figure aloft between them, floating in a cocoon of golden light that streamed from their palms. Gabria dismounted to follow Sir Catrine deeper into the wreckage, leaving Marta to face this new development.

"Milady Chief," one of them stated, reining his horse to a snorting stop, "I present to you the miscreant known as Warlord Durn the Dreaded, bound and secured for your judgment. It is your lands which he has invaded, and your people which he has harmed the most."

Torn between accepting their gift and watching the efforts of the Aurulan mage-warriors, the Arbran Knight, and her best friend to levitate the chunks of metal in their way, searching for signs of Sir Zeilas, Marta forced herself to acknowledge her duty. Facing the murderer responsible for this mess was bound to be more pleasant than staring at the squashed remains of her would-have-been lover.

Marta swung out the rear leg of her motorhorse, leaning the vehicle on the prop so that she could dismount. Turning to the Mage-Captain, who was dismounting as well, she asked, "Being that you are a mage . . . you wouldn't happen to have a Truth Stone or a Truth Wand somewhere about you, would you? I'm afraid they were banned from being used by all but the old priesthood and vanished or were rendered inert when the False God was finally cast down—I suspect because they had been corrupted somehow. None of my mages know how to craft an honest one, just yet."

"I have a spell which will suffice. When he speaks a lie, he will glow red, and when he speaks a truth, he will glow green," the Aurulan offered. Handing the reins of his horse to one of his fellow Aurulans, he lifted his chin at the activity behind her. ". . . I think you should turn around, Milady Chief. It seems your intended has survived. As predicted."

Confused, Marta turned and looked over her shoulder. The crowd of bodies and metal parts was a little thick, but she could just see Sir Catrine stooping to pick something off the ground . . . and an overgrown, unruffled, red-and-cream stallion cropping placidly at the grass beneath what had been the house-sized, hip-joint casing for the motorman. The visibly dented hip-joint casing, its thick metal plates warped in a divot the length and size of an overgrown Arbran Steed.

"Zeilas?" she whispered.

A familiar armored body rose into view, aided by the lady Knight. He unstrapped and tugged off his helm, wincing and lifting a hand to the back of his head. Marta didn't care that there were still half a dozen people between them. She sprinted toward the Knight, pushing people aside, torn between laughing and shouting and crying over the fact that he was still miraculously alive.

"*Zeilas!*" Flinging herself at him, Marta wrapped her arms around him. He was lumpy from armor and his helmet fell from his started hands, banging against her left boot as it clattered onto the ground, but she didn't care. "*Zeilas!*"

He looked just as stunned and just as relieved to see her. "Goddess, *Marta*!"

That was all she gave him time to say. Dragging him down by the back of his neck, Marta kissed him. She didn't care that more and more people were gathering around the fallen machine, that more and more of her fellow Guildarans could see their Consul-in-Chief kissing the Arbran ambassador. She only cared that Zeilas was *alive*. Part of her reveled in his life, in his lips, in his embrace, despite the uncomfortable chunks of rune-carved cavalry armor he wore. Part of her mind did acknowledge that the others were all watching, and that the consequences of it couldn't be damned and set aside so easily.

Part of her, having seen the Aurulans' determination that Gabria return to Aurul with them, was struck with a brilliant, if slightly crazy, plan. One sparked in part by the Mage-Captain's choice of words, though mostly prompted by her own desire.

Their kiss finally ended when he pulled back just enough to caress her face, then lean in again, resting his forehead against her own. Face flushed, eyes wide, he murmured, "So much for courting you discreetly . . ."

She smiled and chuckled, eyes still a bit watery but otherwise feeling much, much better. "I have a solution for that. But, um . . . first, the war field has to be cleaned up."

"Right. Duty first." Drawing in a deep breath, he squared his shoulders, his expression sobering. He winced in the next moment, shifting the hand on her cheek to the back of his head. "Duty, and a cold compress. I think I hit my head when I dived off my Steed, taking cover between his legs."

Not wanting him to *always* put duty first, Marta leaned up and kissed him. Just a quick peck of their lips, but it was enough to put some of the warmth back into his expression. Both from embarrassment and from pleasure. Turning back to the others, Marta lifted her chin, resuming her role as Consul-in-Chief.

"Mage-Captain Ellett, please cast your lie-detecting spell on the prisoner. The chief prisoner," she amended, realizing that some of her people, interspersed with his, were herding groups of other former Mekhanans their way, their hands manacled together and their ankles hobbled by more of the same golden glow that held the warlord aloft.

Bowing, he complied, lifting his hand and chanting a short piece. The syllables meant nothing to her, and Gabria had once confessed most of them were just mnemonics meant to help the mage shape the magic within them to his or her will. The effect was palpable, however. As the other two mage-warriors lowered him and released their levitation spell, the brown-armored man started to glow a dull silvery gray.

". . . The gray is simply the color he assumes when he says nothing," Ellett murmured.

She accepted the explanation with a nod. "Alright. Another request . . . is there a way to make everyone see and hear what I'm about to do and say?"

One of the other Aurulans twisted her hands, fitting forefingers to thumbs in front of her face in a sort of rectangle shape, muttering words under her breath. Light and color rippled into existence overhead, forming a tableau of Ellett, Marta, Zeilas, and the bound man. That enlarged projection showed every detail of his tooled leather breastplate, carved with the insignia he had chosen for his banner, and the equally brown gambeson and trousers he wore underneath the various boiled leather plates. In fact, he wore velvet clothes under his armor, instead of sensible woolens and linens, she realized with distaste, no doubt copying the highest rankings of the False God's wealth-bloated clergy.

Her own choice of common, knitted wool and plain leather was meant to bind her closer to the average Guildaran, not set her apart from them. All she could feel for this would-be conqueror was contempt and disgust, and a tightly reined anger that he had dared harm even a mere square inch of her realm. Suppressing the urge to wrinkle her nose in distaste, Marta addressed him sternly.

"Warlord Durn . . ." She broke off as her voice echoed across the valley. Wrinkling her nose anyway, she continued, focusing on him instead of on the oversized illusion of herself floating high overhead. "Warlord Durn, the so-called Dreaded, you are bound and brought before us under the charges of unlawful invasion, wanton destruction of property, and the willful murder of sovereign citizens of the Guildaran nation. Do you have anything to say for yourself?"

He lifted his chin, one of his eyebrows turning puffy and dark from bruising, and sneered at her. "*I* don't talk to *sheep*. If there's a leader among you worth his bollocks, I challenge him one on one! You had to use *magic* to defeat me. There's not a one of you that can stand against me in a fair fight!"

His words, like hers, echoed over the fields. Not all of his speech glowed green, however. Parts of it glowed red, notably his last statement. Marta heard the answering growl from her people, not magically projected, but audible all the same. She was not swayed in the least by his challenge, and not taken in by his lie.

"Warlord Durn, to hear you speak of a 'fair' fight is, at best, a poor and failed piece of mockery. As for sheep, I wouldn't toss a sick lamb to a rabid wolf, even if that rabid wolf were starving and beaten . . . just like you."

"You little piece of dung!" he snarled, and lunged at her. Or tried to. While most of him was unbound, his hands and feet were still shackled by golden power. All it took was the lifting of a hand from one of his two mage-captors and he jerked to a halt, straining against his glowing, immobile bonds.

"*This* 'little piece of dung' is Marta Grenspun, Goddess-chosen Consul-in-Chief, ruler of the free nation of Guildara," she stated coldly. "Beside me stand Mage-Captain Ellett of the Royal Guard of Aurul, and Sir Zeilas, Knight-Envoy of Arbra. Your offenses against Guildara have affected not only our sovereign selves, but our good neighbors who, like us, only desire peace. You have brought *war* to my nation, and shed the blood of my citizens, the blood of the Arbrans, and the blood of the Aurulans.

"You aren't even a wolf," she disdained. "You are a rabid dog, bringing pain and misery to all you encounter. We have heard how you have conquered much of the northern lands of former Mekhana through fear, intimidation, sabotage, and outright battle. You think to proclaim yourself both a warlord and a king . . . yet no God or Goddess will Manifest to support your bloody methods, never mind your mad ideology." Turning to look first at Zeilas, then at Ellett, she asked, "Sir Knight, Mage-Captain, it is my best judgment that a rabid dog should be put down, to prevent his madness from further contaminating our otherwise peaceful lives. What would you and your governments have to say about this?"

Zeilas looked around at the debris of the battlefield. "This used to be good farmland. It will likely take a full year before it can be used for such again, if not longer. Arbra as a nation will not condone such wanton destruction of property, ours *or* Guildara's. I believe His Majesty, King Tethek, will agree. You do not allow a rabid dog to run loose, destroying everything it meets. But you *do* grant it a swift death, giving it the mercy which, in its madness, it does not comprehend."

"I am *not* a dog!" Durn growled.

"As it was said, so it was written; thus it is proved, and so shall it be," the Mage-Captain stated, his words sounding almost ritualistic. Ellett shrugged calmly. "I have no objections to granting him a swift, clean death. I am here to aid your people specifically because my liege foresaw that he must fall, if there is to be peace within this realm."

A fifth figure joined their projected tableau as Precinct General Stalos joined them. "I would concur, Milady Chief. We have too much healing, repairing, and rebuilding to do to worry about an ambitious madman getting free and starting up all over again." He drew a dagger from his belt and saluted her with it. "I stand ready to execute the sentence."

"*We* are not madmen, nor bullies, nor evil," Marta agreed. "And we should be merciful . . . but you gentlemen are right. He is too dangerous to lock up, in the fear that he might break free. Too mad to be reasoned with. Make it swift, and may the Gods have mercy when judging his soul. We have more important things to do."

Nodding, Stalos dragged the former warlord off to the side. It was swift, with the dagger applied to the other man's spine. Marta dragged her gaze away, glad that part had not been projected. Mindful of her giant illusion-self, she addressed the war field. "Those of you who followed Durn the Would-Be Warlord will be questioned under truth-verifying spell, as administered by our Mage's Guild, by the Arbran Knight-mages, and the Aurulan Royal Guard. If you fought under duress, you will be free to return to your homes in the north.

"If you are here of your own free will, and intend to continue harming the people of *any* of these three nations . . . you will be granted the same swift and merciful death. The rest of you will be treated according to the severity of your participation and war crimes. Expect to labor for the restoration of these fields as payment for your actions, at the very least. Take the time now to make up your minds as to how truthfully you will answer. For those of you set free to return to the north, carry this piece of news for us: Guildara will accept into our nation any village or town or populated expanse of land who votes to join us by a majority of eighty percent of its adult population. Otherwise . . . you're on your own. We have no interest in conquering *you* in return."

She paused to let her words sink in, then turned to Sir Zeilas, letting her speech be heard by all.

"Even in times of sadness, there is often some joy. Guildara has laid the foundations for firm alliances with our neighbors to the east and the west. There is still more work to be done to secure and stabilize that peace, however. Sir Zeilas, some of the greatest ties two nations can enjoy come not from words on parchment, but from the actions and deeds of two of its people. I wish to solidify our mutual peace and understanding, Guildaran and Arbran, with your assistance," she stated, squaring her shoulders and lifting her chin slightly, aiming for dignity in the face of her speech. "I would like to propose an alliance of marriage between a Guildaran and an Arbran, to symbolize the alliance of our borders in peaceful coexistence. What do you say to this idea?"

"I think it's a very wise idea. If I may suggest a particular couple . . . Marta Grenspun, will you 'mage' me?" he asked, giving her a smile.

It took her a moment to realize what he meant. The gleam of humor in his brown eyes helped free the laughter that bubbled up inside, even as his words caused confusion among the rest of their audience. She let herself chuckle out loud only for a few moments, then sobered. Somewhat.

"Your Guildaran needs just a little more practice," Marta teased, smiling at him, "since we say *marry*, not *mage*. But yes, I will *marry* you."

The cheer that rose up across the smoldering battlefield was ragged, but full enough to let her know that most of her people approved. Relieved—if mindful that everything was still being magically projected overhead—Marta accepted a quick kiss from her intended.

"As it was said, so it was written," Ellett murmured as the illusion ended. "We can delay three days, Milady Chief, but no longer, then we must return to His Majesty. It isn't much time, but perhaps with our help, we can set much of today's injuries and damages to rights, and still have time for a celebration of your impending personal alliance before we go?"

"Your help would be deeply appreciated," she acknowledged, eyeing the devastated land. "I wish this battle hadn't happened, and that everyone was alive and well, but . . . I don't regret the alliances that were made."

SEVEN

Left in the front room of the "chief suite" of the palace, Zeilas eyed his surroundings in curiosity. Like much of the palace, the floor and walls were covered in carefully joined strips of wood. They formed diamonds, circles, stars, zigzags, and braids, some dark, some light. Special attention had been paid to those areas that framed the doors, neatly carved in rectangular panels, and the windows, many of which were glazed with stained glass in yet more geometrical patterns. Not that they could be easily seen, since it was now late at night, but they would be similar to the other windows in this place, he was sure.

There wasn't much in the way of artwork on the walls just yet, but he thought the room didn't need any, really. It had some padded chairs, a settee, a couple of tables, and a fireplace which crackled and glowed with a recently stoked fire. Oil lamps, slightly fancier than the lanterns which lit the halls outside the suite, burned in sconces here and there, adding their steady light to the dancing of the flames.

They illuminated a room that was filled with furnishings, but empty of people.

". . . Hello?" he called out as a few more moments of solitude passed. "Milady Chief?"

Footsteps heralded her approach. She hadn't bothered to scrub her face—most of them hadn't stopped for such niceties, cleaning up the aftermath of their short but horrid war—but Marta had taken the time to remove her riding leathers and unbind her waist-length hair. In fact, all she wore was a thick-knitted robe, sort of like an overgrown riding coat, only fuzzy and ankle-length, and fastened with a sash instead of buttons or buckles. Even her feet were bare of socks, though she had slipped them into casual toe-loop sandals, the sort his fellow Arbrans, and even the Sundarans, liked to use in their homes.

It was a good thing he had removed his own battle gear. The first thought that ran through his head was the relief of knowing he could strip almost as fast as she could. The second thought was a blush for thinking such carnal thoughts. "You, ah, wanted to see me?"

"Yes." Holding out her hand, she caught his when he extended it, and pulled him through the next door, which proved to be an office of some sort. Beyond that was a smaller, more cozy parlor, and beyond that . . . the bedroom. Where a pair of tunic-and-trouser-clad ladies were busy turning down the bedcovers on a large canopied bed. They slanted knowing looks at the two of them and exchanged smirks, and giggled when Marta shooed them out of the room.

"Sleep well!" one called over her shoulder as she left.

"*Very* well, when you get there," the other quipped. Marta dropped his hand, mock-chasing the women out of the room for their impudence. Both giggled and darted across the private parlor, closing the door to the office as they left.

"Ignore them," Marta murmured, turning back to face her guest. She eyed him, then glanced back at her office, nibbled her lower lip, then shrugged. "Let me blow out the lamps—that door over there leads to the bathing room. Go on in, and I'll meet you in there."

Zeilas wasn't sure he was hearing her correctly. Not her words—they were clear—but the meaning behind them. "Beg pardon?"

She glanced back at him from the office doorway and blushed. "Well . . . I figured you'd want to clean up from the long day we've had, but I know there's not much in the way of room in your suite. Not with several other Arbrans sharing it, and only one bathing room. And here I am, in this big suite, all by myself, with a big bath . . ."

"Ah." So it *was* what he hoped she meant. Some of his tiredness lifted away at that. "I'll just go and get ready for it, then."

She smiled at him, both sides of her mouth curving up in that beautiful grin. A smile, he realized, she often used around him. Grinning himself, he entered the indicated door.

Rather than the spell-heated pipes he was used to seeing back home, or even a primitive cauldron over a hearth fire, the bathroom had some sort of flame-heated engine thing, with the flames under the copper tank fed by what looked like the same oil as the lamps illuminating this room. That light gleamed on a massive, white-glazed tub, easily big enough for two people, with sloping sides and a frothy mound of softsoap bubbles filling it not quite to the rim. They smelled of something herbal, some scent he couldn't remember inhaling before. It wasn't unpleasant, just unfamiliar.

The rest of the room was tiled in yet more ceramic tiles, glazed and patterned in an echo of the geometry in the other rooms. A second door led, he discovered, to a refreshing room, which he quickly used, not wanting any untimely interruptions. Emerging after a few moments, he fingered the exotic, bleached cotton drying sheets resting on a varnished wooden bench next to the refreshing room door, and wondered at the expense of importing the soft, white fabric this far north.

Other touches bespoke similar aesthetics. Someone had placed a delicately fluted, burled-wood table next to one end of the tub. On it lay a scrubbing cloth and a blown-glass pot of softsoap. A silver tray rested next to them, loaded with plates of bite-sized snacks, a pot of what smelled like fragrant, expensive Aian tea, and two empty mugs. No wine, he noted, but figured it was just as well; wine after a day like they'd just had would have put him to sleep, and sleep was the last thing he wanted to do right now.

It was the site of a seduction for two lovers. Or a pampered reward for a pair of tired heroes. Or perhaps both. He wouldn't mind if it were both. Using the bench briefly, Zeilas unlaced and removed his boots, then his socks. Standing, he pulled his wool doublet over his head, glad this bathing room was warm, even steamy. The heat relaxed his sore muscles, promising a good night's sleep if he soaked up enough of it.

He was in the middle of peeling off his trousers when Marta entered the room. Before he could step out of the fabric, she crossed the chamber and wrapped her arms around his bare chest, burying her face against his skin.

"I thought I'd lost you," she whispered, clinging tightly. "It was awful."

Zeilas hugged her back. "I thought I'd lost myself, too. There wasn't much air under all that metal. Nor much room. Whatever my head hit knocked me unconscious for a little while. If I hadn't been wearing my armor . . . When I woke up, it was so dark, I thought I was a ghost trapped in the Dark, between Life and the Afterlife. Except I could faintly hear sounds of battle, and Fireleaf lipped at my leg, letting me know I was still alive. But I didn't know if anyone else knew I was still alive."

She hugged him harder, then turned her head and pressed her lips to his chest, kissing the hair-dusted flesh of his pectoral muscle. "I saw the horses vanish and thought you were dead."

"No, just unconscious. I didn't know if *you* had made it free," he confessed, kissing the top of her head. "I thought you had, but everything happened so fast . . . You were beautiful—and injured," he added, cupping her chin so he could tilt up her face and examine the scabbed line marring her cheek. With his experience as a fighter, he knew it wasn't a serious injury. "If that's the only place you were injured . . . thank the Gods you won't even have a scar to remind you in a couple of weeks. But I want you to know I'd take you even if you were missing an eye or a leg.

"I promised myself as I waited that I'd tell you I love you," he continued, quickly covering her lips with a finger as she started to speak. "I love you, Marta Grenspun. I was ready to give up my ambassadorship and ask to be granted leave to court you openly as an ordinary citizen—I'll probably still have to give it up . . ."

She chuckled. "Then I'll hire you as my personal consultant on all matters Arbran. Or maybe the government will hire you. Though I think your king would be a fool to insist you step down. You're *good* at your job. After all, you can clearly separate duty . . ." Her hands slid down his back, down past the drawstring for his undershorts. ". . . From desire."

"Mmm, yes," he murmured, enjoying the feel of her fingers kneading his flesh. Part of him felt guilty for wanting to enjoy pleasure, to savor life itself, after so many others had been hurt. Part of him knew that *this* was what all that fighting had been about. To stop the invaders so they could all get back to their rightful lives. *This* was right, and therefore rightful.

"The Precinct General says it's not uncommon for soldiers to experience a . . . rush of *interest* in life, right after a battle," Marta said as he shifted his fingers to bury themselves in her unbound, ash brown hair. "The healers call it the survival instinct, the need to propagate more of one's kind after a close brush with death. But the battle ended hours ago, yet I still want you. I also wanted you before it began, so it's not a temporary rush, nor an instinctive interest. And yet, I want you even more *because* I almost lost you. Enough to find a way to keep you with me, if you were so inclined."

"Trust me, I'm inclined," Zeilas agreed. Dipping his head, he kissed her. The touch of their lips was meant to be soft, seductive, but it quickly turned as heated as any previous kiss. More so, for this time, he was nearly naked, and she was just a thick knitted robe from being so. Nipping his way toward her ear, kissing gently along the line of that little cut, he pulled back with a grimace after only a moment. "Ugh . . . sorry, but you taste like smoke. And something else."

"Munitions powder," she admitted, sighing. "It gets on everything and lingers for hours. Days, if you don't scrub it off thoroughly. We use a special softsoap to neutralize and remove it. I asked someone to send a pot of it to your companions, but . . . I wanted to share this bath with you."

He tried not to smile too much, giving her a mock-serious reply. "I would be happy to let you demonstrate this residue-removing softsoap you've invented. You are the expert on all engineering-related matters, after all."

She tickled him on the ribs for the teasing, then when that didn't make him squirm, gave up and led him to the edge of the bathtub. Or would have, if his ankles weren't still tangled in his trousers. Laughing, she stooped and helped to free his feet. Then stared as he loosened the drawstring on his undershorts, baring himself completely. The sight of her mesmerized gaze fastened on his loins excited him. He didn't pressure her, though, and after a moment, she cleared her throat, helped him step out of the linen garment, and stood back up. Catching his hands, she placed them on the sash of her robe and gave him a somewhat shy half smile.

Untying the bowknot allowed him to coax the other half of her smile up into existence. Before opening the folds of her robe, however, Zeilas leaned in and kissed Marta twice, once on each corner of her lovely mouth. That made her smile all the more, though with a puzzled edge. Deciding he wouldn't tell her just yet that it was her half-to-whole smiles that had first made him fall for her—that was something which could be saved for later, when they had been married for a while—he kissed her full on the lips and slid the thick-knitted wool from her shoulders.

She was lovely. Absolutely lovely, with soft-curving hips and a narrow waist and breasts that would just fit nicely in the palms of his hands. She was also bruised in a few places, mostly along her left arm and leg. His armor was enchanted to cushion him from all but the most severe blows, which was why his brief concussion had concerned him, but her riding leathers apparently hadn't been crafted with magic; her only protection had been the leather itself, and whatever Sir Catrine had managed to imbue into her motorhorse.

"I'm sorry you were hurt," he told her, his tone as soft as the finger he trailed down her mottled arm. "I tried my best to protect you and Gabria. I knew I loved you weeks ago, but . . . I couldn't figure out how to reconcile our careers." Zeilas let the corner of his mouth quirk up. "That was very clever of you."

"That was very *selfish* of me, too," Marta retorted. Catching his fingers, she lifted them to her lips for a kiss. "I had a handful of minutes in which to contemplate the rest of my life without you. I didn't like it."

"I'm glad you go after what you want—and if I may do the same," he added, freeing his fingers so that he could scoop her off her feet, startling a squeak out of her, "what I want is to be clean and warm and tucked into your bed, after finally getting to do more with you than just kiss. A *lot* more."

"Thank the Gods you go after what *you* want, too," she chuckled, wrapping her arms around his shoulders.

Lowering her toes-first into the ceramic tub, he climbed in after her. The frothy foam, herbal, tickled his skin. It also hid a delicious, deep amount of water. Some of the bubbles oozed over the rim of the tub as he settled in across from her, but he figured those giggling maids could mop up any mess from the floor in the morning. Easing back, he relaxed and let the heat of the bath soak into his limbs. Until he felt her fingers ghosting over his feet and calves.

"Are you trying to tickle me?" Zeilas asked, lifting his brows.

She smirked. "Maybe."

"Sorry, but I'm not ticklish."

"That's not fair! You're always making *me* laugh." She pouted, folding her arms across her chest and rearranging the bubbles sheltering them with the act.

It was the pout on her face, the plumped-out lower lip, that made him laugh. It was a glimpse of her bare breast when she sat up and eyed him warily that made him grin. And it was the way she splashed forward, straddling his thighs, that made him groan and kiss her, meeting her incoming mouth willingly.

Except that they both still tasted of smoke and munitions powder. Pulling back after a few moments, she wrinkled her nose. "Bath first. Lovemaking later. Um . . . you have something on your ankle. Did you mean to get it wet?"

It was his turn to smirk. Nudging her off that leg, he lifted it high enough to brace his heel on the rim. "Contraception charm. I bought a fresh one when I was in High Hold, so it's less than half a year old."

She twisted to eye the braided thong with its rune-carved bead. "I've heard of them. But we don't have the knowledge to make them. Yet. Even our healer-mages were hunted down by the priesthood. We tried to hide them in other guilds and worked through herbal healers to get anything done. The closest we've ever had to a contraceptive is a potion they developed—which I took earlier tonight, hoping I'd be able to get you in here—but . . . it doesn't always work."

"These do," Zeilas reassured her. Thinking of their function made him think of the fun things the two of them could do to test the bracelet's enchantment. That led him to look down at her breasts, dusted with slowly vanishing foam. Beautiful breasts.

Lifting his hands from the water, he cupped the soft, slick curves. Her blue eyes widened, but not with shock. Covering his fingers with her own, Marta showed him how to gently knead her flesh. She tipped her head back with a soft moan, enjoying his touch, then blinked and sat back. Disappointed, Zeilas lifted his brows.

She gave him a half smile of reassurance. “We need to scrub away the residue now, before we get carried away.”

“Right.” Twisting, he reached for the scrubbing cloth on the table, and the pot of softsoap. “Want me to scrub your back? And any other places?”

That quirked up the other side of her mouth. “Please.”

Soaping the knitted rag, Zeilas began with her arms. He used long, soothing strokes, being careful of her bruises, but thorough enough to remove the grime of their long, horrible day. In the steamy, herb-scented room, lit by the warm, gentle flicker of oil lamps spaced around the walls, the bathing room seemed half removed from reality. A sanctuary of peace. Not untouched by the grim reality of battle, but rather, a place to rinse it away.

From her arms, he moved to her face, gently scrubbing the grime from her skin. She paused him long enough to rinse her head under the tub’s wall-mounted spigot, then wet her hair so that he could scrub more of the softsoap through her fine, long locks. Zeilas took extra care with her scalp, knowing from past encounters with other women that many of them liked this sort of attention. After that, he massaged her back, caressed her breasts, and stroked her stomach and hips, turning her this way and that.

By the time he had her stand so he could stroke the re-lathered rag down her legs, the look in her eyes had landed somewhere between dreamy and worshipful. Relaxed and aroused. And when he stroked that cloth between her upper thighs, the last place left to scrub, she endured it with a very feminine grin, then growled playfully and stole the rag with an insistent tug. Sinking back onto her knees, she re-lathered the square until the lather foamed over her fingers—then smeared it across his mouth and chin with a laugh, giving him a bubble beard.

Sputtering, Zeilas tried to reach for her hands, but she dodged and dropped another dollop of soapsuds on the end of his nose. Giving up on corralling her hands, he settled for grasping her hips. The soap made her slippery, but he didn't mind. Kneading her buttocks, he pulled her close, planted his face between her breasts, and blew a loud, wet, sudsy raspberry. That made her laugh out loud, her voice ringing off the tiled walls.

Only then did he grab the rag long enough to scrub his face. She recaptured it when he rinsed the soap away and tackled his shoulders and back. Marta scrubbed his skin from scalp to soles, lingering on his shaft last. Leaning over the edge, she fetched a rinsing pail from the floor under the table and used it on both of them as the tub drained, then filled it from the spigot with clean water to get the last of the lather off their skin.

Refilling the broad, glazed basin with more hot water, she reached for the pot of tea. It had cooled considerably, and steeped a bit strong, but just smelling the astringent brew revitalized his tired, relaxed senses. Tasting it helped further. As did the nibbly little pastry thing she pressed to his lips, something crumbly, delicate, and filled with herbed cheese. Zeilas accepted the mouthful readily, then spent several seconds carefully licking the crumbs from her skin. Snagging a small biscuit topped with meat minced in a thick, creamy sauce, he teased her lips with the morsel until she bit into it, and sucked on his thumb in passing.

Together, they ate most of the food on the tray, feeding each other, kissing and suckling and licking on whatever body parts happened to get close enough to taste. Thankfully, the herbal flavor of the soap lingered only faintly on their skin and didn't clash with the miniature feast. He could have wished for a little more of her own flavor, something sweet and salty and feminine, but that would come back with time and perhaps a little sweat.

Hungry for more than food, Zeilas gently caught the hands exploring his flesh and pulled them free. At her disappointed sound, he mustered a smile. Half a smile; the other half of him was struggling for control, mindful of their awkward surroundings.

"Not here," he murmured when Marta tried to touch him again. "Not in a bathtub. In your bed."

She stopped resisting. Flipping the clever lever that drained the tub, she smiled with both sides of her mouth and climbed out. Following her, he took one of the towels from the bench and started drying her skin. She did the same for him, giggling when the lengths of cloth tangled, the two of them working at cross-purposes. After he squeezed the moisture from her hair and she scrubbed it from his, they met over the damp cloths for a soft, laughing, hungry kiss.

The soft lengths of cotton fell to the floor, no longer needed. Thigh to thigh, breast to chest, lips to lips, they entwined and embraced. The feel of his shaft rubbing against the soft skin of her belly, of her breasts brushing against his sternum evoked the need to feel more, to feel other things rubbing together. Once again sweeping her off her feet, Zeilas carried her out of the bathing room. The sudden move made her gasp and break their kiss, but that was alright; he needed to see where to carry her.

She had dimmed or extinguished most of the oil lamps before entering the bathing room, he noted. A mesh screen shielded the red-glowing logs in the hearth, and a lamp burned on either side of the canopied bed, but that was it. Just enough light to see by, but not enough to keep them awake, should they fall asleep afterward.

And it will be afterward, he thought, carrying her to the bed. *Goddesses of both lands, I've waited a long time for this. Ever since I first heard her laugh.*

Good mare, Fireleaf murmured sleepily in the back of his mind as he carefully laid Marta on the feather-stuffed mattress. *Good foals, too. Good night . . .*

Good night, he thought back, not bothering to correct his Steed. Instead, he pulled the covers careully down while Marta adjusted her position on the bed. The mystical stallions bred when and where they wanted to, ignoring some mares who were in heat—an act contrary to more normal stallions—and somehow inducing heat in other mares, depending upon their moods.

According to Fireleaf, sex was all about creating foals that were just a little bit faster, stronger, and better than their dams, no doubt as much by Arbora's choice as by the Steed's whims. But for Zeilas and Marta, this wasn't about procreation. *Just pleasure, and as much of it as we can manage—whup!*

Rather than letting him take his time crawling into the bed next to her, she had snaked her arms around his shoulders and impatiently tugged him down over her. "I want to feel you against me, again," Marta murmured. "I want to feel every inch of you against every inch of me."

Thank the Gods for women who know what they want! That was his last coherent thought for a while. The feel of her, the enthusiasm with which she hooked one of her calves behind his thigh, denied coherency. In retaliation, he kissed his way down from her mouth to her breast, plumping it in his hand. She groaned at the swirling of his tongue and tugged on his hair when he teased her with his teeth.

Slipping a hand between them, he teased her inner thighs with the lightest of touches, counterpoint to the suckling of her breast. She didn't hesitate; after only a minute or so, Marta grabbed his hand and brought it straight to the crux of her thighs. Her curls were warm and slick. His heart skipped a beat, then raced with the need to thrust. Carefully, Zeilas focused on giving her pleasure, first by tracing his fingertips between her netherlips, then by probing slowly, gently into her depths. Slotting his thumb over her node, he curled his fore and middle fingers and circled with the pad of his thumb.

"—Holy Gods!"

Her heartfelt shout startled him, since she had never struck him as particularly reverent. It also made him grin and flutter his fingers harder. Marta bit her lip and strained into his touch, then let out her breath in a gust, panting. Within moments she was moaning again, moans which rapidly became words.

"Oh, Gods . . . oh Gods oh Gods . . . oh! Gods, that's even better than my crankman!" she exclaimed.

The term puzzled him. He stilled his hand and released her breast, giving her room to think. "Than your . . . what?"

She stilled for a long moment, and then the slyest smile he had ever seen on anyone curled both corners of her mouth. It broke into a grin a split moment before she squirmed out from underneath him. Catching his dismayed look, Marta snagged his hand and brought it to her mouth, sucking briefly on the damp digits. Breathless, he was disappointed when she let go moments later and rolled toward the far nightstand. She didn't stay away for long, just the length of time it took for her to open the top drawer, dig around, and pull out a polished metal rod.

Facing him, she sat up and brandished the odd device. It looked sort of like a silvery peppermill, since it had a crank at one end, but the other end was rounded and smooth, with no holes. The shaft was striped in a trio of long, spiraling ridges from crank to tip, more like ripples than creases, and there was a push-button thing at the end, something which he could only identify as a push button because he had learned to do so over the last few months in this land.

Her blue eyes gleamed with an excitement palpable even in the dim lighting of the bedroom. "*This* is the greatest invention to ever come out of the Clockworks Guild. Never mind our collaborations with the Hydraulics and Pistons Guilds to create things like the motormen and so forth. *This* is the absolute greatest."

"What does it do?" he asked, mystified. It wasn't a peppermill, and it didn't look like a weapon. Zeilas was stumped.

"*This*." Smirking, she thumbed the push button—which he saw slotted all the way from one side of the rounded, ridged casing to the other—gripped the shaft, and cranked the handle. She turned and turned and turned it, until it finally slowed and stopped winding easily. Then, with a fierce grin, she pushed the button-shaft to the far side.

The rod began shaking and buzzing, startling him. Startling, and confusing. Zeilas slowly shook his head. "I'm sorry, I don't get it. Is that *all* it does? Rattle?"

"Well, if you push the button to the far side and hold on to the crank, the shaft spins," Marta offered. At his puzzled stare, she smirked and grasped *his* shaft, making him suck in a startled, if pleased, breath. "Here, let me show you what you do with it . . ."

Bringing the buzzing thing down to his shaft, she rubbed it against the head of his manhood. Sparks exploded behind his eyes. He lost all the breath in his lungs, only to suck it back in again quickly. Noise in his ears belatedly resolved into his own voice chanting hoarsely, "—Oh Gods oh Gods oh Gods oh Gods!"

She pulled it away. Shuddering, Zeilas fell down from the heights the machine had driven him . . . only to lose even more of his wits as he watched her stretch out on the bed, bend one leg up out of the way, and apply the tip of the rattling torture device to her own loins. Her moaning, panting breaths made him jealous for a moment. Then inspiration struck. Sliding his fingers up her thighs, he delved gently back into her depths, twisted his palm faceup, and resumed his curling, circling palpitations on her inner walls.

Marta screamed hoarsely, arching up off the bed, only to fall back with a convulsive shudder. Moisture drenched his hand. Removing it, he licked his skin, reveling in the flavor of her climax. She had, he noted, moved the buzzing crankman away from her body. That gave him room to lean over her. Grasping his own shaft, he rubbed it against her folds. She shivered, eyes fluttering open. A moment of alignment was all it took, then he sank into her heat, wringing a soft, appreciative moan from her.

As the mechanical toy buzzed quietly on the bed beside them, he covered her with his body, not wanting to crush her but needing to feel her curves beneath him as he moved. She encouraged him by cradling him within a warm, loving cage made from her arms and legs, by the intimacy of staring into her merry blue eyes, by the way she smiled with both corners of her lips.

Once again, he dipped his head and kissed each of those beautiful, pleasure-quirked corners. She sighed happily and stroked the drying strands of his hair. He thrust a little firmer, a little faster, and her next sigh merged with a moan. Hitching in deep, he circled his pelvis against hers, evoking a little shiver of pleasure. Need burned within him, but he was still in control.

"I love you, Zeilas," she murmured, caressing the side of his face.

He leaned into her touch, then kissed her palm. "And I, you."

She traded palm for lips and tongue. He picked up his pace a little, until she nipped his lower lip, pulling on it briefly, sensually, and demanded, "Faster . . ."

Blood burning, he hooked his wrist under her knee, doubling up her thigh, and braced his weight on his other hand. The move curled up her pelvis, allowing him to thrust in a new position that rubbed him against that spot on her inner wall. He knew he found it when she shouted and shuddered, fingers clawing at his arms and shoulders.

His grin melted away beneath the squeezing of her flesh. Abandoning himself to his own desire, he cantered through her orgasm, then galloped into her, hard enough to make the bed frame sway, until his body bucked with blinding, muscle-tightening release. Panting as his limbs slowly relaxed, Zeilas felt her fumbling for something among the bedding. He opened the eyes he had squeezed shut just in time to see her bringing the still-rattling, silvery rod between their bodies. The tip of it rubbed against her node . . . and brushed the base of his shaft.

In fact, the devious woman *pressed* it there, against his pleasure-sensitized flesh. Eyes wide with shock, Zeilas writhed with a second, near-instantaneous climax. His hips bucked, her back arched, and the two of them—well, mostly him—collapsed onto the bed. Exhausted, sated beyond thought, but vaguely aware his muscular frame was probably crushing her, he managed to roll to one side. Then onto his back, which allowed him to breathe in the air that had gone missing during his second, unexpected orgasm.

The buzzing of her mad, mad invention filled the quiet of the night. A click of the button spun the crank handle wildly around for a few moments, whizzing and rattling, then it slowed and stopped, silencing the infernal machine. Dropping it on the nightstand, Marta curled upright long enough to drag the blankets up over their bodies, then flopped down beside him and snuggled up to his side.

Thought came back, as the fire burned low and the oil lamps glowed. "Please . . ." he murmured, licking dry lips. "Please, *tell* me you don't use that as a torture device?"

She cracked up laughing, snorting and chuckling into his shoulder. He chuckled as well, though his question had been somewhat serious at its core. Humming happily, Marta snuggled closer, hooking one of her legs between his own. "Maybe. If you're really, *really* good."

Laughing, he dredged up enough energy to hug her and kiss her on the top of her still-damp head. He hadn't expected to find love in this foreign land, but it was a good land, better than expected, with a wonderful, inventive, brilliant woman nestled in his arms. "Mmm. I'll try to be."

Once again, he made her laugh. She sighed happily, squeezed him, and chuckled herself to sleep. Zeilas smiled and let himself drift off as well, glad that he could make her laugh.

AURUL

ONE

Gabria watched the last of her trunks floating out the door of her bedroom. Her suite in the palace wasn't much, just a bedroom, a combined bathing and refreshing room, and a small parlor that also served as her office, but it had been an improvement on her previous tenement. A vast improvement on her previous life, prior to the False God's destruction. It felt odd to be leaving Guildara, but not as unsettling as she'd feared.

This alliance is worth the relocation, she reassured herself. The Aurulans were a civilized people, their kingdom long established and quite prosperous. Envoy Pells had sent back reports on the ornate architecture, rich fabrics, and abundance of jewels, fruits, and spices that formed much of the kingdom's wealth, and the wonderful ambassadorial suite he had been assigned. *They won't stick me in a hovel. Not if they clearly want me among them so badly.*

I just wish I knew more spells, she worried, entering her parlor. *If they expect me to be a . . . well, I'll be a sorry one for a long while.*

Maybe I can arrange for lessons? It's not as if I could take Sir Catrine with me. And more lessons in Aurulan, she added, listening to two of the Royal Guards, the mage-warriors who had turned the tide just days ago in their brief but bitter war with a would-be warrior-king to the north. She could only pick out a couple of words, they spoke so quickly and used vocabulary she hadn't learned yet. *Or I'll be lost, trying to negotiate any treaties . . . unless they* want *me to be lost?*

"Are you ready to go, Your Highness?"

Gabria startled, for two reasons. One, she hadn't noticed Mage-Captain Ellett enter the room, and two, his form of address confused her. Glancing around, she didn't see her best friend Marta, the Consul-in-Chief of Guildara, in the chamber. "Uh . . . I beg your pardon? Did you just call me . . . ?"

"Your Highness?" he repeated, clasping his hands behind his purple-and-gold-clad body. "I am informed that is your title."

That bemused her. Mindful of the need to be tactful, Gabria shook her head. "My correct title is sub-Consul, or perhaps advisor. We don't have royalty in Guildara, and that's a royal form of address."

"I was not referring to Guildaran conventions." The tall, ash brown–haired man smiled slightly as her confusion deepened further. "Until His Majesty directs me otherwise, I am instructed to address you as such."

"But . . . why?" Gabria asked, still lost.

". . . I think that is something best left to His Majesty to explain. Now, if you are ready to go, Your Highness, Sir Catrine had kindly offered to assist us in tandem mirror-Gating to the border. From there, it is just three more mirror-Gates to the winter palace on the Jenodan Sea." He gestured at the open door, where her trunks had vanished. "Everything has been set up in the parlor at the end of this hall."

The two Aurulan Guardswomen on the settee broke off their

conversation and rose. Everywhere she had gone for the last three days, these two women had accompanied Gabria. It had felt almost like being treated as a prisoner, except they never stopped her from going anywhere; they just silently invited themselves along. Even into her bedchamber, though after a quick perusal each night, both women had respectfully retreated.

I wonder what they would've done, had I gone to the motorbarn and taken a motorhorse out for a ride? The idle speculation amused her. Her humor faded. *Not that there was time for such things. I was too busy—with their help, admittedly—trying to clear the wreckage from the battlefield.*

That, and attending the private oath-swearing of her friend's marriage. Marta and Sir Zeilas were happily wed in the eyes of the Gods and the law, though the actual celebration had been deferred a couple of months, so that those who had fought would have time to let their wounds and their memories heal before enjoying any festivities associated with their leader's marriage. Gabria didn't know yet if she'd be coming back for that particular party, though she hoped she could.

I just wish I knew why they wanted me *in the Seer King's court.*

Entering the second-floor parlor—the same one where she had interrupted Marta and the Arbran Knight in the middle of a very friendly-looking, private picnic, with the news that the Aurulans wanted *her* to head east and join them—Gabria eyed the mirror. It was a big, tall, cheval-stand looking glass, of the sort rarely seen outside of the ransacked ex-priest quarters, since unwarded mirrors were too dangerous to allow out into the general populace. At least, back when this land had been a part of an aggressive, enemy-rich and magic-poor Mekhana.

Instead of reflecting the room, the mirror looked into a large hall lined with banners and old weapons fixed to its high-windowed walls. There were benches along the edges of the chamber, plus the purple-and-gold-clad figures of yet more Royal Guards, and a stack of her belongings, each bundle, chest, and trunk awaiting their turn to be floated through what looked like another reflection-less mirror a few yards away.

"It's quite safe," Ellett reassured her. "Just don't touch the frame and you'll be fine. You might also feel a bit disoriented as you land on the far side, particularly as a mage. I find it helpful to tighten my personal shields just as I pass through, and keep them tight and close for a moment or two on the other side."

Nodding, Gabria waited for the last of her trunks to be levitated through the mirror that wasn't acting like a mirror. Having already said her good-byes to friends and family earlier that morning, she gathered her courage and her magic, took a deep breath, and carefully stepped through the mirror.

Disoriented was definitely the word for it. Her awareness of her surroundings slid, scraped, and clashed. Feeling more than a touch of vertigo, she hastily cleared her other leg through the frame, focusing her gaze firmly on one of the benches across the way. It only took a few moments for her to stop feeling like the floor was trying to heave like a boat under her feet. By that point, both her shadow-guards and their commander had passed through.

They were in what looked like the Aurulan version of a Guildaran Precinct, the military guildhall for a particular region. Probably the headquarters of a border fortress. She didn't have time to ask any questions, though. Ahead of her, the last few bundles were being floated through the next mirror. Ellett touched her shoulder briefly, offering silent support—or maybe sympathy—then gestured at the frame as soon as the last bundle cleared. Gritting her teeth, Gabria strode up to the mirror, took another deep breath, and stepped through.

Ugh . . . Gods, it's slightly better than the first time, but not really. I hope it gets bearable, if this is how these people move around. Yet another Precinct-style hall, with yet another mirror waiting for her and her goods, and the Royal Guards accompanying her. *What did he say, three more after the first one? So I just have two more to endure?*

Hoping he was right—surely he was right—she stepped through, steadied herself, and then stepped through again.

The last one didn't open onto the equivalent of a Precinct guild-hall. The previous chambers had been no-nonsense in their function, and militaristic in their decoration. This was an ornate reception parlor. Very ornate. She had thought the careful joinery and parquetry of the Woodwright's Guild had made the Guildaran palace a sight to behold, with wood from a hundred species of trees forming beautiful, mathematical, geometrical patterns. But this place, this was stunning.

White marble columns, fluted arches, and pierced screens defined the edges and openings of the chamber, with practically every inch covered in carvings of animals and plants. The walls in between had been cunningly painted with images of garden scenes, clearly meant to look as realistic as pigments could possibly get. In fact, she had to blink twice to realize they *were* flat, painted images, the shadings and tones were so close to the real thing. Deceptively delicate furniture had been crafted from intricately wrought, white-painted iron—with a skill that came close, she noted, to the abilities of her own people—and padded with brightly hued, tassel-edged cushions.

There were people in the room, more than just the purple-and-gold-clad members of the Royal Guard. Several men and women, apparently servants from their uniform of cream edged with lilac trim, were busy carrying her belongings by hand out of the chamber. Others, clad in more colorful brocaded fabrics, were chatting with each other or with the Royal Guards who had preceded Gabria and her baggage. Behind her, one of the mage-warriors shouted something in tones that made her ears hurt, casting some sort of powder at the surface of the mirror. It restored the normal reflectivity of the glass, letting her know the mirror-Gate was firmly closed.

A hand touched her shoulder. Turning to face its owner, she found the Mage-Captain giving her a reassuring look. Ellett cleared his throat, and the men and women in shades of pink, green, blue, gold, and several other hues turned to face him. "Miladies, milords, this is Her Highness, Gabria Springreaver."

She felt like a drab sparrow suddenly thrust into the midst of a bunch of exotic Natallian jungle birds. A roasting drab sparrow, too, for the air was warm and humid, pressing in on her as she stood there in her gray knit tunic and matching leather pants. Practical garb for a former hydraulics engineer living in the chilly early spring weather found in the higher elevations of Guildara. Not so practical for the subtropical lowlands of the southern edge of Aurul. She knew just enough of the geography and climate of this kingdom to know that the Jenodan Sea kept most of Aurul warm even in winter, if considerably wetter than its hot, dry summers.

Still, some of the flush that heated her face was from the dubious, disdainful looks on the faces of the half dozen men and women eyeing her from felt-capped head to leather-booted toe.

One of the men asked something. His tone suggested it was something along the lines of a highly skeptical, "*This* is the woman we're looking for?" only he said it too quickly for Gabria to translate with the little Aurulan she had learned so far. He wore a gold-sprigged blue coat, like a floor-length, leather riding jacket, but stitched from silk and bearing dangling square sleeves instead of practical, close-fitting ones. Those sleeves held things, too, she realized, as he reached into one through the large wrist-hole at the front.

Pulling a double-lensed viewing loupe on a long, gilded stick from one of his bag-like sleeves, he eyed her through the crystals for a moment, then lowered it just enough to tap the frame against his chin. A humming sigh escaped him, and he muttered something equally rapid, flicking out the double-loupe-on-a-stick, indicating points along her body. He then said something else which sounded like an order, and flicked the loupe-on-a-stick off in the direction her belongings had vanished. When she just blinked at him, he repeated more or less the same words with a stronger emphasis. Then again, less patiently.

Lost, Gabria looked back at the Mage-Captain. "I'm sorry . . . but I don't understand more than two or three words of what he just said. I haven't had enough time to learn much Aurulan. Sorry."

". . . Of course. I apologize for my thoughtlessness," Ellett replied, bowing slightly to her.

"Your thoughtlessness?" Gabria repeated, mystified.

"I have had the privilege of drinking Ultra Tongue, a very rare and wondrous potion that enspells the speaker to hear and be heard in a thousand different tongues," he explained. "The magics woven into the liquid spell allow me to speak in my native tongue, but if my intent is for you to understand, the spell projects my meaning into your ears as if you were hearing it in your own. I in turn hear your words in my ears as if they were in Aurulan, if with a Guildaran 'accent.' And if I wish to speak specifically in just one language, I need merely concentrate on my intent and speak with that 'accent.' Naturally, having benefited from it for several years, I forgot not everyone has this advantage. Allow me to make reparations . . ."

Turning to one of the still-dubious-looking women, clad in shades of green, peach, and gold, he rapped out a command in what sounded like Aurulan. An argument broke out at that, one from the woman in green, another from a woman in pink, and rather vociferously from the man in blue. Ellett's own tone sharpened, though unlike the others, he didn't bother to raise his voice. It was the implacable tone of a man who knew and wielded his own authority well, and they subsided. Whatever he said, he ended it with the lilt of a question, and a pointed lift of one brow.

It quelled their objections. The woman in green rolled her eyes, sighed heavily, and stalked off. The front folds of her jacket-like gown parted, revealing gathered peach trousers which matched the peach sash encircling her from shoulder to waist and hip to hip, where it ended in a knot and two trailing ends that fluttered around her knees.

"Lady Lianna, Chief Mage of the Palace, has left to craft and brew the Ultra Tongue potion for you," Ellett murmured. He gestured at the man in blue. "This is Milord Souder, Master of the Royal Retreat. Mmm, you would say he is in charge of the private, familial residence of His Majesty. Sort of a sub-Consul cross between secretary and housekeeper." The Mage-Captain leaned in closer and all but whispered in her ear, "Of course, he thinks much higher of himself than that. Thankfully, he is very good at his job, otherwise His Majesty would not tolerate such airs. Indulge most of his whims, but do not be afraid to stand up for yourself. So long as you break none of the laws of civilized behavior common to all lands, it is doubtful you would truly offend."

Patting her on the shoulder, he nudged her forward.

"Go with Milord Souder, and do as he and his helpers direct you."

Unsure, Gabria glanced back at him. "What will they want me to do?"

"They merely intend to bathe, dress, and prepare you to meet His Majesty. Your appearance is suitable for Guildara, but this is Aurul, and the court of the Seer King." Giving her the same friendly smile from the last three days, he bowed and left.

Gabria wanted to protest that her clothes were acceptable, since she *was* a Guildaran and this was how Guildarans dressed, but faltered as he strode away with the air of a man who had other things to do. The mirror had been pulled back into a pillar-flanked alcove, and all of the Royal Guards, save for the two women who had appointed themselves her watchers, had vanished.

Wordlessly, but with a gesture of half-restrained impatience, the Master of the Royal Retreat gestured with his loupe toward the archway where the servants had taken her things. Giving in, she started walking that way. The woman in pink hurried to get in front of her. Not knowing what else to do, Gabria followed her.

Since the man in blue didn't protest, she guessed it was the right thing to do. As it was, she was hard-pressed to keep up. Her feet kept slowing down, her eyes drinking in the intricate carvings and mosaics outlining yet more of the realistic garden scenes painted on the walls. Despite having to hurry every so often to keep up with the lady in the pink brocaded jacket-gown, Gabria did notice two repeating themes among the animals displayed in wall paintings, mosaics, and carvings: the Eye and the Owl of Ruul.

The Eye wasn't nearly as common as the Owl. The Eye, she knew from her crash course in Aurulan culture, was the official symbol of Ruul, Patron God of Vision. It was reserved for the Seer King, the priesthood, and the higher levels of government. The Owl was His symbol for the common people to use, and was thus in common use. Very common use; owls were cast into the frames of the wrought-iron benches they passed, carved on the pillars supporting the fluted archways, and painted into the boughs of at least one tree in every garden scene.

They walked for several minutes, climbing stairs and passing windows overlooking real gardens with exotic bushes and trees laid in attractive planted patterns. They passed through a set of ornately carved and banded double doors guarded by more Royal Guards in their gilded purple armor. Just as Gabria was wondering when this huge palace would reach an end, they entered a grand parlor lined with the most ostentatious furnishings yet. The wrought-iron furnishings were covered in gold leaf, not paint, the tassels looked to be spun from real thread-of-gold, and the mosaics framing the windows were crafted from polished semiprecious stones.

She felt distinctly Guildaran in this room. As in, from a brand-new, barely started, makeshift kingdom cobbled together by commoners. Even if they *had* managed to Manifest a bona fide Patron Deity. She also felt sweaty, since the door-sized windows stood wide, the gauzy curtains pulled back, revealing the sun-drenched balcony beyond and letting in the heat of midday.

The lady in pink barely paused, however. She strode straight for yet another fluted archway. Hurrying to catch up, Gabria found herself led into a smaller parlor, then a corridor with latticework windows and carved doors, and finally into a bathing . . . well, not a bathing *room*, so much as a bathing *hall*. The first bathing tub was the size of a small pool, half sunk into the floor and surrounded by a raised marble ledge just high enough to act as a sort of bench. It was flanked at each corner by yet more carved pillars, and boasted a fountain which filled it with a constant flow of gently steaming water. The second tub was higher, almost on a pedestal, sized to fit maybe two people, and filled with flowers and a milky white liquid.

Correction, she thought, staring in wonder as the lady in pink strode right up to its steps and turned to face her. *It* is *filled with milk. I can smell it over the scent of the roses. I thought people only bathed in milk in the wilder bardic stories!* A moment later, an amusing thought quirked the corner of her mouth. *Then again, this palace is so ornate*, it *could have sprung from a bard's wildest imaginings.*

Realizing from her gestures that the lady in pink wanted her to strip and submerse herself in the milk, Gabria quickly looked behind her. Master Souder had not followed them into this chamber, however, just her two Royal Guard shadows, who took up places to either side of the bathing chamber entrance. Apparently they were still keeping up the pretense of being her personal sentries, or watchdogs, or whatever it was they believed they were supposed to do.

The other figures in the room, three women, wore the cream gowns of the servants she had seen earlier, but these were edged in purple. Royal servants for the Royal Retreat apparently, and not just palace servants. This could only *be* the Royal Retreat which the imperious Master Souder presided over. It was too ornate for anything else.

Relieved he hadn't entered this particular room, for all he might have been in charge of it, Gabria followed the gestures of the unnamed woman. Removing her cap, she pulled the pins from her hair, twisted up in a bun to keep the hip-length, ash blond locks out of her way. Just removing the gray-felted cap relieved her of some of the excessive warmth plaguing her in this subtropical land. So did raking her fingers through her hair, detangling and fluffing it out.

At the sight of her locks, the woman in pink seemed to look relieved; her own hair was pulled back into a neat plait that reached down past her waist. *Long hair on women must be important*, she thought, remembering the woman in green, Lady Lianna, had worn a similar, waist-length, plaited hairstyle. *On engineers, either you wear it up to keep it out of the way, or you cut it short . . . though the priests of the False God used to rant horribly about the unnaturalness of women going too far in looking as well as acting like men.*

It was a relief to remove her knitted tunic, too. Dropping onto the steps to remove her boots and her socks, she felt cooler as each layer was set aside. She felt a little uncomfortable rendering herself completely naked but knew it was necessary. *I need to be pleasant, polite, and cooperative, so these people will be favorably inclined toward Guildara by my actions. I suppose, if dressing like one of them will make them more charitable toward me . . . well, bathing in milk shouldn't be so bad. Provided they allow me to rinse thoroughly, of course.*

Lady in pink said something and gestured at the pool with a mild but friendly smile. Guessing she was meant to climb in, Gabria removed the last of her underthings and mounted the outer steps. Hesitating, she dipped her toes into the liquid, then started down the first of what looked like an inner set of steps; the liquid concealed all but the topmost stair from her view.

The milk was cool to the touch, and sweet-smelling for its scent. It also had a thin layer of cream floating on the top. She didn't know if that was because it had been partially skimmed after sitting there for a while, or if the pool had been freshly filled and was only now settling long enough for the cream to rise to the top. *Cream*, she realized, noting pools of clearer liquid floating here and there among the milk fats, *and . . . attar of roses? Actual rose oil, and not just flower petals?* The combination felt odd against her skin, but not unpleasant.

Splashing startled her. One of the older maidservants had removed her outer gown, revealing a short, belted tunic that bared most of her shoulders and covered her only to the tops of her thighs. The middle-aged woman descended the steps of the milk bath, and dipped a pearl-glazed pitcher into the liquid. She poured the mixture of milk, cream, attar, and rose petals over Gabria's shoulders, then carefully anointed her head, using a sponge to dab the milk onto her face.

A gesture and a handful of words had Gabria frowning softly in concentration, before she comprehended that she was supposed to crouch down at the far end of the smallish pool and soak for a while. Bemused, Gabria found a bench at that end by bumping into it, and sank onto the marble surface. More milk was poured over her scalp as she sat and soaked, and the sponge patted carefully over her face.

She sat like that, bored and wondering what else would be expected of her, long enough for her fingers to wrinkle. Long enough for the milk dabbed on her face to feel sticky. Finally gestured to stand and exit the pool, she found herself led toward a leather-padded table, rather than the larger pool of water. After a bit of gesturing, Gabria stretched out on the waist-high table as directed, and found herself drizzled with scented oil by the other woman.

Gabria stared at the mother-of-pearl mosaics patterning the curlicue arches of the ceiling, while two more of the servants unnerved her by massaging her legs and arms, her feet and her hands, even her stomach, hips, and breasts. Not in a sexual way, but definitely without regard for Guildaran sensibilities. They even carefully massaged her face, which was an odd sensation. Not unpleasant, just odd.

Urged upright, she was given a cup of clear, sweet-tasting water to drink, then urged facedown on the padded table, where she was drizzled with more oil and the two ladies once again massaged their way from soles to scalp and back. Their touch was near-perfect, somewhere between soft and firm, finding knots and gently but determinedly soothing each muscle until it relaxed. Aches which she hadn't really noticed now twinged, twitched, and vanished, until it was all she could do to keep from moaning out loud.

They finally left her alone for several minutes, until she heard her name being called by the lady in pink. Groaning under her breath, Gabria rolled over, eased up, and wondered briefly why her oily-sticky body should ache in new ways, now that it was thoroughly relaxed. Thankfully, her Aurulan bath companions waited patiently until she felt like she could stand. Crossing to the larger pool, Gabria let herself be directed to stand on the topmost of the inner side steps, where she was sluiced with water dipped from the pool, then lathered and scrubbed thoroughly with coarse sponges until her skin felt like it glowed. Another round of rinsing and she was allowed to sink fully into the pool, where she was handed a goblet of fruit juice and urged wordlessly to drink it all down.

Between the heat of the water and the vigorous scrubbing, her body tingled all over, reviving her from the lethargy induced by her very first massage. The water and the juice had an inevitable effect, though. Dredging up what little Aurulan she had managed to learn and retain in between her many duties as a sub-Consul and advisor, Gabria carefully asked where the refreshing room was. After a long moment of blank looks, one of the servants just as carefully repeated the words with a slightly different inflection and a questioning tone. Nodding fervently, Gabria was gestured out of the water and led to a small chamber to one side.

Even the refresher, she noted with bemused humor, was carved from the finest white marble, and ornamented—at least, on the outside—with bas-relief images of flowers and vines.

Led back to the pool, she was scrubbed one more time, some sort of crème applied to her hair, and led back to the heated water. The woman who had bathed her in the milk directed her back into the pool, though not for quite as long as she had been expected to soak in the milk. The crème was rinsed from her hair and her long locks carefully and gently combed from the tips on up. Urged back out after that, she was led to a fresh padded table—the other one having been cleaned and left to dry in the meantime—and gestured back onto it. The same two servants lightly anointed her with oil and massaged her from head to toe, though they didn't take quite as long about it this time.

Directed back onto her feet, Gabria found herself patted dry and wrapped in a square-sleeved silk robe. She was then led into one of the other chambers branching off of the hallway, first through a sort of private parlor, then into a bedchamber, and lastly into what had to be a formal dressing room. Here, new servants in their cream-and-purple robes quickly pulled open drawers and cabinet doors on the left side of the chamber, displaying the bright hues of local fabrics—clothing, apparently—and some of her personal effects.

Her own clothes, she discovered, had been stuffed into Aurulan-style trunks at the back of the large room, their sides and lids inlaid with yet more polished stones and bits of pearly shell. Gadgets from her personal effects had been placed with greater care on the shelves with no rhyme or reason, but she blushed to see her crankman, a very intimate and personal tool, sitting out in the open next to her equally hand-cranked calculation box. The crankman had been a gift from Marta from their days of collaborating between the Clockworks and Hydraulics Guilds, back when the two young women had first met as apprentices. It did not belong out in the open next to her calculation box, nor her cases of calibrators, wrenches, and pliers.

It almost was enough to distract her from the right side of the room, where yet more clothing and personal belongings—someone *else's* personal belongings—occupied the cupboards, trunks, and shelves. Indeed, she had a hard time craning her neck to look over her shoulder, for one of the servants quickly produced a brush and busied herself smoothing and drying Gabria's hair from the ends up. Another woman brought in a basket of fresh, fragrant flowers, most of them tiny roses no bigger than Gabria's thumbnail, and some of them exotic orchids formerly only seen in books describing and illustrating foreign lands.

The flowers, she discovered, were for plaiting into her hair. Deft hands separated and wove together the strands, while more hands added stems and blooms at just the right moment. The whole process lasted long enough that the heat of her bath had completely cooled and her hair had thoroughly dried before it ended. She was also thirsty once again.

Just as she was going to dredge up the words to ask for another glass of water, the lady in green entered the dressing room. Lady Lianna carried a gilded, chased goblet carefully in her hands. She stopped in front of Gabria and spoke in Guildaran.

"You are lucky His Majesty agrees with Captain Ellett, and that I was given leave to bottle and sell the other half. This brew costs well over five thousand gold to craft. Do not waste a drop." She held out the cup, which Gabria eyed warily, then sighed impatiently. "It is *Ultra Tongue*, woman. If you have any wits in your head, you'll drink it so that you can understand and be understood. Drink up. All of it."

TWO

Accepting the cup, Gabria eyed the milky white contents filling half of the heavy vessel. It smelled like bitter garden weeds and looked like thick, syrupy milk. The taste, when she took an experimental sip, was even worse. Bitter, sour, spicy, and ever so slightly soapy. Grimacing, she knocked it back quickly, then returned the metal cup. One of the servants handed her a crystal goblet filled with more of the sweet-tasting local water, which she used to swish around her mouth until the horrid, nasty, bitter residue was gone.

Lady Lianna, her task finished, took herself and her goblet back out without another word.

"Can you understand me now?" the lady in pink asked, her words lilting with the Aurulan accent, but seemingly spoken in Guildaran.

"Yes, I can," Gabria confirmed. She rubbed at her ears; the other woman's voice had made them twitch rather oddly.

"Good. I am Milady Geno, Mistress of the Bath. We are preparing you to be brought before His Majesty in the Vaulted Chapel for the Acceptance Ceremony," she stated, as if her words would explain all of these elaborate preparations. Which they didn't.

"Acceptance Ceremony?" Gabria asked. She knew a milady was one step lower on the social ladder than a lady, sort of a demi-noble to a full noble, but she didn't know what this ceremony thing was about, nor why she had to be cleaned and dressed so specifically for it.

"Yes, the ceremony where Ruul, praise His Eyes, will accept you. We haven't a lot of time left," the Mistress of the Bath continued briskly. "His Majesty wishes the ceremony completed as swiftly as possible, yet Master Souder decreed you had to be made . . . *more* presentable, at least to Aurulan preferences," she stated tactfully. "Your hair has been properly dressed, which, aside from the bathing, is one of the most tedious and time-consuming tasks. Now we will layer you in the garments of an Aurulan courtier as befits your impending station. As soon as you are dressed and shod, we will journey to the Vaulted Chapel. Please stand so that the maids may assist you into your clothes."

Lost, but mindful of the need to comply and be a good and friendly representative of her people, Gabria stood and allowed them to clothe her in fine, white silk underdrawers, a pale pink chemise fitted well enough to support her breasts once it was laced, pale pink gathered trousers embroidered with white orchids, and not one, but two layers of jacket-like robes. The inner one was the same blush pink as the trousers, while the outer one was a shimmering white scattered with embroidered miniature roses of nearly the same hue as the ones woven into her hair.

The sleeves on the outer robe were extra-long rectangles which dangled almost to her knees; the sleeves on the inner robe were more squarish, suitable for use as pockets. So suitable, one of the maidservants tucked a white linen kerchief into one, and a clever folding fan made from thin sticks of delicately carved wood into the other. Her waist was wrapped with a gauzy white sash, crossed over her breast, and knotted just under her ribs. The layers of silk, while lightweight enough to flutter with every little move, were still tightly woven and thus retained heat. Though she wasn't quite as warm as she had been in her woolens, Gabria fished out the fan and fluttered it in front of her face, wanting to cool herself back down.

Mistress Geno frowned, lips compressing in a thin line. Catching Gabria's wrist, she shook her head. "A lady of the court does *not* whap a fan about her face like a flyswatter in a barn. You hold it like *this*, and waft it gently, like *so*—keep your movements small and slow, as graceful and smooth as possible. We will have time for lessons in deportment, manner, and movement later on. When His Majesty returns to his duties, you'll have time for such things. Until then . . . slow, graceful, smooth. You need to present yourself as well as you possibly can, Your Highness. Everyone that is anyone will be in the chapel, wanting to witness this momentous and long overdue occasion."

Being addressed like that, and finally being free to glance at the belongings on the other shelves, Gabria felt a sinking sensation in her stomach. "Um . . . Milady Geno . . . is this 'Acceptance Ceremony' . . . a *marriage* ceremony?"

"Of course. Don't forget her slippers," Mistress Geno instructed the maids.

Gabria eyed the white sueded shoes being brought over to her, soft and supple, lined with silk and padded, almost quilted, on their soles, but didn't really see them. "Uh . . . I'm, um . . . expected to . . . ?"

"As it was said, so it was written; thus it is proved, and so shall it be," the woman in pink stated with a matter-of-fact air.

Gabria stared at her, balancing awkwardly first on one foot, then the other as the maids silently slipped the suede shoes onto her bare feet. "That . . . that can't be right. I'm the Guildaran envoy, and envoys don't . . . marry . . ."

Her own protest tripped her up. Not even twenty-four hours ago, she had stood witness to her best friend, Goddess-elected ruler of Guildara, marrying the Arbran Knight who had been sent to Guildara as the chief envoy representing his people. More than that, the message which had brought *her* here came back to her. Or more precisely, the opening lines of the Seer King's prophetically phrased response to Guildaran overtures of peace.

Tell your queen what she does is right and just. Seek it further from the west if you wish peace for longer than a day. If you wish the same from the east, send your friend, the girl in gray. Those words had been delivered to Marta and Sir Zeilas while they had been enjoying one of their private, indoor picnics over the winter. Gabria remembered quite well how their cheeks had been flushed and how their lips had looked a little puffy, as if they had been kissing mere moments before the message had interrupted their picnic tryst.

The Mistress of the Bath gestured for Gabria to follow her out of the dressing chamber. Part of her wanted to protest, but the rest of her was too busy thinking about the ramifications of her situation, and there were several to consider.

If by "what she does" His Majesty meant courting with Zeilas, and "seek it further" meant pursuing further Arbran ties literally through the bonds of marriage . . . then "if you wish the same from the east" . . . then he really does *expect me to marry him, as Marta expected Zeilas to marry her. Well, more hoped than expected on her part,* Gabria added silently, honestly. *But* these *people are outright expecting me to . . . to* marry *their king!*

Why me, and why marriage? And why didn't they tell me this back when I was in Guildara, where I could have more easily protested the idea?

That, she suspected, was probably the point. She was now deep in the heart of Aurul, so far away that it had taken four mirror-Gate trips to reach this place, a fabled means of instantaneous travel which Sir Catrine said could span in mere moments the sort of distances it often took weeks to traverse by more normal means, depending on how settled or unsettled the intervening aether might be.

They didn't tell me because they didn't want *me backing out of it. Worse, they* expect *me to go through with it as a means of securing strong ties be-*

tween Aurul and Guildara. Which they told me about, more or less, when they presented the demand that I come here with them or see Guildara's wishes for peaceful coexistence and trade be tossed aside. If I don't go through with it . . . they could use it as an excuse to ignore Guildara, or even peck at our borders. From their impressive display of battle magics against the forces of Warlord Durn . . . my people wouldn't stand a chance in a fair fight. Not without enough time to learn our own countermagics, which would take years.

She *could* say no . . . but she had already damned herself by promising Marta she'd do whatever it took to secure good relations with these Aurulans. *I just had no idea how* intimate *those relations would end up being!*

All the way to the Vaulted Chapel, she worried over what sort of a man the Seer King was, what sort of marriage they would have, and why *her*, of all people. She barely noticed the paintings and the artworks, the tapestries and the curtains, the windows and the columns they passed. Descending a broad set of marble steps, they walked through a set of latticework doors into a chamber so huge and marvelous, it wiped away her worries with the sheer wonder of the place.

Like so many other rooms in the palace complex, the roof was supported by ornately carved pillars and fluted, arched crossbeams. Unlike those other halls and chambers, the walls and roof of this place were forged from glass. Surrounded on three sides by gardens bearing sculpted bushes and rippling, fountain-fed pools filled with hundreds of elegantly, brightly robed courtiers, the chapel seem to float in the sunlight like a crystal bowl filled with flowers.

Gabria was now very glad the Master of the Royal Retreat had insisted she be bathed and dressed "appropriately" for this moment. Her woolens and leathers would have looked utterly out of place otherwise. She also noticed she no longer felt overly warm and in need of the fan still clenched in her hand, and awkwardly tucked it into one of her inner pocket sleeves, unfamiliar with the movements necessary. Shaded only by the marble arches crisscrossing the ceiling like an overgrown stone arbor, it wasn't hot, but instead remarkably cool in this remarkable hall.

The sight of long, banner-like scrolls hanging from those rafters, painted with carefully crafted runes, gave her a clue. In fact, Sir Catrine had showed her and her fellow guildmembers how to modify their crude by comparison cooling spells with runes similar to these. Their presence kept the place from overheating like the glorified, overgrown greenhouse it resembled.

Musicians began playing something soft and melodic as Mistress Geno turned, bowed to her, and stepped aside, leaving Gabria at the start of the long, white velvet runner carpet bisecting the patiently waiting crowd. It took her the discreet, swift flutter of the other woman's hand to realize she was supposed to walk up that carpet and . . . and marry a foreign leader without any fuss, hesitation, or offense.

If I don't . . . Guildara may suffer, Gabria reminded herself, moving one foot slowly in front of the other. *If I do . . . peace for my people, and trade relations with this clearly prosperous kingdom. And . . . and as Zeilas himself joked, the spouse of a ruler has a* great *deal of influence over that ruler's opinions and judgments, if he's sweet enough to her. Or her to him, in my case.* Swallowing, mouth dry despite the water she had so recently consumed, she steadied her stride into something more graceful than faltering. *All I have to do is be sweet enough to this . . . king . . . and he'll think sweetly of my homeland. Whoever he is.*

He wasn't going to be found among the courtiers standing patiently, silently in front of the rows and rows of padded, marble-carved benches lining the chapel. Barely a single cough interrupted their quiet, watchful vigil, despite the fact that there had to be nearly a thousand people gathered in this remarkable place. Her stomach quaked with what her people called "clattering gears" and what she'd heard other lands refer to as "fluttering butterflies," the unsettling side effect of sheer nervousness brought on by the weight of all those eyes.

Turning her gaze to the far end of the aisle, she realized there was one person who remained seated as he waited for her to approach, while all the rest stood, including the minstrels playing their bowed strings and soft flutes. He sat on a throne of crystal-faceted glass, clad in white robes similar to her own, though where hers were pink, his were gold, and where her sleeves reached her knees, his looked long enough to brush the floor when standing. His skin was shaded toward the darker end of the spectrum for these Aurulans, some being nearly as fair-skinned as herself, others not quite as dark as Sundarans were reputed to be.

His hair, plaited much like hers in a braid down to his waist, albeit without the flowers, was either black or dark brown; in the sunlight gleaming down through the tiled panes of the roof, it seemed to hold reddish highlights, though she couldn't be sure. A thin mustache and goatee had been neatly shaped and trimmed, encircling his mouth in a thin, dark line. It surrounded a generous mouth that looked like it was used to smiling a lot, though only the hint of one could be seen now. As she approached the short flight of steps leading up to the dais, she could also see his eyes. His eyes . . .

His eyes were *gold*. Owl gold, as bright and sharp as a pair of highly valuable coins.

Gabria stopped, unable to move a single step more. Her legs wouldn't carry her any closer. Almost all her life, she had feared and hated the False God, loathed Him, dreaded Him, and done everything she could to avoid His unwanted gaze falling upon her. Mekha had been an abomination, an unloved God who refused to fade away, and outright refused to die, though He *had* technically been slain over two centuries before. A Netherhell demon in disguise, sucking out and stealing away the life force which powered the spells of His mages. A False God, who cared only for His own selfish needs, and nothing for His supposed people.

This wasn't a mere mortal man. This was the Seer King, who saw with the eyes of His God. Or rather, whose God saw with *His* eyes. The Eyes of Ruul.

Unnatural, divine eyes which were looking straight at *her*.

She almost turned and fled when he uncurled himself from his throne. His slow descent down the white-carpeted steps mesmerized her, like a mouse caught under the stare of an owl gliding over a meadow. Taller than most Guildarans, he towered over her as he reached the last step separating them. His hand lifted slowly, gracefully to her face. She shivered before he even touched her, eyes wide with fear, but his fingers were gentle. Calloused, too, slightly rough in the way that said he worked with his hands.

The feel of those calluses bemused her, paralyzing her urge to flee from the contradiction. Gods didn't work with Their hands; They were Gods and used Their will to enact great—and sometimes terrible—deeds. Mekha's hands were said to have been cold and clammy, the hands of a corpse dragged from its grave. This hand was warm and dry, and very much alive.

Do not fear me, Gabria.

Her eyes widened. That . . . he . . . He, rather . . . The voice filled her head, soft and low, but echoing as if it rumbled throughout the chapel, though she *knew* she hadn't heard it with her ears. Nor had those full lips moved. It was all unnaturally, eerily, all in her head.

Yes, I speak to you in your mind, hearing your thoughts. All Gods have that right. It is only your fellow mortals who are forbidden. I am pleased you come before Me willingly. Afraid of what you do not yet know, nor understand . . . but willingly all the same. You are what My Seer needs, the right choice for him . . . and, perhaps, I choose you a little for Myself. Those fingers curled and brushed gently against her cheek. The caress was both soothing and unnerving. *You are a beautiful woman, inside and out, and a worthy vessel.*

. . . *Vessel*? she thought, mouth too dry and throat too tight to have made an actual sound.

His mouth curved in a slow, disturbingly male smile. Disturbing, because this was still very much a God staring at her with those unnatural gold eyes. *You will be My vessel, strong and kind, bright and loving. My current Seer will fill you with untold pleasure as you fulfill the honor of becoming the mother of My next Seer King, in a line unbroken for over five hundred years.*

Shock held her still. Descending that one, last step, He leaned down—still taller than her by a full head—and brushed His lips against hers. Watching her with those owl-bright eyes. Somehow, she found the strength to try to speak, though not yet the voice. He took swift advantage of her parted lips, kissing her fully. Tasting like a man, touching like a man . . . feeling like anything but a man as, somehow, He kissed her mind as well as her mouth.

He pulled back after a moment, one hand still lightly cupping her cheek, the other lifting her right hand between them. This time, His voice echoed in her ears as well as her head, rolling like thunder in the distance. His lips framed each word as clearly as the windows framed the garden view, filling the glass chapel with His approval.

"I accept this woman as Bride of My Seer King. She is blessed in My Eyes. Honor her as the Princess Gabria, wife of King Devin and mother of My unbroken line. Let their union be fruitful; let them love long and full!"

The otherwise silent congregation of courtiers spoke up in near-perfect unison at that, startling her.

"As it is said, so shall it be written!"

"Thus it is proved, and so shall it be," Ruul stated, satisfaction coloring His voice. Lifting her fingers to His lips, he kissed the ring that had materialized on her littlest finger. *I will see you soon, Gabria. Hopefully without any more fear in your heart. You are too lovely to suffer from anything.*

Lowering her hand, He leaned down again, kissing Gabria fully on the lips with no teasing or hesitations this time. He also closed those unnerving eyes. A shudder passed through his frame, somehow diminishing him; he pulled back slightly after a moment, just far enough to gaze at her, their mouths not quite brushing. With brown eyes.

Normal, mortal, plebeian brown eyes. With Seer King Devin's eyes, not Patron God Ruul's. He studied her a moment, as if this was the first moment he was finally seeing her face, then swooped in for another kiss. It wasn't quite as masterful, but it was quite skillful in its own way. Shaken and trembling, Gabria leaned into him. Not for enjoyment, though the kiss was disturbingly nice, the nicest one of her life so far, but for physical support as her knees threatened to give way from sheer, overwrought nerves.

By instinct, or perhaps divine guidance—an unnerving thought—he abandoned touching her cheek in favor of wrapping that arm around her waist, lifting and supporting her against his warm, strong body. His other hand came up and cradled the nape of her neck, beneath her flower-strewn braid. Turning her head slightly, he kissed his way to the soft skin just in front of her ear, and whispered into it.

"I must now introduce you to the Prime Minister and the others. Face them with courage and grace, dignity and courtesy," he coached her under his breath. "Once their eyes have turned elsewhere, and we are alone, *then* you may react as you wish." One last brush of his lips against the curves of her ears, tickling them in an unnerving way, and he gently turned her toward the others.

Mindful of his words, of having to make the best of this all-but-absurd situation, Gabria squared her shoulders and leveled her chin. Despite the clanking of her guts and the shivering of her knees, she reminded herself firmly that this was far, far better than, say, the old priests of the False God finding out she was a mage. *Really, by comparison, finding myself unexpectedly . . . married . . . isn't so bad. At least they don't seem to want to hurt me, or drain away my magics. So far.*

She also knew, from her modest handful of lessons in Aurulan culture and politics, that the Prime Minister was the bureaucratic power of this nation. The Seer King had the final say—or perhaps that was more

Ruul having the final say—but from what she knew, his position was wrapped up in the duties of being head priest, prophet, and watchful Guardian of their nation, the spiritual head. It was the Prime Minister who oversaw the day-to-day running and practical governance of Aurul.

So he's sort of like Marta. Appointed into the position, not born, and wielding a great deal of power and respect, Gabria reminded herself, gathering her wits as well as her composure as the closest of the men stepped forward. He wore black robes decorated with thread-of-gold, counterpoint to the Seer King's white, and his mustache and goatee were a full growth, rather than a neatly trimmed line. More than that, he *looked* like the man at her side. Not exactly like him, not like a twin, but quite possibly like a brother, or a cousin.

"This is Lord Daric, our Prime Minister, and elder brother," the Seer King introduced.

Not quite ready to trust her still unsteady knees—and not inclined to bow anyway; she had played similar ranking games within the Hydraulics and Mage's Guilds and knew she needed to establish her own position right away—Gabria managed a slow, hopefully graceful dip of her head. His mouth tightened briefly, but he returned it, placing himself as her equal.

"Next to him is Lord Zuill, Prime Mage of the kingdom." That was an older, gray-braided gentleman in rich brown robes accented with peach and gold. The head bow he gave her in return to her nod was a little deeper than the Prime Minister's. "Lady Lianna, Mage of the Palace . . ." She bowed a little deeper still, as did the rest. Gabria listened and nodded as her erstwhile husband introduced several others, ending with the blue-robed "Milord Souder, Master of the Royal Retreat."

Master Souder lifted his loupe-stick, eyeing her from flowered head to sueded toe. "Hm. Well. At least she cleans up well enough." He lowered it and looked at his ruler. "She'll need deportment lessons. She stands like a laborer."

"I stand like an *engineer*." The words left her, sharp and crisp, before she realized it. Not that she wanted to stop them; his attitude irked her. Gabria held the other man's gaze firmly as he blinked, taken aback. "My education and skills are *far* superior. As for deportment lessons, I would suggest you sit in on them and listen as well. As much as I may need instruction in Aurulan manners, it is also clear that you may need a refresher in how to be civil and courteous in public."

Souder's brows rose, but not in affront. Instead, she had the impression she had pleased as well as startled him. Sweeping into a lower bow than the rest, he replied, "Of course, Your Highness. I apologize for any offense given by my forgetfulness."

She confined her reply to the same slight nod as before, and figured it was best to say nothing more on the matter. At least, unless and until he snipped at her again, or waved that stereoscopic loupe-on-a-stick disdainfully in her direction. Part of her—her engineering curiosity—wanted to know about its optical properties, but the rest of her didn't quite like the man. Yet.

But . . . I do seem to be stuck here, so I should *try to get along with everyone. I just won't let him or anyone else—not even a God—walk all over me.*

"The others," the man at her side was saying, returning her attention to the assembled courtiers, "you will come to know as time progresses. It is time, now, for the Three Days of Grace to begin."

As if his words were some sort of ritual statement, everyone else in the glass-walled chapel bowed, stating as a group, "As it is said, so shall it be written; thus it is proved, and so shall it be!"

They also started filing out, though many of the brightly clothed men and women kept their gaze on Gabria, studying her as they waited for their turn to walk back along the aisle and up into the palace proper. Rather than following them as she expected, Gabria found herself pulled gently to the side, led through a glass door in the wall to one side of the dais. Even though the chapel was roofed and walled in glass, the sunlight was brighter outside, and palpably hotter now that they were beyond the cooling effect of those scroll-scribed runes.

The glimmering waters of the Jenodan Sea could be seen beyond the bushes and trees, and the breeze wafting up from the south smelled of flowers, moisture, and a hint of mud. She knew from her geography studies that the great body of water wasn't a true saltwater sea, but was instead a vast freshwater lake, dotted with islands to the south and crags to the west. Before she could dredge up the names of the other kingdoms besides Aurul that claimed portions of its shoreline, the man leading her along the stone-tiled paths of the garden stopped and faced her.

"Are you hungry?" he asked.

The question caught her off guard. "Uh . . . yes. But what I really—"

His fingers lifted to her lips, silencing her. Those brown eyes flicked around the garden. "We are not yet alone. The nobles and the ministers still watch us. Come. A small feast has been prepared for us in the *fuchsia* pavilion."

"The what?" Unfamiliar with the word, Gabria let herself be led along the path once more. They ascended a curving set of steps flanked by lemon-scented bushes and stepped up to a gauze-curtained, marble-carved structure. The broad roof was covered in solid, blue-glazed tiles, she noted, and the edges of the fluted roof hung with basket after basket of bright red, pale and vivid pink, and even a few purple flowers. More had been planted in large urns, and in planter boxes at the corners of the steps ringing the stone and tile pavilion. Gabria smiled at the bright colors. "Those flowers are lovely! What are they?"

"These are fuchsias," he told her, lifting his fingers to one of the dangling, colorful stems. "They grow abundantly all over our kingdom. Come; your journey may have been short, but your preparations were long. You must be hungry."

Pulling aside one of the aqua blue curtains, he revealed the interior of the pavilion. A low oval table lay in the center of a rug-padded, cushion-strewn platform. Like most of the other things she had seen since beginning that bathing ritual, the table was gilded and inlaid with semiprecious stones. Gilded dishes lined its surface, many of them covered with decorative domes.

Leading her to one side, he lifted her hand to his lips and kissed it. "It is a pleasure to finally meet you in person, Gabria. Until now, I have only seen whatever visions of you Ruul has granted unto me. I am honored the reality is more pleasant than the vision."

She stiffened at the name of his deity. ". . . Are we alone yet?"

"Not quite. And I must introduce myself first. I am Devin, second-born son of Elric and Talinea, current Seer King of Aurul, blessed of Ruul . . . but you may call me Devin, particularly when we are alone. You have met my elder brother, Lord Daric, of course." Gesturing for her to sink onto the cushions, he lent her his hand for balance, then took himself around the table to the far side, continuing his introductions. "I also have a sister, Lady Atena; currently, she is our ambassador to the kingdom of Haida, which lies to the southwest of us, due east of Sundara. You, of course, are Gabria of the family Springreaver. Do you have any siblings?"

"Two sisters." It felt a little strange to be making polite conversation with a near-stranger she had just married, but she had resolved to make the best of the situation. *For the sake of Guildara, of course.* Finding what looked like a napkin on the table, she draped it across her folded legs. "I'm the middle child. My eldest sister is Marica. She works as an accountant for the Glassworks Guild. And, of course, she's a member of the Accountant's Guild.

"My younger sister, Zeda, is a journeyman chef for the Hospitaller's Guild—those are the people who serve in taverns, inns, restaurants, and the like. She was originally apprenticed to the Glassworks Guild, since our eldest sister had some clout and it's a good career for a woman, it doesn't require as much strength as, say, the Iron Smelter's Guild, but she discovered she really prefers working with food." Gabria eyed the dishes between them and gestured hesitantly at the lids. "Are we going to begin eating, or . . . ?"

He lifted his hand, and two men in the cream-and-lavender robes of the royal household parted the curtains on the side opposite from their entrance. They came in, bowed to their king, bowed to Gabria—nearly as deeply, she noticed, though not quite—and uncovered the dishes. Bowls of greens rested on chunks of ice, as did mixtures of exotic, screw-shaped spirals of something vaguely pastry-like tossed with tender vegetables in a glistening sauce. Other dishes held gravy-slathered chunks of meat cooked on skewers. Strange peach white curls of what looked like meat formed rings on another plate, encircling a dish filled with some sort of creamy gold, herb-speckled sauce.

The two servants brought forth bowls of water and little towels. Watching Devin dipping and scrubbing his fingers in the water, Gabria did the same. The water had been scented with lemons and was refreshingly cool. The little drying cloths were soft, exotic cotton, which came from so far away, Gabria couldn't remember the name of the place, other than that it was extremely expensive. *Marta has a set of cotton drying cloths, a coronation gift sent from Sundara. She let me touch them . . . but these are even softer than hers. I think because they've been washed and used many times, like well-worn linen.*

Once their hands were clean and dry, the servants shifted the bowls and cloths to the end of the table, then brought forth pitchers, etched with cooling runes, and poured water into two of the goblets, and what smelled like a pale golden wine into two more, placing one of each in front of the two diners. Bowing again, they retreated to the pillars to either side of the curtains they had entered through, knelt on a pair of cushions laid out for them, and settled in to wait until needed again.

Bemused, Gabria glanced at them, then at the Seer King. He lifted the goblet of water nearest him, cleared his throat, and spoke. "Praise be unto Ruul, who brought you into my life."

Holding the blown-glass cup aloft, he waited patiently. Pointedly glancing at her own.

THREE

Sighing, Gabria lifted her cup, though she didn't say anything. She had a problem with his God and couldn't quite bring herself to lie about it. Thankfully, Devin didn't seem to be offended by her lack of words. Lowering his cup, he sipped from it, so she sipped from hers. It was cool, sweet, and quenched some of her thirst. She copied his moves and started serving herself small portions of this and that, sticking mostly to the foods she recognized.

"There are certain . . . rituals . . . involved in the marriage of a Seer King," Devin stated a few moments later, after having bitten into one of the white peach curls of meat and sipped at the wine placed by his water glass. "Rituals and traditions. Since you are an outlander, I need to enlighten you as to this particular one. We have begun the Three Days of Grace. They are designed to allow the Seer and his bride the opportunity to get to know each other first, without the pressure or expectation of begetting any heirs."

She blushed at his words. *That* was one of her strongest points of objection to this whole mess, second only to the fact he harbored a God in his body, and she was deathly afraid of all deities, thanks to her people's unpleasant past. Gabria opened her mouth to address that fact, only to find herself silenced again when he raised his hand.

"I know, you wish to speak of Ruul's intentions regarding your presence here. There will be time for that, I promise. First, you must know what these three days are. Out in the rest of the kingdom, these are three days of rejoicing for my people, of celebrations and feasts and prayers of well wishes for myself and my bride. Prayers for you, that you will, ah, be fruitful and kind, and prayers for me, that I will be fruitful and loving. But as you and I come to each other as strangers—as most Seer Kings and their brides have been—we are given three days to become better acquainted, and to begin a lifelong friendship.

"In fact, my father dined with my mother in this very pavilion over forty years ago," he added, making her aware that he was, indeed, older than her, mid-thirties to her mid-twenties. "They both still live, and he is still a holy Seer, though obviously, he is no longer the Seer King.

"You would have met them already, but my mother fell and injured her hip last week, and the palace healers have decreed bed rest for her, otherwise she would have been in the Vaulted Chapel. My father chose to keep her company, for they came to love each other very strongly over the years—as was prophesied—or he would have been here himself. Are your parents still alive?"

"My mother is. She works for the Hydraulics Guild, the same as I myself did for many years." She thought about mentioning her father, but refrained. Doing so would bring up her objections to being so close to a God, and he apparently didn't want to discuss such things just yet.

Instead, she spooned some of the screw-shaped dish onto her plate and tasted a few bits. The spirals were indeed some sort of wheat-based pastry, lightly coated in a spiced mixture of oil and vinegar. The vegetables had been blanched and chilled along with the pastry screws, so while they were cooked, they were still crisp and tasty. The combination pleased her.

Devin smiled wryly. "Forgive me. I'm so eager to get to know you, I keep forgetting to finish the explanation . . . As I was saying, for three days, we will spend all our time together, conversing, sharing our backgrounds and our interests, and spending time finding the points of similarities in our educations and interests. We will even sleep in the same bed, but without any intimate congress between us. Once the three days are up, we will have another three, the Days of Intimacy, wherein we explore each other's preferences in pleasure, even as we continue to explore each other's pasts and pastimes.

"On the seventh day, you will begin your instructions in Aurulan protocols, courtesies, rituals, and the like, while I will return to my duties as Seer King and high priest of our people. These are the *only* days, at least ever since the Eyes of Ruul were laid upon me, wherein I am free from all duties and obligations as the Seer King. I intend to enjoy them for as long as they last," he added dryly. "In fact, one week after we finish our post-wedding days of peace and idleness, the whole court will have to pack up and go on tour to the eastern lands, making our way to the summer palace up in the mountains north of here by a bit of a circuitous route.

"I must make my way to the winter palace via the seven major cities to the east," he explained. "The journey takes a full month, and it allows the people of the land to see, and be seen by, the Eyes of Ruul. Naturally you will travel with me, though there won't be much opportunity for privacy, save late at night. Either we'll be traveling all day long to get to each city on time, or I'll be spending all my time in prayers and prophecies in the various cathedrals."

Hearing his apologetic tone, Gabria felt a soft rush of sympathy for him. "Are you always the Seer King, then? With no time for yourself?"

"A few hours every day in the morning and evening, but many of the rest are spent listening to petitions and leading prayers, and laying hands upon those who come before me in the hopes that I may foresee something of their futures—it is a job much like any other," Devin added wryly. "Save that I carry a heavier burden than most, for all I carry it upon my heart and in my eyes, and not on my shoulders or in my hands. The heaviest obligations come when we make the half loop to the east in the spring—which was delayed slightly this year so that you and I could adjust to being wed—and the half loop to the west in the autumn.

"But eventually we will be settled into the winter palace. And eventually your lessons will end. You will have some light duties of your own to attend to, some rituals to preside over in addition to your role as future vessel and mother of the next Seer King. You will also be allotted time for your own pursuits and interests . . . though I'm afraid we don't have one of these Hydraulics Guilds you mention." Devin shook his head slightly. "Frankly, if it weren't for Ruul's clearly stated wishes, the thought of a Mekhanan being the bride of the Seer King would upset my people. We've never had reason to look kindly upon your former kingdom. You will be scrutinized on our trip, and I know that Souder plans to squeeze as many rules of proper behavior and etiquette into you that he can before we head east."

"Blame the ambitions of the False God's priests for all of that," Gabria retorted. "Not the majority of my people. *We* wanted free of the madness of their lust for conquest . . . and we *are* free. You may inform your people that I am a Guildaran, *not* a Mekhanan."

He dipped his head in acknowledgment of her point. "Captain Ellett explained the battle he and his men joined, and how your people handled its aftermath. My people would say, it only takes a few bugs in a basket of fruit to spoil the sale. But we also admit that most of the fruit is usually still good if salvaged in time. And it is quite clear that some of your people are very worthy of our friendship, with yourself as the foremost example."

"Well, I suppose my future duties will include ensuring your people enact treaties and enjoy peaceful trade with mine," she allowed, "though I'm really not trained to be a diplomat. Not like Envoy Pells."

He coughed into his hand. "Well, as for *that* . . . you technically cannot *be* an envoy, since your other duties will be far more important . . . though naturally you will have some definite influence of our opinions regarding your home nation. And I'm sure you could become a good envoy given time and training. My brother, the Prime Minister, would never accept you as an envoy, however. Your position is the vessel of motherhood. It is a holy calling higher than any other, and deeply enmeshed within Aurulan customs and concerns. Since you are not Aurulan by birth, you will have to undergo a lengthy period of training in Aurulan ways, so that you may be an appropriate influence upon our children.

"A kind one, either way," he allowed quickly, "and undoubtedly a good mother without training—Ruul would not choose otherwise—but there are certain expectations of the royal siblings, ensuring that at least one of them is raised to be a worthy enough vessel for the Eyes of Ruul, and another is worthy of being the Prime Minister, that you will need training in the ways of proper parenting. We've had five hundred thirty-six years to perfect the system, after all. Hence all these rituals."

His words dredged up her objections once again. Gabria thought about it for a long moment, then sighed. ". . . Can we *please* be alone, now?"

She didn't have to glance at the two servants kneeling in the pavilion with them. Letting out a sigh of his own, Devin flicked his fingers. "Leave us, and permit no other disturbances until we summon you."

Rising, the two men bowed to each of them in turn and left the pavilion. Gabria waited for a long, slow count to twenty, to make sure they were gone, then spent a few moments more, ordering her thoughts. She was stuck in this situation. Her willingness to be this "vessel of motherhood" *would* have repercussions for her people, ones which corresponded to whether she reacted in a positive or a negative way. But she didn't have to like it, and she didn't have to keep silent about it.

"You have to understand one very important thing, Devin," Gabria told him, looking him in the eyes. "Your God—the very *thought* of your God—terrifies me. The thought of being *noticed* by your deity makes me want to panic and . . . and run as far and as fast as I can possibly flee. The only thing that kept me from running away when I met Him—you—in that chapel was the fact that my fear *paralyzed* me. And the thought of having His attention focused on *me* for the rest of my life, constantly looking at me . . . !"

"Technically, only for as long as I am the Seer King," Devin corrected her. "Once one of our sons is selected and gifted with the Eyes of Ruul, I will become a mere Seer priest, as my father did before me, and his father. At that point, you and I will retire to a quieter life at one of the temple complexes scattered through the land. He would no longer look upon you directly through my eyes, and only occasionally look at you through the eyes of our child.

"I do understand that your people had reason to fear your last deity. The rumors of what Mekha did to the mages in your land were horrible. But even we knew He was generous to His engineers. All of His ambitions centered around your creations. As you yourself said you were one—"

"—I'm a *mage*, not just an engineer," Gabria interrupted bluntly, her voice as tight as the fists her fingers had curled into, resting on the edge of the table between them. The word *mage* wasn't easy to say, but she knew she had to explain. He stared at her. "My father *died* in one of Mekha's hellholes, the living magic sucked out of his body all because a *God* looked at him. You'll excuse me if I have *reason* to fear a similar fate."

". . . I'm sorry." The sober look in his eyes told her he meant it.

"I'm sorry for your pain and for your loss. Your Patron Deity should have been destroyed long ago."

Gabria relented a little, softening her tone to one of quiet resignation. These pains were embedded in the immutable past, after all. "Mekha was no Patron. A plague, but no Patron . . . but we were so tightly ruled by fear and by habit, we were paralyzed. Generation after generation. As much by our own fault as by His greed, in a way. But up until the last two and a half years . . .

"When I was seven, my father was taken from us, and my mother had to smuggle my sisters and me out of our hometown and run away, hiding by day and traveling by night, then sneak us into a faraway town where we could take on new identities and evade the priests who would want to study my sisters and me for any signs of mage-taint in our lives. Between the age of eleven and twenty-three, I lived in fear of my own developing abilities being discovered. Luckily, my mother already knew the Hydraulics Guild was one of the guilds which had ways to hide, disguise, and somewhat train the abilities of those mages born to its members. And other mages did their best to help her disguise the trail of our escape.

"The only thing we couldn't do was flee across the border. Mekha's priests watched the borderlands so closely, only a highly trained mage could pass through them undetected. None of us were that well trained. Not without entering the priesthood . . . and I would rather have slit my wrists," she muttered grimly. Lifting her water glass, she sipped from it, then set it down. "So I have a very deep-rooted set of reasons to fear the attention of a God. Even a foreign one. I *thought* I was asked to come here to be an envoy, an ambassador. Had I known the real reason . . . I wouldn't have come—not to slight you, since you do seem nice, but . . ."

"But I do come with a God attached," he finished for her, sipping at his own cup. He lingered over his wine for a moment, then set it back down. "I cannot change who and what I am, just as you cannot change yourself or your own past. All either of us can do is go forward. And while I can reassure you that Ruul would never abuse you in such a manner . . . I am not foolish enough to believe you will accept either of our word on the matter. All I can ask is that you give us time to prove we are worth your trust and can earn your trust. And I pledge to you, Gabria, if Ruul ever demanded something of you which made you wish to leave, I would fight Him on it.

"I am *not* a puppet of my deity," he told her, his gaze somber, earnest. "For the most part, yes, I am His vessel. But I am still a man, and I still have free will . . . and I *have* been known to exercise it. The proof of it lies in these next six days. Now that you have been Accepted, Ruul will not lay His Eyes upon me again until the seventh day, when I resume my duties as His Seer and high priest. Until then, it will be just you and me. And I'm afraid I'm not very frightening, when I'm just being myself," he added wryly. "I don't even know how to be, and I'm not all that inclined to try."

As far as jests went, it wasn't much. But it did provoke a small smile from her. He smiled back and reached for one of the odd meat-curls. Hesitating, he gestured at them.

"Aren't you going to have a crayfish?"

"A what?" Gabria asked.

"*Crayfish*," he repeated, picking up one of the peach white curls. "This is the tail meat of the crayfish. I'm told it's like a miniature lobster, but those are found in the ocean, and these live in freshwater, in lakes and streams."

"I have no idea what either of those things are like," Gabria confessed. She hesitated, then reached for one. It was cold, slightly spongy, but otherwise tender feeling. The smell was fishlike and the taste mild when she bit cautiously into it. It was also both chewy and tender. Nodding slowly, she finished chewing and swallowed. "Not bad . . ."

"Try some of the *aliolaise*, the garlic-spiced cream sauce, for dipping," Devin instructed her, licking the sauce from his own fingers. "It's also good on the *pasta*," he added, gesturing at the spiral-pastry dish. "They're a type of food that comes all the way from Natallia, which is a land that lies far to the south. One of the advantages of royalty is that I get to sample all manner of exotic foods—I even have some of the new holy-food, *chocolate*, imported all the way from the Isle of Nightfall. That's the land that reconvened the Convocation of the Gods."

"Trust me, Devin, there's not a single person in all of what used to be Mekhana who doesn't know about that Convocation," Gabria retorted wryly, dipping the last bit of tail meat into the sauce bowl. "It's what set us free. That, and the work of Sir Orana. I never met her personally, but I pricked my thumb and signed my guild's petition book as soon as I was old enough to be trusted with the secret of its existence. I haven't had any of this *chocolate* food, though. Not even Marta has had any yet—she's our equivalent of a queen."

"Yes, your Consul-in-Chief, whom I am told was chosen for her position by your Goddess. Somewhat like I was . . . save that I have fewer administrative duties, and a lot more of the religious ones," he amended.

"I wasn't there. A lot of us from the guild . . . the Mage's Guild," she made herself explain, "didn't attend the assembly to petition for the selection of our leader. A lot of us still have trouble saying 'mage' since it often led to discovery and a slow death sentence, before. At the very least, calling someone that threatened them with a lot of very uncomfortable scrutiny by the priesthood."

"On the bright side, you're in Aurul, now," Devin reminded her. "We have a long history of a gentle, kind, and watchful Patron Deity, one who clearly cares about His people. I have confidence you will learn to accept and trust Him as much as the rest of us do, given enough time."

"Six days *isn't* 'enough time' by my reckoning," Gabria stated dryly. She smiled wryly when he gave her a chiding look. ". . . I'll *try*. If nothing else, for the sake of Guildara, and how your people will perceive mine whenever they interact with me. So . . . what shall we talk about next?"

"I don't know . . . what does a Hydraulics Guild do?" he asked, shrugging as he offered it for a topic. "The guilds we have are for ordinary things, metalworking, cloth making, that sort of thing."

"Hydraulics deals with the regulation and flow of liquids. Originally it referred to water, but it has come to mean oils and other fluids as well," she explained, warming to the topic. "Water pressure can do amazing things. The most common use, even outside of former Mekhana, is the use of streams to turn mill wheels, which grind grain into flour. We also use them for powering many other things, such as the bellows for our forges, and pumps which increase the pressure of the water. Forced through a nozzle, it can be used to erode dirt and soft stones, and clean difficult substances from surfaces without badly scratching anything, unlike chisels or sanding stones . . ."

They talked and nibbled and drank until the sun set, and then talked and nibbled some more as the evening sky darkened and the stars came out. Spells scribed on the various dishes kept the iced ones cold and the heated ones hot, and when she needed to use the refreshing room, he escorted her to the nearest one, set in a corner of the garden, then guided her back through the garden paths to the pavilion where they resumed their wide-ranging conversation.

Gabria stuck to water, since even her poorly trained people knew it was bad for a mage to get drunk and potentially lose control of their powers. Devin summoned the servants back with the jingling of a delicate porcelain bell, and they cleared away emptied dishes and served her fruit juice at her request, wanting something unfermented. They also lit lanterns in clever paper-sided shelters, most of them glowing a translucent white but some of them dyed in pastel shades. Similar lights sprung up all over the gardens, making it seem like a scene out of some fantastical bard's tale to her.

Tired despite the remarkably good discussion they were having about possible trade products between their lands—she wasn't officially an envoy, but she could discuss trade goods with a reasonable amount of authority—Gabria couldn't quite suppress her yawns. It wasn't that late an hour, but her day had been exhausting. The sheer wealth of this land, the care and artistry implicit in this palace and all of its decorations, the bright clothes and willing, deferential service of its denizens, all of it added their own extra layers to an already complex, overwhelming day.

As she yawned for a fourth time, Devin lifted one brow. "Tired already? I know, I shouldn't be surprised. You've had a number of upheavals. Come," he murmured, uncurling his tall body from the cushions strewn over the floor. "We will retire for the night. My own day has been relatively light, but I could use the rest."

Crossing to her side of the low table, he offered her his hand. Accepting it, Gabria let him draw her to her feet, only to find her hand saluted with another kiss.

"Thank you for not running away from *me*," he murmured, his eyes gleaming with humor in the pastel glow of the lanterns lighting the pavilion. "Though at least now I understand why you'd run away from my God."

"I'm still holding that as an option," she muttered back, feeling comfortable enough—daring enough—to tease him back. Somewhat tease. Part of her words were the truth.

Another yawn threatened to crack her jaw in half. Smothering it behind her free hand, she let him tuck her hand into the crook of his elbow and lead her through the garden to the palace. Inside, the candle lanterns extended all the way to the royal wing. The few people they passed turned and bowed politely, but though their eyes held many questions, their lips remained sealed. As they passed the third such set of courtiers, Gabria heard Devin sigh happily, and looked up at him, giving him a questioning look.

He smiled beatifically. "They're ignoring me . . ."

His muttered explanation made her want to laugh. Biting it down into a smile, Gabria let him lead her back into the Royal Retreat.

Here, the flickering, paper-shrouded candles gave way to expensive, rare mage-globes, magical light sources which Sir Catrine had told her about. Master Souder was waiting for them in the massive, ornate front parlor. He rose from the settee he had been occupying, loupe-stick dangling at a careless angle from his hand.

"Your Majesty," he greeted Devin, bowing. He added a second bow toward Gabria. "Your Highness. Regarding your schedule tomorrow morning, I was thinking—"

"—Three Days of Grace?" Devin interrupted, his tone mostly light. "Followed by Three Days of Intimacy? As in, *privacy*?"

Heaving a sigh, the Master of the Royal Retreat tucked his loupe into one of his square-dangling pocket sleeves. "As you wish, Your Majesty."

"Yes, I do wish. Her Highness and I have had a long day. We will retire, now," Devin said.

Bowing, the Master of the Royal Retreat hurried ahead of them to the royal bedchamber. They could hear him clapping his hands and issuing a set of orders. Devin guided the pair of them toward the same hall, passing a couple of purple-and-gold-clad Royal Guards standing duty at the entrance to the corridor.

Gabria wrinkled her nose at the sight of the armored man and woman. "Are there always people about?"

"Usually, yes. Servants to attend to my every need, guards to defend me against any enemies, witnesses to any prophecies I may spout—all the servants and the Royal Guards carry spell-shrunk slates and chalk-sticks in their sleeves or tablets and pencils in pouches on their belts to help them record anything I may say when the Eyes are upon me," Devin revealed, strolling with her toward the bedroom. "If it isn't servants, it's bureaucrats with kingdom business which my brother has sent to me for approval, and if it isn't those, it's courtiers currying favor, or citizens seeking prophesies. The Royal Guard are always somewhere around, of course, though they do try to be discreet about it."

They entered the bedchamber, with its gilded bed and equally ornate furnishings. He led her not to the bed but to the dressing room, where three maidservants and two menservants separated the two of them. Gabria, unused to being helped out of her clothes, eyed the silently working women. Too silent, in her opinion.

"Um . . . you ladies *can* talk, yes?" she asked.

The one peeling back the inner layer of jacket-thing from her shoulders looked up with a grin. "Yes, Your Highness, we *can* talk. We just . . . have nothing to say at this point in time."

"Ah. That makes sense, I suppose." Gabria quickly glanced over her shoulder at the men. Neither Devin nor his two servants were paying her state of undress any heed. She blushed when the maids unlaced the corset and slipped it from her ribs, but they replaced it with a thigh-length tunic in a matter of moments. An expensive, luxurious tunic made from soft, imported cotton.

They also removed her gathered trousers and underdrawers. Those, too, were replaced with more cotton, this time a pair of drawstring-waisted trousers not too different from the pants she wore as a Guildaran. She was then ushered toward a door that turned out to be a refreshing room. Her tooth scrubber had been unpacked and laid on the counter. Given a moment of privacy, Gabria took advantage of the refresher, then washed her hands and lifted the scrubber to her teeth. And stared at her reflection.

What a very, very strange day, she thought, eyeing her image. *I don't* look *any different, aside from the clothes and the flowers in my hair . . . but I've faced a God and survived with my powers intact. I've been married against my wit and my wishes . . . but not entirely against my will. And I've had a rich and varied conversation with a near-complete stranger, talking until my voice was almost hoarse, and listening with equal pleasure until his was just as worn.*

A very, very *strange day . . .*

Scrubbing her teeth, she rinsed and set the slender implement aside to dry. Devin took her place in the refreshing room as soon as she emerged. Seeing no maids in the dressing room, Gabria hurried out to the bedchamber, where the maids were busy turning down the covers on the bed. They finished and started to leave, and she hastily spoke up.

"Um, haven't you forgotten something?"

The same maid who had spoken turned politely to face her. "Yes, Your Highness?"

"My hair?" Gabria reminded the cream-gowned woman. She gestured at her flower-woven plait. "Aren't you going to undo it?"

The dark-haired woman smiled. "No, Your Highness. Your flowers stay until His Majesty removes them himself . . . which he will most likely do when the Three Days of Grace have ended. Do not worry; the blooms are enchanted against fading or being crushed, and to keep the plaiting from being mussed." Her smile deepened. "When I got married, my husband waited barely two days before unbinding my hair . . . but then we'd known each other for three years, and knew our minds well regarding each other."

Bowing one last time, she retreated, following the others out of the room. Gabria blinked, mulling that over. *They wait to remove the flowers until the hour they become intimate? Gods . . . is* that *where the meaning of "deflowering a woman" came from? Literally, from removing her flowers?*

The thought was an amusing one. Turning back to the bed, she saw the menservants leaving the dressing room. Both bowed to her, not quite looking at her directly, and left the bedchamber. The last one quietly closed the heavily carved door behind himself. Another yawn snuck up on her.

Time to go to sleep, she thought, smothering it in her palm. Climbing into the bed—it was huge, fitted easily for three or four people of Devin's size, and fitted with soft, fine linen sheets that crinkled faintly under her weight—she pulled the covers up to her shoulders.

The dressing room lights went out. Devin emerged from the dressing room after another moment. He detoured around the room, double-rapping the moon white globes in their wrought-iron wall sconces, extinguishing the magical Artifacts until only the one centered over the head of the bed remained lit. Climbing in beside her, he adjusted the covers over his frame, which had been clothed in a cotton tunic-and-trouser set similar to her own.

"Are you ready to sleep?" he asked, reaching up toward the globe.

She blushed, realizing he had literally meant it when he said they'd sleep together. Which brought up a host of other expectations. Digging up some courage, she admitted, "I've never done this before. Slept with anyone, I mean. Or married anyone, for that matter, or . . ."

He chuckled. "I'm told I don't snore, so it should be fairly easy."

Double-tapping the globe, he plunged them into darkness. Faint light from the gardens could be seen through the lattice-sheltered windows, but it would take them a while for their eyes to adjust, she knew. Of course, the irony of the situation was . . .

". . . Lovely," she muttered, voicing her realization aloud. "Now I'm not the least bit tired!"

Devin's laughter rang through the darkness. Reaching over, he found her hand under the covers and squeezed her fingers. "I'm not sleepy, either, but I think for a different reason than your not having slept with anyone before."

"Oh?" Gabria asked, curious.

"You are a very lovely woman."

Her face grew warm at the compliment.

"And, um . . ." He shifted on the bed a little but didn't move closer to her. "I haven't been with anyone since your image was revealed to me. So . . . it's been a few months."

Gabria wasn't ignorant of physical needs, male as well as female. Until the False God had been cast down, her people had only had access to a certain potion to prevent conception, a potion which wasn't always reliable. She knew that other realms had more reliable, spell-based means. It meant adults could enjoy each other's company without worry or regret for long-lasting consequences. For herself, she hadn't actually been with a man, yet. At least, not all the way.

Marta and her other female friends had described it, and discussed men's needs, which seemed to rise with greater frequency than women's. Considering hers tended to rise three or four times a week, Gabria had once quipped that she felt sorry for men. Women, after all, had clever little mechanical devices like the crankman, which was still sitting openly on one of the dressing room shelves. Machinery couldn't replicate the female counterpart to a phallus, so men were left with fewer options for sating their needs.

She hesitated over one of those options. He squirmed a little more, adjusting his position, but didn't let go of her hand. Gabria listened to the silence stretching between them, until she couldn't bear it anymore.

"If you need a hand—" she said, just as he said: "I shouldn't have mentioned that—" Both of them broke off, then she felt him twisting to face her. "You . . . ah . . . what?"

Glad the darkness hid what were surely bright red cheeks, Gabria explained. "It's, um, not unknown in Guildara for a gentleman to get . . . yes. And it's equally not unknown for a lady friend to, well, lend a hand . . ."

He flopped onto his back, not quite stifling a groan. "You shouldn't tempt me like that!" Devin chided softly. "The sooner we move on to the Three Days of Intimacy, the sooner I have to go back to being a Seer! You are *very* lovely, but these days are my chance to fully and wholly be myself. Something I won't know until the next Seer King is chosen."

She mulled over that. As much as she tried to understand, Gabria couldn't quite get past both his admission and her own background. "If you have free will . . . why do you do it? Why do you let Him take over your life, and your eyes?"

A soft sound that wasn't a laugh escaped him. "I think I've left you with the wrong impression. Being blessed with the Eyes of Ruul isn't a *bad* thing. Not in the least. He is very much a part of me. My closest friend, my confidant, my . . . my *God.* When I give myself to His presence . . . it is as blissful as making love. Only without the sex, of course."

"Of course," she murmured, not quite but sort of understanding.

"Actually, the sex *with* Him is incredible," Devin muttered in an aside. He must have felt her start, for he chuckled. "Not with *Him*, of course, but . . . with Him *inside* of me, when we make love to a woman together. And judging by *her* reaction . . . it's equally incredible for the woman."

"Ah . . . I'm *not* comfortable with that idea," Gabria confessed, staring up at the darkness of the ceiling. Her eyes had adjusted somewhat to the gloom, but she couldn't make out the carved arches overhead. Instead, she imagined those gold eyes seeing her naked, and . . . she shuddered. Thankfully, the man at her side didn't take offense.

"Given the history of your own people, I think I can understand why. But He doesn't ever force Himself on anyone, Gabria. Not even me. He doesn't *take*. He watches, and gives, and I give freely in return," Devin stated quietly. A yawn followed his words, and he squeezed her fingers. ". . . Mmm. You will come to trust Him in time. And, I hope, myself as well."

"Well, I don't fear you," Gabria admitted, squeezing back. She stifled a yawn of her own. "In fact, you're rather nice, and I've really enjoyed talking with you. I just . . . It'll take me a while to get used to all of this."

"Mmm, yes . . ."

He sounded sleepy, and within a few more moments, she was fairly sure Devin had fallen asleep. Gabria stayed awake for a little while more, contemplating the wild turn of events that had led her to this place, and this bed. Gradually, her tiredness from earlier caught up with her, and she slipped away herself.

FOUR

Someone was in her bed. That thought snapped her eyes open, banishing her normal, gradual waking patterns in a rush of alarmed adrenaline. Finding another body actually *in* her bed, evident in the cotton tunic, neckline gaping enough to show a tanned, masculine chest lightly dusted with dark hairs, propelled her back with a shriek. "*Aah!*"

She almost fell off the bed, half tangled in the covers, before she realized *who* was in her bed. A bemused, amused Devin, one eyebrow and the other corner of his mouth quirked upward. Scrabbling for balance, and composure, Gabria stared and panted. Memory of yesterday flooded her head. His God, their marriage, and her presence in his bed. Untouched, rested—save for the pounding of her heart, though that was gradually subsiding—and still wearing flowers braided into her hair. Both of them clad in soft cotton nightclothes.

Gabria expected him to react to her brief display of nerves, to say something reassuring about his intentions, to . . . to do *something*.

Shifting his face so that it rested on his uplifted palm, the Seer King of Aurul simply said, "Good morning."

"Uh . . . good morning," she returned as politely as she could manage. Levering herself upright, she scooted a little more fully onto the bed. Once the pillows at her back somewhat supported her, she curled up her legs under the bedding and scrubbed her face. Now that she wasn't being alarmed by the presence of a stranger in her bed, she could feel the dregs of sleep saturating her brain. Not that the man at her side wasn't still a stranger in many ways, though she had learned quite a lot about his interests and opinions yesterday.

"Did you sleep well enough?" Devin asked her.

"Better than I'd thought, given the, ah . . . I'm just not used to anyone being in the room with me," she explained, apologizing. "I'm sorry for the way I reacted. I haven't shared a bed since my sisters and I were little, and I wasn't expecting anyone to be there."

He smirked. "Well, I wouldn't mind making you scream a second time, if it were a scream of *pleasure*."

Eyes widening, Gabria gaped at him. He grinned back. Grabbing a pillow, she whapped him with it. Laughing, Devin blocked it with his arms, shielding his head, then snatched it from her grasp and tossed it aside. Thrown off balance, Gabria fell over him. His humor faded, replaced by a look of wonder. With a soft murmur, one too quiet for her to hear any actual words, he pulled her down into a kiss. A warm, hungry kiss.

One which ended abruptly just as she was really beginning to enjoy it. Pushing her off, Devin shoved to his feet with an odd exclamation. "—Breakfast!"

Taken aback, lips tender and aching for more, Gabria stared at him. Or rather, at his back. He faced away from her, hands on his hips and head bowed. "Breakfast?" she asked, confused. "You want breakfast?"

"I think it is *safer* for us to have breakfast, now." Turning so that he was in profile to her, he glanced down. Pointedly. Then, just as pointedly, he looked at the bed.

On the bed was a single miniature rose, intact from petals to stem. Gabria quickly lifted her hand to her hair. It *felt* intact, as neatly arranged as it had been the day before, but where the ribbon tying off the braid had been a finger-length from the end, it had shifted a bit higher along her waist-length plait. Now two finger-lengths of it hung free below the knotted ribbon. Glancing up at his body, she saw the peaked front of his sleeping trousers and blushed. "Ah. Yes. Breakfast."

He offered her his hand. Rising, Gabria rounded the end of the bed and accepted it. This time, when their fingers touched, she was very aware of his masculinity. Not just his arousal, but the strength beneath his gentleness. He escorted her into the front room, where she saw a small table being loaded with covered, rune-etched dishes fetched from a wheeled cart by a trio of servants.

Gabria hung back at that. "Devin," she whispered, tugging on his hand so that he leaned over, bringing his ear close to her lips. "*How* did they know we were ready for breakfast?"

He shrugged blithely. "They were probably listening at the door."

This is not *my culture*, she thought, dismayed by his acceptance of such a lack of privacy. Settling herself at the breakfast table, she found herself further disturbed by the approach of Master Souder. Today, he was clad in shades of green and gold, his long brown hair plaited into three braids, which were in turn twined together.

"Good morning, Your Majesty, Your Highness," he saluted them, bowing to each in turn. The servants quietly removed the covers of the dishes and poured fruit juice into their goblets, deftly working around him. "Today's schedule allows for an hour of exercise in the salle with the Royal Armsmaster, two hours in the baths to help correct Her Highness' skin problems, a double *palanquin* ride down to the eastern shore, and a leisurely lunch on the beach."

"Excuse me?" Gabria interrupted, brows rising. "*Skin problems?* My skin is *quite* clear, and I haven't suffered from spots since I was a child!"

Souder bowed. "I refer not to any oiliness of your complexion, Your Highness, which is as clear as the sky, but rather to the dryness of it. The maids will be careful not to disturb your hair, of course, but you will need several herbal scrubs and a good soak in milk baths for at least a week. We didn't bother with pumicing away the calluses on your hands and feet yesterday, being somewhat pressed for time, nor did we do anything about the dreadfully short state of your nails, but today—"

"—I think *not*," Gabria countered firmly. His brows lifted, then lowered again when she met and held his gaze. She lifted her hands. "These calluses are a part of me. They are proof that I am a real person. That I make an honest wage with honest work. That I am *not* some . . . some pampered palace pet! Furthermore, I bathe to be *clean*. Not to 'fix' some imaginary problem with my face. I trim my nails so they will not snag nor get in my way. I dress so that I can move freely and be comfortable. *Not* to be gilded like a . . . a sculpture, or a painting! And I *will not* waste two hours of my life wrinkling my body in a puddle of milk! If milk is to do my body any good, it will do so when I *drink* it!"

The two men in the purple-edged robes of the palace staff eyed each other, then unctuously flowed into action. One fetched a pitcher and a fresh glass from the cart, the other plucked her juice-filled cup from the table. Within seconds, she had a crystal goblet bearing fresh white liquid in its place.

Gabria bit her tongue to keep from laughing at the absurdity of it. And it didn't help that from the gleam of humor in his brown eyes, Devin was also struggling against the urge to laugh. Still, they meant well, and she did like milk. Nodding her head politely, she said, "Thank you. I'm sure it will taste lovely."

A glance at Souder found him smiling, a rather odd reaction to her tirade. Not that she went off on a tirade very often, but this was such a strange culture, and her presence in it still such a shock, the only thing she could think to do about it was establish certain boundaries. If nothing else, for her own comfort while she adjusted to all these changes in her life.

"What would *you* like to do today?" Devin asked her before the Master of the Royal Retreat could speak.

"Well . . . I wouldn't mind exploring the palace," Gabria admitted. "All the carvings and the inlay work, and the paintings . . . they're incredibly beautiful. And I wouldn't mind seeing the gardens, and maybe some of the countryside, too." She glanced at Souder, who was back to looking like he didn't enjoy having his schedule disrupted. "Though that lunch on the beach does sound lovely."

"Then we'll explore the countryside, have lunch on the beach, then retire to roam through the shade of the palace as the afternoon heat rises," Devin stated, picking up his utensils. "Souder, please instruct Captain Ellett to prepare an escort, and the stables to ready my horse—do you ride?"

Gabria lifted her brows. "A real horse? No. I never learned. The only kind I know how to ride is a motorhorse, but I doubt you have any of those here."

"Then you'll ride with me. Behind me," he added, looking briefly but pointedly at the flowers in her hair. He started to cut into his food, then eyed her in curiosity. ". . . What exactly is a 'motorhorse' anyway?"

Chuckling, Gabria sipped from her goblet of milk—which was indeed tasty—and launched into an enthusiastic, if simplified, explanation of Guildaran-style transportation.

"I really am sorry about that," Devin apologized for what had to be the fourth time. He followed her into the dressing room of their suite. "It was just supposed to be a simple dinner with my brother and his family, but these pirates keep attacking our ships, and . . ."

"It's alright, truly," Gabria reassured him, smiling wryly. She twisted around and started unknotting the sash holding the open folds of her floor-length jackets in place. "I *do* understand. My best friend is the Consul-in-Chief, back home. We've had more than one meal interrupted by kingdom business. And I can't blame your . . . what did you call her? Her title?"

"Admiral, and it's a rank. Like Captain, only higher, and pertaining to the sea instead of the land," Devin explained, seating himself on the silk-padded bench in the center of the dressing room. Servants entered the room, trailing in their wake.

"I can't blame your Admiral Arrevi for wanting some sort of prognostication on how to deal with them in the near future—no, thank you," Gabria added as the maidservants started to remove her sash for her. "*No*, thank you," she repeated as they pulled on the sash anyway. "I am quite capable of undressing myself—you can fold my things up neatly, if you must have something to do. I can tell you have some special sort of way for folding all these lovely clothes, and I haven't a clue where to begin. Devin, you say these pirates are mostly based in some city among the islands?"

"Jetta Freeport, on the largest of the Jenodan Isles. It's a fortified city, but a barbaric one—they've refused to be claimed by any of the kingdoms surrounding the sea, yet they also refuse to turn civilized and gain a Patron Deity," he told her, standing so that his menservants could remove a few layers of his own sashed garments.

"I'm not ready to retire yet," Gabria murmured. "Could I have a riding jacket to wear, like the short one I wore earlier?"

"It's called an *eta*, Highness," one of the maids replied, giving her a soft smile. "The long-coat is an *etama*, the long-coat with the sash of nobility is an *etamana*. The *eta* . . . it is a commoner garment. It is only worn by the nobility for riding because the long hemline is awkward for riding, and the longer sleeves can sometimes startle the horses."

"Well, then that will suit me just fine." She waited for an *eta* to be fetched from the shelves, since while her corset and trousers were decent enough, there were other men in the room, still.

The woman blinked, her smile faltering. "But . . . you are a princess. You must appear as your station requires."

After a lengthy afternoon tour of the palace, replete with impromptu history lessons, Gabria was beginning to learn that visual presentation was important to these people. Glancing at her husband showed him being eased into a plain, golden silk *etama* with sleeves that . . . yes . . . still reached below his knees, even if they didn't wrap a fancy sash several times around his chest. He did have a short, simple one that knotted in place around his waist, but that was it.

"Look . . . your Patron is the God of Vision, right? And His Eyes see everything? Well, then, I am quite sure His Eyes can see way down into my soul, and thus He—and by extension, everyone else—does not need to see me, in the privacy of my own chambers, prancing around like a princess." They didn't *feel* like her chambers yet, but they were as close as she was going to get, and Gabria didn't want to endlessly argue the semantics. "Short *eta* jacket, please."

The two maids attending her exchanged looks, then the older one rolled her eyes and fetched a jacket from the shelves. A short, thigh-length jacket with thigh-length sleeve pockets, in the same golden-dyed shade of silk as Devin's garment. She let them help her into it, then took the short sash and knotted it with her own hands. To her relief, Devin fluttered his fingers, silently dismissing the women as well as his own menservants.

He also looked mildly amused as he stepped around the bench.

"You will send my people into fits of offense, if you keep insisting upon your foreign ideals and foreign ways." One of his fingers stopped her defensive protest before she could start. "You do have a right to be yourself to an extent, but try to remember that my people are not from a brand-new kingdom, struggling hard to throw off the old customs of the old land. Our ways have been fully developed by now, and we like them this way."

Stepping back, she bumped into the shelves holding her goods, but it did free her lips. "Well, I wouldn't want to offend out in the rest of the palace, and I'll try to comply, but *here*, this is supposed to be a private place. At least, by my standards and my culture. Try to understand that *my* ways are not *your* ways, and that to ignore and trample over them is equally disrespectful. Which is what I suspect those so-called pirates are feeling."

Devin blinked and frowned. "What do you mean?"

Leaning back against the shelves, Gabria folded her arms over her chest. She half tangled them on the sleeves as she did so, before managing to get them pushed up so that the position was comfortable. "I mean, I listened to Admiral Arrevi when she kindly explained to me the previous attacks on the other Aurulan merchant ships. They claimed to have had a free-merchant ship boarded and stripped—*robbed*—and when they brought their complaints to the nearest Aurulan port authority, those complaints were ignored.

"Simply because their ways and methods are foreign, you treat them like those ways and methods are worthless. Simply because my values and customs are different does *not* mean they are worthless. Just because I am a commoner by birth does not mean I have no value. I *do* have value," she asserted, touching her chest, then flicking her hand out as she continued. "And just because these so-called pirates have no Patron Deity does not mean they have no rights. They *do*. Arrevi said the city's been an unaffiliated freeport for over four hundred years—do you realize that's almost as long as Aurul has been a kingdom? If they've managed to last *that* long as a cohesive identity, the Freeport of Jetta, then clearly they have a system that works, and works very well. For *them*.

"It is *valid*. For *them*. And if you wish to gain their attention and find a way to stop them from retaliating against your ships, then you need to respect *them*. Open your eyes to *more* than just what you see on the surface," she added quietly, if tartly. "It is said that the Gods can see into the hearts of mortal men. Not just look at their faces. My ways are different, but they have value, and they work for *me*. I may think the length of your sleeves is a bit ridiculous by my standards—for all that I think the fabric is lovely—but I won't deny you the right to wear them. Because they work for *you*. More than that, I will not disrespect you if you choose to wear these *etamana* garments, or something else. *You* are the person I respect. Not your clothes."

He studied her with a thoughtful look, his brow softly pinched. "I think I finally see what Ruul Sees in you. A certain . . . common," he teased softly, lingering on the word, "sense reminiscent of my late grandmother. May she rest in the arms of the Gods."

"May she rest, indeed," Gabria murmured in reply. At least that much of their two nations' customs was similar. "Look, if you want to make progress in your dealings with these free-merchants, try treating them as if they were citizens of a nation."

"But they don't have a Patron Deity!" he reminded her, spreading his arms. He glanced down quickly to either side, then sighed roughly. He lowered his arms to his sides. ". . . Now you have me wondering if I look silly when I do something like that."

"You look graceful, but then you're used to the way those things move." Gabria lifted her own arms and flapped them. "*I* feel like a molting chicken, and probably look like one, too."

He chuckled and leaned in close enough to press a kiss to the tip of her nose. "A prettier molting chicken has never been seen."

The playful compliment made her blush. He pulled back before the kiss became anything more and changed the subject. Lifting his chin at the shelves of her Guildaran goods, he asked, "So, are any of these . . . things . . . some of the objects you told me about, this morning?"

Pushing away from the shelves, she turned to face them. Right in front of her sat her crankman, its steely spiral and curved handle making her blush. Clearing her throat, she moved to the side and picked up one of her less volatile belongings, a bucket-shaped object with an inner metal bin and a handle of its own at the top.

"This is an iced-cream maker. It was one of my projects as an apprentice engineer. Hydraulics concerns the movement of fluids, and that included writing a paper on churning sweetened, flavored cream as it freezes.

"You put your ingredients in the middle and chunks of ice in the outer section, and pour salt over them, which lowers the freezing temperature and keeps it cold long enough to freeze the cream," she told him, cranking the handle and moving the paddles inside the inner bucket. "But you have to keep it moving so it forms very small crystals, which makes it taste smooth and uniform in flavor. It's a dessert, a big favorite in the summertime. Obviously we couldn't use . . . you know, magic, to freeze the confection. I still use it, even if I do speed up the process a little with a spell or two these days."

"And all those balls of yarn?" he asked, looking up at the skeins of wool.

"Those are for knitting. *Everyone* knits in Guildara. Or crochets," she allowed, putting the machine back. At his blank look, Gabria moved over to one of her tunics, touching the soft gray wool. "See this? I knitted it myself. Knitting is done with long needles, and crocheting with a special hook. I can do both. I can even teach you, if you want to learn. It's very soothing—it gives the hands something to do while relaxing the mind, and a lot of people like to sit and chat while they knit in the evenings. Unless you're trying for a complicated pattern, of course, then it's best to pay attention."

"What about this thing?" Devin asked as she smoothed a wrinkle from the tunic. Glancing over, she caught sight of the silvery shaft in his hand and flushed, face and body growing hot with embarrassment. He lifted one of his brows in return. "I'm very good at observing things . . . and I've observed that every time you look at this thing, you blush. Now, why would that be?"

"It's . . . it's personal!" Flustered, Gabria grabbed for it, but he lifted it out of her reach. Since he was a full head taller than her, that lifted the crankman well out of her reach. She tried jumping for it, but that just bumped their bodies together, making him grin and wrap his other arm around her waist. "Devin! Give that back!"

"Not until you tell me what you do with it," he countered, smirking.

Embarrassed and unwilling to share something so very, very personal just yet, Gabria screwed up her mouth and spat out a word. "*Ziggit!*" The crankman jerked out of his fingers and slapped into her upturned palm. Angry that he'd made her do that, she poked him with it. "*Don't* make me use my magic again!"

Then she blushed even harder when she realized what she was doing. Turning in his arms, Gabria moved to place it back on the shelf. He grabbed for it, which meant she had to fumble to keep it in her grip—and accidentally thumbed the switch. There probably wasn't much of a crank-charge left in the workings from its last use, but it promptly buzzed to life anyway, rattling vigorously in her hand.

She was too mortified to retain a firm grip on the shaft. Plucking it from her fingers, Devin released her so that he could examine the throbbing, vaguely phallic device. "What . . . ? Ohhh. *Fascinating*. So that's why you're blushing. *That's* what it's for."

"Oh, Gods," Gabria muttered, burying her face in her palms. Unfortunately, no deity was kind enough to open up the floor and swallow her into the ground, not even a demonic one from a Netherhell. Instead, she felt him turn her around by her elbow and found herself backed up against the shelves once again. Summoning her courage, she lowered her fingers just far enough to peek at him over their tips. He was eyeing the buzzing device with a distinct look of cunning calculation. Masculine calculation.

"The question is, where do you apply it?" he murmured. Lowering it to the curve of one breast, he rubbed the buzzing tip against her silk-clad flesh. "Here?"

She *had* applied it there, in the past. But always by herself, in private. Now she knew why some of her fellow females had giggled and insisted that letting their men know of their crankman's existence hadn't turned out to be such an embarrassing thing. Pinned by his gleaming brown eyes, knowing she wasn't the one controlling it, circling it around and around her increasingly tight nipple, was incredibly arousing.

When she didn't say anything, just swallowed and breathed heavily, he smiled and trailed the buzzing tip over to her other breast. He didn't tease that one for long, however. Just enough to make her bite her lower lip, before shifting it down her abdomen. The short folds of her *eta* jacket did nothing to stop him from sliding it between her silk-covered thighs, where the vibrations combined with the intensity of his gaze, making her dizzy.

The clattering slowed down, faded, and stopped. *Thank the Gods*, she thought. Her mind sighed with relief, though her body whimpered with disappointment. Pulling the crankman back up into view, Devin frowned and shook it gingerly. "Ah . . . did I break it? I didn't *mean* to . . ."

His baffled concern brought a welcome touch of humor into the moment. Still blushing, though not quite as embarrassed, Gabria took the shaft from his unresisting fingers and pushed the switch. "You didn't break it. It just ran out of energy, is all."

Turning, she placed it firmly on the shelf. A soft sound and the feel of his fingers plucking something from her shoulder made her turn back around. He had a rose stem in his hand, and a wry look wrinkling his tanned face. "I suppose it's just as well. We *should* take one more day to get to know each other better. Especially after your little speech. Though I still don't see how it should apply to Godless pirates."

"They might not *be* Godless; have you considered that?" Gabria asked, grateful for the change in topic. "Look at Nightfall. They acknowledge no one particular God or Goddess as a specific Patron Deity, yet they're clearly not Godless. They permit the worship of *all* the known Gods. *And* they're prosperous. And I'm quite sure they're an even smaller nation than this Jetta place, if the city of Jetta has been around for four hundred years—learn to see them through *their* eyes, not your own, Seer King," she urged, nudging Devin out of the dressing room and back into their bedchamber. "Now, you promised me earlier how to play that one game . . . *tafl*, you said?"

"*Tafl*, yes. Something nice and cerebral," he muttered, guiding her over to the small table by one of the windows. "And not the least bit carnal."

"Or buzzing," Gabria found herself teasing. She blushed at her temerity, then grinned when *he* blushed. Not that it was easy to see on his naturally tan cheeks, but he did blush. Seating herself at the table, she settled in to listen to the instructions on how to play.

FIVE

"So," Devin murmured as soon as the door shut behind the last of their servants. His brown gaze swept down the length of her body, clad in a pale-green-and-silver *etamana* robe-and-sash set. "How many flowers have you lost, today?"

Gabria blushed, remembering their prolonged lunch in the fuchsia pavilion. A brief rainstorm had driven the servants farther away, giving them enough privacy to kiss and caress. When the shower had passed, they had struggled to smooth out the rumpled folds of their clothes, but it hadn't been easy. Nor could she exactly hide the stems that had fallen from her braid, or the way the ribbons now confined her ash blond hair only down to her nape, instead of a couple finger-lengths from the waist-long ends. "Three roses and an orchid. But . . . we did have our hands almost everywhere."

He smirked. "Hm. I shall have to do better than that. What sort of a husband am I, if you lost only four of your blossoms during lunch?"

Her brows lifted. "What kind of a *husband*?" She might have been a virgin to actual intercourse, but she wasn't entirely an innocent. Gabria lifted her chin a little, hands going to her hips. "If *your* hair were braided with flowers, maybe *I'd* have removed *five.*"

That made him laugh. Strolling across the distance between them, he grinned, teeth white against the tan of his lips and the dark line of his mustache. "You do realize that at least *two* of those flowers fell from your hair because of where *your* hands were located?"

Her face heated again, but Gabria didn't back down. "A pity I couldn't lose any more of them during dinner. But it was still a very good conversation. Mage-Captain Ellett is a good man. Very loyal to his king, and very knowledgeable about spells and such."

"And Lady Lianna?" Devin asked, stopping just sort of kissing distance.

"I don't think she likes me very much. Or at least, doesn't respect me, deep down," Gabria told him. "It's nothing I can pin down, just a subtle sort of attitude. I think probably because I'm an adult, yet I don't know as much as she and Captain Ellett know."

"Then we will find you teachers in the art of magic," Devin promised, cupping her upper arms in his palms. "Have you considered what you would like to do, as Royal Wife?"

Gabria blinked. ". . . Do?"

"Yes, do. The Royal Wife often takes up certain causes, using her station and influence to bring awareness to certain needs around the kingdom. My mother was and is a proponent of good agricultural practices, particularly when guarding against bad practices which could lead to erosion and floods—her parents died in a flood, so it was a cause close to her heart. My grandmother, who was an architect, insisted on preserving and upgrading our older public buildings, the temples and market shelters, town halls, and so forth. My great-grandmother focused her efforts on our textile industry, and my great-great-grandmother invested her energies in upgrading our roadways."

"Maybe I should invest my energies in education, then," Gabria quipped, slipping her hands around his waist. "Though I should also invest some effort in bringing Aurul and Guildara closer together. That's what I originally thought I was supposed to do, in coming here."

"You can still do that to some extent," Devin murmured, sliding his fingers along her arms, then around her back. "Though your envoy does a good job."

She snorted and leaned back, eyeing the Seer King in her arms. "You mean, now that you're deigning to *talk* with him?"

He chuckled. "We listened, every single time. When nothing important in his message changed, we knew both he and your fellow Guildarans were sincere."

As much as part of her knew this was a good opening for influencing his opinion further about her people . . . she couldn't bring herself to do it. "As much as I like talking with you about everything under the sun," Gabria stated, giving him an earnest look, "I don't think I'd care to mix politics with pleasure . . . and this *is* the end of the Three Days of Grace, isn't it? Shouldn't we be thinking of other things right now?"

He smiled and lowered his mouth to hers, murmuring, "It is, and I agree."

Gabria didn't argue. There really wasn't need for further debate, unless it was the kind shaped by lips and tongues, by palms and fingertips. Somewhere in there, she lost her sash, but then so did he. She also lost two or three blooms. Devin murmured something about the bed being a good place for this, so they disengaged long enough to retreat from the parlor.

After arguing that morning with her would-be dressers, she had only two layers of *etamana* to remove, though she did have the corset and trousers beneath the garments and sash. In contrast, he wore a full four layers, though at least the innermost layer was discreetly stitched with runes for comfort, since that much silk could get rather warm after a while.

As much as a part of her wanted to examine the stitching spells, they were nothing more than an extra bit of texture against her fingers, an obstacle to get past. Beneath that layer, his bare chest and the crisp hairs scattered across it deserved far more of her attention right now. Gabria all but buried her face in his chest, inhaling the scents of sandalwood, a hint of her rose attar from their earlier interactions, and pure male.

It was that lattermost scent she wanted to smell; it reached into her sinuses and entwined itself down her spine, touching places mere scent alone shouldn't touch. But it did, and it augmented the path of his hands as he removed her corset, trousers, and suede slippers, until he tipped her down onto the bed to aid his efforts.

Wanting to divest him of his own remaining clothes, Gabria tried to sit up, pulling the increasingly ragged remainder of her braid out from under her back, but he licked the insides of her knees. Squirming at the ticklish sensation, she giggled and collapsed onto the soft bedding, hair flopping and tangling around her shoulders and face. Devin held her legs open and rapidly licked his way up the soft skin of her thighs, making her squirm and laugh and squeak the closer he came to their crux.

Just as the level of intimacy started to alarm her, he retreated suddenly, leaving her stewing in a mixture of both relief and disappointment. With a few quick movements, he removed his trousers, slippers, and underclothes, leaving him bare of everything but the black ribbon wrapped around the tail of his braid. Anticipating more of the same, Gabria parted her thighs a little wider; she'd heard from Marta and other female friends how much fun it was to have a man kiss a maiden at their apex.

Instead, he picked up her right foot, making her squeak and try to kick it free, for the soles of her feet were very, very ticklish. He didn't let go. In fact, he stroked her sole briefly with his fingertips, making her shriek, then kneaded it firmly, soothing the unbearable tingle roused in her nerve endings. To her surprise, he was very, very good at massaging her feet, and within minutes had her relaxing enough to turn her giggles into moans.

Or maybe not a surprise, she thought distractedly, arching her head back as he gently tugged and twisted her toes. *All those morning massages, he's bound to have paid—Oh my* Gods*!* In fact, she might have shouted that thought out loud, but Gabria honestly couldn't tell. The Seer King had suckled her toes into his mouth and was tonguing between them, and every single little scrap of her foot that he bathed connected itself to every other part of her body, rendering her dizzy with the unforeseen bliss of it. Back bowed, head digging into the covers, she clawed at the bedding.

And then—and then!—he reached out with one hand and slid his fingertips through her nether-curls. Gabria shouted, undone by his sneaky attack. Pleasure wasn't the word for it; delirium might have qualified, if a delirium came with a rolling, bed-shaking spasm. Between the suckling attack of his lips and tongue and the circling attack of his fingers and thumb—*when did he get two of them inside of me?*—she could barely think. Then he sucked strongly, swirling tongue and fingertips and thumb, and she lost all sense of self in mind-blowing bliss.

She drifted back to consciousness, stunned by the strength of her pleasure. Taking pity on her, he released her right foot, gently lowering it to the edge of the bed. Panting heavily, Gabria calmed down. Or as much as she could, given he still had two fingers tucked into her depths. She could feel her flesh clenching around those fingers with each spasm of her stomach, and felt little tremors of arousal echoing in their wake.

"Gods . . ." She sighed, staring at the ceiling. "All this time . . . I never knew!"

"That your feet were sensitive?" Devin asked. There was enough satisfaction in his voice that it bordered on smug. "I knew."

Gabria managed to lift her head and saw that there was an unmistakeably smug smile curving his lips. She blinked at him.

"*How?* How did you know my feet . . . ?"

"Because I'm a Seer?" he reminded her, indisputably smug.

"Ohh, that's just not fair!" she groaned, letting her head thump back onto the mattress. A moment later, he withdrew his fingers. Part of her was disappointed at the loss, but the rest of her was relieved. The combination foot and . . . and . . . had been overwhelming. Still breathing a little heavily, Gabria focused on regaining her strength. She heard suckling sounds, heard him moan softly, and felt her belly clench again.

This time, he touched her with his other hand, brushing his fingers along her netherlips in a featherlight caress. She jumped a little, breath hitching in anticipation of more pleasure.

"Ready for more?" he murmured. Without waiting for an answer, he slid first one, then two fingers into her body. Into, and out of, over and over. Her hips started flexing in time with his slow, steady touch. Then, with the slightly damp fingers of his free hand, he caught her left ankle, lifted her leg up, and *licked* the sole of her foot.

Gabria lost control. Not just of her voice, which shouted loudly, nor of her body, which arched and strained against the mattress, but of her magic as well. Startled and scared, she tensed, scrambling mentally to control it before she damaged anything, and worse, revealed herself to . . . to . . . There *weren't* any priests of Mekha waiting to pounce on her for being a source of food for the False God . . . and her magic wasn't burning up the bedding.

Blinking hard and fast, Gabria focused her vision on where that burst of energy had flowed. Not exploded, but flowed and drained . . . into the man nuzzling her toes with the tip of his nose. Dark brown eyes met her startled gaze. *He* had absorbed her powers. *Oh . . . right. Sir Catrine said that . . . that Seers can* channel *magic, even if they cannot summon nor purpose it themselves . . . wow. Nice to know I* can *let go, in both senses. Passion . . . ohGodsohGods he's suckling my toes again . . . and . . . and magical . . . self . . . bastard!*

Incoherent as her thoughts were, she felt a twinge of discomfort in the midst of her bliss. Her flesh stung a little. She realized vaguely it was because he had eased a third finger in beside the other two, but the loving he was giving her middle and fourth toes, with occasional flicks of his tongue to her littlest toe . . . she didn't really care. The stroking circles of his thumb on her outer folds weren't quite as skillful coming from this hand as from his other one, but they were still good enough to strain her eyelids shut.

Just as she was getting near her peak again, he withdrew his fingers and pressed something else against her flesh. It was a bit smoother, a bit rounder, and definitely more blunt. Eyelids flying open, she found her left ankle lifted to his shoulder, his neck craning so that he could press a kiss to her skin.

Slowly, steadily, he sank into her body, stretching her passage until it stung. But no more than stung, thankfully. Undoubtedly the use of her crankman had eased the way in the past, as had the careful plumbing of his fingers. Now, snugged groin to groin, joined as one, Gabria could feel the difference between the slender shaft of stiff, unyielding, cool steel and his warm, full, somewhat more giving flesh. *Ohhh, that's much more wonderful . . . Why didn't anyone tell me it was this . . . this nice?*

Unbidden, her hands let go of the covers she'd clenched into disarray. Sliding them down over her stomach, she pressed her palms low over her belly, savoring just how full he made her feel. His hand slid over the top of hers, his fingers covering and twining with hers. Joining her in silent reverence for their connection.

For a moment, she thought his eyes were starting to turn gold. But then he blinked and they were merely a warm, deep brown. A mischievous brown, for he smiled in the next moment, shifted his grip on her foot, and returned to the task of suckling her toes. Gabria clutched at the covers once again, her world coming dizzily undone, and his thumb resumed its gentle stroking.

He finally moved within her, withdrawing partway and pressing back in. Moaning, Gabria succumbed; it was just one more layer to her delicious delirium. When he finally released her legs and lowered his chest to hers, she clutched at him, capturing his mouth in a kiss that tried to convey every bit of her pleasure right back to him. It didn't last; with every stroke, his breathing increased until he pulled back, panting heavily, his gaze just as dazed as hers felt.

Using the leverage of his feet on the floor, he rode her with increasing speed and vigor, until the bed creaked from the sideways stresses it was being subjected to. That stung her again, but not enough to distract her. Gabria's pleasure rose, spiraling up and washing over her in a rolling, repeating peak augmented by every thrust, until she broke just before he did. In fact, a dim corner of her mind was pretty sure that it was the tight clenching of her inner muscles that triggered his own peak, for no sooner had she sagged back into the bedding than he stiffened, prodded, and shuddered into a limp, sweaty weight that blanketed her overstimulated flesh.

Like their first moment of joining, when their hands had spoken in silent, eloquent reverence, this moment of rest seemed equally reverent. Something had taken place between them just now, something which no amount of magic could duplicate. Something as old as male and female. Gabria summoned just enough strength to stroke the dark locks spilling down over her shoulders and face . . . and wondered in the next moment how his hair could have come undone, when her last awareness of it had seen it solidly braided.

Rousing slowly, Devin breathed in deeply, then let it out in a soft groan. His head tilted, his lips brushed the side of her throat, then he carefully levered himself onto his elbows. And quirked his brows at the mass of dark hair curtaining them from the bedroom. Sweeping it off to one side, he *pffffted* a few stray strands from his lips, then gave her a warm, lopsided smile.

"Well. *That* doesn't happen very often."

"That, what?" Gabria asked, distracted.

"It's not often that a first joining of husband and wife unbraids not only *her* hair, but *his* as well. Then again, you are a mage, and a rather passionate one. I'm pleased I could help you let go." Leaning down, he kissed her on the lips, then eased himself out and away.

Gabria felt a little bereft when he left her, but relieved at the same time; he was rather muscular, solidly built. Still, his comment had to be addressed. Sitting up, she closed thighs which felt a little tender from being held open in such an unfamiliar—if enjoyable—position for so long. "Um, yes . . . I've never . . . that is, it was always *dangerous* to . . . to lose my mind so fully. Wow. *Very* fully . . ."

He smirked as he helped her to her feet. That gave her a chance to pad, somewhat stiffly, to the private refreshing room, located across the bed from the dressing room door. When she came back, he had turned the bedcovers down—at least, she hoped it was his work, and not that of some servant—and fetched two goblets of water. Not to mention, he had piled all the loosened flowers, their petals slightly crushed, onto the nearer of the two nightstands. Sliding an arm around her waist, he gave her a somewhat brief kiss, then released her and took his own turn at refreshing himself.

Unsure what to do now, Gabria climbed onto the bed and picked up one of the glasses. Drinking half of it in one go, she was surprised at how thirsty she was. At least at first, then she felt smug. *Given how much sweating we did just now . . . Gods! What a lover! I don't think I'll ever be satisfied by my crankman again. Or rather,* she admitted in a touch of honesty, *that I'll never be satisfied by my crankman* alone, *again.*

It was with that thought lurking as a smile on her lips that she watched her husband emerge and stroll her way. Her smile broadened until she figured she looked about as smug as he had, earlier. Or as smug as he did now, returning that smile with a very warm one of her own. Taking the cup from her hand, he drained the remaining half, set it on the nightstand next to the flowers their passion had removed, and kissed her until she sank down among the pillows.

Not wanting to be merely a recipient in all of this, Gabria nudged him over until he was the one cradled among the pillows, and she was the one kissing her way down his chest. Given how he gasped and clutched briefly at the covers, she guessed his nipples were *almost* as sensitive as her feet.

Almost, however, wasn't enough. Body humming with repleted but not quite sated pleasure, Gabria made up her mind to find every possible erogenous zone on his body. Even if it took her all night. She didn't have the advantage of being a God-blessed Seer to guide her efforts, after all. Thankfully, he didn't seem to mind her exploration efforts.

SIX

Gabria woke to an annoying glow of bright sunlight off to her right, a warm presence to her left, and a body that ached in wonderfully, painfully, deliciously tender ways. Drawing in a deep breath, she let it out in a sigh and found enough energy to open her eyelids. The angle of sunlight streaming in through the lattice-framed windows said it was midmorning. Looking the other way, she smiled at her gold-eyed hus—

His hand covered her mouth with lightning speed, muffling the shriek that tried to escape. "Shhh! Devin is still sleeping," Ruul stated quietly. He smiled, manipulating that familiar, and now stubble-ringed, mouth with the ease of long use. "You wore him out. I'm rather proud of you."

She stared at Him in fear. He frowned softly, and shifted His palm so that it merely caressed her cheek.

"Do you still fear Me, then? I am *not* the False God," He chided her. His golden, unnatural gaze slipped down from her face to her chest. Gabria promptly clutched the covers in place. ". . . You would deny Me the pleasure of seeing you directly, in your greatest glory?"

"I am *not* comfortable with You being here, like this," Gabria stated, managing to sound calm, if a bit tight-voiced.

He returned His gaze to her face. "I have seen the wives of sixteen generations of Seer Kings. Seen, and shared bliss with each of them. You fear something which I know you would otherwise enjoy, all because you cannot let yourself trust. This is a sad thing. I only wish to give you unbridled joy."

"I am married to *Devin*, not You!" she retorted, fighting hard against the urge to flee.

"We are as one. He is my Seer, I am his God," Ruul reminded her.

"Maybe in a chapel—but *not* in my bed!" Fighting her lifetime of fear, Gabria shifted one arm far enough to push at his chest with the edge of her wrist. "I don't want You in it!"

He blinked, shook his head, and stared at her with plain brown eyes. "What . . . ?" Looking around, at his position on his side, half supported by one elbow, at the fear in her gaze, he blinked again. His gaze unfocused for a moment, then he sighed, focusing on her again. ". . . Ruul asked that I convey His apologies. He is . . . disappointed . . . but will abide by your wishes, and stay away from us when we make love.

"He adds that He apologizes for intruding on our privacy . . . but that He finds you a fascinating, attractive woman for whom He only wishes great pleasure. I myself hope you'll eventually reconsider," Devin added, giving her a smile. "After all, if you thought last night was fun . . ."

Gabria shuddered. "I can't . . . I just can't."

"Shhh," he soothed, sounding different from his God. Stroking her sleep-tangled hair back from her face, Devin shook his head. "Neither of us would force you. He *will* stay away, unless and until you ask for Him. That is, He'll stay away when we make love. Unfortunately, I have only the Three Days of Intimacy left before I must return to my duties . . . and that does mean channeling Him again. At least, in the daytime."

She lifted her other hand, rubbing at the frown creasing her forehead. "I know . . . I *know* He's not the same, and I know you trust Him . . . and maybe one day I can get over this fear, but . . . I'm still afraid. Some of us . . . mages . . . got over our fears quickly enough after Mekha was dissolved, but . . . myself . . ."

His finger covered her lips, hushing her fears. He followed it with his own lips, soothing her nerves with a perfectly normal, warm, succulent kiss. As a distraction technique, it worked well. Aside from a few wary peeks to make sure his eyes were still mortal brown, Gabria was eventually able to let go of her worries and enjoy a repeat of a few of the activities which had made her so deliciously sore upon waking.

When they finished, she cuddled against his side, silently fighting her fears in the aftermath of her bliss. Only time would tell, however. She knew it, down to her bones. Time, and the God of Vision keeping His promises to her.

A stray thought wafted through her head a few moments later. A disconcerting stray thought. "Devin?"

"Mmm, yes?" he murmured, softly stroking the arm she had wrapped around his chest.

"Did you . . . of course you probably *know*, but . . . did you know He made love to your *mother*? And your *grandmother*?"

The fingers stroking her skin stilled for a tense moment before he answered her. "I try not to think about it."

Disconcerted more than a bit herself, Gabria tried not to think about it, either.

Granted entrance into the private parlor of the palace section known as the Royal Retreat, Mage-Captain Ellett greeted his liege with a deep bow, and his liege's bride with an equal bow, the morning after their Three Days of Intimacy had come to an end.

"Knowing what I do about Guildaran magic—which is more than most in our land—and after having consulted with our own equivalent to a Mage's Guild, I have found the best possible tutor for Her Highness," the head of the Royal Guard stated. "In fact, she taught a full quarter of the older members of the Royal Guard, with myself as one of her last pupils. I refer, of course, to Milady Samia—one and the same as Milord Souder's great-aunt," he added in an aside. "She is amenable to the idea of coming out of retirement for this task, though she says she would rather wait until the royal court is settled into the winter palace before making a habit of it."

Souder sighed and fiddled with his loupe, but shrugged. "I *suppose* she'll do. She can also teach the basics in Aurulan etiquette, and slay two spiders with one shoe."

It was obvious from the way he lifted his loupe to his eyes and gazed through them that he was comparing those spiders to a specific target.

Gabria put down her fork. "Enough." Her voice wasn't loud, her tone wasn't sharp, but it halted the Master of the Royal Retreat. "*Why* do you keep picking on me, Milord Souder? *Why* do you insult me? And then *smile* when I confront you over it? At least the Mage of the Palace is more consistent in her dislike of me."

This time, the same as the others, he smiled. The man also had the grace to blush a little, and since his skin was on the paler side of the Aurulan spectrum, it was quite obvious that he blushed. "I am merely doing my duty, Your Highness. I must test your mettle, to see what sort of a mother you would make. It wouldn't do to raise a spoiled or slovenly child, after all. Sons of poor character will never be chosen to become the next Seer King, and daughters of the same are equally uncomfortable as family members.

"Since every child born to a Seer King automatically becomes a noble, it is important that each one be raised well—that is my compatriot's foremost complaint about you, that you are not only a foreigner but that you take pride in your commoner status. Lady

Lianna disdains your origins. She will be polite because of your new station, but until you prove yourself worthy, she will not give you much leniency. I, however, am more concerned with your character, which will determine your suitability as a mother," Souder explained.

Gabria nodded slowly, trying not to take offense. This was very much a different culture, after all. "I suppose that makes sense . . . And your judgment of my suitability?"

"A bit rough in the etiquette department, a bit common in the personal tastes . . . but I think you'll do well enough as mother material. At least, you won't need too much in the way of guidance. As for the etiquette, Great-Aunt Samia will suffice for your initial lessons—be mindful of those lessons," Souder added, pointing at her with his stereoscopic loupe-on-a-stick. "She wields a mean wooden ruler, and your knuckles don't need to earn more of those dreadful calluses still clinging to the other side of your skin."

"If I may continue," Captain Ellett interjected smoothly. "Milady Samia is mostly retired from teaching, but has indicated she is willing to undertake the proper instruction of Her Highness. Provided, of course, that the two of them *can* get along. Milady admits she is a good teacher, but much set in her ways, given her age. And, given her advancing age, her knees are not quite up to the amount of walking that a visit to the palace would entail.

"I will therefore make myself available to escort Her Highness to her initial lessons, to personally ensure her safety," he offered. "At least until such time as another teacher needs to be found, or milady can be convinced to travel to the winter palace and take her lodgings in the royal court, so as to be closer at hand."

Devin opened his mouth to reply, but paused. Gabria, glancing up at him, caught him just as the brown drained from his eyes, turning gold. Off to one side, the two menservants who attended their breakfast quickly scrabbled for their pouches, pulling out the tablets they kept inside.

To stay the hand
Of the pirates' pride
You must set sail on
The Parrot's Ride.
To keep the peace
And fell your foe
Your gentlest touch
Will be your hardest blow.

The gold faded. He blinked twice, shook his head, then looked over at the servants. They finished scribbling, compared notes in hushed murmurs, then the shorter man dutifully recited back the words to him. Devin absorbed them, shrugged, and glanced up at the head of his Royal Guard.

"Well. I guess you've been temporarily reassigned, Captain Ellett. Find out when this *Parrot's Ride* sets sail, and where it is going . . . and if you can find a way to get the people of Jetta to stop raiding our ships, all the better. I give you permission to speak on the kingdom's behalf; my brother and I will trust you to know what is acceptable, and what is unacceptable, should you have to seek a compromise in order to secure peace.

"But do your best to secure some sort of surety that they *will* behave, while you're out there. Even if it has to be a hostage in the guise of an honored guest," Devin added. "Or however you can manage it. These things are open to more than one interpretation, after all—do make sure whoever you pick is treated as an *honored* guest. Even better, bring them here *as* an honored guest," Devin emphasized. "And best of all, an actual envoy or ambassador with whom we can officially treat. Perhaps if we finally show them some respect, they will resume a more respectful behavior themselves."

Gabria thought he sounded something like his elder brother, the Prime Minister, with those pragmatic words. Ellett bowed, accepting his liege's words with more equanimity than she could have mustered.

"As it is said, so shall it be written. Thus it is proved, and so shall it be," he murmured. "I will seek out this ship immediately. But, I would not abandon my duty to the safety of Her Highness, either. I would defer this quest by a few minutes so that I can hand-select an appropriate escort, but I am uncertain how urgent my departure may be . . . ?"

Devin negated that concern. "That is a matter easily settled. Master Souder, send a *palanquin* to pick up Milady Samia. One sized to fit through the corridors of the palace, to give your great-aunt's knees a rest. Arrange also for her to have escort and transport among us as we travel to the seven cities of the eastern half of the kingdom. She may not be of noble blood, but she has earned the right to such an honor through the efficacy of her teachings. Our Royal Guard is second to none, thanks to the efforts of men and women like her, and I trust the judgment of our Mage-Captain."

"Your Majesty's praise is most kind. I shall inform my Leftenant about your prophesy, give her some instructions on handling my tasks in my absence, and then I will seek out my destiny." Bowing once again to Gabria and the Seer King, the Mage-Captain left them to their breakfast.

Gabria blinked. "Well. He's *very* loyal. I'm not sure *I* could just drop my duties and just take off like that."

"I wouldn't send him away so precipitously, either, if I had a choice," Devin agreed. "But Ruul has spoken, and spoken urgently—I can tell His attention is focused mostly elsewhere in the kingdom, but this one moment was important to Him." He shrugged and picked up his fork. "Some days I am close to my God, while other days I am but a cushion for Him to briefly rest upon."

"A prettier cushion never waited for a more holy bottom to sit on it," Gabria teased dryly.

Devin narrowed his eyes, mock-glaring at her, and flung a soft bun at her. She laughed and flinched, letting it bounce off her forearm. Souder groaned and jabbed his loupe-on-a-stick at her.

"*You* are a disrespectful wife, *and* I see you are a terrible influence! And *you*," he accused, pointing next at the Seer King, "need remedial lessons on breakfast etiquette!"

Plucking the roll off the table, Gabria tossed it at him, next. "And *you* need to relax, Master Souder. This is breakfast in the private royal quarters, not some public feast!"

Glaring sternly, the Master of the Royal Retreat carefully brushed any possible, miniscule crumbs off his thigh-length sleeves . . . and then peered through his loupe lenses and stuck out his tongue at her, raspberrying her with a distinct lack of his usual decorum. Gabria giggled, delighted, and Devin almost choked on his drink. Even the servants off to one side had to stifle their mirth into mere snickers, while Souder himself laughed outright.

Three months later, Gabria didn't object to being clad in the excessive layers of full noble dress. They had moved to the cooler mountain climate of the summer palace, but that wasn't why she allowed the maidservants to layer her in four *etama*, each one an increasingly darker shade of purple. They wrapped the layers carefully in place with a pale lilac sash which matched her gathered trousers and the sueded slippers beneath, crossing the sash over both of her breasts and thrice round her waist.

She did not object to her hair being plaited in dozens of little braids, nor of the artistic way they were twined up together and dotted with tiny little lilac blooms, forming a flower-studded waterfall at the back of her head. And she did not object to the young serving girls who were pressed into duty, tossing rose petals and lilac blooms in front of her as she descended the steps to yet another glass-walled temple, this one nicknamed the Chapel of Arches from the ornate marble spans that supported the glass-tiled roof. It was three times as large as the Vaulted Chapel, with an equally larger number of pews, and an equally larger crowd occupying them.

By now, she had learned quite a bit about both Aurulan magics and Aurulan customs. This particular one was too important to these people, and more important, to the Seer King, to skimp on the expected traditions. This time it was Lord Daric, Prime Minister and sibling of the Seer King, who led her into the chapel and bowed himself to one side. Somehow, he had timed it so that the current petition was just leaving, granting her the full attention of everyone. Necks craned, heads tilted and swayed, and she felt the Eyes of Ruul upon her, even from so far away.

No one spoke as she paced slowly and gracefully up the carpeted aisle. The flowers in her hair, the color of her robes, all bespoke the message she brought, but no one even whispered to his or her neighbor. It was up to her to reveal the message she brought. Stopping at the foot of the stairs, she bowed to her watchful, golden-eyed husband.

"I come before the Eyes of Ruul as a vessel which has been filled," she stated, using the ritual words. "It is my honor to be filled with Your holy grace . . . and may I one day become the mother of the next Seer King."

"You are a most worthy vessel," He stated aloud. Then added in her mind, *Though technically, I have not filled you. Nor will I, for I will keep to My word, as promised. But I am pleased My Seer finds deep joy in you, and that your union is proving fruitful on many levels.*

The smile that graced His lips was a gentle one. A loving one. Briefly closing His eyes, He vanished from the Seer King's body. Devin, gazing at her with his own warm brown eyes, rose and descended from his throne with a warm smile of his own.

". . . And I myself am pleased. Ruul has graced me with a day's freedom, to properly celebrate this news. Petitions will be heard on the morrow. Tonight, let the whole kingdom rejoice!" he called out, reaching her side and lifting her hand for a brief kiss. With his free hand, he touched the section of stomach outlined by the lower two swaths of her sash. "We have a future son or daughter on the way."

Looking up at him, loving him, Gabria realized she was no longer afraid. *Ruul?* she thought, shaping the name carefully. *Ruul? Can You hear me?*

Always.

Um . . . You've kept your word . . . and I'm not afraid. If You want—if you both want—You can share our joy. Even, um, in bed.

One eye blazed gold while the other remained brown. Devin flicked up his free hand, the one on the golden-eyed side. Gabria blinked and stared around her, taking in the colorfully inlaid walls of their winter palace bedchamber, which had abruptly replaced the body-filled, glass-walled chapel. Not to mention the startled faces of the maidservants, who were caught in the act of changing the bedding. One look at their sovereign and they quickly scuttled out, not even bothering to finish straightening the covers. Within seconds, the bedroom door banged shut, and moments after that, they could hear the muffled sound of the parlor door closing as well.

Devin-Ruul smiled and lifted her fingers once again to their shared lips. *You will not regret this . . . and since I can tell you want to comment on it,* no, *it is not incest. Neither I nor My hosts have been related by blood to any of the women We have loved. Nor have My Seers loved more than one woman at a time. The right woman for each of them, hand-selected by Me.*

I have simply loved all of them . . . just as I love you. Just as he *loves you.*

She blushed, but cleared her throat and spoke her mind. Knowing that she safely *could*, with this particular God. "Just so long as *You* understand that I love Devin more than I love You. I'm not afraid of You anymore, and I do . . . I do love You. I just love *him* more."

I can live with that, the golden-eyed half of her husband teased, while the brown-eyed half pulled her close and kissed her deeply. The two of them merged . . . and suddenly she felt like she was being kissed all over, all at once, by a dozen hungry mouths.

Oh, dear Gods—and I thought having my toes suckled was . . . wow!

Ruul chuckled in her mind, and the sensations increased. *Indeed. You can return the favor by introducing Me to this "crankman" machine of yours . . . after the second or third round . . .*

Gabria shuddered at that particular thought—but not, thankfully, from fear.

JENODAN ISLES

ONE

If I weren't such a faithful man, Ellett thought to himself, watching the crew of the *Parrot's Ride* hauling on the ropes that shifted the cargo ship's colorful sails, *I might have given up by now. But that does beg the question, Ruul,* he added, aiming that thought at his Patron Deity. *You prompted my king to tell me to set sail on* this *ship . . . but this will be my fifth trip around the rim of the Jenodan Sea. When are these Jettan pirates going to show up, so I can* do *something about their predations?*

For that matter, what am I supposed to do?

He didn't expect an answer. Even if his friend and liege were there beside him, he wouldn't have expected a reply from Devin. Gods could help, but it didn't mean they always would. Not after having given mortal men and women free will. *At least I can take comfort that Ruul* does *see all that happens in and around our borders. Which includes this sea. So I know I* will *encounter the pirates while on board this ship. Eventually.*

Hopefully soon. As Captain of the Royal Guard, leader of the finest mage-warriors in all of Aurul, he really shouldn't be assigned to a simple task like this. A good part of him itched to be back in command of his fellow guards. He did believe his Leftenant was competent, though he thought she was a bit too zealous as an organizer and not quite personable enough to lead with the greatest effectiveness.

I suppose it's a good opportunity for Rahina to try her hand at command, he allowed. *Not that I expect I'll be giving up my post any time soon. But she needs to know just how difficult it is to lead people, not just command them. It takes flexibility to deal with different kinds of personalities, and an understanding of human nature. If she simply barks out a command and expects, say, Sergeant Briss to follow it without questioning . . . well, I myself* earned *the right for him to follow me, by listening to his complaints, taking them seriously, and explaining in terms he could understand why certain things needed to be done in the Royal Guard way, rather than the way he thinks best. Some of his ideas have been quite good enough to implement, and* that *softened him . . .*

Ellett's thoughts trailed off as the bo'sun shouted up at him from the middeck. "Hey, mage! Stop daydreaming and start working! We're almost clear of the breakwater!"

And thus begins circuit number five . . . Lifting a hand in acknowledgment, Ellett sighed and straightened, tugging the folds of his plain, pale blue *eta* jacket more neatly into place. Brushing his fingertips over the forecastle railing, he traced strengthening runes onto the wood, tightening the hull and supporting the masts so that they would withstand the coming stresses.

Learning in his initial investigation that the *Parrot's Ride*, a common, broad-bellied, Aurulan cargo ship wasn't due to pull into the port nearest the winter palace for a handful of days, Ellett had given his prophecy a bit of thought. He'd realized quickly enough that if he tried to ride around on the ship as a member of the Royal Guard—captain or otherwise—every single sailor around the entire sea would talk about it.

That meant subterfuge, and it meant establishing himself as a more common sort of man. He had known he wouldn't make a very good trader, though; most of the cargo carried by the *Parrot's Ride* was purchased and hauled by its owner, the independent-minded Captain Livit, and very little of it freight bought by other people. Nor did Ellett think he had the right mind-set to be a good trader, since that required a different sort of diplomacy than juggling the personalities of some of the best battle-trained spellcasters in the kingdom. And he definitely couldn't hide the fact that he was a mage for very long, though at least he could hide most of his magical strength.

The best option, therefore, had been to present himself as a ship's mage. It had also meant a bit of maneuvering. Not only a two-day crash course in various nautical spells, but also a thorough investigation of the ship's mage currently serving on board the *Parrot's Ride*. A bit of manipulation, a letter from "an addendum to the estate of your late great-uncle, only just now uncovered" which detailed the funds to send said mage to one of the best Mage Academies, and the mage in question gleefully jumped ship as soon as he finished reading his mail and explaining this once-in-a-lifetime opportunity—room and board and books included in the tuition price, which were actually being provided by the government and not any dead relative—to his captain.

Ellett had then arranged to be on hand when Captain Livit sent out word for any interested parties to audition for the vacancy in a series of tests ranging from a display of nautical spellcrafting to a set of Duels Arcane. The only part he had sweated was the display of spells. One did not become a member of the Royal Guard, never mind its commanding officer, if one were magically weak . . . and one did not become a ship's mage if one were exceptionally strong. There were far more lucrative positions available to the truly powerful spellcasters, after all.

More lucrative, and more interesting. Any mage who could

manage the power and the responsibilities would go after the best possible job he or she could get, and ship's mage wasn't exactly the highest-paying career.

Once the ship was strengthened, Ellett cast two more spells. One was a downward curl of his left hand and a mnemonic murmur of words, which lowered the water pressure in front of the ship just a little bit. The bow dipped downward slightly, giving them a touch more in the way of speed.

The other spell required a swirling, cupping twist of his right wrist, fingers and spell spread to capture and entwine the winds blowing in from the west. Not that much was needed in the way of redirecting the wind, but in order for the ship to travel swiftly to the east, it actually needed to blow in slightly from one side or the other, and blow consistently. The bright red, green, and yellow sails snapped and filled, straining at the sheets—which weren't the sheetlike sails, but which were instead the nautical term for ropes—holding them in place. He still didn't know all of the terminology involved in sailing ships and other seaworthy things, but he was learning.

Tying in the threads of power to the rigging, which would anchor the spell and allow it to funnel the wind more accurately, Ellett relaxed his arms. Part of his mind had to stay cognizant of the trio of spells, but only as long as it would take them to reach the next port, half a day's steady sail from here. Relaxing, Ellett leaned on the rail again, the short, pocketed sleeves of his *eta* bumping lightly against the rails.

In one of those pockets, he had tucked a kerchief and a viewing loupe, similar to the sort used by the slightly nearsighted Master of the Royal Retreat, back at the royal court. Unlike Master Souder's looking glass, his was enchanted to act like a telescope, giving him an enlarged, stereoscopic view of the horizon. It was a very popular tool among those sailor types who could afford the expensive Artifacts. In the other pocket, he had tucked a small, hastily scribbled grimoire filled with his notes on nautical spells.

After having traversed the entire circumference of the great Jenodan Sea four times and a titch—their next port of call would be a city in the neighboring kingdom of Keket, and four ports farther along than his original starting point in Aurul—Ellett didn't have to refer to his notes very often. Unless the weather changed noticeably, he would have nothing else to do. Of course, the sky was more cloudy than clear, with some tufts moving faster than others. That might herald the beginnings of a windstorm, or it might simply mean rain. Right now, the wind was in their favor, and a little rain wouldn't hurt, given how hot and dry even the months of early summer could be.

I will have faith in my God . . . I will have faith in His prophecy . . . I will be bored out of my wits . . . Sighing, Ellett pulled his loupe-on-a-stick out of his sleeve. Giving the lenses a cursory polishing with the scrap of linen serving as his kerchief, he peered through the eyepieces at the shore. They were pulling away from the eastern half of the port city of Cerulean Cove, easternmost town of any size on the Aurulan coast. From this angle, the magnification spells on the lenses allowed him to peek into the upper floors of the houses and other buildings they were leaving behind.

Such as the inn at the edge of the docks, which had several of its second-floor windows open, letting in the midmorning light. *Oh, here we go!* Ellett bit his lip, stifling the urge to laugh. *Someone not only loves the morning sun, but apparently has no compunction against making love to his or her companion . . . up against the wall, if I'm not mistaken. Although it's such a small view, I* could *be mistaken.*

The loupe came with a rune-chased band near the bottom of the shaft. If he chose to do so, he could have twisted it and heard an amplified version of whatever he was hearing, at a distance suitable to the focal point of the lenses . . . in other words, just barely close enough to have heard, faintly, some of the louder, lustier sounds the pair were undoubtedly making. *Especially with her mouth that wide . . . but I think I shall refrain.*

Lowering the viewing glass, he sighed for a different reason.

That's another thing I haven't had in a while. The crew is off-limits; Captain Livit carefully, monotonously explains it every few days, no fraternizing among the crew or the few passengers we may take on board. At least while on board the ship. We can romp all we like onshore, but that sort of thing isn't meant to be brought on board.

Not that he'd had a lot of that lately. There had been a few casual liaisons with fellow Aurulans before he and thirty of his fellow Royal Guards had been sent into the somewhat new kingdom of Guildara to fetch the Seer King's foretold bride. In the interim, nothing had happened. Barely a week had passed from his fetching and presenting the charming Gabria Springreaver, mage and engineer, to her new life, to the day when his king had prophesied his place on this vessel.

Stuck on a ship for the last two months, staying in various ports of call only for a night or two at a time, Ellett hadn't cared to find a stranger. Not only would it have run the risk of missing his ship if he got too distracted, plus the threat of possibly letting something slip regarding his mission—not that there was much to tell about *that*, given how vague a prophecy it was—but there were certain health risks he didn't care to take. As convenient and widespread as contraceptive amulets might be—including the fact that Ellett could and did enchant his own—there were certain diseases associated with pleasures that were shared too freely. He knew *some* medical magics, but didn't care to test his prowess, designed for a battlefield, against ailments from a dockside tavern.

I hope whoever that is, he or she knows a good healer, just in case, he thought. Curiosity had him lifting the stereoscopic loupe back into place. The angle of the speeding ship, however, precluded a second view. Idly, he turned his attention to the coastline ahead. The view was a little blurry, so again he fished out his kerchief, polishing the lenses more carefully this time.

The view was still a little blurry. Or rather, not so much blurry as just . . . odd. Frowning, Ellett tried to pinpoint what made the combination of shoreline, waves, sunlight, water, and cloud-cast shadows tug at the back of his mind. All he could see were the rock-strewn beaches, the wind-stirred ripples on the surface of the water, and the shades of blue green and green gray that delineated the portions where the morning sun fell on the water and where the clouds blocked its rays.

Shadows . . . something about those shadows . . . He stared at those patches of cloud-shadow in the distance as the *Parrot's Ride* sailed closer. They were now far out enough from the shoreline, the possibility of shoals and sandbars shouldn't be a problem. *So there shouldn't be any anomalies of shadow under . . . that's not* under *the water*, Ellett realized as one of the shadows bobbed against the horizon. Bobbed much like another *ship* would, if it were sitting at anchor in semi-shallow water.

A cloaked ship, disguised by illusion. Squinting, he evoked mage-sight, looking for the telltale glows and other traces of a spell in action. With the sun slanting in from ahead, it was hard to tell. Only by comparing the two views, with the loupe and without, did he note the slightly brighter-hued patch where the sun-and-shadow shape of that ship might be. Impressed, Ellett carefully refrained from making any sort of startled reaction. Just in case someone on that hidden ship was watching *him* through an enspelled, telescopic loupe.

I am impressed. Very impressed, he decided, shifting his gaze to other parts of the horizon. A bit of careful searching showed nothing else out of place. *Whoever cast that hide-me spell is* very *good. Where there is nothing but sunshine, I can't see a thing. Where there's nothing but shadow . . . the same. Only at the borderlines of all four, sun and shadow, water and sky, do the hues and the tones subtly change.*

It was quite possibly one of the best camouflaging illusions he had ever seen, on or off a battlefield . . . and this would be a battle. He bit his inner lip a second time, this time to avoid a satisfied smile, rather than a mirthful one. *The only reason a ship* would *be cloaked this close to a port city is to disguise itself for an ambush . . . because if it needed shelter from being attacked, it need only sail within the protective range of our port authority mages and signal for help. All the crews who ply Aurulan waters know we don't tolerate piracy along our shore. And how audacious of them, to establish this ambush so close to those protections!*

The pain in his lip kept him from grinning. *No, I do not doubt You, Ruul. I may have been impatient, but You do indeed see all, even through this particular piece of witchery. Now . . . given how we'll be approaching within striking range in . . . mmm, a quarter of an hour . . . what to* do *about it?*

The previous reports of Jettan piracy had said the attacking vessels had appeared out of nowhere, attacking from the east in the midmorning and from the west in the afternoon. Never at night, never at dawn or dusk, never at midday. *Because only that particular angle of sunlight which produces rainbows can hide most of the glow of a spellcast aura from a well-trained, observant mage, powerful or otherwise. Skill trained to a specialized degree can make up for a lack of sheer strength. And, within its own field of expertise, can be preferable.*

Clever, clever mage. And undeniably skillful. The biggest questions remaining are whether or not this mage is as powerful as he or she is skilled, and how trained in combative magics?

Shifting his loupe-augmented gaze to the right, starboard of that not-entirely-perfect blend of daylight and cloud-shadow, Ellett considered the section of water where the *Parrot's Ride*, with its golden hull and colorful sails, would most likely pass. *How are you going to ambush us?*

There was no question in his mind that he would let it happen, or at least let it begin. His destiny lay in a conflict with the pirates plaguing Aurulan ships, not in avoiding one. *The residents of Jetta Freeport claimed it was because we did nothing to stop predations against* their *merchant ships. But it's gone well past a simple reprisal of a cargo for a cargo. Not when this will be the . . . eighth such attack? Presuming what I've heard is the most recent and accurate report on such matters.*

Someone *has to stop the cycle of violence. And according to His Majesty's prophecy, that someone is me. Which is highly ironic,* he thought, squinting through the loupe at a tiny, bobbing object further rippling the rolling, flexing surface of the sea. *I'm a warrior by profession, yet I'm supposed to defeat these pirates with my "gentlest touch," whatever that means. At least I can guess with some confidence it'll be a confrontation with* this *mage, because someone this skillful is surely the source of their pride.*

Shifting away from the railing, legs braced against the steady bobbing of the foredeck, Ellett made a show of stretching, scratching his back with the end of the loupe-stick, then strolled over to the other railing. With the aid of the loupe, he peered up the length of the bowsprit and the lines holding the jib sails in place. Whatever that object was in the water, it wasn't very big. In fact, it looked like a simple piece of driftwood.

Ellett started to lower his loupe, then lifted it again, frowning. Squinting through the lenses, he tried to make out what the lump at the midpoint was. *Is that a . . . rope? Yes, there's a rope knotted around it, I'm sure of it. But . . . why would a piece of driftwood have a rope knotted around it?*

He wasn't a lifelong sailor, but even he could reason that a chunk of a wrecked ship, maybe some spar or beam or even a bit of railing, might have a rope knotted about it. But not something that looked like a weathered piece of beach trash. Squinting, he tried mage-sight. The angle of the sun wasn't as much of a bother on this side of the ship, and he was reasonably sure he saw the faint glow of a spell.

Possibilities flashed through his mind, at that. *Some sort of entrapment spell? Something to entangle the ship? Or something that requires a spell set on both sides? Something from the ship? No, that driftwood is closer to us than the ship-shadow.* Carefully, as if he were simply bored, he strolled back to the port side. Even without the loupe, he could see a similar dot in the water, and with the loupe . . . another piece of plain, weathered tree limb bobbed in the water, knotted near the middle with a bit of rope. It, too, glowed faintly, though discerning that cost him precious minutes.

If the rope stretched between the two pieces, he couldn't tell. Not even with the augmentation spells of the lenses, allowing him to peer somewhat under the waves. Concerned, he murmured a true-seeing spell over the Artifact and lifted it back to his eyes.

The shadow-blur of the lurking ship was now quite prominent from this close, but it was still just a blur, as if a smear on the lenses. The driftwood looked like driftwood. In fact, there was another one farther along, and another beyond that, forming a line that curved out around that ship-sized blur. Ellett couldn't figure it out.

There wasn't any time left to do anything about it, anyway. The *Parrot's Ride* sailed blithely between the two scraps—and Ellett felt his spells falter. The bowsprit creaked, the jibs fluttered and snapped, and the hull bucked and rose upward, the ship shuddering and slowing as it lost both strength and speed. At the same moment, the world fogged around him, turning thick with sudden mist. As the ship continued forward, the sounds of his fellow crewmen shouting in alarm rippled down the length of the mid- and poopdecks.

Hastily raising the loupe back to his eyes, Ellett saw the reality behind the mist.

The blur was now a ship, a long, sleek, white-sailed, black-painted vessel that would probably cut through the water nearly twice as fast as the *Parrot's Ride* could run, with or without magic. Black was the hull color for Jettan ships, painted on from some sort of resin that was far less sticky and more water-resistant than mere tar.

He could also see its crew, clad in black-dyed clothes augmented by what looked like boiled leather armor, preparing hooks, lines, and weapons for a boarding party. Their faces were covered from the nose down in black kerchiefs, further obscuring their identities. In fact, the only point of identification on the ship was the name of it, painted in trade-tongue lettering near the bowsprit. The *Slack Sails*. That was the name reported by the captains of the Aurulan ships which had been attacked. He hadn't heard any rumors of this particular ship docking at Jetta, though several Aurulan captains had searched for it among the docks and wharfs of the walled freeport city, but the name was familiar.

At least the line of rope-tied driftwood made sense, now. In essence, it was a net. Not one meant to capture fish, but one meant to snare and haul in a much different sort of prey. *Given the complexity of these illusions, I'll bet we either vanished from view of the land the moment we crossed it, or there's an illusion of us just sailing merrily on our way. Probably the former; the latter would be difficult to maintain from all directions. It's also complex enough that their crew doesn't seem to be affected, even though we ourselves are.*

"Ellett! *Ellett!* Damn you, mage! Can't you see we're under attack?" Captain Livit yelled, charging up the ladderlike steps from the middeck. "Dispel this fog! Shield the ship!"

"Prepare to repel invaders!" hollered the bo'sun from somewhere near the aft end of their ship. He blew a pattern on his pipe, too, just in case some of the other sailors couldn't hear.

"Speed us up, man!" Livit shouted. Grabbing Ellett by the elbow, he shook the taller man. "Damn you, *do* something!"

Ellett almost lost the loupe, at that. Clutching it firmly before it could fall into the water, he turned his head and leveled a stern look at the upset merchant-captain. Livit got the message and released him, but only to lift a finger and shake it in his face.

"I hired you not only because you could speed this ship on its way but because you *seemed* to be a competent battle-mage!" he threatened. "We're losing speed, and I just know we're about to be boarded. If you don't do *something*, and do it *right now*—!"

Making up his mind in a flash, Ellett straightened and tucked his loupe into his sleeve. "You're right. I should do something. I resign. *Sartorlamanit!*"

Shouts from belowdecks were followed by a sturdy linen bag flying up out of the hold, the bag containing the few belongings he had brought on this trip. He didn't have to pack anything, since it was already stuffed into his duffel sack; his "bunk" was nothing more than a hammock belowdeck, anyway, the same as the rest of the crew, save for the captain.

"You . . . you *resign*?" Captain Livit sputtered.

"Yes. Don't worry for your ship," Ellett added, catching his duffel as it swerved up onto the foredeck. Setting it at his feet, he fished his nautical grimoire out of his other sleeve. "I'll send it on its way in a moment . . ."

Gaping, the merchant-captain drew in another breath to protest, but it was too late. Grappling hooks came flying through the air. With a curse that blistered Ellett's ears, the merchant-captain hurried down to the middeck to start cutting the lines before the other ship could heave to, literally pulling the two vessels together.

Left alone for the moment, Ellett quickly found the spell he wanted. It stood to reason that, if the net was a spell laid on the rope-lashed driftwood in the water, then it caused its slowing and mist-cloaking and whatever other effects because the ship was connected to these things by touch. If nothing else, by the *Parrot's Ride* touching the same water that touched those spellbound ropes. *Remove direct contact, and you negate the majority of the spell's strengths. Ah, here it is. The glasswater spell, the one with the shaping variant . . .*

Casting the spell, he tucked the book back into the plain beige square of his pocket sleeve, shouldered his bag, pulled out the loupe again, and stepped up over the railing just as a column of flat-topped water rose to meet him. He could feel the net-spell trying to sap his energies now that he was touching the water, but it couldn't break through his personal shields, nor could it dissolve the column of water swaying him away from the Aurulan ship.

A peek through the loupe lenses showed the two vessels within a few body lengths of each other. Close enough that some of the pirates were hauling up boarding planks. Enough was enough. Raising his free hand, ignoring the way the strap of the duffel bag threatened to slide off his shoulder, Ellett chanted the words of his second-most-powerful levitation spell.

The last time he had used it, he had been helping the people of Guildara lift and remove the chunks of their humongous battle-machines from the fields near their capital. The *Parrot's Ride* was easily as large as any of those strange war-engines, and just as slowly lifted. In fact, there was enough time for a good five or six, maybe seven pirates to have scrambled onto the decks of the Aurulan ship before the planks slipped free and the grappling hooks stretched to their limits, before the cleats they were lashed around broke free with crunching cracks of broken wood.

Some of the Jettan pirates were even lifted off their feet, hollering and still clinging to the ends of their ropes, while others narrowly avoided a tumble into the sea. The ones on the ropes gave up and let go, crossing their ankles and covering their noses as they plunged several body lengths into the sea, where they bobbed to the surface and started calling out for rescue, treading water.

A slow, hard shove of his hand sent the *Parrot's Ride* spinning sideways just enough to put the sails parallel to the wind to reduce drag, and another shove sent it sailing backward over the water. Back toward their last port, the Aurulan docks with the Aurulan mages who would be watching for any anomalies. Like a ship flying several yards above the waves.

Not that it would stay up there for long; his spell would let it sag slowly downward until it scraped the waves, then it would drop fully into the water. By then, he gauged it would be about a mile or so away. And by then, he intended to have the attention of these would-be pirates.

TWO

Leaving the cargo ship to sag slowly into the west, Ellett directed his column of glass-hardened water toward the other vessel. He had to do so while still looking through the loupe lenses. The moment he looked with his own eyes, the thick mist was back, obscuring everything beyond the reach of his arms. The sailors who were still on board that black-painted ship didn't have his problem, however. The nearest of them drew their weapons and faced him as he approached, while the others did their best to haul their fallen comrades and tumbled boarding supplies out of the low-rippling waves.

They didn't attack him, which was a good sign. In fact, they backed up enough to give him room to step onto the foredeck of their ship. They didn't release or sheathe their weapons, but they didn't strike, either.

A quick peek without the loupe showed what he had suspected was true; touching *this* ship negated the mist-illusion. Since no one was attacking him, Ellett took the time to tuck the loupe back into his sleeve once more.

The black-clad men and women, their expressions half obscured by those kerchief-masks, were joined by a tall woman clad in a much more elaborate, highly tooled version of their black armor. The deference they gave her as soon as they noticed her told him this was someone important. Squinting with mage-sight revealed the shimmer of personal shields, and the glow of several protective runes subtly carved into her armor. They were as intricate and as elegant as the whole mist-illusion net. *I wonder if she's not only the mage behind those spells but also the mind behind all those raids.*

"Well." She planted her hands on her hips, facing him. Her voice wasn't muffled much by the black cloth covering half her face; it was low, feminine, and piqued with curiosity. "You seem rather determined to spoil our fun. Not to mention rude, coming aboard without an invitation. You also have no right to interfere in our business."

"Robbing ships of their rightful property isn't *fun*," Ellett chided her. The other sailors bristled, but he continued smoothly. "Which, I think, was your original point, wasn't it? You started these raids as acts of retribution for the theft of your fellow Jettans' cargoes. The only problem is, a lot of people think you have lost your way. That you have gone well beyond restitution by now, and are as bad as the original pirates who plagued *you*. If you want to be considered a *civilized* nation . . . perhaps you should return to your original civilized ways?"

"You Aurulans still owe us a considerable amount of restitution," she countered sharply, giving the square pocket sleeves of his *eta* jacket a disdainful look. "And what *you* call civilization, I call overbearing arrogance!"

That accusation lifted one of his brows. "It could be argued that, as you were so eager to board the *Parrot's Ride* without waiting for permission, it would only be fair that I should be equally free to board the *Slack Sails*, here. It could be argued that your arrogance began first, in *this* particular encounter, for we offered no insult whatsoever. Then again, I merely think you're projecting someone *else's* arrogance onto my own actions.

"Be careful, milady," he cautioned her, lifting a finger in gentle warning. "Be very careful, that you do not become so wrapped up in your efforts to tar the hulls of your ships, you end up tarring every other piece of wood in sight. You might not find it so easy to walk around, should your overzealous efforts glue your chair to your . . . pants."

One of the others *snerked*. Ellett couldn't have said who it was, for their mouths were masked, and by the time his gaze traversed the lot, there were no shaking shoulders to be seen. The mage-pirate dropped one of her hands from her hip, flicking her fingers at him. "At least you have a reasonable sense of humor. That's more than your bastard of an ambassador can say. I find *his* jokes to be utterly unfunny."

Ellett blinked at her words, taken aback. ". . . Ambassador? There is no ambassador to Jetta Freeport. Not from Aurul."

"Yes, there is," she countered.

"No, there is not," Ellett repeated.

"Yes. There *is*," she insisted.

"And I say that no, there is *not*. In fact, *I* am the closest thing Aurul has ever had to an ambassador," he stated crisply, cutting her off before she could argue the rest of the matter. "I have been sent to find the Jettan pirates—which I have—and put an end to your predations on Aurulan ships. Which I will."

That caused a growl from the other crewmembers, and the lifting of more than a few weapons which had been lowered, though not yet sheathed.

"—*In my own way*," he asserted quickly, loudly. "I can do it via violence, *or* I can do it via discussion. I would *prefer* discussion."

They subsided, though their mood remained palpably unpleasant. Ellett kept his expression calm, his stance relaxed, swaying gracefully with the movement of the anchored ship under his feet.

The clouds in the west had darkened half the sky, and rain was falling in the distance, but this moment was more important than the weather, however wet they were about to get.

"Now, I *am* a reasonable man, and I am willing to *listen* to your complaints . . . which I'll admit is more than you've received from Aurul in the past. I suggest you calm yourselves, order your thoughts, and present your cases and complaints to me in a peaceful, factual, and nonviolent manner," he said, holding the mage-lady's gaze. "Starting with *why* you think Aurul has an ambassador assigned to your autonomous city, when we do not."

Her free hand returned to her hip. "We do, because we *do*. Lord Stelled, ambassador for and second cousin of His Majesty, Seer King Devin."

That narrowed his eyes. "Lord Stelled, who was His Majesty's *third* cousin, died two years ago in the northeast mountains while gathering rare herbs for his alchemical work."

"Lord Stelled is very much *alive* and causing massive headaches for my people!" she countered heatedly. "His outrageous tariffs on importing Aurulan goods have forced our merchants to sail to other lands in search of replacements—if anyone is robbing anyone, it is *your* people robbing *us*, and on a daily basis!"

"Milady, I was *there* when they brought his remains back for identifying," Ellett countered just as firmly. "The healers and scryer-mages were able to determine he died of a heart attack, and his body half eaten by scavengers before it was found and recovered. If there is anyone in Jetta Freeport pretending to be Lord Stelled, then that is exactly what he is doing. *Pretending*."

"So you *say*," she scoffed.

"Yes, I do. *This* is why we need to talk like two civilized beings, rather than thugs interested only in a bit of theft and a street brawl. Something wrong is going on here," he told her, "and it is beginning to look a lot worse than a few pilfered cargo holds. Now, put your weapons away, and let us *discuss* the problems at hand."

She stared at him, her hazel eyes mulling over his blunt request. Her tone didn't sound very convinced. "So you *say*. You *say* you have the authority to 'deal' with us . . . but all I see is a ship's mage bluffing his way out of combat, and buying his crew the time they need to escape back to a safe port. Just who do you think you are, the son of the Seer King?"

"Considering he only just married his destined bride, that would be physically impossible," Ellett retorted dryly. "As for my status, all that matters is that I was sent here by His Majesty to seek out why you Jettans are targeting Aurulan ships, and put an end to your thievery. *How* I do so is entirely up to my own discretion . . . which in turn depends on *your* level of aggression."

"So you say," she repeated. She lifted her black-swathed chin. "If you want *our* respect, give us your name and your title."

"My name is Ellett. As for my title . . . that does not matter."

"Why not?" she challenged him. The approaching rain started pattering down around them, dampening the deck and the crew in darkening splotches.

"Two reasons. You clearly don't know much about Aurul, if you think Lord Stelled is still alive. And you're pirates. You might think my title valuable enough to try to hold me for ransom," Ellett said, smiling slightly. He didn't trust any of these people, and had no reason to do so. He wanted them to know it. "All that would do is make me a lot less inclined to *discuss* how to put an end to your excessive thefts and more inclined to act in an *un*civilized manner."

She snorted and lifted her chin at him, though she addressed her crewmates. "Listen to him! He thinks he's powerful! He thinks he can take on a whole shipload of us—Netherhells, he probably thinks he can take me!"

That caused a wave of laughter in the others.

". . . Fine. You think you can take me? *Provocave, pacicave!*" Her words physically pushed the others back and to the sides in a small, glowing semicircle. She lifted her hands in a formal dueling stance.

"I, Mita, challenge you, Ellett, to a Duel Arcane! Mage against mage, might against might, mind against mind."

Dropping his duffel bag onto the deck, Ellett wordlessly called up the other half of the Dueling shield. Its edges met and matched hers as he spoke. "I, Ellett, accept your challenge, Mita, to a Duel Arcane. Wrath against wrath, word against word, will against will."

Phantom hands flared into existence. Glowing fingers interlaced and clasped. Braced for a hard, swift squeeze of sheer magic, Ellett found instead that his opponent ramped up her energies slowly, almost probingly, rather than opting for a swift, crushing defeat.

They rose slowly enough that the deck was thoroughly wet and the winds of the rainstorm were tugging at the rigging, tilting the ship sideways, before he had to work to maintain his own magical efforts. The crewmembers who had crowded onto the foredeck grimaced and glared at the clouds drenching each of them, but they didn't move. Wrapped in their Dueling shield, the two of them remained quite dry. Stress for stress, he matched her efforts, letting her set the pace of their duel. The fact that he did so made her eyes widen with what looked like dawning wonder.

A corner of his mind noted the change from her former narrow-eyed belligerence. *She almost looks pretty. At least, from the eyes up. I wonder . . . what does she look like from the nose down? Certainly her figure, armor notwithstanding, looks to be rather nice. And probably quite fit, given she's a ship's mage. She's also wearing a pair of long daggers and looks like she knows how to use them . . .*

Such thoughts were somewhat distracting. They did, however, give him an idea. The Royal Guard of the Seer King were, one and all, mage-warriors without compare. One of the things they did on a near-daily basis, as part of their training, were Duels Arcane very similar to this one, but with one notable exception. Rather than just standing in place while their minds battled, Ellett and his fellow Guardsmen and -Women were expected to *move* while their minds met and fought.

Increasing his own side of the pressure, he tested her. She fought back with force of her own. He increased it further, until his fingers threatened to tremble, and he could see a slight tremor in her own. Once he saw them shaking subtly, Ellett made his move.

Lowering his hands, he deliberately stepped closer to her. The other black-clad men and women exchanged quick, puzzled looks. Ellett *looked* like he was no longer fighting mind-to-mind against her, but their illusion-hands were still visible, still clearly locked in brute-power combat over their heads.

Two more steps closed the distance between them, until he was barely a hand-span away. Lifting his fingers—which did tremble, since she increased her magical pressure sharply, no doubt in an effort to warn him away—Ellett reached behind her head and gently teased apart the knotted ends of her kerchief. Brow furrowing, she strained harder. The pressure between her effort and his resistance formed more than just a giant pair of illusory hands; tiny sparks formed and dropped, glowing bits of expended life force compressed into existence between the hammer and anvil of their clashing wills.

Unfortunately, he had picked the wrong kerchief. That was the knot for the cloth that covered her hair. Given her tanned skin, he wasn't expecting the rich, dark auburn hue of her hair. Trying again, he found the other knot under her shoulder-length locks and lowered the other scarf, the one covering her from nose to throat.

The sight of her lower face pleased him. Her suntanned nose was slightly hooked at the tip, her mouth more than a bit generous, her lips wider than most, but he liked them; they went well with her broad cheekbones and the sharp jut of her chin. With those large hazel eyes and that broad forehead, she seemed larger than life, like the illusory palms representing the powers held locked in combat between them.

A lot of power, in those hands over their heads. More than he had expected, even given the complexity of her illusions. Certainly far more than the average ship's mage possessed, and probably equal in strength to the weakest member of the Royal Guard. If not more powerful.

To keep the peace, and fell your foe, he reminded himself, shifting one of his real hands so that he could glide a finger down the soft curve of her cheek, . . . *your gentlest touch will be your hardest blow. So say the words of Ruul, as prophesied by His Seer King.*

He stroked her cheek again, seeing more than just her hands tremble, while feeling the sharp increase in her power. His caress was part his own effort and part the effort of the wind-tugged deck tilting beneath their braced feet. As lightly as he touched her, she didn't falter, let alone fall. *Alright, so that isn't it. What, then, would be my "gentlest touch" if not the lightest stroke of my hand?*

Rain washed over the deck, while the relatively gentler waves of earlier grew coarse and choppy, turning that chilly, murky shade of gray that made even seasoned sailors move carefully abovedeck. The Jenodan Sea, while reputedly not as salty as the great oceans of the world, was large enough that one could not see the far side, and its waters could get quite cold and rough in bad weather, even in the summer.

Inside their spell-shielded bubble, the two of them were growing hot. Beads of sweat dusted her forehead and cheeks, while the folds of both his jacket and his trousers clung to the warmer spots of his skin. Over their heads, sparks fell in silent sprays, further warming the air.

Panting audibly with her effort, Mita licked her lips. Somehow, she managed to speak. Not to move, for her physical hands were caught in the invisible vice of his power, body locked into the illusion cast by her mind . . . but she did speak. "You're . . . *very* strong. You're wasted . . . as a ship's mage."

"It was a temporary job at best," Ellett murmured, watching her moisten her lips a second time. He, too, was beginning to sweat, though given how much he and his fellow Guardsmen had practiced such things, he didn't have to struggle to speak. "One which I took on just long enough to find *you*."

"Find me? You knew who . . . to look for?" she panted, looking into his eyes as if she could read the answer written in them.

She was tall enough to look him in the eyes, for hers were within a few inches of his own, and he wasn't a short man. Their bodies almost brushed with each ship-rocking gust of wind. Ellett gently stroked her cheek, considering her words, her features, and the strength of her magics. Her very strong magics. She hadn't stopped increasing her power, though her muscles shook with the effort of it, trembling like the sparks sputtering their silent points of light overhead. As did his, though at least he could still move.

The worst thing he had to fight was how the sight of her licking those full lips distracted him, weakening his concentration. "Not who, just what . . . though I am very happy I found *you*."

Wanting—needing—to end this conflict without either of them getting hurt, Ellett leaned in just far enough to close the gap between their heads. His lips touched hers, more of a brushing brought on by the swaying of the deck underfoot than any deliberate press . . . but by her reaction, it was a devastating blow. Crying out, she buckled and dropped hard to one knee, her magical strength faltering.

Instantly, he gentled his mental pressure, not wanting to break her fingers. She tried to recoup her energies, to resurge them into another attack, but it was too late. The Dueling shield vanished, popping like a soap bubble and letting in the lashing rain. The moment her leg had bent to the deck, she had lost, for it was a very rare mage who could regather enough strength to continue. Keenly aware of the stunned looks and dark glares being aimed at him by her crewmates, Ellett dipped to one knee as well. He caught her hands as she flexed life back into her fingers, and gently chafed them between his palms.

"You are incredibly strong and incredibly talented. Your cloaking illusions were near-perfect, the best I've ever seen," he praised her quietly. "I'd consider it an honor if you'd teach me some of what you know."

She looked up at him, startled by his words.

Ellett struck his next unconventional blow by slicing one hand horizontally through the air, silently carving the very air. A cupping flex of his fingers forced the wind up and over the black-hulled ship, quelling some of the waves and calming the unruly rocking of the deck. The move lessened some of the falling rain, too.

It was a showy display of his power, for not many mages could have cast such a demanding spell so soon after arcane combat. Not that it didn't cost him, for it did—it was all he could do to hide his trembling, though he couldn't do anything about the sweat trickling down his face—but it impressed the woman Mita and her startled crew. Helping her to her feet, Ellett cupped her hand in his and held her wary, wondering gaze.

"Now. Let us set sail for Jetta, where you will point out this impostor who claims to be the late Lord Stelled. Once I have confirmed he is an impostor, he will be dealt with appropriately. In the meantime, you and I will fill the hours and the days of our trip with conversation. You, by discussing in detail each and every offense that Jetta feels has been wrought against it by the people and the government, and me, by listening and giving what facts I can from the Aurulan point of view in all of these matters. Like *civilized* people do."

She blinked at him, then narrowed her eyes. "And do *civilized* people go around kissing other people without either invitation or permission?"

Leaning close, Ellett murmured in her ear. "Only when first defeated by your beauty."

With her hazel eyes wide with surprise and her tanned cheeks flushed with pleasure, she looked very lovely indeed. Not the loveliest woman he had ever seen, if one counted strictly by facial features, but she was quick, intelligent, and strong-willed. Such things held an attraction of their own. Which meant that no sooner had he said the words than he realized they were true, and not just a method to distract her. To an extent. He hadn't earned the rank of Mage-Captain by being easily distracted or swayed.

Apparently, she hadn't earned the respect of the men and women around her by being easily swayed, either. Narrowing her eyes, she gripped his hand tightly in hers, though at least she spoke equally quietly in his ear. "*Not* without knowing the authority you carry to do such a thing, and *not* without it being tested on a Truth Stone. One which *I* have made, for I do not trust anything Lord Stelled has claimed on his own."

"*Not* in front of your crew," he countered. "You have earned some of my respect and a chance to earn my trust. They have not. And you will give me your word of honor you will not mention it to them."

"You want me to swear a mage-oath?" Mita scoffed.

Ellett shook his head. "No. I want you to give me your word of honor. Just you *saying* that you will keep my full identity to yourself, until I deem it appropriate to tell anyone else. If you break it, then I will *know* you are untrustworthy. Forcing you via magic to keep your word does nothing to help you prove your good character."

She studied him a long moment, then pulled her hands free and picked up her fallen kerchiefs. Straightening, she turned to face her crewmates. "Pick up the mist-net, and weigh anchor. Head south. For now. *You*, come with me."

"Captain . . . ?" one of the crewmen questioned.

"I'm going to interrogate him. If I like what I hear, we'll head for Jetta. If I don't . . . he'll be sent down below—I do hope you know a good water-breathing spell," she added to Ellett over her shoulder.

He smiled back, amused by the threat. "It's not raining *that* hard."

Humor gleamed briefly in her eyes, then she descended to the middeck. Ellett picked up his bag and followed. One of the men on the foredeck shouted an order to the middeck crew, which their bo'sun picked up, blowing first an odd melody on his pipe, then the by-now-familiar tune for hauling a ship's anchor out of the water.

At least I'll no longer have to go round and round the rim of the Jen-

odan Sea, waiting for these people to show up. And I won't have to listen to that shrill whistle being piped day and night for much longer. Following the armor-clad mage all the way back to her cabin under the aft deck, Ellett closed and latched the door behind him. The room wasn't large; in fact, it took up barely half the space. Another door led off to the right, possibly to private quarters, or maybe to storage, he didn't know.

Unlatching one of the drawers at her desk, she pulled out a familiar, palm-sized disc. There were several variations on truth-sensing Artifacts, even some spells which could be applied in an impromptu manner, but the stones, while not as cheap as Truth Wands, were the most commonly used. The balance of truth versus lie could be seen by just how much a lie darkened the purified marble.

She came back, picked up his hand, and placed the stone in it, curling his fingers around the edges. "Tell me true. Is Lord Stelled, cousin to your Seer King, truly dead? And did you confirm this with your own eyes?"

"I am a blue seagull."

THREE

At her bemused look, he glanced pointedly down at the stone disc cupped in his fingers. She released his hand, allowing the blackened imprint of his digits to show. That proved the spells embedded in the Artifact were still viably strong.

The marks faded after a moment. Re-gripping the edges, Ellett gave her the truth. "I was present when the search team brought his remains down from the mountains, and when the healers and mages had scried the truth of his identity, and the means of his death.

"I also personally carried word to His Majesty, Seer King Devin, just under three years ago that the son of the daughter of his great-uncle, his third cousin, Lord Stelled the alchemist, died of a heart attack while gathering rare herbs in the mountains." Uncurling his fingers, he displayed the all-white stone. Clenching it again, he added, "Furthermore, to the best of my considerable knowledge of such matters, *no* ambassador, envoy, or official government representative is currently assigned to Jetta Freeport to represent any official Aurulan interests. Our last envoy of any sort, before myself of course, was sent after the fourth of our ships was pillaged this year."

A brief revelation showed his words were true. Ellett continued briskly.

"Our envoy reported that he was forced to retreat rapidly no more than half an hour after landing. He had found himself being pursued by a mob determined to paint him with your black Jettan tar and hang him for his 'crimes,' claiming at the top of their lungs that he was a child molester. Needless to say, he didn't consider it safe enough to stay in port long enough to prove the falsehood of such claims . . . and His Majesty didn't care to endanger any of his other subjects."

The disc remained white. Outside the cabin, they could hear the muffled sound of the anchor chain clanking its way up the side of the ship, and the orders being barked by the bo'sun to unfurl the sails, adding to the pattering of the rain falling on the deck.

"So *you* are the new envoy, is that it?" Mita asked him, leaning back on the thick-lipped edge of her desk. Like most furniture on a ship, it was bolted to the deck and didn't move.

"Not quite. I have been directed by His Majesty to put an end to the piracy plaguing Aurulan ships and Aurulan shores," he corrected her. "*How* I am to do so is mostly up to me. And you."

This time, when he revealed the Truth Stone, the polished marble surface was mottled by a silver gray imprint of his fingers. Mita arched one of her brows. "*Is* it, now? Care to clarify why that's ever so slightly a lie?"

Clutching the stone, Ellett restated, "Correction. How I am to do so is partially dictated by one of His Majesty's prophesies . . . but being a prophecy, the wording is vague, and the interpretation of said words is still very much a matter of my free will."

Now there was no blemish on the stone. He started to hand it back to her, but she folded her arms across her leather-guarded chest. "We're not done just yet. You haven't said who *you* are, nor what rank or authority you have, that you can claim to speak on behalf of your king."

"Give me your word you won't mention it to your crew, and I'll tell you," he countered. The ship swayed sluggishly. Guessing it was now under power from the wind reduced by his most recent spell, Ellett lifted his hand and withdrew the magic dividing the wind, tapering its effects down as he pulled the energies back into himself. The rigging creaked audibly, reverberating through the ship, and they could hear the sails fluttering and snapping as they were hauled up into place.

Mita eyed him for a long moment, then lifted her pointed chin. "Alright. You have my word of honor I will keep your identity a secret from my crew. For now. For as long as it takes us to sail to Jetta."

"For longer than that," Ellett bartered. "If this impostor has fooled all of you into believing him—and nothing I have heard of you Jettans makes me believe you are lifelong fools—then it's clear he's taken pains to make sure his identity will not be unmasked by any Aurulan official. He *might* even have spies among your crew."

"Not *my* crew," she boasted. "I handpicked them myself. We don't discuss our secrets with outsiders."

Ellett smiled wryly. "That may be, but this isn't one of *your* secrets, so they may not consider it important enough to keep. And they may not spy directly for this impostor, but if even they just talked about me within the hearing of one of his actual informants . . ."

"Fine. I give you my word I'll keep silent about your source of authority until you give me leave to discuss it and you. Now, who are you, Ellett of Aurul?" she asked. "Presuming that *is* your name. Ellett is a fairly common one among both Aurulans and Keketites."

"I am *anything* but common, milady. In specific, I am Mage-Captain Ellett, head of the Royal Guard of the Seer King." That much widened her eyes. He confirmed it by displaying the unblemished stone in his grip. Ellett gave her a small smile, enjoying her reaction. "As I said, I am sent by His Majesty . . . speaking with the words of our God, Ruul. I can do almost anything I like regarding you and your people to get you to stop pillaging our ships, and it will be acceptable in the eyes of my liege and my Patron.

"Be happy I'm interested in *talking* with you, rather than 'sending you down below' as you so charmingly put it." Lobbing the all-white stone at her, he watched her catch it. "Now, a few questions for *you*. What is *your* position in all of this? What rank or position do you hold in Jetta, and who or what gives you the authority to take up vengeance against Aurulans in the name of your people?"

She eyed the disc in her hand, then him. "How much do you know about the freeport?"

"Not much. You're a closemouthed lot. It's a way station for a lot of cross-sea trade. You have massive warehouses, you guarantee the safety of all goods held in storage—some of it expensive stasis-enspelled storage, which is often used for food products and delicate herbs until more profitable times of the year come around. You build some of the fastest ships on the sea, magic notwithstanding. You also don't have a Patron Deity, though you've somehow managed to retain your freedom from would-be conquerors for over four hundred years," Ellett recited, listing the highlights. "And the most peculiar thing of all, when asked who your leader is, you Jettans change the subject. Repeatedly."

Mita stared at him a long, long moment, mulling something over. She seemed to make up her mind, drawing in a deep breath and letting it out. "Swear on your powers as a mage that you'll keep the identity of our leadership and the source of our freedom a secret, and I'll tell you."

Curiosity prodded him into agreeing, but Ellett didn't do so carelessly. "I, Mage-Captain Ellett, bind unto my powers this vow: That *if* the identity of the leadership of Jetta Freeport and the source of its freedom from outside conquest all these years does not harm the sovereign kingdom of Aurul or myself, I shall keep the secret of both these things from non-Jettan sovereign citizens, until given leave to discuss them by Captain Mita or anyone else of an equal or higher Jettan rank . . . but I do reserve the right to both speak and act freely as needed in the defense of myself or my homeland, should that need arise. So say I, Mage-Captain Ellett of the Aurulan Royal Guard."

His skin tingled, and the glow of energy sweeping over him briefly brightened the interior of the cabin.

"So you're a law-sayer, too?" Mita asked sardonically. "Do you really think that's the best vow you could make?"

He shrugged. "It's the best you'll get."

Again, she studied him for a long moment. The hissing of the rain hitting the deck overhead, the creaking of the wind straining against the sails, and the splashing of the waves breaking against the hull filled the silence between them. Finally, she spoke. "The island on which Jetta is built shelters a Fountain. One of those rare and extremely powerful singularity-wells of magical energy. Its exact location isn't important to you, but its Guardian is the leader of our city and the defender of our lands. We do not *need* a Patron Deity to defend ourselves.

"We also have a higher-than-average ratio of mages born to our population, small though it is, and thus we run a local, private Academy to train our mages. A number of them are agriculture specialists, as the rocky terrain of the Jenodan Isles isn't the most hospitable for growing food—wine, yes, but food, no. Most of the rest either work for the various warehouse, merchanter, and transport companies, or as Aquamancers, ship's mages, shipbuilders, and other forms of spellcasters," Mita informed him. Then she smiled slightly. "And *all* of us are trained to defend our homeland. Even if we must be aggressive about it, sometimes."

"A little *too* aggressive," Ellett pointed out. He held up his hand as she stiffened, her hazel eyes narrowing. "However it came about, you now have official Aurulan attention. Open-minded attention. I suggest we focus on creating peaceful ties between our lands. Speaking of which, you've mentioned your leadership, but not *your* position in it. I presume it has something to do with the strength of your magic?"

"Something like that. I'm the commander of our flagship, the *Jetta's Pride*," Mita said, spreading her hands and giving him a slight bow of self-introduction. "Not quite the admiral of the Fleet, but *he's* still in the prime of his life, and a better strategist than I am. Not to mention his wife is our Spymaster, with contacts in every single port around the sea—we trade in information as well as goods, you see. It's one of the factors that helps keep any would-be conquerors in check while they're still just thinking about heading our way."

"A clever use of your resources. So what are you doing on board the *Slack Sails*, if you command the *Jetta's Pride*?" Ellett asked. Now that they were headed south into deeper waters, the ship was starting to rock harder underfoot, forcing him to ease his knees and sway with the rolling of the deck.

She smirked. "*All* Jettan ships are black with white sails, and very sleek and similar-looking in build. All it takes is just a few minutes to swap out the bow and aft boards on which our ship names are carved and painted, and a few minutes more for my crew to change from all-black shirts to all-white. Or any other color we choose."

"And with your faces covered, your identities are further obscured," he agreed. "That explains why I haven't heard of the *Slack Sails* ever docking in Jetta Freeport."

"Yes. You annoyed me and angered my crew when you took off my scarves," she added. A frown pinched her brow. "*How* did you move? No one can move during a Duel Arcane! You stand there and you throw everything you have into it!"

It was Ellett's turn to smirk. "That's a secret of the Royal Guard."

She pouted slightly. "Oh, but I *must* know."

He suspected it was deliberate, because she looked too lovely doing so not to have practiced such a perfect look of pleading disappointment. Mulling it over, he rubbed at his chin, feeling the slight scratch of a day's worth of stubble forming across his skin. "I suppose I *could* teach you . . . in exchange for mage lessons from you in things you can do well. So long as you understand that learning how to move during a Duel Arcane does *not* give you the liberty to attack your opponent. Physical attacks negate the outcome, after all."

That widened her eyes. "So you *cheated*!"

"Ah, but I didn't attack you," he countered, smiling. "A 'physical attack' in a Duel Arcane is one which *harms* the opposing spellcaster. Even by the broadest definition, a kiss does not harm anyone—distractions *are* allowable in a duel, so long as they cause no physical harm."

She narrowed her eyes again, but the corner of her generous mouth curved up. "So you *are* a law-sayer in disguise."

That made him laugh. "That," he agreed, "or I just found your mouth irresistible."

The look Mita leveled at him was dubious at best. "Maybe I should make you repeat that while holding this Truth Stone. I am well aware, Captain Ellett, how large my lips are, how tall my frame, and how unfeminine my hands. I am not a beauty, and I do not need for you to pretend that I am."

Giving her a chiding look, Ellett crossed the space between them. Plucking the Truth Stone from her fingers, he gripped it firmly. "I think you *are* a beauty. That you are lovely in my eyes." Uncurling his fingers, he showed her the all-white marble. She stared at it, taken aback. "As we say in Aurul, beauty is in the eye of the beholder, and I behold a beautiful, strong, intelligent woman when I look upon you."

One step closer would have allowed the swaying of the rainstorm-driven ship to brush their bodies together. Her bits of leather armor wouldn't have been comfortable, however. Dropping his gaze to her tooled leather pauldrons and breastplate, he smiled.

"You have some interesting battle runes, too. Of course, I'd also like to see you in something more comfortable, since that armor isn't necessary around me anymore."

"Oh, it isn't, is it?" she challenged, hands shifting to her hips.

Reaching past her, Ellett set the marble disc on the rail-guarded surface of her desk. It slid a bit as the ship bobbed through the waves, but he didn't care. The movement had brought their bodies close enough for his next attack. "You don't need to be protected from *this*."

This time, though the movement of the ship did brush their lips together, more of it was from his own effort. Bringing his hands up, he cupped her head, sliding his fingers through her thick, auburn hair. At the same time, he sucked on her lower lip. A soft sound escaped her, then Mita slipped her arms around his back. As expected, her armored body wasn't the most comfortable thing to embrace, but she did know how to kiss.

A knock on the door was followed by an increase in the hissing of the rain and a voice calling out, "Captain, First Officer Peany wants . . . *What* are you doing with our captain?"

Mita, he saw as he pulled back, looked a little flustered by the interruption and accusation. He was more amused than embarrassed, himself. Turning to face what looked like the bo'sun of this ship, Ellett gave him a calm, firm reply. "Anything she wants me to do."

That earned him a scowl from the middle-aged man. Mita stepped around him. "Peany wants *what*, Jukol?"

"He wants you to strengthen the rigging, Captain. The weight of the rain accumulating in the sheets and sails has him worried. The crew also wants to know what to do with *this* thing," the bo'sun added, lifting his chin at Ellett.

"Milord Ellett is our guest. Tell the crew we sail for Jetta," she added. "He has things to say which we as a people need to hear. I'll be out as soon as I've shed my armor."

From the look the bo'sun gave him, Ellett guessed the man wanted to order him out of the cabin. Instead of complying with that unspoken glare, he lifted his fingers to the most worn-looking buckles holding the tooled breast and back plates in place; their condition told him they were ones she used the most to get into and out of her armor.

The bo'sun bristled at his efforts, though Mita merely turned and lifted her arm a little, giving Ellett better access. She unbuckled her vambraces and elbow cops herself, calloused fingers making short work of the task. The sailor stepped fully into the cabin, letting the door swing shut behind him in time with the rolling of the ship. "You *don't* need to be doing that, man! You won't be touching her—and if I had my way, you'd be sleeping in the deeps for all you've done!"

"*Enough*, Jukol. Go tell the crew I'll be out in a few moments."

Grumbling under his breath, the bo'sun left.

"For 'all' I have done?" Ellett asked mildly, unfastening the straps that attached the breastplate to her pauldrons next.

"You *did* cost us a ship filled with rare timber and spices," Mita reminded him, slipping sideways out of her upper armor. Lifting a knee to one of the lower railings bracing the legs of her desk, she unbuckled her greaves and knee cops, and lifted her chin toward an armor rack bolted to the wall dividing her cabin from the rest of the ship. "You can hang that over there."

"The advantages I can bring to your future far outweigh the loss of a single prize in the present," Ellett reminded her, before carrying her upper gear to the wooden rods waiting for it. Re-fastening one shoulder strap to secure it in place, he turned back in time to accept the leggings. Once they were secured as well, he turned back to the redheaded captain. "Are the rest of your crew going to dislike me as much as your bo'sun Jukol apparently does?"

She shrugged, re-buckling her belt and its daggers around her hips. "Until they think they can trust you? Probably."

"Can I trust them to leave me alone in my sleep?" Ellett asked her next. "I can fend them off without injuring anyone if I'm awake, but if they attack me in my sleep . . . well, I can't guarantee their safety if they try. Do you think I'd be safe if I slept in the crow's nest?"

She eyed him thoughtfully. Finally, Mita nodded. "I'll have Jukol bring you a hammock. You can set it up in the corner by the door, there. Normally I'd have a cabin girl in that spot, but I don't take younglings when I know we're going to . . . you know."

"Defend your people aggressively?" Ellett finished for her. "Mind if I follow you and watch how you strengthen the rigging? I'm sure you know far more ship-based spells than I do."

Mita laughed at that. "A land-bound man like you? I'm surprised you even have sea legs with *your* background."

"I wouldn't, if I hadn't just sailed around the entire sea four whole times, and then some," Ellett grumbled. "You *could* have shown up a bit earlier, you know. I was growing rather bored."

"You *could* have loaded a more worthwhile cargo, before now—a cargo you still owe us, in recompense for the plundering of the *Island Maid*," she retorted. "And I'll give you a whole lot more to worry about than being *bored* if your people don't stop bothering ours!"

"The *Island Maid*?" Ellett asked, following her out to the mid-deck. "When did this happen, and where?"

"It happened last week, and it happened just south of the Keket border—you may think you're so clever, attacking us so far from Aurulan waters, and using plain white sails instead of all those colorful ones, but you *forgot* to repaint the water-line something other than Aurulan purple," she accused, facing him. It forced her to squint into the rain, but she ignored it. "Or maybe not *you*, personally, if you've been on board the *Parrot's Ride* long enough to circle the sea four or more times. But it's been either an Aurulan merchanter with the bright-colored sails or an Aurulan warship trying to disguise itself without them. Sails can be swapped and different uniforms donned, but everyone knows that Aurulan warships are painted purple below the water-line, and the last two ships have been purple!"

Ellett caught her elbow when she turned away again. He was conscious of the crewmen, many of them clad in oiled, *eta*-like rain jackets, nearby, straining to hear their argument. "I swear to you that there were *no* warships unaccounted for in the last five months, never mind last week. If anything, the more I hear about this 'Lord

Stelled' and these purported warship attacks, the more inclined I am to believe they're an elaborate ruse. Hulls *can* be enchanted to *look* purple—or even repainted if need be, and then covered with an illusion whenever they need to look normal in port. *We* have no reason, as a nation, to pick a fight with you!"

"Ha!" she retorted. "You've always looked down on us!"

"Milady Mita, we *didn't care enough* about Jetta to pick a fight with you," Ellett argued. "First of all, the Aurulan nation is wealthy in its own right. We don't *need* to steal from others—look to the southlands for that, since they're resource-poor compared to us. Second, the whole kingdom's been wrapped up in the news that the Seer King's bride had finally been foreseen, and then in waiting for her to arrive, which she has. Now that they've wed, the whole kingdom is waiting breathlessly for her to produce the next potential heir.

"Or rather, I should say the *government* is waiting, as well as the average citizen," he allowed, glancing around as some of the other crew moved closer, skepticism warring with interest in their expressions. "If this is the work of any Aurulan, then it is a private group under the direction of some madman—I would suspect your false 'Lord Stelled' of masterminding it, if no one else.

"The first rule of battle is, what is the enemy's motivation for attacking? And the first rule of politics is, what does anyone stand to gain by a particular action? Jetta Freeport and the Jenodan Isles have no *value* to my people, therefore, no motivation . . . and our government has nothing to gain by attacking your merchanting ships. Nothing could be gained but war, and war isn't on our list of things to do this decade," he told her, wincing as the wind shifted direction a little. It wasn't enough to need the sails adjusted, but it did drive some of those cold droplets of rain into his ear. "Randomly picking off Aurulan ships simply because you *suspect* Aurulan attacks makes as little sense as Aurulans picking off random Jettan ships."

"Well, it wasn't exactly as if we could *talk* with you about it, since you *didn't care enough* to open *real* diplomatic relations with us," Mita retorted.

"Well, you and I are talking *now*, aren't we?" Mindful of the storm, he released her arm. "We have, what, five days of sailing to get to the freeport? That should be plenty of time to go over every attack you know about, and see if there's a pattern. And I can mirror-scry my own contacts in the Aurulan navy, and get every scrap of information I can about any domestic ships with port manifests that match the attacks, or those of foreign ships which could pass closely enough to masquerade as an Aurulan vessel."

"Four days, if these winds stay steady—and if the *rigging* is going to hold, I have to get to work." Turning, she strode away. Then she stopped, turned, and swept her hand toward the foredeck, giving him a pointed look. ". . . Well? You *said* you wanted to learn more about nautical spells. Move it, sailor!"

"Aye, Captain." Glad this was just a mildly windy rainfall and not a true storm, Ellett followed her carefully across the bobbing, sloping deck. He wiped the water from his face and muttered a warming charm as he did so, but he followed.

FOUR

The sharp jolt woke him from his sleep. Ellett didn't have time to process it, however, for it was immediately followed by the hard crack of his skull hitting something immovably solid, and the bruising thump of the rest of him following suit. An expletive escaped him, and he curled up protectively onto his side, arms sheltering his aching head from the rocking of the hard surface under his body.

Light bloomed as the door to the inner cabin flung open, dazzling his eyes.

"What's going on in here?—Ellett? What are you doing on the deck?" Clad in a white, loosely gathered shirt that contrasted with her suntanned limbs, Mita crossed to his side.

Half blinded by the bright white light of the small globe in her hand, Ellett winced and blinked. He started to say something, but she crouched right next to his head . . . giving him a second dazzling shock, this time from what he saw, thanks to the way her hem had shifted position. *By the Eyes of Ruul . . . she's not wearing any undergarments!*

Her hand touched his face, tilting his head away from that stunning view. She pried back his eyelids while he struggled with that second—if much more pleasant—blow, and held the miniature light-globe up to his face. "Well . . . you don't *look* like you're heavily concussed . . . but you're not exactly responding. *Ellett*, are you all right?"

Her crisp, hard demand broke through some of his daze. In a flash of insight, he realized this was an opportunity not to be missed. *Injuries garner sympathies, after all.* Affecting more of a stunned demeanor than he felt, he wittily responded, ". . . Uh?"

Not that it gained him much in the way of immediate sympathy. With a disgusted sigh, she rose and padded away, taking that lovely, inadvertent view with her. The light bobbled behind him, casting her shadow in a weird dance across the rest of the cabin. "Well. It seems my bo'sun picked out the oldest, most dry-rotted hammock he could find for you. I'm sure you were too much of a land-man to know what to look for, and I didn't check it myself."

She returned to his side, crouching behind his back. As much as he wanted to roll over and see if the view were the same, he didn't dare. Her fingers probed gently at the back of his head, making him hiss in pain when they encountered the very real bruise.

"Well, I don't think your skull is cracked . . . but you're definitely out of it. Come on, wake up!" She tapped him on the shoulder. Ellett obligingly rolled onto his back and blinked up at her, not quite focusing on her face. "You fell on your head, Captain. It's knocked some of the sense out of you. Come on, respond."

Mita brought the light near his eyes. Lifting his arm to ward off the too-white glow, Ellett groaned. "Owww . . . what . . . what happened?"

"Your hammock broke. Come on, sit up, so I can see how bad it is—but if you cast up, you're holystoning the whole deck in here."

With her help, he managed to curl upright. Nausea did well up inside of him at the shift in position, but thankfully not enough to make his stomach protest violently. "Ugh . . . Gods . . . I just want to lie down again."

She brought the light close to his eyes, prying them open a second time when he winced away. "Nope, you're not concussed. I can see your pupils dilating. But you're shocked from the blow, I'm sure. Sleeping on a hard deck won't do you any good, and I wouldn't trust any other hammock the crew might find in the middle of the night. Particularly with how they feel about you."

Ha, sympathy is *working*. Ellett carefully kept his expression vague. He blinked and focused on her face. "It's . . . okay. I don't want to . . . to put you to any trouble. I can sleep on the ground. Done it before . . ."

"And have you getting sick from all the rolling, and cast up all over my cabin?" She snorted and traced a rune on his forehead. "You need a stable, unmoving bed. If I can't trust a hammock, it'll have to be my own bed."

Maybe a little too *well*, he thought, realizing that he hadn't exactly thought through to *what* kind of sympathy she might give him, or where it might lead. "No . . . I'll be all right. I don't want to put you out of your bed."

She snorted again and hooked her arm under his, hauling him to his feet with surprising strength. Ellett allowed her to drape his arm over her shoulders and guide him toward the door to her cabin. "Trust me, that bed is big enough for a small orgy. More important, it's spell-stabilized. Just because you don't *look* concussed doesn't mean you automatically aren't. My healing spells are more geared toward rope burns and battle wounds, but I do know I need to keep an eye on you for the next few hours . . . and I don't think I can trust the ship's healer."

"Why not?" Ellett asked, wincing as she bumped him into the doorframe in the effort to get the panel open and the two of them through. He could have helped her, but he was enjoying the feel of her linen-clad body snug against his. A pity that he was wearing sleeping trousers; his chest might have been bare, and most of her legs, but their flesh only touched in a scant few places.

"Because he's the bo'sun's brother, and they think too much alike to trust him with you right now. Into the bed with you," she added, lowering him to the broad, wood-framed mattress taking up the back of the small cabin. Its covers were rumpled from her hasty exit, and she quickly shoved them out of his way. "Completely into the bed with you, so I can turn on the stabilization spell. It's odd, but the only time I ever get seasick is when I'm lying down. So I spent a week mastering the spells necessary to craft a stabilization warding, since I love everything else about sailing."

Easing his legs up, Ellett sank back into the feather-stuffed pillows. Then winced from his bruises and rolled onto his side. He could tell exactly where she slept when he did that, for she had left a warm spot down the middle of the mattress. *Middle . . . which means she isn't used to sharing a bed with anyone. Or has fallen out of the habit. Like me.*

It was clear from the way she kissed that she was no stranger to intimacy, but he was glad she seemed to be single. Seemed to be. That thought turned over in his mind as he felt her climb in behind him and touch something at the headboard. Instantly, the rocking of the ship quelled and eased, until the bed seemed to be lying still. Some of his sea-legs feeling remained, making him a little queasy, but it didn't last long, thankfully.

He heard her doing something with the light that steadied it; from the sound of it, she was clipping it into a holder of some sort. A moment later, he heard the soft double-thump that shut off the necessary Artifact. Flame-based light ran the risk of setting something on fire, which meant most ships worked hard to afford the expensive items so that they could have clean, steady light belowdecks.

"Uh . . . Mita?" he asked, distracting himself as the nausea faded. He tucked his arm over the blanket and sheet she drew up into place.

"Yes?" she asked.

"I'm not going to be attacked by . . . by a jealous husband, once we reach land? Or a crewman? For being in here?" he added in clarification, still trying to seem like he was more injured than he really was. If someone *did* attack him, they'd get a nasty surprise; Ellett was fully capable of fighting even with a mild concussion, since he had done so in the past.

"The closest you'd get is probably my bo'sun, and he's already attacked you once tonight. He's also happily married, with three children," she stated, pulling the covers up a little higher. Mita paused a moment, then added, "Mind you, *I* might attack you in my sleep. I tend to sprawl a bit. I haven't had to sleep in a hammock for two years, now that I've made captain—and I definitely do *not* sleep with my crew. They might with each other, but not with me.

"I won't play favorites, and I won't disrupt their discipline." She paused, then added, "I also checked you for diseases. You're clean. And you have a contraceptive amulet, like I do. Which is good, since one can never be too careful about such things. Um . . . not that there *will* be such things. You *do* have a concussion, right now."

Ellett merely grunted, since there wasn't much more that he could add to that.

Silence descended between them, broken only by the creaking of the ship and the splashing of the prow through the milder waves, the only thing left of the midday storm they had suffered. He felt her squirming behind his back, shifting the feather-stuffed mattress a little with each movement.

"Ugh. Heave to," she finally muttered. Unsure what she meant, Ellett cautiously rolled back toward her. She poked him in the shoulder. "The *other* way? Heave to the gunnels, land-man, not to the captain—in this case, the gunnels mean the edges of our little boat."

"And here I thought it was a bed," he retorted, squirming forward on his side. That brought him up to a pillow which smelled like her. Ellett couldn't remember noticing it before now, but there it was, a mix of warm woman, linen, feathers, and the pervasive scent of the somewhat salty sea. It was a surprisingly good combination. And a somewhat confusing one. His mind wanted to relax at the scent, but parts farther south wanted to wake up.

"Don't make me keelhaul you," she warned, though she chuckled as she said it. A moment later, he heard Mita yawn, then sleepily order, "Go back to sleep, land-man. I'll keep you safe from any more rotting hammock ropes."

"Aye, Captain." Though as he lay there, Ellett wondered who or what would keep him safe from her, or her safe from their destiny.

The temptations of this moment go far beyond a "gentlest touch" and well into the realm of . . . of matchmaking, for lack of a better term. Everyone knows Ruul is a romantic. He loves every one of his Seers' brides. He also loves foretelling happy marriages to His petitioners. So . . . was His prophecy an attempt at uncovering the real troubles and settling the peace between our two peoples . . . or an attempt at matchmaking *a peace between us?*

It wasn't without precedence. Princess Gabria had originally thought she was being summoned to the Seer King's court as an envoy, only to discover she was meant to be Devin's bride. *And as much as I'd like to claim this concussion idea was just to make her feel more sympathetic toward me . . . after that kiss in the front cabin, I don't think I can honestly say my motives were aimed purely at mere sympathy.*

She is beautiful, after all. And a very good teacher, explaining the specific spells she used throughout the progression of the storm. That, however, drew up a very good point in his mind. *If Ruul pointed me in her direction for matchmaking reasons, if He thinks we'd be compatible as more than just friends or temporary lovers . . . what would happen to our careers? I'm not quite ready to hand over the Royal Guard to my Leftenant—or rather, she's not quite ready to take on the responsibilities just yet, though I could always hope she's finally learning how to handle disparate personalities as a leader—and I'm fairly certain Mita loves being a ship's captain.*

That is, presuming we are are *meant for each other. Nothing's guaranteed, and the logistics would be awkward . . .*

He normally wouldn't think of himself as a romantic man; he was a mage-warrior, a practical man. But lying there on her stabilized bed, feeling the warmth of the woman sharing it with him, inhaling her scent with each breath, Ellett found himself daydreaming potential solutions to each scenario. Closing his eyes, he assessed the troubles of various match-made possibilities and worked through strategies to surmount them, until his daydreams turned into real dreams and he slept.

Someone was fondling his rod. It took him a few moments to crawl up out of the erotic dream that was trying to consume him and come fully awake, but he did, and it was because someone was definitely fondling him. In fact, that someone was plastered all over his left side, head pillowed half on his chest and half on his bicep—numbing his left arm—with their knee and calf curled around his left leg. He could even feel a soft breast pressing into his lower ribs . . . and its owner's hand on his groin, tucked inside his sleeping trousers.

He opened his eyes, dazed and unsure what to do.

For a moment he couldn't see anything. Not because it was dark—there was some light filtering into the cabin from outside, with that gray shade that said dawn wasn't far away—but because her thumb was rubbing slowly back and forth across the little arrow-dimple on the underside of the tip, and her fingers were lightly squeezing him where they had wrapped around the shaft. Mouth dry, panting, he blinked until he could focus on the planks of the ceiling overhead. The subtle, gentle movements of her long, strong fingers threatened to shatter his wits, but he clung to them, trying to figure out what to do.

Craning his neck allowed him to confirm that, yes, it was Captain Mita who clasped him so intimately. Her auburn hair spilled over his chest in a short, tangled mess, obscuring most of her face, but it was definitely her. Lying on his back as he was, the bruise on the back of his head still hurt a little from his fall, but the soft bedding cushioned the worst of the pain. The rest of it was no match for the pleasure evoked by that lazy stroking from her thumb.

It was all he could do not to lift his hips up into her hand. Worse, he didn't know if she was awake and conscious of what she was doing to him. *If she's aware, and therefore taking advantage of me in my sleep . . . well, that's dirty play, and something I'd expect more from a pirate than from the captain of a flagship. But if she's doing this in her sleep, she might wake up embarrassed, or worse, accuse me of coaxing her into it, when technically I'm the victim, here.*

Worst of all, he thought, closing his eyes in the effort to restrain the urge to rub crudely up into her hand, *she might* stop . . .

Her body tensed, and her hand stopped. A moment later, her head lifted slowly, warily from his chest. Ellett was not quite ready to meet her gaze, but he knew he had to speak.

Looking up at the ceiling once again, he confirmed her suspicions. ". . . Yes, I'm awake."

"Oh." Half levered up onto her elbow, Mita very carefully opened her hand, releasing him. "I, ah . . . uh . . . sorry?"

His rod throbbed, protesting at the lack of warmth and stimulation. His cheeks flushed with embarrassment and disappointment. His left arm tingled, blood and feeling returning to his limb. Other parts of him could find some humor in their situation, mainly his mind. "If *this* is what you meant last night by 'attacking' me in my sleep . . . I'm not in any shape to object right now."

That startled a chuckle out of her. ". . . Sorry. I was, ah, having some rather nice dreams in there. Very nice. But it wasn't my intent to molest you in either of our sleep—how's your head this morning?"

"Aching," he admitted. Then added candidly, "Both of them."

She laughed again. "Well, considering I inadvertently made *one* of them ache, would you like me to fix the problem?"

"Yes, please," he replied politely, if a bit breathlessly. She started to get up out of the bed. Ellett snagged her sleeve. "Where are you going, woman?"

She turned back and winked at him. "To fix the hammock, of course."

Ellett tried to laugh, but his rod ached too much to do more than groan. Thankfully, she slid her fingers slowly down his torso. She also leaned over far enough that he got a glimpse of her breasts through the gap in her loosely gathered neckline. Close enough that he was torn between cupping one through the age-worn linen and pulling her tousled head down into range.

Her hair, barely shoulder-length and thus short by Aurulan standards, lured his fingers up to play with the tangled strands. They were very soft. A corner of his mind wondered what she would look like with wedding roses braided into her hair, while another corner wondered what the Jettans did for their marriage ceremony, particularly if they had no Gods to bless their unions.

Breath catching, he tensed as she slipped her fingers under the waistband of his sleeping trousers. It stayed caught as she pushed the material down out of the way with her wrist, fingertips feathering over his hot skin. All that pent-up air left his lungs when she smoothed her palm gently over the curve of his sack, cupping his flesh. It sucked right back in again, making her chuckle.

That firmed his determination. *She may have power over me right now . . . but I can have power over her, too.* Sliding his fingers through her hair, he pulled her head down to his. Pulled that generous, soft mouth down to his. Mita didn't resist; she met him kiss for kiss, each taste and nip as hungry as his own.

Once she was participating, he freed his fingers from the soft strands of her hair and slid it down her throat. He couldn't push aside her shirt as she had his trousers, but he could slide his fingers over the linen, teasing her breasts. Mita purred into his mouth and slid her fingers up to his rod, encircling it. Squeezing it. He retaliated by abandoning her breasts in favor of points farther south. It helped that she scooted closer, bringing her mound into reach.

What he found, once he eased his fingers into her folds, was enough to make him shudder and bite his lip. Slick and hot, her body gave him ample proof she was enjoying this early morning interlude. Ellett did his best to coax more of her liquid essence from her body, rubbing the edge of his forefinger gently through her folds. Mita squirmed and tightened her grip on his shaft, arousing him further.

"Ah—Gods!" she hissed, pulling back from their kiss. He frowned at her, since the move pulled her out of his reach, but not for long. Yanking back the bedding and tugging down his trousers, she quickly climbed over his hips. Ellett hastily grasped and guided his tip when she lowered herself; she teased him for a few moments, rubbing and nudging, then sunk slowly onto his rod.

Heaven. Absolute heaven. More so, when she pulled up the hem of her nightshirt and tossed it aside. While her face and throat and arms, and even a bit of her chest were tanned from years spent on the water, her breasts were a paler shade, tipped with dusky rose discs that begged to be kissed. She didn't lower her torso into kissing range, however. Instead, she closed her eyes, drew in a deep breath . . . and *squeezed.*

Ellett choked on his own breath. She moaned as she did it again. So did he, eyes rolling up as he struggled with his body's demand to pound and pound and spend himself. Just as he reached for her hips, needing the leverage gained by gripping them, a noise nearby startled both of them.

"Captain? Captain!"

"Gaah! *Skodeth!*" Lashing out her hand, Mita zapped the door handle with a red spark. It washed over the latch in what Ellett guessed was a locking spell. A bare second later, the man on the other side of the door tried to open it, but barely jiggled the lever. He pounded on it, calling through the panel.

"Captain, are you in there? The Aurulan's gone! The slimy sea-spy's gone missing, Captain!"

She bared her teeth in a cross between a snarl and a grimace. "No, he *hasn't*, Jukol."

"But he's not in his hammock!"

"You mean the *rotten* one you dug up out of the bilge for him?" she shot back, glaring at the door. "Bo'sun Jukol, your little trick gave our *guest* a nasty concussion. I've been forced to tend him all night because I don't trust your asinine attitude not to have rubbed off on your brother, and I haven't had a lot of sleep as a result. You also know that First Officer Peany has the night watch! You are *not* to disturb me in the mornings unless we've run aground, are being pursued, or the ship is on fire! Maintain *discipline*, Bo'sun Jukol."

". . . Aye, Captain." The bo'sun sounded subdued, rather than belligerent. Mita released a heavy sigh after they heard the front door to the captain's cabin shut.

With some of his own urgency diminished by the unwelcome intrusion, Ellett wondered if she'd lost hers. Before he could ask her if she wanted to stop, she rolled her eyes, shook her head, and looked down at him.

"Sorry for the interruption. How's your head? Does it still ache?" The gleam in her eyes matched the curve spreading those lovely lips. "If it does, I was thinking a massage might help."

She tightened her inner muscles just as he started to reply. Losing his breath, Ellett could only gape at her. He drew in another lungful of air, only to lose it a second time when she repeated the intimate squeeze. Mita laughed softly.

"Poor thing, looks like you've been struck speechless," she murmured.

That narrowed his eyes. She could torment and torture him with the delights of her body all she wanted, but she would not mock him and get away with it. Gripping her hips, Ellett pushed her up a little, then pulled her down, circling his hips as he lifted them to meet her.

Her hazel eyes widened and a delighted smile curved her mouth. A squeeze of her flesh met his next spiraling stroke, as did the ones that followed.

Holding her gaze, Ellett made love with her somewhere between languid and heated. The bo'sun hadn't spoiled their mood so much as tempered it, thankfully. But as the sun rose in the east, gleaming through the port-side windows, their tempo rose as well. Gripping his hands for balance, she started curling her pelvis forward with each downward stroke.

With the sweat of their efforts sheening her skin, her hair glowing red in the intermittent rays of the sun peeking through the windows—the bed they were on felt as steady as if it were on land, but the ship still bobbed up and down with each passing wave—Ellett thought she was the most beautiful woman he had ever seen. He wanted more than anything to see what she looked like when she came undone.

Shifting her hands to his chest made two things available: his own hands and her breasts. They swayed enticingly with each stroke of her body. At least, until he cupped them. The soft mounds weren't overly large, but they didn't need to be. In fact, the best part was how the pebbled tips of her breasts slotted perfectly into the gaps between his thumbs and forefingers. That allowed him to knead and gently roll the various bits of her flesh, until she shuddered over him, gasping his name.

The feel of her breasts in his hands connected itself down through his arms to his abdomen, joining with the squeezing bliss of her inner muscles, heightening his own pleasure. When she sagged, replete, Ellett lowered her to his chest and wrapped his arms around her waist. The angle was different in this position, not quite as deep, but still enjoyable. Listening to her pant as she recovered, he reveled in the way she covered, even clung, to him, leaving him free to thrust as he wished.

She sighed against his neck, then shifted her head. An exploratory lick of her tongue along the lobe of his ear broke his careful pacing. It caused a shock wave of pleasure which exploded both down through his chest and up from his toes, gathering in the heavy fullness of his rod. Pulling on her hips, Ellett held her close and poured himself into her heat, groaning with each mind-reeling pulse.

Slowly, his muscles relaxed. Before any post-bliss lethargy could lure him back to sleep, Ellett shifted his hands from her hips to her face. A tilt and a nuzzle allowed him to find her lips, kissing her in thanks for their lovemaking. She sighed and kissed him back for a few moments. Sitting up, Mita smiled down at him.

"Feeling better?"

"Mmm, yes." Ellett paused thoughtfully, then added, "Unless I should have a relapse later tonight. I just might need more of your tender ministrations to make me feel better, again."

She chuckled. "We'll see." Climbing off of him, she steadied herself at the side of the bed. "Oh—you may want to just stand by the side of the bed for a couple moments so you can get used to the movement of the ship again."

Nodding, he watched her move across the cabin. There were three doors in this inner chamber; one led back to the captain's office, one led to the head, the charming nautical term for the closet that passed for a refreshing room, and a heavily locked and rune-warded door which Captain Mita had dismissed as "the ship's vault" last night. If they had succeeded with their raid on the *Parrot's Ride*, no doubt the most valuable of goods would have been locked behind its stout walls.

She came back after a few moments. His turn, he rose and braced himself beside the bed for a few heartbeats, then crossed the room once he felt his sea legs returning. Using the same door she had, Ellett relieved himself at the refresher, then used a dribble of water on a clean scrap of cloth, scrubbing the sleep from his face and the evidence of their lovemaking from his skin. A muttered spell scrubbed and dried the fabric, which he tucked back over its hanging rod under the small square of mirror fastened to the bulkhead.

The silvered glass, he noted, had been carved along the edge of its wooden frame with anti-scrying wards. It reminded him of the small palm-mirror in his bag of belongings, and the fact that he really should contact someone back in Aurul about having found the pirates, and having found a more serious problem than just some disgruntled Jettan sailors playing restitutions games.

Later in the day, he promised himself. *None of my contacts back at the palace would be awake this early. Well, maybe Leftenant Rahina*, he corrected himself, rubbing his hand over his stubble-dusted chin. *She's an early riser.*

His musings from last night came back to him. *If Ruul thinks we're meant to be together . . . then either Captain Mita or Mage-Captain Ellett will have to give up their career. I love my work, and I am proud to serve my king . . . but she loves her own as well, and is proud to sail for her people. And I'm not sure how* I *would decide, let alone her.*

Not one to keep fighting an opponent that hadn't yet materialized, Ellett murmured a shaving spell. His hair needed tending, too, since little wisps of brown were escaping its braid, but that would have to wait until he could dig his brush out of his bag. With nothing left to tidy, he returned to the sleeping cabin.

His half-formed thoughts of getting dressed and starting the day vanished at the sight of his hostess. She had redonned her nightshirt and crawled back into her bed, cuddling one of her overstuffed pillows with a contented smile. Amused, Ellett approached her. "Permission to climb aboard, Captain?"

FIVE

She quirked a brow, though she kept her eyes shut. "Me, or the bed?"

"The bed," he clarified. Then couldn't resist adding, "For now."

"Permission granted—but be careful," she added as he eased through the transition from moving ship to unmoving bed. "I take prisoners."

"So do I." Shifting so that he spooned up behind her, he allowed himself to cuddle her. This was something he hadn't done in a very long time: snuggled in bed with a woman without it being a prelude to a session of lovemaking. There was something of a post-lovemaking feel lingering in the air, but not by much. That thought did prompt him to speak, however. "Thank you for making love with me. I enjoyed it very much. I hope you did, too."

Mita chuckled. "Oh, I did. You're quite good. Unless you think you can do better, of course?"

"Naturally. But later." Honesty prompted him to gently squeeze her, adding, "I like *this*. I don't get to do this very often."

"Neither do I." A bell off at the prow of the ship rang, counting the hour. She sighed. "Fifth bell. Breakfast will be ready in an hour. I usually eat with the second watch at the end of the meal, but if you're hungry, we could cadge something early."

"I can wait. What do you do after you eat breakfast?" Ellett asked.

"After that, I usually spend a little time going over the course and the charts with my First Officer, discussing what happened during the night watch, and then I spend about two hours overseeing the off-duty crew in their weapons practice. We're not quite a full-time warship, since we do occasionally take on cargo—legitimate cargo," Mita clarified, "—but we're as close as any ship in the fleet ever gets, considering how all Jettan vessels and their crews are expected to serve in the defense of our isles.

"Once that's done, it's usually ten bells of the morning, and I take over the day watch from Peany, my First Officer, until ten bells of the evening. He's nicer than Jukol . . . to a point. You may have noticed he wasn't entirely friendly toward you last night, but neither was he rude."

"I noticed. My mornings are a little different," he offered. "But not too different from yours."

"Oh."

"Well, when I'm not chasing down mad Jettan pirates," he teased, squeezing her again with the arm he had wrapped around her waist, "I rise early, break my fast and dress, then look over my correspondence until I receive word His Majesty is awake. Then I hold a brief consultation with the Master of the Royal Retreat—the man who schedules His Majesty's day and oversees the doings in the royal wing of the palace—and both of us report to His Majesty over his breakfast.

"*Then*, depending upon that schedule, I either spend a couple hours at the salle, practicing weapons and spells with my fellow Royal Guards, or I oversee His Majesty's defense practice, or I arrange escort for His Majesty if the Seer King needs to travel anywhere. And of course I do these things now for Her Highness, too. Or I would, if I weren't busy chasing down angry Jettans."

"And later in the day?" Mita asked, squirming onto her back so that she could look at him. "What does the Mage-Captain of the Royal Guard do?"

"Stand around looking pretty," he quipped, and laughed at her confusion. "From tenth hour—your tenth bell—to noon, His Majesty attends to the days' prayer-petitions and leads services in one of the glass chapels attached to every royal residence. Then there is lunch, followed by petitions for prophecies. It's a custom for parents to bring their children to the capital for a blessing between the ages of twelve and fourteen. At least, those who can afford to travel. Otherwise His Majesty makes a royal tour twice a year, circumnavigating the kingdom as he travels between the winter and summer palaces. More serious petitions are heard in the later afternoon, along with council sessions attended by the various heads of governance and the Prime Minister. Supper is followed by early evening prayers.

"And all the time these things are happening, I'm either organizing things in the background, or serving alongside my fellow guards, 'looking pretty' as bits of background decoration," Ellett said. "Our uniforms aren't designed for subtlety, but we do our best to be forgotten by everyone. That way we can spend our time looking for whatever potential danger might lurk in the royal court."

"Danger? I thought everyone in Aurul loves your king," Mita offered, frowning at him.

"Most citizens do, but sometimes certain people take exception to him. Either they're angry with our God for prophesying something unhappy, or for *not* prophesying it, or they're angry at their king for agreeing with the Prime Minister that taxes needed to be raised, or that funds had to be shifted from road repair to bridge building after a sudden flood . . . or they're enemies of the nation. Before Mekhana fell, the agents of their False God would try to sneak the occasional assassin among us, and the Keketites in decades past haven't always cared for certain Aurulan trade taxation policies." Propping his head on his hand, Ellett gave her a wry smile. "Since every Royal Guardsman and Guardswoman is a highly skilled battle-mage, we're also sometimes sent into areas of conflict to quell them more directly, whether they're internal or external.

"Most recently, it was the new kingdom to the west, Guildara. I was sent with an escort of thirty guards to secure peace for our neighbors, and fetch back Her Highness." He smiled. "Unless you count being ordered onto a ship to go hunt down a bunch of wily Jettan pirates."

"*Technically* we're privateers. We're not in this for our own profit, but rather, for the welfare of our people," Mita countered mock-primly.

"So what do you do when you're not privateering?" Ellett asked.

"We patrol the waters around the isles, and occasionally take on very expensive cargo that needs to be run swiftly and safely to its destination port. Because I'm such a strong mage, we can get away with just the healer on board as backup," she told him. "Normally our ships run with two mages and a healer, if not three. There are too many lucrative jobs on land, which is where most of our more powerful mages tend to be employed, so we use the lesser ones at sea."

"It's the same with Aurulan ships' mages," he agreed. "The worst part about auditioning for the post on the *Parrot's Ride* was memorizing and displaying all the necessary spells to prove my competence. I had the power, just not the practice."

"Mmm. You're certainly stronger than almost any other ship's mage out there, excluding myself—and for the record," Mita added, the corners of her mobile mouth curling up, "I hadn't reached my peak strength when you disarmed me with that kiss."

Ellett smirked back. "Neither had I. Not that I'd care to get into a Duel Arcane in earnest with you, but . . . if you like, I could teach you how to move during a duel. Once you learn how to move, you're far less likely to let a physical collapse lead to a magical failure."

"Isn't that some sort of arcane secret of the Aurulan Royal Guard?" Mita drawled, twisting onto her side so that she could plant her elbow on the bedding and her cheek on her palm, mirroring his position. "Wouldn't you get in trouble with your government if you taught it to me?"

"As I said yesterday, a physical *attack* nullifies the results of a Duel Arcane," he reminded her. "But a distraction doesn't count. Many a duel has been won or lost based on distractions. Most mages train themselves to ignore anything *outside* the Dueling shield, but very few are prepared for troubles *inside* its circumference. As for any 'secret' to the trick, there isn't one. It just takes concentration and practice."

"If physical attacks aren't allowed, then why bother doing it?" Mita asked.

Ellett wrinkled his nose. "Because while they aren't *allowed* . . . they aren't unknown, either. It was a good . . . two hundred and thirty years ago? Somewhere back then. A mage from Haida snuck into Aurul, pretending to be a native. He hung around the royal court for a few years, ingratiating himself, then challenged a Royal Guardsman for his position. Back then, it was easier to get into the Guard. He was known, supposedly trusted, and if you were known and trusted, and powerful enough, you could challenge a Guardsman to a Duel Arcane. If you won, you became a Guardsman yourself.

"This fellow cheated. Naturally the Royal Guard screened all applicants under truth-spell, but the fellow wore a special talisman that allowed him to lie and get away with it," Ellett told her. "Then, once he was a member of the Royal Guard, he started challenging the other members to private duels. 'Practice duels,' he called them. Held without witnesses, he was able to move while they were trapped in the effort of the duel, and killed them with a needle dipped in a very toxic poison. Three Guards were declared dead of a heart attack before we grew suspicious."

"So how did you catch him?" Mita asked.

"My predecessor quietly rounded up a small army of lower-ranked mages and had them scry upon each and every one of his fellow Guards. This man was *very* clever, though. Very skillful and well prepared, as well as powerful. He had cast spells against scryings to make it look as if he was somewhere else—usually in the gardens—while he killed three more Guards, with the intent of infiltrating even more secret Haidans into the Royal Guard. His targets simply seemed to be walking around, meditating, reading, whatever, before they keeled over."

She frowned. "It's said the Eyes of Ruul see all. Why didn't He warn your ancestors?"

"Because the Gods gave us free will. These were things we *could* notice, and could handle on our own," Ellett pointed out. "Aurul was also embroiled in a border war with Keket at the time, if I remember right, which was probably why the Haidans saw fit to attempt their infiltrations during our distraction."

"So if his spells were so good, how did they catch him?" she asked.

"The only child of the Seer King, a very young daughter, escaped her nurse and ran right through the illusion of the Guardsman. Naturally, the girl didn't see anything, because the illusion was only in the scrying mirrors of the Mage-Captain's spies. But the spies saw it happen, and quickly accounted for every single Guardsman that was both alone and far enough from possible witnesses, *and* who had recently come in contact with the illusion-Guard. There was just one," he said. "The real Haidan Guardsman was off trying to kill his seventh victim down by the beach, east of the winter palace. My predecessor raced down there with several of the Guards he trusted, caught the man, and . . . well, after a bit of rather unpleasant trial and error, found and destroyed the talisman, and extracted a full confession.

"That confession included the means he had used to deceive everyone, and the Haidan identities of four of the new Guards he'd managed to get into place. The others were Aurulans who had beat out the other applicants." Ellett rubbed at his face, glad such ancient headaches weren't his. "I thank Ruul that none of them had been assigned all as a group to escort duty, yet, since they were all still being paired with more experienced Guards. If they had been the only ones on duty, the moment they got His Majesty all alone . . ."

"Without a son to take up the Seership of the kingdom, the confidence of the kingdom would have faltered and the Haidans would have poured in over the border. I haven't been too happy with the *current* version of Haidan expediency, either," Mita offered wryly. "They've toned down in the last year or so, but even a law-sayer would have a hard time pinning them down, unless it was to word the law in such a way that benefitted *them* the most. Theirs is not an altruistic deity, and the ways of Hai-shu, Patron Goddess of Diligence, are not always *moral*.

"*Exacting*, but not always moral," Mita agreed. "Not to throw stones at our own windows, of course, but with that for an example, is it any wonder my people have shied away from picking out a Patron of our own?" she quipped dryly.

"When you put it that way, no," Ellett agreed. He started to say something more, then stopped and frowned. "Wait . . . you said the Haidans have grown quiet over the last year, correct?"

"Yes. They've given up testing our defenses for now," Mita repeated.

He sat up, frowning. "The Haidans don't give up easily. They're always searching for something to do. When they have a good king or queen on the throne, they're a joy to deal with. When they don't, they're a pain in the neck. They haven't bothered Aurul during this reign, let alone in the last year. Yet they still have the same king as before. I can't imagine his attention would have faded so easily from your people, unless he had something else to focus his attention on . . . but I haven't heard any rumors among the ports that the Haidans have turned their attentions south or west, either."

Mita sat up next to him, wrapping her arms around her blanket-draped knees. "So the Haidans are up to something. The question is, what?"

"They can be very subtle," Ellett muttered. He lifted a brow at her. "Maybe they're the ones behind the impostor Lord Stelled and the fake Aurulan warships?"

"Or they could be from another country, or they could be independents working together, or they could be independents working separate agendas . . . though considering some of the things 'Lord Stelled' has said *could* be construed as subtle threats, they're probably working together," Mita said. She picked a nub of lint off of the top blanket and flicked it away. Her tanned brow furrowed. "The more I think about it, the more everything seems to be coming to a head, like he's planning on 'encouraging' us to pay high import/export taxes permanently, in order to ensure our ships are never attacked by Aurulan vessels again."

"Either that, or it's an encouragement to get Jetta Freeport and the Aurulan government embroiled in a war, which could be politically advantageous for another country," Ellett pointed out. He placed his hand on her linen-draped back and rubbed gently. She leaned into him, making him feel good. Making his rod twitch and regain some life to it, too. Sighing, he focused his mind on the problem at hand and continued. "The *good* thing is that your prior attacks have been remarkably polite. Very few injuries, very few lost lives. And you don't scuttle the ships or seize them, sending the crews out in longboats to try to make it to some shore. You just round everyone up, transfer the cargo, damage the rigging so they cannot pursue quickly, then set them free as you sail away."

"We're vengeful, not stupid," she muttered, nudging him with her elbow. "Besides, ever since we turned to trading for our main source of income, we've always known it hurts worse to hit someone in their wallet than to hit them in their stomach."

A mischievous thought crossed his mind. Ellett eyed the woman at his side. "Oh, really?"

She lifted her chin from the arms clasped around her knees, loosening her grip on them. "*Yes*, really."

"Even when you attack them like *this*?" Pushing her back onto the bed, Ellett raised her nightshirt and wormed his head down between her arms and legs, raspberrying her belly. She shrieked, laughed, and fought back.

Somewhere in there, his night trousers got torn at the hip and her shirt pushed up over her head. When Ellett finally managed to pin her to the mattress, fabric-tangled arms secured in place over her head, his rod had wound up pressed against the warm, slick folds of her loins. From the warmth in her eyes and the way her hips flexed, rubbing herself against him, he knew she wouldn't protest. But he had to ask.

"May I . . . ?" he inquired politely, nudging her gently.

Mita smiled. "Be my guest."

More mischief made him grin. Prodding carefully, he sank in the tiniest bit and said, "My, what a lovely, warm entry hall you have. So very *welcoming*."

That sparked another fit of laughter in her, which squeezed the head of his shaft. His eyes rolled up into his head. Delving deep, Ellett rode her spasms of laughter until they became shudders of pleasure. For both of them.

Collapsing in the bliss of aftermath, he remembered to brace some of his weight on his elbows and knees. But it was alright; she cradled him close, stroked his braided hair and his sweat-damp shoulders. Pressed her lips to the side of his throat. He liked that. Drawing in a deep breath, he shifted enough to the side to rest on the bed, though he pulled her close.

"You are an incredibly beautiful, funny, intelligent, passionate woman," Ellett murmured in her ear. "And I cannot remember the last time I had this much fun with anyone. You make it special."

The casual look in hazel eyes melted and her mouth curved into a smile. Looping an arm around his shoulders, she pulled him close enough to kiss the tip of his nose. "I like you, too." Her smile spread into a grin. "Even if you are a land-man. And I'll take you up on that offer to learn how to move during a Duel Arcane. *And* teach you how to be a proper ship's mage, in exchange.

"One of these days, you Royal Guard types just might have to know these sorts of thing for real, after all. Plus, if we're to put our two lands on even footing with plenty of trust shared all around, someone should teach you how to do it right." Her smile took on a touch of shyness. "That, and it's a lovely excuse to spend my free time in your company, since we still have a few days of sailing ahead of us before we reach the city. If you don't mind?"

"I'd like that," he told her, knowing it was the truth.

SIX

Bo'sun Jukol stepped between Ellett and the gangplank just as the Aurulan started to follow Mita down to the dock. The middle-aged man eyed him up and down, taking in Ellett's plain blue linen clothes, then sighed. "I don't know if you're right about the ambassador up there, but you've done right by the Captain, teaching her your land-man tricks. And taking shots from her, and being polite to the rest of us, despite, ah . . ."

Ellett offered his hand, cutting off the other man. "My pleasure."

"Right." Clasping it, Jukol shook hands, then clapped him on the back. "Watch your land-man legs on the dock for the first few moments, or you might fall off into the water. If you're a diplomat for real, it'd be a shame to lose you."

It wouldn't have been diplomatic to point out that Ellett had spent the last several nights in the captain's enchanted bed, and had grown used to the transition from sea to stability and back. Instead, he nodded, eyed the walled city waiting for him, balanced his duffel bag on his other shoulder, and picked his way carefully down the rail-guarded ramp. This was a city of mages and merchants, farmers and sailors, all of them self-reliant, independent, proud, and wary, and steeped in the magical traditions of half a dozen lands, plus the various spells they had developed on their own.

What he wanted to do was meet this Guardian of theirs who led . . . Ellett stopped dead, just two steps onto the boards of the wharf. Someone or something was scrying him. *Enemies do that when preparing for an ambush or setting up a battlefield . . . but this is a deeper probe. A specific probe, with parameters that feel different. But, how?*

Mita came back to him, weaving around several of the *Jetta's Pride* crewmembers who had been given leave to disembark now that they were at their home port. She gave him a concerned look. "Ellett?"

He raised his hand to ward off her questions, but the tendrils of the scrying spell seized on his name, digging their hooks into it. Dissecting his identity. A flash raced outward in the next heartbeat, so faint that if he hadn't been staring down at the boards of the dock, and thus at the shadows of the sailors making their way ashore around him, he wouldn't have seen it.

But he did, and his gaze followed it as it flared up the legs of the crew and raced toward the shore. One of the stevedores helping to load crates onto a smaller ship tied up closer to the base of the wharf stopped and peered back up the length of the dock. The moment he spotted Ellett, he scowled and set down his crate.

"Hey! You!" Striding forward, he pushed aside a couple of the *Pride*'s crew and pointed a finger at the confused Aurulan. "I *know* you! You're that Gods-be-damned *murderer* that burned that family of Haidans to death five years ago!"

Movement past him showed several others heading Ellett's way. Even the crew of Mita's ship, whom he could have sworn he'd won over, were turning and glaring at him. Including Mita, who was frowning at him in suspicion. A flash of memory passed through his mind. *The previous envoy . . . accused of child molestation . . . chased by an angry mob—the spell!*

It was already at the city gates, with who knew how many more innocent people waiting to be snared by its effects.

Not for nothing was he a mage-warrior, and not for nothing the Mage-Captain of the Royal Guard. This was *not* the first sabotage spell he had faced, though it was disturbingly cunning. And disturbingly fast. *No time for subtlety!*

Snatching one of the long daggers from Mita's belt, he let his bag of belongings fall to the planks underfoot. Without hesitation, Ellett grabbed the blade with his left hand and pulled his palms apart, then knelt and slammed the blood-coated steel into the wooden dock with all of his might, releasing his power in a single, willful word.

"*Break!*"

Blood-red power flared out of him and raced up the length of the dock, chasing after that pale golden glow visible at the edge of his mage-sight. It whipped past crates and barrels—some of which broke open—past cranes and pulleys—whose rigging creaked and snapped—and kept going, moving as fast as he could pour his life's magic into the command. Fisting his left hand to control the bone-deep ache of his wound, squeezing more blood out from between his fingers, he concentrated on shattering whatever it was that scrying spell had triggered.

It worked, in that the people already affected slowed, stopped, and shook their heads. Now they frowned from confusion, rather than outrage. Mita started to crouch next to him, then straightened, staring over his head at something that made her eyes widen. She quickly looked to either side.

"The docks . . . are on fire? Bright Heavens, *all* of them are catching! And the spells are all failing!"

Ellett didn't move. All of his attention poured into his counter-spell, chasing down every last bit of that scrying enchantment. Only when he couldn't sense it anymore did he ease his mental pressure and withdraw his energies back into himself. It was crude countermagic, what he had done, but nevertheless powerful. Feeling dizzy, he sagged back on his heel and rested. Someone came down the gangplank and grabbed his arm, lifting his injured fist.

"Idiotic land-man!" Jukol's brother chided him. The ship's healer wrapped his large, calloused palms around the Aurulan's fingers and murmured, pouring his own magics into Ellett's severed flesh. That hurt even worse than cutting it had, for it added a burning sting on top of the painful ache. Enduring it stoically, Ellett peered past the broad-shouldered man at the damage his counterspell had wrought.

Anything magical which had been touched in passing by the scrying spell had suffered. Every last spell had been broken. Blood magic was incredibly powerful, and incredibly dangerous. Not just because it had bled most of his energies out of his body with the force of his will but because it always ran the risk of an evil taint. *That way lies madness, and the whispers of the Netherhells. It may have been a self-sacrifice and thus* not *inherently evil, but I suspect I'm going to have to repair each and every damned, damaged enchantment to make* sure *nothing ill is attached to my soul, because of it.*

Mita had moved to the end of the dock, where several of her crew had grabbed whatever cloth came to hand, shirts, sacks and the like, and had beaten the flames down to smoldering cinders. He heard her chanting something, and heard the splash of water on the underside, extinguishing the last of the flames. A glance at the other wharfs showed similar scenes. When he looked back behind himself, she wasn't in sight for a long moment. Then he saw her, rising up on the same sort of spell-stiffened water he had used to cross to her ship days ago.

A frown pinched her face as she stepped onto the charred boards. Mita strode back to his side just as the healer was prying his hand open, checking the healing of the cut for flexibility. He winced, but let the man probe the injury; he had some minor healing magics of his own, but this was a deep wound, requiring an expert touch.

Crouching, she touched his shoulder. "The part that caught on fire, it looks like it had runes scratched into the underside of the planks. I suspect *all* of them were marked. I'm not familiar with half the markings that were used, though."

"I'm not surprised. I believe this was the same spell used to chase our last envoy off the docks under the spurious claim he was a child molester." Ellett paused, gritting his teeth as the ship's healer muttered another spell over his palm, making his fingers tingle with cold, pain, heat, and ticklishness all at once. The new spell faded, giving him room to speak without grunting. "In fact, I'd say it probably was designed to attack the reputation of any Aurulan arriving here in an official capacity . . . and that the more official backing an arriving person had, the stronger the effects of the spell."

"Hence the accusation of you being a mass murderer, instead of just a child molester. That makes sense," Mita allowed. "Disturbing sense, but sense. You come here with so much authority, the spell literally blazed to life, determined to destroy you before you could reach the shore."

"No, my counterspell caused the runes to catch on fire," he corrected her, shaking his head. "It's like the sparks you see in a Duel Arcane, my magics versus the power of whoever carved them into your docks. *All* of your docks, because he or she would *have* to make sure any emissary sent from my people would be caught and targeted before they reached the city."

"There, your hand's better," the healer murmured. "You'll be hungrier than a starving dog in a few moments, and everything will ache and be tender, but there's no fear of infection. You did lose a fair bit of blood, though. Try not to spill any more, and drink plenty of water with your next meal."

"Thank you," Ellett murmured. He glanced at his palm, bisected by an especially straight, pink-healed line, and guessed it would finish healing without any noticeable scarring. He switched his gaze to Mita, who looked worried. "On the bright side, I'm pretty sure this was a passive scrying spell, and that it wasn't connected directly to its caster, which means he hasn't been alerted to its destruction, yet. There's only one person who would be afraid of a *real* envoy coming to Jetta Freeport. Let's pay him a visit."

She shook her head, fluffing out her auburn locks with the movement, and spoke under her breath, leaning close enough to keep her words private. "First, a visit to the city leader. That much magic—blood magic—will have alerted the leader to your presence. It's best if we reassure our leader as to your intentions. And if L . . ." She stopped herself from mentioning the name, showing some discretion in the quick flick of her eyes around the dock. "Well, if your clever foe hasn't been alerted as you suspect, we can simply summon the person in question, and deal with them then."

Grasping the hilt of her dagger, she worked it back and forth, grunting with the effort until the point, embedded firmly in the planks from the force of his blow, rocked itself free.

"And if they have been alerted?" Ellett asked, digging a kerchief out of the square blue sleeve of his *eta* so that she could wipe the blade clean.

She grinned and accepted the cloth, rising from her crouch. "Simplicity itself. I may not be the admiral, but I am the captain of the flagship, and it is my right to demand that all vessels stay in port . . . at least for twenty-four hours. Unless it's a very clear-aether day—and it doesn't feel like it, thanks to your little blood spell just now—our quarry cannot mirror-Gate out of here."

In just a few firm strokes, she had the blade clean enough to sheathe. He occupied himself with finding the drawstring to his duffel bag so that he could sling it back over his shoulder. Ready, Ellett accepted the hand she offered, letting her pull him to his feet. "You can sense the aether?"

"It's like weather-sense, or mage-sight, if a bit more difficult." She shrugged. "It's something that can be developed with practice."

"Ah. Like moving during a Duel Arcane," he murmured, following her across the dock. As much as he wanted to make amends for the broken spells around him, they had a bigger problem to contain, an impostor who clearly didn't want a real Aurulan official to show up on his doorstep. Mindful of his commoner clothes, and the stains from his wound which had made their way onto his thigh, he thought of the carefully wrapped bundle at the bottom of the bag bouncing at his back. "Should I clean up a bit, first? I did bring one set of court clothes with me."

"When we send for our quarry, I think," Mita told him. "The person you are about to meet doesn't stand on formality."

The person he met didn't even *stand*, Ellett discovered.

The person who held the position of Guardian of Jetta Freeport was barely tall enough to reach Ellett's shoulder, had a head of golden hair more curly than anyone Ellett had ever seen, and a pair of lively blue gray eyes which gleamed behind a nose-pinching version of a pair of single-lensed, gray-tinted viewing loupes. She didn't stand, because the entire time she held her interview with him, the young woman constantly moved. And she didn't walk so much as flit. Nor did she hold the title of Guardian, officially.

Instead she was, officially, the Chief Librarian of the Freeport University. The university, he learned, was something like the Academies found more commonly elsewhere, but instead of following one primary discipline of study, such as healing, spellcasting, military skills, a particular craft skill, it contained all such disciplines. The library was therefore the largest building in the whole city, and well guarded behind rune-carved walls.

The young woman didn't even bother to wait for introductions when Mita led him deep into the stacks of shelves on one of the upper floors. Instead, she assessed him in a swift look from head to foot, then stuck out her hand. The one not carrying an open book, that was, which happened to be her left hand. Ellett, perforce, had to shake hands with his own left hand.

"Callaia, Chief Librarian of the university. Captain Mita didn't say what position you hold, but I think I can guess. From the scar I can feel on your palm, you're the author of that rather powerful piece of primal blood magic not half an hour ago. You also have the finely crafted, subtle shielding of an Aurulan Royal Guardsman about you. Since I doubt they would send a peon, you're either a Sergeant, the Leftenant, or the Mage-Captain . . . and if your name is Ellett, then I welcome you, Captain, to Jetta Freeport. I trust you'll not run out of here screaming at the accuracy of my assessment?" she asked, before releasing his hand and moving farther up the row of shelves.

Mita tipped her head, silently urging Ellett to keep up with the short woman. He hastened to do so, catching up in just three long strides. "Ah, yes, that would be my identity, and, no, I don't intend to flee. I'm actually impressed, rather. I should also apologize profusely for the disruptions to the various dockside magics, but . . ."

"No apologies necessary. I'm afraid some of the fault is mine. I've been rather preoccupied with my studies, and foolishly assumed the docks were still fine. The author of that particular spell was *very* audacious, carving it upon *my* planks."

For a moment, she scowled at nothing, then looked into her book, flipped through a few pages at a steady rate, sighed, and snapped the book shut. A swing of her elbow sent it lofting up into the air, where it floated up and back several feet before slotting itself neatly into place somewhere near the ceiling. She didn't stop to see if it did reshelve itself properly, but continued on, forcing Ellett and Mita to keep pace or be left behind.

Lifting her finger, Callaia continued bristly. "Mind you, I do realize that the people of Aurul also have a claim on the offending spellcaster's hide—Captain Mita was kind enough to mirror-scry me and inform me about the lovely little chats you've been having. But considering most of his offenses have taken place on Jettan soil, and have tarnished the Jettan name, I'd like to think we can claim some precedence in the matter."

Holding out her hand, she caught another book that came deftly sailing down from another spot overhead. Opening it, she skimmed a few pages, spending nothing more than two or three heartbeats per pair of pages, then sent it flying back into place. She moved on with another flurry of short but quick steps, and once more Ellett had to keep up with the woman. He couldn't quite decide if she was a hummingbird, from her swiftness, or a butterfly.

Hummingbird, I guess. If she wore a noblewoman's etama *coat, with . . . thigh-length sleeves, I think her rank would be rated at . . . then she'd definitely look like a butterfly*. The thought amused him, but only for a moment. He organized his priorities and addressed her.

"Yes, about the whole set of incidents that brought me here, Chief Librarian," he stated, mindful of his oath not to mention the word *Guardian* out loud. "I've exchanged scryings with my own people, and we're very confident none of the Aurulan vessels described as the attackers on your merchant fleet are ones that actually exist within the known registry of Aurulan ships. At least, the lawful registry. I can also reassure you upon a Truth Stone, or a wand, or whatever spell you deem fit to cast, that Lord Stelled, cousin to Seer King Devin, is most assuredly dead."

"Whereas the 'Lord Stelled' we have here is certainly a powerful enough mage to have crafted the spell on the docks, which I studied from afar while you were still walking all the way up here," Callaia agreed. "As well as strong enough to have spell-shaped his face. Assuming he bothered to *look* like the original Lord Stelled, which I do not doubt." Catching another book, this one a slender volume, she tapped one corner of it against her chin. "Such magics as were carved onto our wharves were a subtle lot. Very exacting. Very deep in the details of their search parameters, yet without a single excess rune."

". . . As subtle as Haidan magics?" Mita asked, lifting one brow.

"Perhaps." The Chief Librarian eyed the tome in her hands, then sighed and waved it in a negligent circle. "I'm hardly the level of mage that my colleagues Sheren and Tipa'thia are. Powerful, yes, but both ladies are decades ahead of me. This is going to cut into my allotted studying time for today, and that makes me feel rather vexed.

"If Lord Stelled's spy network is as efficient as his scrying spell, then he'll have heard of the aborted attack on that Aurulan ship you were on, Guardsman Ellett," Callaia stated, turning a corner and entering a new row of shelves. "Captain Mita, inform the City Council that they need to call the good Aurulan ambassador to a meeting. Jetta Freeport is dropping anchor and giving up her cargo. We want peace between ourselves and Aurul, and are willing to discuss the honorable ambassador's recommendations on how to secure it permanently with his people. *That* should make his avaricious lump of a heart thump with joy."

She paused and looked Ellett up and down, sliding her nose-perched viewing lenses partway down so that she could peer over them all the way to the toes of his boots. Ellett realized belatedly that the inner sides of the lenses, the sides closest to her eyes, had been lightly silvered.

"Hm. That outfit will never do. I trust you brought *something* impressive enough to wear as an envoy of your people? In that bag you dropped off at Mita's house, on your way up here?"

"I left my armor at home, since it's too distinctive, but I did bring a set of *etama* to wear, as befits my station, milady," Ellett reassured her, wondering how she knew what he had brought ashore.

The answer hit him in the very next breath. *How very clever. I'll bet the cost of all my court silks, both here and back home, that she uses those silvered lenses as her personal scrying mirrors. Just enough silvering to reflect when needed, plus the gray tint to cut down on any distracting incoming light, without getting in the way of actually being able to see through them. It takes a talented glazier's hand to make a half-silvered mirror, never mind such tiny ones . . . but then Jetta is rumored to be a wealthy freeport, and she's their leader.*

"Well, go and don them then!" the Chief Librarian ordered him. "Mita, don't forget to tidy your own appearance, too. And reassure the council that *naturally* their secretary will be on hand to record the proceedings for posterity." A graceful half bow from the petite woman somehow managed to simultaneously introduce herself as said secretary and dismiss the two of them from her presence. Diary-sized book in hand, she opened it and skimmed through its pages as she strode down the aisle, her attention clearly no longer on either of them.

Sighing, Ellett turned and followed the captain of the *Jetta's Pride* out of the library. Only when they were descending the steps outside the huge building did he speak. ". . . Is she really as young as she looks?"

"If by that, you mean twenty-three? Yes. She was picked to be the next Chief Librarian at the tender age of sixteen and took over the position two years ago at the age of twenty-one, when the previous Librarian decided he was more than old enough to retire. But it isn't a bad thing. Callaia is very smart, very observant, very wise in knowing when to listen to the counsel of others, and thus takes her academic duties very seriously," Mita replied. "She's done well enough for us in managing her duties."

Her words were carefully couched to avoid the real topic of Callaia's identity and station. There were plenty of students crossing the grand courtyard in front of the library, walking from building to building. There were several of them nestled within the walled campus of the university grounds, which perched on the best hill in the city. The greatest was the library, a full six times the size of the next-largest structure, and three times as large as any single such library Ellett had seen in Aurul. Mita had reassured him on the walk up through the city that the Jettan library was only a fraction of the size of the Great Library of Mendham far to the east, but it was still impressive on its own.

As was the rest of the campus. The walls of each structure had clearly been whitewashed several times and decorated with black-painted knotwork at the corners and along the edges. Windows gleamed as if frequently cleaned, and summer flowers bloomed in the garden beds lining every path, as well as around the bases of half the trees. The other half, he noted idly, were ringed by students with books and tablets and shrunken slates in their laps, studying between classes. Much like a few of the Academies he himself had seen in Aurul, including the Academy of the Royal Guard, just on a larger scale.

"Well, our own version of a 'Chief Librarian' was selected by Ruul at the tender age of twenty-four, and has done well in managing our own academic interests, too—with his brother's counsel—so I can hardly protest," Ellett replied mildly. Thinking of the Seer King reminded him of his duty to his king, and the fact that his quest would soon come to an end. Which wasn't an entirely happy thought, though the hope of securing a solid peace between their people should have been happy enough on its own. "Mita . . . once we confront the gentleman in question . . . I am authorized to represent my people here on several matters for a short while, but eventually I must return to my own duties."

The smile she attempted to give him wasn't a very good one and didn't suit the generosity of her mouth very well. "I know. I've been enjoying your company quite a bit, even though I know it's only temporary. You probably won't get everything settled for at least a couple of weeks, though, surely?"

"Probably not, but with grace and agreement on both sides, it shouldn't take more than a couple weeks at most. At least, the preliminary agreements. The court would no doubt send a more official representative than I could ever be and won't be sending me back. Plus, it's still summer, and the royal court is tucked up in the cool air of the mountains at this time of year," he said, studying her for her reactions. "However, from late autumn to early spring, we're down by the coast in the winter palace. I was wondering if you'd consider finding the time to come visit me on the coast in the winter months. At least, once in a while? Tucked in among your own duties?"

This time, her smile was a little more natural. "I'd like that. I'll see what can be arranged. A pity we'll be far apart for half the year, but I like your company, and I'd like to think of you as a friend. A close friend. If you don't mind?"

Ellett chuckled and tucked his arm around her waist. "Far better a friend than an enemy."

"Well, I certainly don't sleep with my enemies," Mita pointed out dryly.

"Thank the Gods," he muttered and got poked in the ribs by her elbow for his teasing. They approached one of the academic halls near the gates of the university; the summer sun gleamed across the windows, half blinding him for a moment. The reflected light was bright and therefore painful, but it did give him an idea. "Here's another question."

"Yes?" she asked.

"Do you have a glazier's guild in the city, or a glassmaker's shop?"

"Of course. Actually, we have a Glazier's Academy, which teaches both common and spellcrafted glassmaking techniques." Twisting against his arm, she pointed off to the side at one of the buildings to their left. "It's located over there. It's set back from most of the others so that if anything burns up, it won't cause problems with the other facilities. The Spellsmith Academy is not too far from it, either, and both are as far as one can get from the university library."

"Good. I'd like to drop by and see if I can purchase a pair of linked palm-mirrors." He gave her a lopsided smile of his own. "It may not be that long before the court packs up and heads west on its semiannual tour of the kingdom, but it's still going to be a long set of months before I'll be back on the coast again. Scrying mirrors can travel the aether a very long way when they're linked, and I'd like to be able to keep talking with you, if I may. When our duties allow it, of course."

"Of course," she agreed. "And I'd like that, too. In fact, I'll buy my half of the mirrors—or even both of them, if you'd like."

"Only your half," Ellett countered. "I may dress like one at the moment, but I am not a pauper."

"Does this mean you'll offer me the position of 'kept woman'?" Mita teased him.

He grinned. "And here I was hoping you'd offer me the position of 'kept man.' "

She elbowed him again. He kissed her on the cheek.

SEVEN

Lord Stelled *looked* like Lord Stelled, to the point where it deeply disconcerted Ellett . . . but he didn't *act* like Lord Stelled.

The man portraying him was late middle-aged, with the right hazel brown eyes and the right shade of dark brown hair streaked at the temples with silver, which he had plaited in a proper, waist-length Aurulan braid. He even wore the right shades-of-brown silk robes which the real Lord Stelled had favored, long, pocket-sleeved layers of floor-length jacket which, wrapped by the gauzy sash of nobility, made it an *etamana* ensemble.

However, he didn't stand like the late alchemist-mage, with the slightly stooped shoulders of a man who had spent too many years of his life at a workbench, reading grimoires, preparing ingredients, and brewing the potions needed by some of the healers and mages and Artifact-crafters in the winter palace region.

Instead, the man strode into the City Council hall with his shoulders back and his head tilted ever so slightly up, cloaked in a subtle air of arrogance. His voice was strong and smooth, not roughened by years of working with self-tested drafts, and his joints weren't half swollen and thus stiff-moving from the long-term exposure to steam boiling up from all those bottles and pots.

Lurking in the back of the council hall, in the shadows of the corridor that led to the public refreshing rooms, Ellett watched the impostor greet the collection of men and women politely, unctuously apologize "once again" for all the troubles his "unruly fellow Aurulans" had been causing, and then hint ever so subtly that chasing down the seafaring thieves plaguing Jettan merchant vessels was an expensive proposition which the royal fleet would love to do in full, if only they had more funds.

". . . But I understand your council has reconsidered His Majesty's offer to expend his navy's budget in chasing down the miscreants responsible? With Jettan coins paying our sailors and soldiers to be diligent in guarding your interests, I'm sure it would be more than sufficient motivation for our people to extend their protection against piracy all the way down to the Isles," the false Stelled reassured. "I know this isn't what you'd want, but we are men and women of reason, and we all know such things have a cost. Our ships must carry extra provisions when patrolling so far away, our sailors must brave extra hazards when defending foreign crews . . ."

I wonder how the real Lord Stelled would have reacted to his good name being used in a fraudulent case of racketeering, Ellett thought idly, waiting for his cue. *He'd probably be tempted to have the miscreants bound over to him for potion-testing subjects.*

The Chief Dean of the university, whom Ellett had met briefly before this meeting began, enduring a second round of Truth Stone questioning to reassure the others that he was indeed legitimate, answered on behalf of his fellow council members. "Yes, well, we have indeed reached the limits of our tolerance for piracy against our fellow citizens. And we are tired of the 'fines' your government insists on imposing for any and all Aurulan goods brought onto the freeport's docks, simply because ships who may or may not have been Jettan in origin have pilfered some of *your* vessels."

Lord Stelled spread his hands. "The flow of money has long been known to be a far more effective means of leverage, either in encouragement or discouragement, than the might of an army. At least with money, no one loses an arm or a leg." Fishing a scroll from the inner pocket of one of his thigh-length sleeves, the impostor bowed and stepped closer to the Chief Dean's section of the U-shaped table hosting the Jettan council. "All this treaty requires is the approval of the council and the signature of your leader to make it binding."

Ellett narrowed his eyes, squinting at the scroll. A half step to his left positioned it so that the dark, tooled leathers worn by Captain Mita provided a background for the rolled object. He wasn't completely sure even then, but there did seem to be a faint glow of magic to the document. The Dean reached for it, then withdrew his hand before touching the parchment.

". . . There's just *one* last reassurance we need," the gray-haired scholar hedged, tucking his hands back together on top of the council table.

To his credit, the impostor Stelled didn't scream or growl or flinch at the last-minute gambit. He didn't even roll his eyes, let alone sigh. "And what reassurance would that be, milord?"

The Chief Dean unfolded his hands and held them out to either side. His fellow council members clasped hands, forming a chain around the table . . . and a silvery white shield around the impostor. Power flared up, obscuring the man for a moment, then died down low enough that they could see him from the knees up, though from the knees down, the brilliant glow remained, locking him in place with far more magic than most mages could overcome on their own.

That was Ellett's cue. Stepping into the light cast by the chandelier of lightglobes overhead, he let the impostor get a good look at his one set of formal robes. The inner two layers of golden and lavender silk matched the golden patches appliquéd on the outermost violet layer, patches that echoed the gilding, and the function, of the enchanted armor he had left back in Aurul. While the silk wouldn't do as much to stop a purely physical blow, it was the look of his clothes that mattered.

From the widening of those hazel eyes, Ellett knew the impostor recognized the distinct design of his garments, marking him as a member of the Aurulan Royal Guard.

He smiled. "The council would love to know how a very *dead* man can claim to still be alive."

The false alchemist twisted a ring on his finger . . . then paled when nothing happened. He twisted it again, then looked up at the air. The Chief Dean and his fellow Jettans dropped their hands, though their binding shield remained firmly in place.

"Don't bother looking to your cohorts for rescue, 'Lord.' This entire room has been warded against mirror-Gate travel. As we speak, the university's top magecraft students are working to trace the origin points of any and all scryings upon this building, and specifically centered around your person." The Chief Dean smiled. "They have been told it is an extra-credit project which will affect their grades for this semester. Naturally, they are being rather diligent in the matter."

Scraping back his chair, the stout, gray-clad Dean rose, squared his shoulders, and clapped his hands together. A murmured spell released a sparkling green globe of energy. It zoomed forward, penetrated the shields holding the impostor in place, and impacted on the other man's chest.

The magic vanished inside his body even as the impostor clutched at his robes. An odd look came over his face, not quite bulging his eyes, then the man belched loudly. Green gas issued from his mouth, hovered in midair for a moment, then formed misty lettering in the Jettan alphabet.

Thanks to his sip of Ultra Tongue years ago—a necessary expense for the Royal Guard, so that they could overhear any possible plotting in foreign languages—Ellett could read the characters that formed. Not that there was much to it, just a single word which identified the other man's nationality.

Haidan.

"It figures," he heard Mita muttering in disgust. She raised her voice slightly. "You were correct in your assessment of the situation, Mage-Captain. Jetta Freeport wishes to apologize to the Aurulan government for all the troubles that were caused when we fell for the lies of these Haidan scum."

"As it is said, so shall it be written. Thus it is proved, and so shall it be," Ellett replied philosophically, ritually. He folded his arms in their hip-length sleeves and shrugged, keeping his gaze on the mage caught in their extraordinary shield. "Had our God wished it otherwise, this matter would have been cleared up a lot sooner. The Eyes of Ruul can pierce all disguises and see even into the very heart of darkness. But I have faith there is some greater good to be found in unveiling these matters here and now, rather than earlier or later. We need only grasp it, as *true* allies, and turn this would-be disaster into an advantage for both sides."

"Well spoken, good Captain," the Dean of Spellsmithing stated, rising from his spot at the large, nearly circular table. He fetched a casket from the floor, opened it, and fished out a set of what looked like silk-wrapped manacles. Ellett didn't have to actually see the metal to know it would be engraved with anti-magic wards. "We'll make sure there's enough left of him and his accomplices so that *some* of them, at least, will be available to face Aurulan justice. Once we're done exacting our pound of restitution, of course."

"As I told Captain Mita and some of the other members of your council, my people will be happy to let your people go first," he allowed, bowing politely to the men and women ringing the room. "My only request is that you consider the possibility of teaching *our* mages such finely crafted spells. I didn't even know there *was* a spell that could force a man to literally belch his true allegiances."

The Chief Dean chuckled. "It's a rather popular one among our students, since it can be crafted to belch out any manner of truths regarding its impacted target."

The sour look on the false Stelled's face amused Ellett to no end. *Unmasked by the equivalent of a student's prank, of all things.* That *has to sting the impostor's pride.*

Looking pretty wasn't easy, anymore. As attentive as he was to his duties, Ellett couldn't wait for his day to be over. Only at night, when His Majesty and Her Highness had retired for the evening, could the Mage-Captain set aside his vigilance and do what he longed to do: Contact Mita on the linked scrying mirrors they had bought back before he had left Jetta Freeport.

Today was even worse. Mita told him that her ship, *Jetta's Pride*, had been elected to escort the newly appointed ambassador to the docks of the winter palace. They had barely settled into the winter palace a handful of days ago when she had scryed him through the mirror with the news that the Jettan council had finally selected a representative to send to the Seer King's court. Apparently there had been quite some difficulty between what the council thought was an appropriate representative and what His Majesty preferred. Ellett hadn't been privy to those discussions, so he hadn't been able to advise her on what Devin, or perhaps Ruul, wanted to see.

But she's finally coming. She said last night she thought it might be possible for them to arrive sometime today, even though she wasn't quite sure when. He resisted the urge to look over his shoulder, through the glass walls of the Vaulted Chapel. All he would see would be the royal gardens, more of the royal gardens, a bit of the palace walls . . . and nothing of the sea from his position near the holy dais. No tall black masts, no crisp white sails, nothing of the *Pride*.

A palace servant approached along the outer wall. Ellett eyed the cream-and-purple-clad man, gauging him for unusual or furtive behavior, a possible disguise, or anything else that could hint at a threat to his king. Or to the king's staff, for the man whispered something in Master Souder's ear. The Master of the Royal Retreat waited until the Seer King lifted his hands from the shoulders of the youth brought before him for a chance at prophesying his future, then lifted a couple fingers, subtly signaling his liege.

Devin nodded slightly, finished what few words he had to give to the barely pubescent boy and his proud-beaming mother, and dismissed them with a bow of his head. As they backed up the aisle and turned to leave, the Seer King raised his hand and his voice.

"There will be a brief pause in the afternoon's viewings and blessings of our youth. We have received word that the ambassador of the Jettan Freeholders has finally arrived. We wish to receive their delegation at this time. Please extend all due courtesy to our honored guests."

Ellett felt his heart skip a beat. His stomach tightened with the hope that Mita would be among the delegates escorting their ambassador into the glass-walled, marble-vaulted hall. Firmly, he reminded himself that now was not the time to let his vigilance slack, and peered over the heads of the seated families waiting to petition their king for a glimpse at their children's futures.

The sight of an armed, armored redhead descending the stairs to the chapel doors, accompanied by two equally armed and armored gentlemen, both thrilled and dismayed him. But they stopped on the landing above the last set of steps and carefully removed their weapons, setting them on the carpeted floor. It wasn't the first time that armed dignitaries had done the same, so someone must have instructed them in the proper protocols.

A pair of servants opened the great glass doors and the trio strode inside. Ellett watched them approach, drinking in the sight of Captain Mita. Her hair was a little bit longer—the mirrors they used were small and thus didn't always show head and shoulders—and she had pulled it back in a braid, perhaps in deference to Aurulan fashion. Other than that, she didn't look much different than the last time he had seen her in person, which was when she had personally delivered him to Aurul a few months ago. As for the last time he had seen her in a mirror . . . well, she was fully clothed this time.

She gave one of her broad, charming smiles to the Seer King and bowed, as did the two men accompanying her. "Greetings, Your Majesty. I am Ambassador Mita of the Jettan Freeholders, and these are my assistants, Kulden of the Mage's Academy, and Reltor of the Merchant's League."

Each of the gentlemen bowed in turn. Ellett forced himself to assess them for potential threats, but it was hard to concentrate, given the news she had dropped into his lap. *Ambassador Mita? She never told me that* she *was the new ambassador! And she never said anything about giving up her career as a ship's captain.*

Devin nodded and made the necessary speeches of welcome and introduction. Struggling to pay attention, Ellett blinked twice and moved belatedly when His Majesty beckoned *him* forward.

". . . Mage-Captain Ellett will personally show you to your ambassadorial suite. I place you in his very capable hands. Captain," Devin added, giving his stunned Guardsman a slight smile, "I trust you will show her everything she wishes to know about her life here?"

"Of course, Your Majesty." Bowing, he gestured for the trio to retreat back up the carpeted aisle. It was unusual for a Royal Guard to be given this sort of duty. Even more so for their leader. He didn't protest, however. Not when it allowed him to walk out of the massive, glass-roofed chapel at her side.

They paused at the landing to pick up their weapons. Sheathing her daggers, Mita grinned at him. "Surprise! . . . I hope you don't mind I kept it a secret?"

"I might have, if I weren't *very* happy to see you at the same time," Ellett confessed, then reined in his enthusiasm, glancing quickly at the two Jettan men flanking her. Mindful of his duty, he gestured at the doors leading back into the palace proper. "This way, if you please. We've set aside a suite for you. Hopefully it should be large enough for your needs."

She nodded and walked beside him, the other two following, as he led the way. Ellett filled the time with a discussion of various palace amenities and points of interest, then gave them a tour of the multiple-room suite. He added plenty of information which would be of interest to the mage and the merchant accompanying Mita, but most of his attention circled around the woman at his side. Once the other two men were settled in their bedchambers and she had been shown to hers, alone with him, he found himself feeling a bit awkward.

Mita cured that feeling as quickly as the time it took her to remove her ornate armor. The moment the tooled leggings were dropped onto a chair, she turned and caught him in a hug. His own armor got in the way, but he didn't care. Nor did she. Snuggling her cheek on his shoulder guard, she peeked up at him.

"I hope you don't mind?"

"The hug?" he asked. At her nod, he dropped a kiss on her brow. "I can't think of anything I wanted more. At least, while I'm wearing armor. And on duty."

She chuckled. "Yes, your duty. And mine, too. The council was rather dubious over His Majesty's insistence that *I* be the ambassador. I was, too, at first. But then the more time passed, the more I missed you. Mirror-chats are good and all, but . . ."

"But not enough," he agreed. "I didn't ask for you to be the ambassador. I know how much you enjoy sailing."

"And I couldn't ask you to give up your job. It's slightly more important than mine. Peany's the new captain," she added. "Jukol was offered the First Officer position, but he says he likes ordering around the crew too much to give up being a bo'sun just yet, so they promoted a Second Officer from another ship to serve under Peany. As for myself, I'm still a commodore of the fleet. I heard you have pleasure-boats, both here and at some lake up near your winter palace. If I ever get the urge to go sailing, I could always commandeer one."

He grinned. "Just so long as you don't turn privateer on His Majesty's lake."

"Oh, there's no worry of that. I just got my hands on the only booty I really want."

Her words, and the pat of her hand in a pertinent place, warmed him from the inside out. Devin's instructions floated through his mind. "So . . . I'm supposed to show you everything you wish to know about your life here. Is there anything you're wishing for, right now?"

"Well, aside from the wish that you weren't on duty—which I know you take very seriously," she reassured him, "—I'd love to know is if it would cause difficulties between our peoples if the Ambassador of Jetta Freeport was caught sneaking into the quarters of the Captain of the Royal Guard?"

He mulled that over, enjoying the feel and the scent and the sight of her in his arms. Whether or not the Seer King's prophecy *meant* for this to happen didn't matter. It had, and he intended to capitalize on it. "They *might* be more forgiving if, say, the Jettan Ambassador and the Mage-Captain had something of a formal agreement between them regarding such things."

"Formal agreement?" Mita asked, lifting her head so she could look him in the eye.

"Yes." He smiled at her. The thoughts and words that had been racing around in his head for the last several weeks were remarkably easy to say, now that she was here in person. "One bound by love."

She blushed. The phenomenon fascinated him, since she hadn't seemed like the type. He didn't get much time to study her pink cheeks, however, for she kissed him very thoroughly. *That* was more like the Mita he knew, a bold woman willing and able to go after what she wanted, intelligent enough to keep him on his toes, and utterly beautiful in his eyes.

Pulling back after a long moment, she frowned softly at him. "Wait . . . isn't that some sort of ethical conflict, if an ambassador and the head of the Royal Guard . . . ?"

"Ruul may be the God of Vision," Ellett informed her, "but He is also very much a romantic at heart, and He was the one who set things up so that you and I would meet . . . and the one to insist that you should come here. Nor are we the first pair He has nudged together. For that matter, Devin's wife, Princess Gabria, is still counted as an official adjunct to the Guildaran ambassador. If His Majesty doesn't have a conflict with a foreigner for his mate, why should we?"

She mulled that over, then nodded. "Fair enough. But if anyone ever tries to split us up before we're good and ready, I'm not only dropping diplomatic ties, I'm kidnapping you and dragging you off to Jetta as my war-prize."

Ellett chuckled. "Just give me enough time to appoint someone else in my place, that's all I ask."

Kissing him one last time, Mita stepped back out of his arms. "Well. You have your duties—which you take very seriously, and I admire you for it—and I have some duties of my own. Like unpacking and such."

"Then I'll see you tonight, after evening prayers," he promised, and stepped close enough for a brief kiss. A sort of brief kiss. She finally laughed and pushed him gently away, fluttering her hands in a shooing motion.

He knew her actual presence in his life would probably be just as distracting as simply longing for her had been, but Ellett didn't care. His faith in his deity's wishes had brought him a great deal of happiness. *As it is said, so shall it be written*, he thought, letting himself out of her suite. *Thus it is proved, and so shall it be.*

Thank the Gods.